MW00626056

The Wolf's Shadow

Jennifer,
Thanks for the
support and the
chance to visit!
,K.W.

The Wolf's Shadow

Book One of the She-Wolf Saga

By: K. W. Kenny

Stone Wolf Publishing

Copyright © 2020 K. W. Kenny All rights reserved

The characters and events portrayed in this book are fictitious.
Any similarity to real persons, living or dead, is coincidental
and not intended by the author.

No part of this book may be reproduced, or stored in a
retrieval system, or transmitted in any form or by any means,
electronic, mechanical, photocopying, recording, or otherwise,
without express written permission of the publisher.

ISBN-13: 978-1-7349257-1-5

Cover design by: Covers by Izzy

Printed in the United States of America

Table of Contents

Chapter 1

There were three men there with her in the dark. She could sense their presence. After two days alone in this prison, she was almost grateful for the company. At least, she thought it had been about two days. Her sense of time was still hazy, owing to the fact that she had been slipping in and out of consciousness.

Briga risked opening her eyes and quickly shut them again as the dim light sent pain lancing through her head. She sucked air through her gritted teeth and groaned. It had been enough, though, to catch a fleeting glance of them. One of them was the man who had slammed the hilt of his sword into the back of her head in battle and sent her crashing into this throbbing darkness. She would recognize that face anywhere. They were talking amongst themselves in their unfamiliar language.

A jangle of weapons and armor sounded as one of them moved across the room toward her, followed by a rough hand that grabbed the front of her tunic and hauled her upright. She cried out again as the sudden movement caused such an intense shockwave of pain that she nearly passed out. The warrior spoke again, so close this time that she could feel his breath, hot against her cheek. Briga didn't need a translator to realize he was threatening her. The hand released, and she dropped back down like a stone, blackness welling up once more to pull her away from all this.

***

For too long now, the signs had all been ominous. Storm clouds had hung low over their settlement for almost a week, but the last few nights had been plagued with constant lightning and occasional hail. Cathbad was worried, which meant all the druids were worried. Several of them had suffered troubling dreams, but unlike the others, Briga's had been recurrent. She sat now before the chief druid, disturbed by her visions.

"Epona appears to me," she explained to Cathbad once again.

"The horse goddess favors you, child," he answered quietly.

Briga shook her head slowly. "Perhaps, but I don't think that's the message."

She squinted into the darkness, as if summoning the images from her dream to life once more. "She rides before a terrible army…There's no escape, and their horses run me down. Her horse is made of fire, and ignites the land in her wake."

Cathbad looked away as she shuddered, frowning into the fire as if he could divine the dream's meaning by staring into the flames. "Epona is not destructive. Is it the same dream every night?"

"Mostly, yes."

He looked up then. "What changes?"

"Sometimes I fight, sometimes I don't. Once, I ran toward the fury with my daggers, screaming our war cry. I felt no fear. Sometimes…" Briga blushed slightly and shifted her own gaze down into the fire to avoid meeting his eyes. "Eamon is there, and he tries to save me. But the ending is always the same."

She could feel the weight of his gaze on her, but refused to meet it. Her infatuation with the chieftain had endured since she was a small child. This was not a new topic, and they both already knew what he would say. A peal of thunder broke the silence, and both glanced reflexively to the rooftree as if they could observe the dark sky beyond. After several long minutes, Cathbad finally spoke again.

"It is strange that we've had no travelers recently to bring news. Tomorrow I will ask Eamon to send out riders. If news will not come to us, we must seek it out. Then we shall pray in the grove. I fear there is a great enemy that threatens our lands. With luck, we may have recognized the gods' warning in time."

Briga blinked at him. "Because of my dreams?

"In part," he confided. "In truth, I have felt this for some time now. A...disturbance to the Pattern. Go and rest now, child. There will be time for worry later."

Cathbad threw some sweet herbs on the fire as Briga stood to leave. She gathered her cloak and pulled up the hood as protection against the rain. In the doorway, she stopped and turned as Cathbad called to her. He watched her in silence for a moment, then shook his head and waved her out without another word.

Uncertainly, she stepped out into the night. Cathbad's look had been inscrutable, but something about it made her uneasy. Lightning flashed overhead, but the rain was nothing more than a steady pattering, absent of wind for the moment. The rhythmic pattern served to soothe her mind and calm her thoughts during the short walk back toward the settlement. The hut she shared with Amergin and Owen was on the other side of the camp. She opted to take a shortcut through the center of the settlement rather than subject herself to the rain longer than necessary. Besides, this path took her past Eamon's hut. He was still awake, sitting outside with some of his closest warriors around a fire. They were partially sheltered by an animal skin that had been stretched on poles for the purpose. The men stared at her as she passed. She glanced to Eamon, but forced her gaze away again so it wouldn't linger.

"Briga," he called, taking advantage of her glance.

She shivered despite herself and pulled her cloak tighter as she turned to them once more. He signaled for her to approach, and she obliged her chieftain. The men made space for her near the fire, and Eamon indicated a dry stump beside him for her to sit. Carefully, she sank onto the worn surface and removed her hood.

3

"Have you been to see Cathbad?"

She nodded, hesitant to volunteer information.

He placed a hand on her arm, gently urging. "What does he say? Are the storms an omen?"

She glanced to his hand briefly, taking comfort from his touch, no matter how small. "I think he should like to speak with you himself, my lord. But aye, the storms are an omen. I cannot say of what. All the druids sense it."

His jaw clenched for a moment, a habit of his when he was thinking quickly. "For ill, or for fortune?"

"I cannot say, my lord. I've had no visions of prophecy."

She had a sudden flash of memory from one of the dreams where he had attempted to rescue her. It certainly didn't feel like a good omen, but it wasn't her place to say so.

"Briga!"

All heads swiveled toward the sound. Owen was standing just outside the light of the fire, his expression a mix of relief and concern. Briga was relieved and irritated all at once at his appearance, but she placed her hand over Eamon's and stood.

"Excuse me, my lord, I am needed. Speak with Cathbad in the morning; he will be expecting you."

He squeezed her fingers briefly and let them slip through his own, nodding. She favored him with a smile meant for him alone and turned to join Owen. She did not need to look back to know the chieftain's eyes followed her until she was out of their sight. The silence around the fire was enough. Protectively, Owen ushered her through the village and into their hut. Amergin was still awake as well and sat tending the fire. He stood as they entered, disapproval stamped clearly on his fine face.

"I know, brothers," she remarked with a sigh before either of them could scold her, "but I had to speak with Cathbad. I've had the dream again."

The two exchanged a look, but neither broached the subject of Eamon. Instead, the three of them dined on a thin broth in companionable silence before retiring to their sleeping pallets. Owen's breathing soon slowed to the deep pattern of easy sleep. Amergin lay facing the fire, which he studied with a faraway look in his eyes. Briga watched him for a time, but uneasy sleep eventually claimed her.

Two weeks had passed, and still no news, though there was talk of some great storm to the east. Eamon's messengers had ridden for days in all directions, and still no one had any news at all—a fact everyone found strange. They did discover one thing just as important as news, however. Travelers through the area were just as scant in the neighboring tribes and villages as they were in Eamon's camp. Something was disrupting the usual trade routes that brought many travelers from the east. *Could it be from the storms?* Briga wondered. Everywhere the messengers traveled, there was a general sense of vague, nameless unease.

***

A few days later, two guards came to escort her from the *ger*, the round-walled felt tent that served as her prison. She had been recovering nicely, and was no longer sensitive to the light, though the back of her head still ached. Briga wasn't certain how long she had been here. She had not been allowed outside, nor had she been fed, and she was visited by only the occasional water-bearer, and someone who had checked the knot on her head once or twice. But now, here they stood, blocking the small doorway. They still wore their armor and weapons, though this time their helmets had been removed. She considered fighting back, resisting, trying for escape even, but her body would only stand rigid, facing them warily. She wouldn't allow them her fear. She refused.

Obstinately, she raised her chin and puffed out her chest in a gesture of defiance. The savage on the left only grinned in the manner of a man who enjoys a challenge. She paled as he crossed the small space in two great strides and seized her by the arm. The suddenness of his action seemed to break the spell of immobility, and she instinctively drew back, mentally urging herself to stay as far as possible from the sleeping pallet due to the hazy memory of the warrior in the dark. Surely they hadn't waited all this time for her to regain consciousness only to…no, men wouldn't care about such details. *Velkcic* men would care about such details, she amended, and silently vowed to fight them to her last breath if they tried to take her. But her small act of resistance was in vain. In no more than the time it took to blink, the second guard was already at her side.

Roughly, the duo pulled her out of her small prison and dragged her across the camp. She complied haughtily, fighting to retain a shred of dignity before the scattered groups of staring barbarian warriors.

They led her to a *ger* that was larger than the rest and bore decorative patterns along the sides and the top of its felt dome. The barbarian who had leered at her before now grabbed her by the back of the neck as he lifted the heavy door covering and shoved her inside. She stumbled and caught herself, blinking rapidly in the dim light to adjust to the gloom. The guards did not follow her in.

She was already dizzy, and the tender spot at the back of her head throbbed dully. A fire blazed in the center, its light illuminating the space in the most remarkable way. Opposite her, four musicians were performing for a group of generals ranged around the walls of the circular tent. No one so much as glanced at her—no one except the man playing a peculiar-looking stringed instrument topped with an elaborately carved horse head. She recognized him instantly as her captor, the man who'd dragged her from the battlefield and had nearly killed her with a blow to the head. She was frozen to the spot, blood turned to ice at his gaze. He wore no armor now, but a richly adorned red and gold tunic, and straight black hair streamed loose over his shoulders. The effect was of a man completely at odds with the warrior she had encountered at the height of battle fury only days before. The musicians started to sing, and the warrior-musician looked away, indicating with a quick gesture an empty space among the generals where she should sit.

He played the instrument with a bow, and she realized it was a kind of fiddle, larger and with fewer strings, but with a similar sound to those with which she was acquainted. Its music was pleasant, but at the same time eerie and commanding. He stroked the fiddle, causing it to neigh exactly like a horse. The sound was so lifelike, it stopped her in her tracks. Shaking herself after a moment, she drifted to the seat indicated and slowly sank into her place. She watched him play, transfixed by the instrument. Eamon's clan had nothing like this, and the throaty, guttural sound of the singing was both exotic and alluring. She was fascinated despite herself. He smiled while he sang, and the joy transformed his face into something entirely different from the man he'd been on the battlefield. A servant brought her a hot beverage of some kind, which she accepted gladly, feeling more like a guest than a prisoner. Confused but seemingly out of danger for the moment, she relaxed somewhat and decided to enjoy the music while she could.

In many ways, it reminded her of home. The words were foreign, but the music itself held shadows of her own people's sounds. The neighing of the fiddle, expertly interspersed between stanzas of melody, sent shivers down her spine. It was as if the instrument held captive the soul of a horse, plaintive and angry by turns at its torment, so real was the effect. Such a sound must surely be magic. She had a disheartening flashback to her recurrent dream of Epona from the nights before the battle and wondered if this might be somehow connected.

After two more mesmerizing songs, the fiddle player stood, and an attendant materialized to take the instrument. A warrior's demeanor now replaced the musician's bearing, and he stood in quiet authority, his earlier mirth having completely evaporated with a startling suddenness. He grunted and waved his hand in a dismissive gesture. The generals stood as one, and bowed, then began filing out of the room. Briga took this all in distantly. The music had a heady feel, as if she were somehow disconnected from her body, leaving her almost feeling intoxicated. Perhaps it was the strange drink in her hand…or perhaps it was only the dizziness from her lingering head injury.

As she stood, the warrior's gaze flickered to her once more, and she felt an uneasy current of true fear. The intensity in his eyes arrested her, rooting her to the spot. She could easily read his intent, and a sense of dread slowly built. As the last general departed, the warrior stalked toward her slowly. The intensity of his gaze froze her to the spot. Shaking herself loose, she retreated a step, unwilling to meet his eyes, but unable to look away. Without breaking gaze, his hands drifted to the gold sash tied around his waist and deftly unwrapped the belt. Her mouth went dry, and she could feel her face growing pale. Blindly, her hand groped at the small table beside her, searching for something, anything that could be used for defense.

He dropped the sash on the sleeping pallet. With savage swiftness, he grabbed the back of her neck and pulled her to himself, kissing her roughly. She struggled, trying in vain to pull her head away, pushing against his shoulders with her hands, and attempting to drive a knee up between them. The resistance seemed only to inflame him. He purred something, a string of sounds against her lips. The foreign words sent an involuntary and unwelcome shiver down her spine. Feeling this, his hands drifted down to caress her low back, and ventured lower still, crushing her hips against his. His mouth worked at hers, demanding.

Pressing against her, he scooped her up, easily holding her weight, and fell with her onto the piled furs atop his sleeping pallet. She thrashed beneath him, determined not to let him mount her, despite one hand pinning her hip in place. A whimper escaped her then, more terror than rage. The sound caused him to stop. He drew back slightly, searching her face

8

with his eyes. Her hands were still at his shoulders, feebly attempting to remove the weight of him. He watched her for a moment, then captured one of her hands in his own and guided it inside his robes.

"No fear."

The deep voice forming her language was enough to shock her into stillness for a moment. His eyes were serious, hungry, but strangely without malice. Firmly he placed her hand around his manhood, and she gasped in surprise and fear. She tried to pull away, but his strong fingers crushed her wrist until she could feel the small bones cracking.

"No fear," he repeated and let go of her wrist.

She began to shake then, despite herself, and a hint of tears glistened at the corner of her eyes. He brushed one away with a rough thumb, one corner of his mouth turning upward in the approximation of sly victory. He simply watched her in silence for a moment, then stood abruptly, retrieving his sash and leaving her a huddled mass of dizzy confusion among his piled furs.

Chapter 2

It had been over a month since Briga had discussed her dreams with Cathbad. An entire month on top of the weeks without news. The general sense of unease had gradually faded as the clansmen adjusted to this new condition. It was becoming normal, if uncomfortable, to be isolated from what might be happening beyond their small territory. Today, however, the settlement held an almost festive air.

It was nearing the end of autumn, which meant the Trading Season was upon them. While Eamon's people raised some crops, they weren't farmers. Their growing consisted mostly of vegetable and herb gardens within the village itself. These crops would last them a while, but would not see them through winter. Once a year, clans like Eamon's and people in the rough country from all around would gather at the nearest village to trade provisions that would see them through the winter.

Rowanar wasn't a remarkable town, but it was the largest in the area, and folk had been gathering here for the autumn markets longer than anyone could remember. Magyun farmers willing to trade their crops for good pelts or woodcrafts were plentiful as well, before the remainder of the crops were gathered and sent east. The young men and women found it particularly exciting, for it was also an opportunity to meet new partners and potentially strike marriage bargains outside of their clans.

"My lord, it is too dangerous," Cathbad warned quietly as Eamon began saddling his mount.

Eamon sighed, not shifting his attention from the horse. "Dangerous? We have no enemies left here."

"No? What about—"

"We are too small in number for any of them to care about us these days, my old friend," he amended, cutting off the chief druid's complaint before it could be further voiced.

It was an unfortunate truth. Infighting for regional supremacy between the local Velkcic clans had decimated Eamon's forces. Of those left, he had been forced to marry off several of the women as hostages to ensure peace.

"And this close to winter, the Emorians will remain in the south," he continued with a bitter note. "Their fighting season is over."

Cathbad blew out a breath and attempted a different tactic. "A large party on the road is ripe for attack by every bandit and brigand in the region."

Eamon abandoned the buckle he'd been adjusting on his horse's bridle and turned to face the chief druid. "Cathbad, safe or no, the people need it. We have had a hard year, and it will be a harder winter. How can I deny them an opportunity to escape this pall that hangs over us, if only for a day? Those who wish to stay may do so, but I will not forbid those who wish to come."

Cathbad recognized a losing argument when he heard one. The chieftain was young, confident, and determined. There would be no turning him now from his chosen path.

"At least take more warriors."

Eamon eyed him with the ghost of a grin. "We are Velkcic, my friend. Half of us were born with a sword in our hands, but I will divide the warriors enough to protect those who stay and those who go."

The chief druid nodded once, acknowledging the point. It was the best he could hope to achieve. His concerns had nothing to do with the size of the traveling party. There was danger to the east. He could not see its nature, but he was filled with a creeping dread whenever he thought of Rowanar. Eamon clapped him on the shoulder before turning to finish with his mount. Cathbad turned to see to his own horse, then noticed all three of the apprentice druids riding into the clearing beside Eamon's bannermen. He scowled as they approached.

"What do you think you are doing?"

Briga reined her horse to a stop beside her teacher, flashing an easy grin to the chieftain and the chief druid. Owen and Amergin rode on either side of her, smiling placidly.

"We're accompanying the clan, of course."

"No, you are not."

"Let them come," Eamon drawled as he mounted his horse and turned it to the group of druids, flashing a smile at Briga. "The gods wouldn't let harm befall four of their druids at once."

Cathbad opened his mouth to remind the chieftain that the apprentices belonged to him, and the gods would do as they pleased, but stopped short at what he saw on Eamon's face. The young chieftain appeared calm enough, but Cathbad could see the tension held in check by his studied, easy bearing. Eamon was afraid.

"Cathbad," Briga offered with quiet sincerity, "our place is with the clan, is it not? We must protect them in our way."

The chief druid turned to look at her. She sat atop her horse easily, one hand resting on the hilt of one of her twin fighting knives. A current of dread coursed through him at the sight of that dagger—old memories, and new fears. Tragedy waited in Rowanar. He could not see its source or its nature, but he could feel the threads of discord echoing through the Pattern even now. However, Eamon was right, the clan needed reassurance, whatever might come. And so he only nodded, trusting in fate to protect them.

***

12

Briga awoke sometime later with the startled jerk of one who had tried and failed to resist the pull of sleep. The warrior was still there, seated at an elaborately painted table situated along the curved wall near the bed. He'd been penning something but paused to glace up at her sudden movement. The look on his face was speculative. After a moment, he muttered what sounded like something about thorns and returned to his writing. She chose to interpret it as, "Good morning." Indeed, she could see through the opening in the ceiling the sky beginning to lighten, and hear the horses and men beginning to move about beyond the warm felt walls. One of the generals entered then, stealing the warrior's attention. They exchanged clipped greetings, and her captor looked at her sharply.

"Ayrak," he commanded.

She stared at him stupidly, not understanding. With a slight frown, he gestured expansively to an area across the tent that housed cups and a few wooden casks of…something. Guessing he wanted whatever it was, she rose and filled a cup with what turned out to be a cold, strong-smelling white liquid. He accepted the cup from her and passed it to the general, while she observed what she could of his body language toward the general. Her captor seemed to be of some importance, but beyond that, she could interpret nothing. He grunted irritably to regain her attention, and she registered that the general was watching her with a disapproving, but mildly curious air.

"Ayrak," he grunted again.

Frowning, she pointed to the bowl she had already brought. He cracked his wooden writing scribe across her outstretched knuckles painfully, then pointed with it to the wooden cask. Wounded more in pride than body, she snatched her hand back and moved to fill a second bowl with a scowl.

"So I'm to be your servant then," she grumbled and set the second cup before him with blazing eyes.

He watched her coldly, and she imagined he was trying to determine if she deserved some sort of punishment. She met his gaze levelly, indignation fueling her courage.

"You're in for a surprise. Briga is no one's slave," she growled.

Both men stared at her for a moment.

"Chon," the general said into his cup.

The ghost of a smile touched her captor's face fleetingly before he raised his own cup to his lips. His dark eyes held for her a promise, and a threat. After a moment, the two men resumed their discussion, jointly pouring over maps and whatever the warrior had been writing. Seemingly dismissed, she wandered the round room, examining its contents, knowing it would be futile to try to leave, for almost certainly there would be guards outside if a general was within.

The *ger* had its own sense of order, in a way. Kitchen things were kept here, beside the door. The trappings of a horselord sat opposite, armor and saddle neatly arrayed in their designated place. Beside that sat a small altar with a terrifying deity, and beside *that* were his weapons. His table was arranged at the back of the tent, opposite the door, with his bedding beside it.

She'd been eyeing his sword, remembering bitterly the pair of fighting knives some savage had taken from her after capture, when a solid hand on her arm startled her back to the present. Reflexively she flinched into a fighting stance, reaching for the daggers she no longer carried. Just as quickly she remembered her dignity and straightened, face aflame under her guard's patronizing smile. He said something aloud, eliciting hearty laughs from the general and her captor. Her captor parried with a comment of his own, and she endured the sudden leering smile of the burly guard. It made her skin crawl, but she bit the inside of her cheek and refused to let them see her disgust.

After a few more exchanges, the guard led her outside. Despite the early hour, the camp was a hive of activity. All around her, the forest of *gers* were in various stages of disassembly. It seemed the horde would be moving today, and soon. But in the direction of her home, or theirs? She stared into the west, wondering if she would see familiar banners in the distance, willing them to appear. Briga cringed inwardly. She was no helpless thing to wait meekly for rescue. She was a druid, a warrior in her own right, and capable of rescuing herself. But at the moment, surrounded by hundreds of enemy fighters, she had to focus on preserving herself and her dignity. No, escape for her would have to be through a gift of opportunity, or through the help of her clansmen. For now, she would bide her time, learning all she could about these savages. Perhaps she could identify a weakness she could use toward her eventual escape.

The previous night had been a near thing. She had been ruminating on the curious set of events she'd undergone, when she realized with alarm that she was not being led to her old *ger*, where they'd held her prisoner while she recovered from her battle wounds. They neared a pen of sorts, where other captured women were being held. They clearly were not of the warrior class, nor were all of them from Velkcic tribes. They were of mixed breeding and clans. Some were crying and clutching one another. Some were sullen. A handful were haughty, but resigned. One unfortunate girl was being dragged away behind three horsemen. It didn't require a druid to divine their intentions, and Briga tensed with mingled pity and disgust. The guard sensed this and growled something at her, warning her not to interfere as his knuckles tightened around the hilt of his sword.

To her surprise, her guard led her past the slave pens and kept on walking. They came eventually to a long string of horses, which stood ready under saddle. Her guard, whom she'd decided to call Joren, led her to a stunning gray gelding. She had known a Joren once. He was a brute, and dimwitted. The name seemed to fit. Polished silver baubles shone from the gray horse's bridle and reins and glistened from the high cantle and horn of the saddle. Joren was asking her something. After a comical pantomime, she divined he was inquiring as to her ability to ride. Briga nodded that she could, and he untied two horses from the line. A second guard swung easily into the saddle of a spirited palomino. Joren held the gray's head while she mounted, then vaulted astride a white steed of his own.

By now the camp was almost ready to move. Servants and warriors alike were loading disassembled tents, provisions, and plunder onto ox and wagon. The entire camp had been taken down in remarkably little time, a testament to the horde's efficiency.

The two guards rode on either side of her. They gave her horse its space, but remained close enough that she couldn't easily escape them. Briga laughed quietly at this. Around her, hundreds of horsemen were mounting up. Escape was decidedly unlikely at the moment, if not outright foolish. Kicking into a trot, the guards guided her toward the front of the caravan. Here, the warriors were moving out in a loosely organized column. They were armored and armed, but seemed vaguely relaxed, apparently not expecting any sort of trouble. She noted grimly that they were headed east, away from her clan and her home. She estimated in a day or two, they would cross the Danu river, and then her chances of escape would drop to almost nothing.

Turning in the saddle, she scanned the horizon, hoping to see a gleam of metal or a flash of wolfskin in the distance. Estimating her time in captivity, Eamon's clan would have had a few days to regroup, and surely the horde camp couldn't have been difficult to find, as large as it was. There had to be a thousand riders here, at least. When her clansmen lacked numbers, their tactic would be to follow discreetly and attack with stealth during the night to free their women. If enough of them had survived, she amended. She tried not to dwell on the faces of her clansmen, especially that of Eamon. Had he survived? She had lost sight of him at the very start of the fighting. With a heavy sigh, she slumped in the saddle and attempted to reach out with her other senses, her druid senses.

But the motion of the horse and the chaos of the massed warriors around her were too great a distraction. What she needed was a sacred grove.

As a means of passing the time, she decided to choose names for the warriors riding near her. The second guard, Joren's ever-present shadow, sported a tuft of short hair on the top of his head that stuck up in such a way she was reminded of a hatchling baby bird. Smiling to herself, she repeated his new moniker quietly.

"Baby Bird."

Both guards swiveled their heads toward her at the noise. Baby Bird cocked an eyebrow in puzzlement. Joren just seemed irritated. He probably hated guard duty. Briga laughed softly and picked her next target out of the crowd.

After a time, they crossed a wide meadow. Sharp-eyed, Briga picked out a cluster of oaks not far away standing as sentinels over one side of the clearing. Unsure of how to communicate her need, she gently guided her horse in that direction. Joren looked at her sharply and kept his mount in line, effectively barring her intended path. Pinched between the white and the palomino of her guards, her horse was forced to continue plodding eastward. Deciding to risk that they would try to stop her but not harm her unduly, she altered strategy. Briga pulled gently on the reins, slowing her horse slightly so it gradually fell half a length or so behind her guards. Satisfied with the distance created, she reined sharply to the right and kicked her horse into a gallop. It cut behind Joren's white and eagerly accelerated into a dead sprint.

Uttering foreign curses, the two guards reacted instantly. Thankfully none of the other warriors intervened, and she made it about half a mile before Joren finally caught up. In an impressive feat of balance, he reached out and grabbed her horse by the bridle and stopped both mounts sharply. Rather than fight for control, Briga surrendered, but urgently gestured in the direction of the grove.

"Please, I must go there!"

Joren looked at the rider of the palomino, who shrugged and shook his head. Sighing in irritation, he spoke a command to Baby Bird, who drew his sword in response and raced off to check the grove. Still holding her bridle, Joren allowed their horses to approach at a more cautious walk. Baby Bird met them near the tree line, apparently indicating that all was clear. Dismounting, Joren took the reins of the white and the gray and waited while Briga dismounted herself. With the horses in one hand, and her arm in the other, he steered her into the grove. Thinking she needed to answer a call of nature, Joren turned his back, but would not allow her to wander. Briga had a different call in mind altogether.

It soon became clear to Joren that she hadn't come here to relieve herself, but he would not allow her to stray deeper into the grove. It was all she could do to keep him from dragging her off again. After somehow convincing him to wait a moment, she sank to her knees in the bare soil. Chanting the old words, she beseeched the god of the oak to aide her search. She held in her mind an image of Eamon, letting her thoughts travel and expand through space, seeking. She thought she felt his thread, but she was rewarded only with the image of a running wolf. It seemed near. Through the vision she could hear its breathing, smell its fur. Joren was forced to turn his attention to the horses, which were suddenly nervous, rolling their eyes and dancing fearfully. She tried once more to reach her clan, seeking out the threads of Amergin and dark Owen, but try as she might she couldn't single them out from the great Pattern. She could only hope the surviving druids had felt her, somehow.

Gradually she became aware of another sound. It was something not heard with the ears, but with the soul. She pressed one hand to the earth, and another to the stout oak, seeking guidance. The horses were still skittish. Joren, impatient, yanked her up to leave, but she had already glimpsed enough to know.

"Emorians," she stated simply and gestured to the southeast.

That was a word Joren understood, and he eyed her skeptically. His horse danced away from her, but she calmed the gray with a look and a gentle hand on his velvet nose. The horse was still blowing, but stood to let her mount, and the pair rode out of the trees to rejoin Baby Bird. The palomino was skittish as well, and the trio of horses were all too eager to put distance between themselves and the trees. They ran eagerly, and without need of encouragement from their riders, back to the relative safety of the column.

***

They had lingered long enough that the formation had fallen into its natural order. Mounted warriors rode at the front, arranged according to their station. Further behind were the herd animals used for milk and meat, tended by horsemen of their own. Behind these were the laden oxcarts. In the rear were more mounted warriors. Some led strings of bound slaves; others guarded them. This group was interspersed with the injured and the warriors who had lost their horses during the fighting. She'd noticed they had not attempted to ride any of the spare horses herded in their group and fleetingly wondered why. Surely it would be faster than walking? Perhaps they'd been disgraced somehow. Shrugging to herself, she resumed her observations. Several minutes to the rear of the column rode a small but capable rear guard. Despite the apparent success of their recent campaign, the horde was still in enemy lands. Briga's warrior-captor was nowhere to be seen, but likely he was somewhere toward the front, with the greater warrior contingent.

The hours ticked by tediously. The horses in the column were unaccustomed to the slow pace of walking, but any faster speed, and they would lose the slaves and the cargo. A sea of twitching ears kept the horsemen occupied, controlling their agitated mounts. They passed remarkably few settlements, and Briga found herself wondering if this was why there had been so

19

little warning of their attack. The few settlements they did pass seemed hastily abandoned. With luck, the owners were hiding somewhere nearby, waiting for the danger to pass, but somehow she doubted it. Any stray animals were quickly absorbed into the guided flocks and herds of the nomad warriors. They were taken without resistance.

As the sun reached its zenith, Joren withdrew a long strip of dried meat from somewhere on his person. Briga eyed him curiously, mostly wondering what it was and where it could possibly have been stored. Joren caught her looking and favored her with a disapproving gaze, which lasted long enough that she began to feel uncomfortable. With a grunt, he tore off a piece and tossed it to her, along with a chunk of bread.

"Thank you," she murmured, catching it.

She hadn't realized she was hungry until she chewed off a piece. Joren ignored her gratitude and resumed his mastication. The bread was thick and raw, but filling, and she chewed happily. The gray tensed suddenly beneath her and swiveled its ears to the side. A moment later, the head followed, and he called shrilly to something off to the south. An answering neigh floated out of the distant tree line. This was nothing new. They had resumed their place near the front portion of the column, and her horse was usually the first to spot another horse in the distance. They'd encountered one or two wary herds in this manner, but most of the unfamiliar horses kept their distance. This time, however, the answering call made Briga uneasy. Her other senses were roused by the call, searching.

"Emorians," she recalled aloud, drawing yet another irritated and disapproving frown from Joren.

It seemed to be his favorite—perhaps his only—expression.

Instinctively she followed the line of her horse's attention and scanned the tree line. Something flashed quickly, so quickly in fact that she wondered if it might have been imagined. A few seconds later, an arrow thudded into the ground twenty paces from the column.

"Archers!" she called reflexively, but the warriors near her had seen it as well.

Joren and Baby Bird drew their curved swords, while the warriors around them nocked arrows of their own in preparation. The enemy was yet out of range. Briga had never entered a battle unarmed, and the prospect made her uncomfortable. Briefly she considered making her escape during the chaos of fighting, but decided falling slave to the Emorians, if that was actually who they were, would be even less desirable than her current predicament. The Emorians were sure to recognize her as a druid, a rival to their own religious beliefs. If the horselords were aware of her status, they didn't seem to care. No, it was more likely they thought her nothing more than an anomalous female warrior, a novelty. On the other hand, it might be her clansmen, though this was not a tactic they were likely to employ. She opted to watch and ensure she was prepared to seize any opportunity that presented itself.

Baby Bird must have been reading her mind, for he snatched her reins with his left hand and kept her horse close alongside his, out of the way of his sword arm. A cloud of enemy arrows rose into the sky, followed not by an Emorian war cry, but by one that was distinctively and curiously Magyun. But the legion was still out of range, and most of the arrows fell harmlessly short of their targets. For a time it seemed as if nothing more would happen. Both sides knew the horselords held the advantage when they could remain mounted. They would not willingly concede that advantage to fight among the trees. Neither would that other force venture out into the open against superior numbers. Gradually they seemed to melt back into the forest, presumably to regroup and strategize.

Without warning, they burst from the trees in a wide horse column, shields raised and spearing for the slower oxen section of the line. With a cry of their own, the warriors near her drew swords and rode out to meet the enemy. Briga could see now

21

that they weren't Emorians, though they were clothed and armed in that fashion. No, these were Magyuns, though clearly they emulated the fighting style and dress of their southern ally. There were several such clans in this area loyal to Emoria, to include some Velkcic she'd heard spoken of often enough by her own clan with no trace of respect. The enemy drove on in a mad rush. It seemed they hoped to outpace the warriors by striking quickly at the cargo and running off with what they could. But appearances were deceiving, and even without the warrior phalanx, the ox drivers and shepherds accompanying the cargo were capable fighters themselves.

The resulting scuffle was intense, bloody, and short. Only four nomads had been slain, but a goodly number were cut or otherwise wounded. By contrast, at least a third of the attackers littered the ground. The rest had lost their nerve and retreated. One ox and its packs were missing, but otherwise the raid had been successfully repulsed.

For the rest of the day, Joren regarded her with wary suspicion, and Baby Bird refused to let go of her reins. Had they sensed her powers in the grove this morning, or were they simply watchful, lest she try to escape? Did they think she had somehow summoned the attacking force? She couldn't tell. The column traveled with slightly more haste, and the horsemen at the flanks were a shade more vigilant after the failed raid. It would take a sizable force to truly threaten the horde, especially out in the open, but small raids and harassments were a risk not to be tolerated.

Chapter 3

Late in the afternoon they stopped to make camp within sight of the Danu. The river need not be close to protect their flank, for the land here was open, and the warriors enjoyed a view of the surrounding area for several miles up and downstream. An enemy foolish enough to attempt crossing the river within sight of the camp would still have to cross several kilometers of relatively open ground before its archers would be in range.

Despite the early afternoon skirmish, the column hadn't ridden hard today, so the pack animals and provisions trailed only a few minutes behind the warriors. Briga and her guards had ridden on to water their horses from a nearby stream. By the time they returned, the first animals were already being unloaded. She could smell the smoke from the cook fires and wearily dismounted. Baby Bird led the horses away, while Joren hovered at her side. Ignoring him, she gingerly massaged her legs. She was unaccustomed to spending an entire day in the saddle, and her muscles were tight with protest. It felt good to stand and walk a bit, and even better to splash the dirt from her face in the cool water of the stream.

The ornamented tent of her captor was being erected nearby, and she watched the process curiously. The skeleton had already been assembled, but they were now pulling a thick layer of felt around the outer wall, and another over the roof. A clattering of hooves announced the approach of a rider. Briga turned to see her captor approach, flanked by two other warriors. He reined up sharply and swung from the saddle with fluid ease, exchanging words of greeting with the unsmiling Joren. He handed off his horse to Joren as the other two riders dismounted and stepped away to supervise construction of the *ger*. Or at least that's what she assumed they were doing.

Joren seemed to be giving a report on the day's events, for her captor regarded her once or twice during the speech with a look of mingled surprise and amusement. Briga caught only the word "Emorians," and tried in vain to study their body language. Surely he would report her detour to the oaks, but what had he seen? More importantly, what had he *thought*? Druid gifts might seem like witchcraft to the uninitiated, and being labeled a witch in any society was often dangerous. Her captor nodded solemnly as Joren finished speaking, then dismissed him. Turning back to Briga, he took her by the elbow and led her to his tent.

Servants had already emplaced most of his furniture. They made way for him respectfully, but continued with their duties. The fire had not been lit, and in its absence, a woman entered carrying a steaming wooden cask and a ladle. She watched Briga expectantly. When she failed to move, the woman made an irritated sound and searched the tent with her eyes. Feeling awkward, Briga hurried to snatch a stack of small bowls and carried them to the woman, who stared at her aggressively for a moment before accepting a small, polished silver vessel.

"Ayag," the woman instructed as she held up the bowl.

"Ayag…" Briga parroted weakly, unsure what the word indicated. "Bowl?" she guessed.

"Ayag, ayag." The woman nodded and ladled a healthy portion of a white, salty smelling liquid. She then gestured to Briga's captor, directing her to serve him the bowl.

Briga carried it in two hands to where he stood leaning against the table. The corner of his mouth turned up in a faint smile as he watched her, and he accepted the beverage with the slightest inclination of his head. When she turned around again, the woman had a second bowl waiting for her. With no further instruction, she assumed this one was hers, and raised it to her lips experimentally. She hadn't been sure what to expect, but hot, salty milk was the last thing she had imagined. It tasted surprisingly good after a long day of riding. The warmth seemed to pool in her muscles and bones, easing them somewhat. The woman grunted her approval, then topped off Briga and her captor's bowls before departing.

The warrior was watching her intently, his attention making her nervous once again. He smiled suddenly and pointed to his bowl, asking her something that she interpreted to be, "Do you remember the word for this?"

"...ayag?" she ventured uncertainly.

He nodded and flashed a toothy grin in an expression resembling pride. She smiled, pleased, and felt herself blush slightly. With an immediate self-reproach, she scolded herself for feeling pride at making him happy. He was the enemy, and she, his slave. She must not forget. Undeterred, he placed his free hand flat on his chest in the universal sign of introduction.

"Mini ner Batu Khan."

"Min...minnerbattan?" she stumbled over their foreign syllables.

He shook his head and tried again, speaking more slowly. "Batu Khan."

Khan? She wondered if she'd heard that correctly. The word seemed faintly familiar.

"Batu Khan."

He nodded confirmation and stared at her, waiting.

"Briga," she offered, laying a hand on her own chest, mimicking his gesture.

"Breeg," he repeated.

Gently he grasped her chin between his thumb and forefinger, examining her face. To her immense relief, one of

25

the generals entered at that moment to speak with him. Batu released her quickly and turned to greet him. She backed away, thankful for the opportunity to put space between them. He had been patient and tolerant of her resistance last night, but she knew that couldn't last. He glanced at her again for a moment before guiding the general to his desk and spreading out some parchment or another. As the two bent to their task, she used the opportunity to slip out of the *ger* behind a servant. No one stopped her. *Can it be this easy?*

Walking with a purpose, she threaded her way to the edge of camp. The area was hilly and densely forested, saving the swath of open high ground currently occupied by the developing camp. The forest here was mostly pine and cedar, but there were a few sacred trees of oak and ash scattered about. The afternoon light was beginning to weaken, but that would be no problem. Inside the tree line, she rested one hand on the sturdy trunk of an ash tree and inhaled deeply.

Most people weren't sensitive enough to feel it, but trees had heartbeats. A dull, electric pulsing transmitted through her fingertips in silent communication. Oak and ash had different properties, and therefore different uses. Her skills were more suited to oak, but she drew what she could from any tree. Closing her eyes, she reached out with her senses to listen. There was still a faint feel of Emorian presence, but it was barely distinguishable. She could feel a slight tingling, almost like a quiet buzzing at the base of her skull. Experience told her this was another druid seeking her pattern, and a powerful one at that.

A twig snapped loudly ahead of her. She didn't move, but her eyes flicked open instantly. She could see as well as feel the wolf crouching in the shadows, watching her.

"Easy, brother," she breathed soothingly. "I'm no harm to you, nor you to me."

The wolf growled, but to Briga's ear, the tone was uncertain rather than hostile. She sank to her knees slowly, demonstrating that she was no threat. The wolf was alone, but he was a large specimen. His ears flicked forward, and the growling changed pitch as he focused on something just beyond her shoulder. Briga snapped her attention around to see Joren standing there with his bow half drawn, fixated on the large predator.

"Shhhh!" she urged, motioning frantically for him to crouch.

She could easily read his inner debate, plastered as it was across his face. After a few shallow breaths, he finally complied, though the bow remained at low ready. The growling subsided quickly. After a moment the wolf cautiously padded out toward Briga, watching her carefully. Briga waited, not meeting his yellow gaze, but tried to project calming thoughts. She could sense Joren's tension as the beast inched closer and sniffed at her hands and face. As if recognizing her scent, his rough tongue scraped her face once and he nuzzled her hands. Grinning, Briga petted the beast and scratched its great, shaggy head. Her druid senses recognized Cathbad in his fur. *So this creature has been sent to find me.* She grinned at the thought, then turned her attention to Joren, who tensed visibly. With a pleased smile, she stood and gestured to the wolf. Joren frowned and stood as well, watching her closely.

There was a bush nearby sporting dark-colored berries. She picked a few and, crushing them one at a time between her fingers, drew an ogham symbol of protection on the wolf's flank. It was a message seeking help from her clan. Returning to Joren, she tried to pantomime eating, remembering the dried meat he carried with him. He shook his head, either indicating he had nothing, or he didn't understand. She stroked the wolf's head and looked directly into his eyes.

"Sorry, brother, I have nothing to offer you."

The animal snorted as if offended and drew back. Sniffing in Joren's direction, he finally turned and bounded off into the trees once more. She watched after him silently, delaying the moment when she would have to face Joren. When she did finally turn and look at him, she was surprised by the lack of emotion on his face. She had been expecting a reaction, any reaction. He was watching after the wolf, but his face was a blank mask.

Could this sort of thing be commonplace among the horse people? No, surely not, or the rumors would have reached druid circles. No, what little was known about the horsemen wasn't spirituality or druid gifts, only fighting prowess and ferocity. As she watched, Joren collected a few stones and created a small pile where the wolf had stood. His purpose was impossible to guess without knowing more about the man, and she vowed to find out in time.

At least one mystery had been solved. It had been so easy to walk out of camp earlier because she had a silent escort. Distantly she wondered if Batu had declared her ransom price yet, and how long she could linger away from the camp before he sent for her again. Surely he wouldn't be occupied entertaining the generals all night.

"Not long" was apparently the answer. Joren had finished building his cairn and was watching her expectantly. With a heavy sigh, she turned and made her way back to the camp. She had no idea how far away her kinsmen might be, but she was certain the wolf would return to Cathbad. She lacked his talent with animals, but the berry stains in the ogham symbol for a rowan tree would convey her message. And the wolf could retrace its steps, leading them back to her.

She was distracted by these thoughts upon reentering the camp, when a rough hand shot out of the dimness and took hold of her wrist. She whirled to face the hand's owner, indignantly drawing back. The stranger only grinned malevolently and pulled sharply against her attempted withdrawal. His strength sent her crashing against his bare chest. The stranger's arm encircled her shoulders automatically, holding her close, while his other hand released her wrist and squeezed her breast painfully.

She squirmed against him, seeking leverage with her arms to push him away. Briga was instantly aware that he was far too strong for her, and unsuccessfully tried to ram her knee into his groin, settling instead for kicking at his shin and knee. She was rewarded by a sharp tug on her hair, which pulled her head back and exposed her neck to his unwanted attentions, and she cried out involuntarily. An arm snaked around her stomach from behind with iron-like strength. It pulled her back, away from her assailant, and against Joren's startlingly solid torso. Shifting, he tucked her behind himself protectively, and held his unsheathed sword at the ready.

A heated and loud discussion followed, in which Joren emerged victorious without having to swing his blade. Sheathing it, he took an insistent but gentle grip on her elbow and steered her directly to Batu's tent. She was still shaken when they arrived, moving half dazed as her mind processed the rapidity of the whole encounter. With sudden clarity of thought, she realized the men around her to date had treated her with singular civility, a condition she had taken for granted around the rest of the horde. The meager safety she enjoyed didn't extend beyond those felt walls. In reality, the common soldiers viewed her no differently than any other foreign slave—an object with certain uses. Nothing more. She realized suddenly that Joren and Baby Bird were there not only to guard her, but to protect her as well. She watched Joren with appreciative shock as he ushered her into the tent, but his expression never wavered.

Batu caught the look on her face and left the generals around the table, crossing to Joren in a few great strides. Joren made his report quietly, but the full extent of his report would remain a mystery to Briga. She stared at Batu curiously. Had he arranged for her safekeeping? If so, why? Batu kept his attention on Joren as he spoke, though she could see a muscle bunching in his jaw with controlled ire. He narrowed his eyes and turned to her, taking her chin in his hand, and examining her face and neck as if checking for injury. He let out a short sigh and clapped Joren on the shoulder, apparently dismissing him for the time being. She noticed that Joren stopped in the doorway to look at her before taking his leave. Batu had noticed it, too. He took her by the arm and led her to the piled furs, encouraging her to sit before rejoining the generals at their work.

What now?

Her stomach growled, and she realized she hadn't eaten since the few bites of dried meat at lunch. At a look from Batu, an attendant brought her a bowl of noodle soup with mutton, and a bowl of the hot, salty milk. She accepted both gratefully and settled in to eat. At the meeting, a disagreement was brewing. One of the generals stood and pounded his hand on the table. He had a long but wispy mustache, which seemed comically out of place with his full, groomed beard. Batu responded to him calmly. Whatever he said seemed to placate the other man enough for him to sit down again. She wondered what they were discussing. Perhaps she could catch sight of a map sometime, which might provide insight as to their intentions.

After finishing her meal, the attendant brought her another bowl of milk, this one cool and strong-smelling. It was fermented, and she recognized the smell from the drinks she'd served Batu and his guest this morning. Hesitantly she raised it to her lips for a taste. Everything about it was strong—the smell, the flavor, and the alcohol content. But for all that, it was strangely appealing. She sipped contentedly, watching and listening to the unintelligible discussion at the table, and enjoying the tiny warm ember forming in the pit of her stomach.

The meeting didn't last much longer. The men were all grim-faced, especially the one with the wispy mustache, but she sensed no malevolence in them. Of course, it was hard to be certain. As a people, they commonly displayed a dour face, but she suspected that was only indifference. Perhaps it was just the way their faces were arranged.

One or two of the generals eyed her on their way out, but said nothing. Batu sat watching her silently from the table, sipping a bowl of fermented horse milk that had appeared seemingly from thin air. An attendant had topped off her own bowl, and she took a healthy swallow for strength.

"Hurt?" he asked after a lengthy silence.

She looked at him, wondering if he'd actually spoken. It was only the second time he had attempted her language, and the effect was unsettling.

"No." She shook her head for emphasis and subconsciously rubbed her shoulder at the memory.

With an incomprehensible grunt, he stood and crossed to her. Reaching down, he peeled the clothing away from her shoulder. She grabbed at it reflexively, indignant.

"Shh. No fear."

Frowning, she relented, but her nerves were still on edge, and she was ready to react again if necessary. He bared her shoulder, but nothing more, examining her flesh for injury. She watched him, puzzled. Why all this tender concern? Were slaves treated so well here?

"Men…wild, after fighting." He waved a hand vaguely, indicating everything around them.

She nodded slowly, thinking she understood the warning. If it was a warning, that is. He spoke again in this own tongue, not having words she could understand. He tapped his temple and under one eye to illustrate his point.

Think and watch, she translated silently, then nodded.

He stared into her eyes, seeking comprehension. Finding it, he moved to smooth the hair back from her face. She flinched away by habit. His hand paused mid-air, and the small muscle in his jaw was bunching again, but his eyes betrayed no emotion except a brief flicker she couldn't read. He tried again, and she forced herself to remain still, but couldn't help squeezing her eyes shut. This man had saved her from the fate of the other women. She must not anger him, though the thought of

31

submitting to him turned her stomach. Still, in this case, better to submit than to be conquered. At least her dignity would still be somewhat intact. He brushed her hair back tenderly, allowing the loose, tawny tresses to play through his fingers.

When she opened her eyes again, he was staring at her, waiting for something. She bravely tried a smile, but it faltered quickly. He pressed the bowl of fermented milk into her hand, stood, and crossed the tent in search of something. She sipped at the milk gratefully, and was surprised to see him produce the horse-headed fiddle.

Batu took a stool from the table and placed it near her, then settled himself, and with an expert hand, tuned the fiddle until the sound was to his liking. He smiled at her briefly, then launched into a calm and faintly sad melody.

Briga realized what he was doing for her and was genuinely grateful. She sipped at the milk and settled into the furs, allowing the music to calm and soothe her. She realized, listening to him play, that she felt safe for the first time during the whole of her captivity, even if the feeling only lasted a moment. She closed her eyes and let the music paint pictures in her mind. The song made her think of crossing mountains in the winter, though she couldn't say why. Briga had never seen a mountain in her life, though she had heard stories of them. Nevertheless, it was remarkably vivid. The pace of the song increased slowly as he played, building. By the end, she imagined herself running, breathless, down a spring-greened slope onto a wide pasture that sparkled with dew under a cold morning sun. The music faded, and she opened her eyes with a smile. Whatever he might be as a warrior, he was a skilled musician.

The next song made her think of running horses. It could be nothing else. She watched his fingers on the strings, fascinated with his skill in coaxing music from simple wood and horsehair. The fiddle approximated a neigh so precisely that it gave her chills. The sound was even more realistic than the first time she'd heard it, and she wondered more seriously what kind of gift he might be harboring. The song stopped abruptly and resumed at a slower pace as the horses ceased their running, then finished on a sharply haunting note. Smiling grimly, he set the instrument aside and approached her. She could feel herself paling as he looked down at her, and she set the half-drunk bowl aside. She steadied her breathing and resolved to endure what was to come with all the dignity of her station. She would try to think of Eamon. Maybe she could even pretend it was him here with her.

He sank onto the furs beside her and gently caressed her shoulders. His touch felt like lightning, and her breath caught in surprise. His fingers traveled up her neck, exploring her skin with the same tender respect he used on the horse-headed fiddle, gently massaging the base of her skull and the tender area behind her ear. Her body responded to his touch of its own accord, tilting her chin down slightly and angling away from him to expose the length of her neck. He leaned closer and kissed the side of her throat, hand sliding down to caress her ribs. The sensations were remarkable, but she couldn't bring herself to enjoy it, and she tightly shut her eyes. He paused, feeling her tense, and looked at her.

"Breeg," he commanded quietly.

She opened her eyes and looked at him with carefully contained fear. He stroked her ribs with his thumb for a time, simply watching her. Finally he sighed heavily, kissed her briefly on the forehead, and stood up. She watched uncertainly as he disrobed and returned to the sleeping pallet wearing only his skin. He lay on his back and pointed to the empty space at his side. Feeling half frozen, she nodded and crawled up beside him. Gently he grasped the back of her head and guided her down until she rested on his shoulder. His arm curled around her back, holding her, while his free hand flicked a shaggy yak pelt over them both. Briga lay on her side against him, head pillowed on his shoulder obediently. Trembling, she waited for something to happen, but he seemed content to let her sleep. Feeling her tremors and correctly interpreting them as fear, he smoothed her hair back and rested his cheek against the top of her head. The hand around her back caressed her soothingly.

"No fear," he murmured, so quietly she thought she might have imagined it.

Chapter 4

The early morning found them in much the same position. Her hand was splayed across his muscled chest, covered by his own. She simply lay there for a moment, listening to Batu's slow, steady breathing. This was the closest she had ever been to a naked man, really the only time, and it made her acutely aware of her own clothing, and grateful for it. Though sleeping fully clothed had never been her custom, it was suddenly less uncomfortable, under the circumstances.

An attendant crept in silently to stoke the fire, and Briga tracked his progress with her eyes. A stick of wood popped loudly in the brazier, and Batu's arm tightened protectively around her. The attendant was staring. Briga glared back at him hotly enough to bring him to his senses and send him on his way. A few moments later Batu inhaled sharply and deeply as his body roused itself from sleep. He looked down at her, quietly pleased that she hadn't shied away from him during the night. He squeezed her hand affectionately and kissed her forehead before getting up. Saying something, he looked at her and gestured drowsily to his discarded clothes. She assumed he wanted her to retrieve them and got up stiffly to comply. She picked up the robes and held them out to him. With a grunt, he shook his head and held his arms out to the sides.

She stood blinking at him. "You want me to dress you?"

He merely watched her, waiting, the small muscle in his jaw beginning to tighten. With a sigh, she slid the robes over his arms and smoothed the collar flat around his neck. Tucking one side under the other, she secured the fastenings at his shoulder and his side. Batu nodded his approval. He stood as she retrieved the winding that served as cinch and belt and patiently

35

guided her hands through the correct way to tie it. It was really a clever method of tuck and fold more than it was an actual knot, which Briga found markedly distinctive in its simplicity. Batu seemed content to begin his morning routine without donning weapons or armor and slipped outside to relieve himself.

For the first time, Briga was alone in his tent, without even a servant to observe her. Seizing the opportunity, she scampered over to the table, searching for anything useful. None of the writings were in a language she could read, rendering them useless to her. At least for now. In the center of the table, however, was a map. Clearly it wasn't of local origin. Lands to the east were fairly detailed, while those in the west, occupied by Magyun and Velks, were shapeless and indistinct. A few scribbled edits were apparent, either from Batu's own advance through the area, or from a scout network. The settlement of Rowanar was marked, she noticed grimly. Frustratingly, their current position was not marked—at least not in a way she could recognize. She guessed one prominent, meandering scribble to be the mighty river Danu, but surrounding terrain was nonexistent. Farther east there seemed to be another horselord force encamped. Perhaps that was where they were heading. It appeared to be several day's ride beyond the Danu, perhaps even a week.

A noise near the tent flap startled her, and she fled back to the sleeping pallet, feigning stretching. It was the serving woman from yesterday, bearing two bowls of hot soup. She handed them to Briga one at a time, along with a string of instructions whose meaning she could only guess at. Without waiting for acknowledgement, the woman left again, and Batu wandered back in, trailing one of the seemingly ever-present generals. Not for the first time, she was curious as to her captor's role here. He had the ear of several generals, and enough authority to claim her, though she was relatively certain they did not understand what she was, with respect to Velkcic hierarchy. Could he be a strategist, perhaps? Noticing the general carried a bowl of soup already, she quickly handed one to Batu, who smiled as he accepted it.

She tried to remain off to the side and out of the way as she drank her soup. Already, servants were creeping in to retrieve various items from the tent in preparation for its disassembly. So they would be on the move again today. Briga couldn't put her finger on it, but she had the impression they had not originally planned to move again so soon. From the horselord perspective, it would be good to cross the Danu as soon as possible. Delays at this point would only give any enemies time to mass their forces for an ambush at the vulnerable crossing point. Presumably they had determined the way, at the moment, was clear. By the time she finished eating, Batu was shrugging into his armor and speaking animatedly with the general. He sucked down the rest of his soup and followed the general outside, handing Briga the empty bowl as he passed. Noticing with a frown that they had taken the map with them, she placed the empty bowls on the table and boldly strode outside to see to her morning ablutions in the cold stream.

Joren materialized not far behind, but his following distance was less discreet than it had been last night. She paused long enough for him to draw even with her.

"Good morning," she offered, to no response. "Did you sleep well?"

Joren looked at her quizzically but offered nothing.

"Where do you sleep, anyway?"

His look slowly morphed into one of concern.

"Oh, I see. Well, I slept reasonably well, all things considered. Thank you for asking."

His mood was quickly transforming into irritation as she continued her one-sided conversation. She dallied at the stream, washing her face and as much of herself as she dared in his presence, noting with a frown that her clothing was showing the effects of battle and road dust. The first of the pack animals were beginning to move out, solidifying Joren's ire. Patience expired and brooking no argument, he took her firmly by the arm and led her back into camp. Baby Bird was already mounted and leading the white and gray horses, looking for them. Joren called out to catch his attention, and all three of them were soon mounted and riding toward the gathering column of warriors. As they picked their way through the throng, Briga wondered if she would recognize her assailant from the previous evening. *Probably not*, she decided, but his anonymity was somehow worse. She felt suddenly cold scanning the crowd, then decided to ignore all of them en masse.

She'd just started thinking about Cathbad's wolf when a thunder of hoofbeats demanded her attention. Everyone turned to look at the rider approaching from the rear. She realized suddenly that it was Batu atop a gleaming black stallion, running at a dead sprint. He was being followed by a standard-bearer carrying the black horsehair banner of an army at war, and there were three more riders behind him. He reined to a hard stop beside her, making her horse dance nervously. In full view of all the men, he rode up beside her, grabbed a handful of her hair, and kissed her full on the mouth. She tried to push him away, but the fist in her hair twisted painfully, demanding compliance. There was a fury in his eyes that frightened her when he finally drew back.

Allowing his stallion to pace restlessly, he made a great loud speech to the men, at one point gesturing to her with his drawn sword, and then waving it at the masses. A battle cry issued from them unexpectedly, and her horse flinched, sensing her unease. Trotting back to her, Batu seized her horse by the bridle and took off at a dead run. Joren and Baby Bird fell in behind them, joining the standard-bearer and the three other riders. The rest of the column followed as Batu led them on recklessly. They ran all the way to the river, slowing at last to rest the blowing horses and let them drink. Most of the riders were panting as well. They had covered at least six breathless miles, but the men and the horses had both needed the release, short-lived as it was.

Farther back, the oxcarts, slaves, and a healthy contingent of warriors were turning north at a more sedate pace. Briga assumed they needed a shallower place to ford. Scouts emerged from the tree line on the opposite side, confirming that now was a safe time to cross. Batu, still holding her horse's bridle, led her aside to a low rise, leaving their contingent to supervise the crossing. At the crest of the hill, he finally released the bridle, and the two of them sat side by side atop their horses, watching the first riders enter the water.

"Breeg," he quietly commanded her attention.

She eyed him warily in response, but he merely touched his temple and below his eye. *Think and watch,* she remembered, nodding. He removed an object from his belt and pressed it into her hands. With a jolt of shock, she realized she was holding one of her sheathed fighting knives, and she stared up at him in open-mouthed astonishment. She'd assumed they were lost forever once she was captured. This knife and its twin were her oldest possessions, and she touched it reverently before returning her gaze to him. He waved away her thanks and helped her tie the scabbard to the saddle in such a way that it wouldn't bother her horse. Without a sword belt, it was her only option at the moment. He looked her over for a moment, then nodded in satisfaction, and led her back to their cohort.

Briga's mind was churning at this sudden turn of events. Batu had offered her protection and trust. She realized by kissing her and dragging her off in front of the men, he was staking his claim on her. Perhaps that would prevent another attack by some battle-drunk, lecherous soldier. But what had his speech been about? It couldn't have all been about her; their frenzied and enthusiastic response indicated something more motivational than merely a captured woman. She would have to puzzle it out later. Additionally he'd returned one of her daggers, and she recognized that instantly as a gesture of trust. Neither action on his part seemed fitting behavior from a master toward his slave. An icy lump began forming in her stomach as she imagined what might really be going on here, but she swallowed her fears and refused to think about it just now.

Ahead, the first contingent of riders were emerging on the far bank. Judging by the wet patches on their legs, the water was about belly-high on the horses. With a frown, she looked down at her garments. Her leather boots would dry eventually, but there was a chill in the air that was sure to make its presence felt. The horses were dancing on the far side, excited by their cool dip in the water. Batu led their group to cross now, not wanting to be too far back in the column. Struck by inspiration, Briga pulled off her boots, secured the leather thongs together, and hung them over her shoulder. Her feet would still get wet, but at least she wouldn't have to ride in soaked boots all day. Batu glanced at her sidelong, and the corner of his mouth turned up in the ghost of a grin.

The water was cold, colder than she had expected, and she sucked in a breath involuntarily. Her horse picked its way across a slick, rocky bottom and had to be urged on through the deeper water. He kept trying to swim, but his hooves struck the bottom, which resulted in an odd jerking, stumbling progress. As he neared the far bank, he lunged excitedly, slipping a few times for his efforts. Finally emerging, he shook himself vigorously, and pranced along the bank, eager but unable to run. Briga carefully slipped the boots back on, thanking the gods for inspiring her to take them off in the first place.

Batu and the first part of the column pressed on, moving into the trees to free up space on the banks. Separated from the encumbered pack animals, the horsemen were free to ride through the forest instead of broadcasting their presence on an open swath of ground, and they seemed to enjoy this new kind of freedom. The horsemen fanned out comfortably and trotted through the trees. Ahead, a cry of warning sounded and cut off abruptly. The forward-riding sentries had encountered something. The tension level around them increased perceptibly, but nothing more was heard. Frowning, Batu spurred his mount forward to investigate. Briga followed close on his heels, curious about what had happened. All the warriors on this side of the river were generally headed in that direction at various stages of alert. They all parted to make way for Batu.

Several horsemen were clustered up ahead, serving as clear indication of the trouble. In the center of them, the earth had opened up and swallowed one unfortunate rider, and the dismounted warriors were treating it with reverent wariness.

The poor horse had been killed almost instantly. Sharpened pikes at the bottom of the pit had done their job all too well, and the horse had been skewered fatally. The rider was wounded and unconscious, but looked to Briga as if he might survive. He lay draped over his horse's lifeless neck, one pike having grazed his side, while another protruded from his calf. None of the warriors moved to help him, but milled tensely near the mouth of the opening. It was almost as if they were afraid of it. Batu was speaking to one of the riders, presumably asking what had happened. Briga slid off the gray's back and handed the reins to the ever-present Joren, who regarded her uncertainly. Drawing her dagger, she thrust the naked blade through her belt and shouldered her way to the opening. Batu leaned down from his horse and caught her by the elbow, forbidding her to get any closer with an emphatic shake of his head.

"Bad spirits," he managed to say, clearly struggling for the correct words.

She stared at him for a moment, realization slowly dawning. They'd never seen a boar pit before. No wonder they were so hesitant. To them, it must have looked like the earth had simply opened up and swallowed the man. She shook her head once, firmly peeling his fingers from her arm. Having freed herself, she was determined now to do the same for the injured warrior below.

The man stared up at her as she circled the pit, searching for the recessed hand holds that would allow her safe descent. Spotting one, she swung over the edge and onto a shallow ledge about two-thirds of the way down. The pikes usually killed any boar that fell into the trap, but the ledge was there just in case it wasn't dead. Boar were notoriously hard to kill, and a hunter had no desire to face an angry, injured pig on equal footing, let alone in the confines of a pit trap. The ledge was there to provide the hunter with a position from which to dispatch his prey.

Briga's quarry was no such threat. Gingerly she patted the dead warhorse and picked her way over to the rider. His breathing was rapid but steady, which she took for a good sign. Blood oozed from his hairline, suggesting he had smacked his head on something. Tearing a strip of fabric from the bottom of her skirt, she bound it around his head gingerly, and moved to address his calf. The pike had entered from the side of the shin, narrowly missing the bone, and poked out of his calf. Healing had been part of her druidic instruction, and she had shown a natural talent for it, but this would be difficult without supplies.

To her uncertain eye, the wound looked manageable enough. The pike appeared to have missed the vital parts of the leg, but time would tell. She knew better than to remove the stick; it was actually helping to staunch the bleeding for the moment. Drawing her dagger, she sawed at the pike to break it off. This wasn't what the dagger had been designed to do, so it was slow progress. At last the pike gave way with a snap. She grunted in satisfaction and carefully repositioned the leg. A quick examination of his side showed no serious injuries, much to her relief. The leg would be bad enough. The warrior groaned as she attempted to move him. He was clearly too heavy to handle alone. Briga glanced up into the crowd of anxious, watching faces and allowed her irritation to show.

"Don't just stand there, help me!"

Joren had dismounted at some point and looked to Batu for guidance. He nodded once, his attention rapt and fixed on the spectacle in the pit. Joren and a warrior standing beside him carefully lowered themselves onto the ledge, then moved to help her lift their brother.

"Mind his leg," she warned, guiding it gingerly.

Despite slightly awkward methods, they finally lifted the wounded man out of the pit, with assistance from those at the top. Briga followed her patient while the two others remained behind to examine the trap and the horse.

"Water," she requested, looking up at Batu, who translated.

Someone handed her a waterskin, and she set about putting her limited healing skills to work. Now that the incident seemed to be over for the most part, Batu was growing tired of delay, and began urging his forces to carry on. Briga stood quickly, suddenly concerned the riders might accidentally discover other pits. They wouldn't all be so lucky if they fell headlong into the pikes, and she didn't have enough skirt left to treat many more. She reached out and put a hand on Batu's knee to catch his attention, knowing better than to grab a half-wild stallion by the bridle. Batu regarded her irritably, but she shook her head meaningfully and pointed from the pit to the forest beyond. He stared at her for a moment, puzzling out her message, but then caught on to her line of thinking and stared into the forest with a narrowed gaze. With a sigh that was equal parts ire and resignation, he turned a cold gaze back to her, plainly expecting guidance. Shrinking slightly from the weight of his attention, she took a few steps toward the open forest, trying to figure out how to explain what to look for.

Luckily she spotted another trap nearby and led him to it. Whoever had dug these pits was clearly skilled in concealment. A scattering of acorns and mushrooms in the center of the square was perhaps the best tell. Crouching down at the trap's edge, she brushed away a covering of dried leaves to reveal thin sticks below. They would snap under the weight of anything larger than a dog. Batu circled the trap carefully, acquainting his horse with the strange, covered chasm. Perhaps the horses could be taught to recognize them as well. Finally dismounting, he crouched beside Briga and poked at the camouflaged opening for himself.

"You don't use traps?" she attempted to ask, pointing at the trap, then to him and shaking her head with a questioning look.

He cocked his head to the side much like a dog, uncertain. She tried again, raising her fingers to her mouth to imitate tusks, and grunted in what she hoped was a decent approximation of a boar. She felt ridiculous and lowered her hands self-consciously as a few nearby soldiers looked at her.

"Gakhai?" he seemed to confirm, imitating tusks himself briefly.

She nodded and pointed to the bait again, then patted her stomach. He seemed to understand and shook his head gravely. He imitated firing a bow. Briga understood.

"No honor," he admonished, nodding toward the pit.

She didn't quite understand what he was trying to convey, and returned her attention to the pit, picking at the camouflaged covering idly. He laid an affectionate hand on her knee and squeezed it lightly in thanks. She patted his hand in return, and stood to return to her patient, but was stopped by a firm grip on her wrist. Batu was staring at her, his expression unreadable. He was searching her face for something but gave nothing away himself. After a few moments, he released her, and she turned away, feeling uneasy.

When she returned to her patient, he was beginning to regain consciousness. Someone had cleaned the superficial wound at his side and had given him a skin of wine to drink. The wounded man watched her skeptically as she knelt on the ground to examine his leg. The pike was perhaps an inch in diameter at its thickest, remarkably thin for the nature of such a trap. The man was luckier than he could ever know. Some of the pikes that had impaled the horse were as wide as her forearm. The one in his leg had lodged under a thick layer of skin, likely causing little if any damage to the muscle beneath, and it had been cut smooth, so few jagged splinters would tear his skin on the way out.

Taking careful hold of the thicker end, she glanced at another nameless warrior crouched beside her patient. The man understood and laid a hand on his shoulder as both encouragement and restraint. As gently as she could, she pulled on the stick to extract it from his leg. At first it wouldn't budge, then it suddenly came loose with a disturbing sucking sound. To his credit, the man didn't move, but he paled noticeably, and beads of sweat formed on his brow. She took the wine from him and flushed the wound as best she could before binding it tightly with another strip of cloth torn from her skirt. That would have to do for now. She could stitch it later, but there were no supplies available here on the march. Riding would almost certainly be better than walking, at least it would bleed less, but she did not envy the man. Already, someone was bringing him a spare horse.

Behind her, Joren made a sound to catch her attention. He was holding her horse and appeared anxious to be on the move again. Baby Bird was nearby as well, his attention focused back the way they had come. Briga mounted and took back her reins, modestly organizing a much-shortened skirt around her knees. Once or twice she caught Joren staring at her exposed calves. He wasn't alone in his attentions. She loosened her dagger in its sheath, just in case. Baby Bird saw her do it and smirked, though it didn't seem to be a patronizing gesture so much as it was amused.

As the horsemen picked their way through the forest, she found herself wondering if her wolf messenger could fall prey to such a trap. Pits were used for wolf, elk, and deer, in addition to boar, so it was possible. Silently, she wished the beast safe journey and continued on with the column.

Chapter 5

The rest of the day passed without incident. The sky remained dark and overcast, but no rain fell. The trees began to thin somewhat as the horsemen climbed rolling hills, slowly but steadily gaining elevation. Around midday, Joren offered her a bit of his dried mutton. Likewise, Baby Bird gave her a piece of bread and an apple he'd found somewhere along the way. She accepted the food gratefully, aware it had probably been given freely rather than on Batu's order. Once or twice she turned in her saddle, curious how the wounded man was faring, but caught no sight of him. Likewise, she had seen nothing of Batu himself since the incident at the boar pit. After leaving the immediate vicinity of the river basin, the prevalence of the pit traps declined sharply. In fact, signs of human settlement were thinning into nonexistence, as well, which seemed strange. Even the wildlife was becoming quieter.

Midway into the afternoon, a lone eagle passed low overhead, calling. The nomads around her seemed to take it for a sign, as all eyes turned upward, and a hush fell over man and horse alike. The eagle circled once, then set off toward the north. At some unknown signal, the loose column turned to follow. Briga looked to Joren and Baby Bird for some indication of what was going on, but they gave nothing away.

Before long a messenger was sent back to them from somewhere ahead. The stranger and Joren exchanged a few words before the latter reined in his horse and passed a set of instructions to Baby Bird. Baby Bird nodded and rode off back along the column. Face set grimly, Joren selected roughly a dozen horsemen and led them out of the column. It was clear Briga was meant to follow, and she guided her horse with a loose rein after her protector. Three of the horsemen rode ahead, obviously scouting. The rest fanned out a respectful distance behind. Joren rode at her side protectively. The sounds of the column fell away behind them. It was remarkable that such a mass could move so quietly when the desire was on them. She watched her surroundings curiously, wondering where Joren was taking her. He seemed tense, but it was difficult to read the nomad's body language. Ahead, she caught sight of snatches of brilliant red glimpsed through the trees.

Joren reined up abruptly and dismounted. When she didn't follow suit, he crossed to her side to help her down. Puzzled, she slid from the horse's back gracefully. Joren gestured ahead to where she'd seen the bits of color, and she strode quietly in that direction. Gradually, she became aware of a hum. It was faint, something felt more in the blood than heard with the ears, but undeniably present. It was a sensation she recognized; she had felt it often enough, but never so strongly. It was the heartbeat of an oak. Following the sound, she emerged in a peculiar clearing. It wasn't a sacred grove, but a single tree. A single enormous tree. Nothing grew beneath its branches, and no dead leaves covered the dark, loamy soil, but most remarkably, the leaves were a vibrant, fiery red. Around them the rest of the forest was thinning, but the leaves had all lost their vibrancy. This tree showed no signs of preparing for winter slumber. It felt undeniably alive…almost conscious. Awed, she crossed to the tree, whispering a blessing, but paused before entering the bare ground beneath its wide branches.

She turned to Joren, plainly astonished that he would bring her here. Had he somehow divined her relationship with the trees? Or was it mere coincidence? He was watching her in the most peculiar way. His countenance was slightly stern, as usual, but there was an undercurrent of something else reflected in his features. He pantomimed shielding his eyes with his hand as if searching the forest around them, then fixed her with a look of frank expectation. A cold fist of dread encircled the base of her spine. She glanced around at the trees, following his gaze, and noted none of the horsemen were within sight. They were alone.

She looked him in the face, searching for understanding. His jaw tightened slightly, and he stepped forward, reaching for her.

The icy grip on her spine transmuted suddenly to liquid fire pulsing through her veins. She would *not* be abused in this sacred place. Rather than shrink back in fear, an explosion of outraged fury made her feel as if she had tripled in size. She bared her teeth in a snarl, muscles tensing in readiness, not to run from him, but to fight. He stopped suddenly, blinking at her in clear surprise. After a moment he gestured to the tree, watching her carefully. When she didn't respond, he mimed again as if looking for someone in the trees and gestured to the red oak once more.

The fury lifted away as swiftly as it had descended on her, understanding slowly dawning.

"You want to know what I see?" she questioned, hoping he would guess the meaning of her words.

He nodded once, a bit uncertainly, but didn't reach for her again.

Briga studied him for a moment, but didn't sense malevolence in him. Then why had he brought her here? Her captors had tolerated her foreign ways and foreign dress, but did nothing to cater to or even consider her customs. So why now? Deciding to accept the gift of the tree, she relaxed and felt its hum surround her once more.

"Water," she demanded. "Ooc."

Joren carefully handed her the waterskin from his belt. Accepting it, she turned and warily approached the tree. The humming grew into a buzz as she approached, and she had to concentrate on the words of blessing she spoke over the water. The noise calmed somewhat as she finished her preparations and spilled the water on the bare earth, circling the wide trunk three times. The tree's song shifted subtly as she spoke to it, flattering and cajoling the god within by turns, for there was no doubt a powerful force dwelt here. The sound was overpowering, and she was beginning to feel dizzy. Her awareness was becoming fuzzy. Images of streaking fire flickered in and out of her sight. Somewhere a raven called out in the distance. A field of crops lay dry and withered to nothing. Drowsy and drunk on the flood of disconnected images, she sank to her knees, still struggling to chant her prayers to the god of oaks. The tree was overwhelming her.

"Briga…"

The voice was distant, weak. She felt it like a hand reaching out from the darkness. She tried to turn toward it, but her limbs felt heavy.

"Briga."

The voice grew more insistent. She wasn't sure if her eyes were open or shut, and it felt like she was trying to move through water.

"Briga, come to me."

She shook her head, trying to clear her vision, and the darkness around her lightened somewhat. The sense of heaviness lingered, but she was slowly adjusting to it.

"Where are you?" she called, realizing dimly that the voice spoke her language. Her own voice sounded muffled to her ears. She was clawing through the thick darkness, limbs moving with maddening slowness.

"Here, daughter."

Ahead, a pinprick of light swirled and grew from the gloom, revealing a hazy but familiar face. She squinted, straining to clear the image.

"Cathbad?"

"Yes, child."

"How did you find me?"

"The red god found you. The god of oaks revealed you. We haven't much time."

Red god? Faintly she recalled a red-leafed oak and a latent sense of malevolence.

"Yes, Briga, there are Others here as well," he responded as if reading her thoughts. "It is dangerous to remain."

"Are you coming for me?"

The high priest was silent, hesitating.

"We are very few, child."

She felt her heart sink. He hadn't said it, but she knew her clan was abandoning her.

"Do not despair. The water will guide us."

"Us?" She squinted; the image was fading. "What water?"

"Amergin and Eamon send their love."

"Cathbad, I must know—"

A sudden violence severed the link savagely. There was a snarling, and her world filled with fire and a strange red mist. The beast pounced on her, its tails scattering Cathbad's image into obscurity. With effort, Briga set aside her fear and endured the wrath of this unfamiliar god. A small part of her longed for death in this way, rather than a return to captivity. Even a comfortable captivity. The dark creature growled in her face, its breath hot and rotten, as one clawed hand closed around her throat. Wicked fangs tore into her shoulder. Its tails lashed her leg and her side. She saw the wasted croplands again, followed quickly by a wolf swimming across the wide sea. It looked at her sharply, fearless.

She woke suddenly, unaware of her surroundings. She lay face down, the moist earth pressing against her face. There was pressure on her shoulder where the creature had bitten her, a tight grip that shook her urgently. She opened her eyes with effort. Joren was crouched beside her, concern clearly stamped on his face. She blinked once and allowed him to lift her to a seated position, wincing at the dull ache in her shoulder. He moved to touch her face, but she drew back reflexively. Her own hand drifted up and came away slick and red. She was bleeding.

"The tree demands blood…"

Briga's gaze flickered over Joren's shoulder at the feminine voice. Behind him crouched a dark-haired girl with delicate features and a wary look. "…for the god within, my lady."

Briga's shoulder flared in fiery pain, reminding her of the creature she had encountered. Had that been the god? She wiped blood from her nose and throat and spread it on the ground.

"You speak my language?"

"Yes, lady…a little."

Joren reached back and urged the girl forward. She was too pale to be one of the horse people, though she dressed as one. And she wore an iron collar welded around her neck. A thrall then, a slave most likely.

"Emorian? Magyun?" Joren questioned softly.

Briga shook her head. She had seen no people in her visions. One corner of his mouth turned up in grim satisfaction. The girl said something to him sharply, and the grin faded.

"They fight soon," the thrall explained in her strange accent. "He wants a sign of victory."

Briga frowned. Her vision wasn't clear. It would take time to puzzle out any meaning. She turned her attention back to the tree, examining it silently. There was still a steady buzz emanating from it. The light was growing dim beneath the thick branches, and Briga realized with a start that she had been in that Other place for longer than she'd thought.

51

"My lady…" The girl crept forward, offering a white rabbit carefully. "For the god."

Briga eyed the creature, felt the tree's thirst, and noticed a slight increase in the tone of the tree's song. Not all gods craved blood, but those who did must be sated. A stoat would be better, but this would have to do. Briga took the rabbit by the ears, shaken, but chanting the words of prayer she used for her own gods softly. The rabbit calmed, lulled almost into a trance by the soft and rhythmic cadence of her prayer.

Briga's knife was still attached to her horse's saddle, she had forgotten to take it with her. Recognizing that she lacked a tool, the slave girl took one of Joren's smaller blades and offered it to the priestess. Taking what was left of the waterskin, Briga cleansed the blade and sprinkled the rabbit's forehead. With a quick prayer, she drew the blade deeply across its throat and allowed the blood to splash on the ground, the trunk, and then seep into the roots. The buzzing faded into an almost pleasant hum. Dipping three fingers in the blood, she smeared it thickly down the side of her face. Likewise, she anointed Joren as a mark of the god's favor for bringing her here. After cleaning his knife on the animal's pelt, she stood and returned it to Joren, then followed him and the slave girl back to the horses.

The horsemen had appeared once more, clustered around Baby Bird and their three mounts. They were looking at a single patch of clear sky in which shone the first of the twilight stars.

"It is a good omen," the slave girl explained. "The Drev'an, they worship the sky. You've brought them good fortune."

By the time they had reached the main body once again, the camp was fully established. They dismounted, and Baby Bird took the horses. Joren hovered at Briga's side, while the slave girl followed a pace behind. She could see Batu seated at a large fire near the center of camp. Around them, a hush fell as the warriors noticed the blood marks on her and Joren's faces. Batu looked around, sensing the change, and his eyes fixed on her. He too noticed the blood and stood as she approached.

Emblazoned by the firelight and anointed by blood, she was the very image of a savage goddess. He touched the blood on her face, then looked to the skies clearing in the north, and she caught the gleam of keen understanding in his dark eyes. Understanding…and desire.

Joren started to speak, but Batu silenced him with a gesture, his eyes never straying from Briga. Batu spoke, his voice low and confident, addressing the silent warriors around them. He allowed his gaze to drift from man to man as he spoke, resting finally on Joren. There was a prolonged silence, then finally one man called out a battle cry and was instantly joined by his fellows. Batu smiled, a very subtle gesture, and passed his gaze between Joren and Briga. She saw his features change subtly and realized he had made a decision. Batu angled his chin toward the *ger* in a way that needed no translation. Briga obeyed, feeling slightly numb, but her blood was humming from contact with the god and fired by the chorus of battle cries around her as the men resumed their feasting. Batu followed her, his presence a protective if unfamiliar shadow.

Once inside the tent, he pulled one of the little stools up to the fire and bade her sit. He filled them each a bowl of ayrak, the fermented milk, and took up a position near her and the fire.

"Breeg," he started, pressing one of the bowls into her hands.

She accepted it gladly. His now empty hand caressed the side of her face, thumb smoothing over her cheek gently. The gesture struck her as vaguely fatherly. Grasping her jaw, he leaned in and delivered an affectionate if possessive kiss. That was decidedly *not* fatherly, but it only lasted a moment. A noise at the entrance distracted them both. Joren had entered, followed by the slave girl. Batu gestured for them to approach and handed Joren his bowl. The slave girl was already fetching a new one for the khan. Joren pulled a stool up to the fire, and the girl settled on her knees across from Briga.

Joren spoke first, eyes lowered respectfully. Briga assumed he was relaying the afternoon's events. Watching Batu's face, she tried to determine what Batu had ordered, and what Joren might have done on his own. Batu remained stoic, peppering in a few questions here and there. Briga looked to the slave girl, but she pointedly avoided her gaze. Finally Joren concluded his report, and Batu sat back, considering. When he spoke, the girl translated.

"My master wishes to know how you know of our gods."

Briga hadn't been expecting that question. She sipped her drink slowly, ordering her thoughts.

"I don't know your people," she began slowly, "but the gods belong to no one. They make themselves known to us in their way, and favor those who honor them."

Batu nodded slightly as the girl translated.

"You are one so favored?"

"I am a druid. A priestess. Do your people have this word?"

"You are a shaman," he confirmed. "And a warrior?"

"I am."

"And a woman."

"Which of these is most troubling to you, Batu?"

"Khan," the slave corrected sharply. "You must address him as Batu Khan."

Batu waved his hand, inferring and dismissing the correction. The girl shifted uncomfortably.

"My master wishes to know what you saw beneath the tree?"

Briga frowned. "I'm not certain."

In truth she would need time to reflect on the series of images she had received. They were disjointed, unrelated to one another in time. The only certainty was Cathbad, but she would not share that with her captors.

"There were prophesies."

Batu's eyes narrowed, and she sensed a sudden tension in the room, but his voice seemed as carefully controlled as ever. "Victory, or defeat?"

She shook her head, thinking of the decimated crops. "I must pray over what I've seen. Victory for one is defeat for another, perhaps."

"Is the god satisfied?"

She nodded, certain. "He has accepted the blood sacrifice. You have seen the sky clearing."

Batu nodded, smiling. "A good omen. I will make you a gift."

He stood and crossed the room to an ornamented box beneath the shrine. From it he withdrew a gleaming wolf pelt cloak and draped it around her shoulders.

"Thank you, Batu Khan."

The pelt was indeed handsome. As he lay it across her shoulders, a memory flickered unexpectedly through her mind. Her mother, flinging a wolf pelt around her shoulders in the dark. She felt an inexplicable chill of fear as she touched the fur. His fingers encircled her chin, breaking the memory's hold and tilting her face up toward him.

"You have brought us fortune since the day I captured you in battle. I was right to claim you."

He kissed her possessively, and she noticed Joren stiffen with discomfort.

"Tomorrow you will have proper clothes. Dagmer will see to it."

The slave girl lowered her eyes respectively. "Would you like to bathe, my lady?"

"I would."

With a few quiet words to Joren, the girl stood and led him out of the *ger*. They returned a few minutes later carrying a large wooden tub and several hot kettles. Batu stood behind her, watching the proceedings with interest. His hands rested comfortably on her shoulders, and he spoke something quietly into her ear. The slave either hadn't heard or chose not to translate.

It wasn't long before the basin was full and steaming. Batu peeled the wolfskin from her shoulders and laid it across one of the stools. Strong arms reached around her, inexpert fingers tugging at the lacing of her bodice. She jerked reflexively, her own hands flying to her breast in protection of modesty. His grip was iron, trapping both of her hands in one of his own. The slave girl shook her head, silently cautioning against further protest, and she lowered her gaze once more. Beside her, Joren looked on stoically, slight disapproval etched into his features. With an effort, Briga relaxed and allowed her captor to undress her. Gathering her tattered shreds of dignity, she stepped out of her pooled garments and lowered herself into the bath. What use was modesty here? Three men held her life in their hands, and two of them were in this room. It was harmless enough, at least for the moment.

Joren moved first, retrieving her stool from beside the fire and taking up a watchful post near the door. It seemed there would be no further audience, at least. Batu picked up his discarded bowl and took a seat near the fire. He watched her, eyes glittering darkly. The slave dipped a rag into the basin and reached out to wipe Briga's shoulder. This she would not tolerate, and she took the rag from her.

56

"I prefer to bathe myself," she explained, hoping to lessen any sting to the girl. It wasn't her fault for being here, anyway. Briga might submit, but she would not be cowed.

She soaked the rag and began cleaning her arms, gaze fixed on Joren defiantly, until he finally submitted to her will and looked away. She turned her sight then on Batu, who was half smiling over his bowl in the most peculiar and unnerving way. There was something secret and predatory in his look. Undaunted, she continued her ablutions, reveling in the feel of the warm water as it streamed down her neck. She dipped the rag again and brought it to her face.

"No," Batu said in her own language.

She paused, curious, the rag frozen midway to her face.

"My master wishes you to keep the blood mark," the slave translated.

"Why?"

"It suits you."

Briga was suddenly reminded of the warriors of her clan. Not Eamon's clan, the first one, across the waters of her childhood. She had hazy but certain memories of that time that would float to the surface of her mind, unbidden and unexpected. She recalled that the warriors would sometimes paint themselves before battle using ashes, blood, or dyes to make themselves appear fearsome. It was an old custom, effective against new enemies in particular. It hadn't been effective enough the night she was taken from them.

Meeting Batu's gaze levelly, she brought the rag to her hairline and dribbled the water down her face. The dried blood loosened in flakes, spreading in a thin stream down her cheek as they slowly became liquid again, down onto her chin, neck, and breast. It was only a little bit of water, enough to spread, but not wash the blood away entirely. She sensed more than saw the pulses quicken in both of the men and hoped she hadn't

57

provoked them more than she had meant. His expression unchanging, Batu sipped from his bowl and dismissed both Joren and the slave with a gesture. Joren waited and held the tent flap, hesitating. Briga could feel his gaze on her but dared not look. At last he left, leaving her alone with Batu and the dark look in his eye.

Briefly, she wondered at the wisdom of baiting him, but it was too late for that. She felt strangely heated by her boldness, breath coming a bit shallower as she watched the khan, waiting to see what he would do. Batu remained beside the fire, watching her over the rim of his bowl, clearly employing the same strategy. She could feel tension mounting between them, and was beginning to regret her decision, but found herself unable to look away. After what seemed an eternity, he drained his bowl and set it aside, then crossed the short distance between them. He looked down at her for a moment, then suddenly grabbed her at the base of her skull and hauled her upright.

Briga cringed but regained her composure quickly, panting slightly with fearful anticipation. His hand remained fisted in her wet hair, eyes tracing the path of the watery blood as it trickled down her exposed flesh. One finger lightly traced its path, slowing as it traversed the curve of her modest bosom. She bared her teeth ferally, but he tightened his grip in her hair to keep her still. His flesh was hot against her air-chilled skin and caused an explosion of gooseflesh in its wake. Somehow, the lightness of his touch was maddening. The fist tugged sharply in her hair, forcing her face upward and exposing her bloodied neck. The tracing finger vanished, only to be replaced by a hand that clamped roughly onto her breast. She gasped involuntarily, and he kissed her, demanding, the fist twisting in her hair painfully until she reciprocated.

Then the fist in her hair loosened to drift lower, seizing around her lower ribcage and lifting her against him, dragging her free of the wash tub. She caught his bottom lip in her teeth, seeking to regain some measure of control over the situation. He paused for a moment, then squeezed her firmly. It felt as if a small jolt of lightning ran through her, and she released his lip, gasping again despite herself. The fingers released and sought out her hand, guiding it to his belt. With trembling fingers, she began to untie the cloth. The hand around her back slid lower, clasping her backside and kneading it. She shied for a moment, but focused with growing understanding of what was being demanded of her in dread and, strangely, anticipation. He rewarded her with a light nip on the side of her neck that nearly turned her knees to water.

Think of Eamon, she counseled herself.

How many times had she envisioned him doing something like this to her? *No, not like this.* Her visions of Eamon were tender. This was more…primitive, somehow.

Impatient, Batu finished ripping loose the belt himself, and his robes fell open, exposing a well-muscled torso. The firelight gilded his contours alluringly. No, this wasn't like Eamon at all. And yet…Stepping back, he shrugged out of them, watching her reaction.

She shivered slightly, and not entirely from the chill in the air. Unconsciously her hands slowly drifted to her chest, shielding herself. An odd expression flitted across his face, and she remembered this was a power struggle between them as much as anything else. With an effort, she slowed her breathing and forced her hands to fall to her sides, favoring him with the most defiant look she could muster.

His face was unreadable for a moment, then slowly cracked into a sly grin, as that of a warrior accepting single combat. He wore breeks beneath his robes tonight, and expertly loosed the lacing. His desire became obvious, and Briga caught herself staring. She'd never seen a naked man in such a state before and was suddenly fearful. He watched her as a cat stalks its prey, circling her slowly, admiring the curves of muscle and flesh. She could feel his gaze like a hot ember but forced herself to endure.

He said something, then came up behind her, pressing her back against him. Both hands came around to caress her. One slid down her abdomen, seeking. Her composure broke, and she thrust her hips back against him in a mad desire to escape his attentions. With a snarl, he dragged her backward to the furs. One hand low on her throat, he threw her down onto the pile. She screamed despite herself as he fell on top of her. He landed with one knee between her splayed legs and a hand at the base of her throat.

She struggled wildly, seeking to close her legs, but the hand returned and found what it had been seeking. She whimpered at the intrusion, fighting with her hands until the choking grip at her throat brought blackness to the edges of her vision, and she felt herself go limp. The fingers ceased moving abruptly, and he looked down at her with clear surprise. They withdrew and began stroking soothingly in small patterns that were uncomfortably pleasant. His other hand removed itself from her neck and smoothed back some of the hair from her face. The abrupt shift from violence to tenderness confused her. She shifted her hips, trying to escape the stroking, but he was undeterred. He said something, a question, but she couldn't understand.

"Vur…ghen?" he tried again, haltingly.

She nodded up at him, wide-eyed and trembling. Pale streaks of blood marked his face and chest, transferred from contact with her. The stroking was beginning to give her a heady feeling, and she endured it with only token protest. He sighed, the sound somewhere between irritation and bemusement, and closed his eyes, collecting himself. Bending down, he kissed her forehead.

"No fear. Little hurt."

He smoothed her hair again, then sank onto her. He kissed her gently, holding himself back for the moment. His free hand drifted to her breast, sending little jolts of lightning through her core. He broke the kiss and raised his head for a moment to look at her, but she followed, wanting to get on with it. Her hips moved against his hand of their own volition, and he nipped a tender spot on the side of her neck, causing her whole body to arch pleasantly. Shifting carefully, he brought his other knee up, driving her legs further apart. She tensed, resisting, but relented. His hand withdrew and he sank onto her, the weight of him somehow both pleasant and menacing at once. There was a pressure then, painful and acute. She moved her hips to escape it, to no effect.

"No…" she breathed, reaching to push his hips away.

"I must," he panted against her and gathered up her wrists, pinning them safely out of the way.

She whimpered as the pain increased. He pushed a little harder, and suddenly the pain was gone. She drew breath sharply in sudden relief, and he released her wrists, moving slowly at first so she could adjust to the feel of him. She was aware of his restraint and whispered her gratitude into his ear. The gesture shattered the tenuous control he held over himself, and he responded to his own needs. She bit into his shoulder, hands clawing into his back as she struggled to accept him. It seemed he would last forever, and she felt herself slipping away, bit by bit. When she thought she could endure no more, he finally reached his peak. A great shudder went through him, and his body went rigid for a moment before collapsing bonelessly on top of her.

Chapter 6

Gansükh had been reluctant to leave the tent in the first place. The image of her pale flesh stained with blood was seared into the back of his eyelids. He had suspected after the first encounter with the raiders that she was a seer. When she'd tamed the wild wolf with only a look, he had known for sure. She was a shaman, a dangerous one, and she was alone with his Khan. He touched the blood mark on his face, strangely reassured by its presence. Yes, she was a shaman, and that was why he'd taken her to the red tree.

The eagle overhead had been a sign—not one sent by the gods, but sent instead by Sartaq. It circled the main body, marking the place where thousands more warriors awaited their Khan. That would place them on the outskirts of the Magyun capital. Battle was imminent, and he'd tried to make use of her gift to seek the gods' blessings on the horde. Frustrated by his limited ability to communicate with the foreigner, he had sent Bayanaa back along the column to find a translator. They had captured a number of pale foreigners in the last few months; surely one was her clansman.

Behind him, he heard his Khan growling in fury, then a shrill feminine scream of fear. He drew his sword reflexively, whether to defend his lord or the seer, he couldn't say. His lord had claimed her, but to force the body of a shaman was dangerous, like handling fire. Everyone knew this. There were plenty of women in the slave ranks—why did Batu Khan insist on the shaman? He heard the muted sounds of struggle giving way to quiet murmuring and realized he'd been holding his breath. The tension left him. Bayanaa clapped a reassuring hand on his shoulder, and he sheathed his sword.

"He beds a wolf, Gansükh. Best to say out of it."

Gansükh didn't respond, but stood and strode off in search of a fight. Circling the khan's *ger*, he caught a group of soldiers straining to hear their Khan locked in the oldest of battles with the savage woman. He grabbed the closest of them by the neck of his robes and hurled him to the ground.

"Are you dogs?" he demanded angrily. "Have you no respect?"

The pack scattered quickly, wisely avoiding a fight. He kicked after them, frustrated, then completed his circuit of the tent. Bayanaa was waiting for him beside their small cook fire, holding a cup of ale. They had acquired some of the strange beverage raiding homes along the way, and both had developed a taste for it.

"Sit, brother," Bayanaa called out, offering the cup to his comrade.

Gansükh sat grudgingly and accepted the drink, taking a healthy swallow of the golden liquid.

"All will be well, you will see. Look, the sky is clearing."

Indeed it was. The small patch of stars had widened to fill a quarter of the sky. By dawn it would be clear, and Tengri would smile down on them.

"That was your doing," Bayanaa confided. "You and the she-wolf."

Gansükh nodded absently, his mind clearly elsewhere. After a moment, Bayanaa took the cup from him and drank deeply. He refilled it from a clay jug and handed it back to Gansükh, standing.

"Where are you going?"

"To find a woman," the younger guard replied with a grin. "Why should Batu Khan have all the fun?"

Gansükh's jaw clenched at that, and he took a sip of ale to conceal it. "Be back by moonrise. That will be your watch."

Bayanaa clasped his hands in a little half-bow of acknowledgement and set off in the direction of the slaves, hand resting casually on the hilt of his sword. Brooding over the cup of ale, Gansükh was left to stare into the fire and lose himself in thought.

"Gansükh?"

It seemed his uneasy peace was not to be long-lived. The guard blinked into the dimness behind him, gaze locking onto the form of General Khuyag.

"The khan is resting. He wishes not to be disturbed until morning. Have you news?"

The general nodded and evaluated Gansükh silently, evidently weighing whether or not to trust him with whatever information he possessed.

"His brother's scouts have returned. The report can wait."

Gansükh nodded and offered the general his ale cup. Khuyag accepted politely and sampled the unfamiliar contents. He made a face and handed the cup back, causing Gansükh to laugh despite his foul mood.

"I will tell him you were here, General."

Khuyag nodded once and took his leave. Gansükh noticed his gaze lingering on the khan's tent flap as he passed, as if Khuyag could see through it. The guard snorted derisively, then resumed his watch, eyeing the clearing sky distantly.

***

Briga lay on her side, staring into the felt wall. Behind her, Batu was curled around her, one arm draped over her side. She wasn't sure how to feel. She had done what was necessary, but it somehow felt like a betrayal of Cathbad. Of Eamon. The act of coupling wasn't what she had expected. What *had* she expected? She was sore, but not unpleasantly so. Batu had held back out of consideration for her. She knew it—whether woman's intuition or druid, it mattered not. Batu was awake; his arm tightened around her slightly.

"Sain?" he asked.

She thought he was asking if she was all right, and she nodded wordlessly.

He inhaled deeply and turned onto his back, pulling her with him. One hand guided her head onto his shoulder, and she nestled reflexively into his side.

"Untakh," he commanded, closing his eyes.

But sleep was elusive. She heard a wolf calling in the distance and longed for her kinsmen, for the familiar.

***

"You must learn to feel the earth, child. To see through its eyes." It was a female voice; one she knew well but couldn't place.

Tiny Briga, who had seen only five summers, pressed her hand into the damp soil, listening intently. This time, a raven appeared to her, perched on the wooden gate marking the entrance to their settlement. Its talons marred the carved whorls and lines of her people. Her father's people. The world shifted suddenly, and the raven was now perched on the rump of a black stallion before the towering gates of an unknown city. Its stone walls rose out of the field, gray and forbidding. She recognized the horse as Batu's.

A nudge at her hand drew her attention down. Beside her, the hairy creature she'd encountered at the tree nuzzled her hand and rubbed itself against her leg, catlike. But it wasn't a cat. Nor a dog. Nothing she could name, yet she felt she knew this creature. Had always known it. She opened her hand, palm turned upward. The creature nuzzled her again, then took her wrist gently between its jaws, forked tails swishing. And bit.

She woke with a start, heart hammering in her chest. Batu was awake and looked at her over the parchment he was studying. She rubbed her wrist absently, noting the dim light filtering in through the sky hole. So she'd slept through the night after all. Batu frowned at her, quietly watching her confusion, then bade her good morning. He was draped loosely in his robes. No remaining flecks of blood marred his skin; they must have worn away during the night. She blushed suddenly at the memory and averted her gaze. Standing, she wrapped herself in one of the large hides, and retrieved his belt. He paused at the table as she moved to stand behind him, halfway turning his head to watch her over his shoulder. She reached around his waist, folding the edges of the robe as he'd shown her, and wound the belt tightly around him, fumbling slightly in her efforts to secure the loose end. Batu laid a hand over hers reassuringly as she corrected an error in the knot and offered her a small smile. Knowing what was expected of her, she moved to retrieve his bowl. The soup woman would be here soon with breakfast.

"No," he admonished gently, catching her arm and gesturing her back to the furs.

Puzzled, she complied, and watched as he stuck his head out the door, issuing orders to someone who must have been waiting outside. A few moments later, the slave girl—Dagmer—and another woman entered, carrying armloads of furs and fabrics.

"Good morning, my lady," Dagmer offered, settling the items at Briga's feet. "My lord wishes for you to be dressed properly."

Without waiting for a response, she took Briga by the hands and stood her up, removing the modest fur she'd donned. She handed over a pair of breeks made of some kind of dark, cured animal hide, almost like leather, but softer, and lined on the

66

inside with soft fleece. Briga slid them on quickly, allowing Dagmer to tighten the laces at each side to hold them at her hips. The slave next produced a cream-colored robe, which she slipped over Briga's shoulders and fastened with loops at waist and shoulder. She wound a cloth-of-gold belt around Briga's waist, tying it expertly. Most of the women wore their sleeves loose and billowing, but Dagmer gathered the loose fabric at Briga's wrists and covered them with the leather bracers she had been wearing when she was taken, lacing them tightly. She also produced the leather jerkin and wide leather belt that served as her armor and helped Briga slip into them. Briga touched the effects reverently. They had been removed sometime after her capture, and like her knives, she'd never expected to see them again.

The other woman had been working at her hair, struggling to comb out the prolific tangles and snarls. Having succeeded in taming the mass of fawn-colored fury, she was now ordering it into elaborate plaits. The plaits held the longer pieces back from her face, and Briga felt every inch a barbarian princess.

Kneeling, Dagmer offered a small bowl of charcoal paint, eyes averted.

"What's this?"

"For your face, my lady. Shaman wear paint, do they not?"

Briga frowned slightly. Shaman...priests, she meant. "Only for important occasions. Or battle."

"Today is important," Dagmer assured her. "You will meet Batu Khan's brother."

Briga's glance flickered over to Batu. He was smiling faintly at her, something fierce lurking behind his eyes.

Politics, she thought. She was familiar with the game, but what was her role? She dipped one finger into the paint and drew a black line beneath each eye, tapering slightly upward onto her temples, and two parallel lines down her chin, fading onto her

67

throat. The other woman had finished her hair, having tied two black feathers in, and was offering a bowl of breakfast to Batu. The khan said something, laughing quietly.

"What did he say?"

"He thinks you will strike fear into his brother's heart," Dagmer stated, smiling on one side of her mouth.

The second slave pressed a bowl of broth and noodles into her hands, and Briga drank deeply, suddenly hungry. When she finished, Dagmer draped the wolfskin over her shoulders, and they followed Batu outside.

Joren stared at her, composure lost for a moment, but soon recovered himself. He held out her fighting knife, which she accepted and fitted into place on her leather girdle. As usual, Baby Bird was nearby, minding the horses. He too stared at her, his expression unreadable.

Calling for his horse, Batu mounted fluidly and waited for Briga and the others to follow suit. The gray stood placidly as she mounted, then obligingly moved up beside Batu's stallion. She stared at his horse for a moment, grasping at the threads of a dream, but he moved off, her horse automatically keeping pace. Baby Bird and Joren fell in behind her, with Batu's standard-bearers, two of his personal guards, and Dagmer.

The procession trotted easily through the camp, warriors moving aside to clear their path. She hadn't noticed last night, but the camp was much bigger now. They must have met up with another force while she was at the tree. *His brother's force*, she realized suddenly. Around them warriors stood to watch the procession, and she guessed they had crossed into his brother's portion of the camp, where the warriors would be unaccustomed to her presence. She looked at a few of them, generating as much ferocity as she could muster, but mostly focusing on the path.

There was a small clearing ahead, ringed by tents, and dominated by one similar to Batu's. A small party of men waited, watching the procession mildly. Batu halted his column in the center of the clearing, a scant few paces from the waiting men. In the center of the group was a bare-chested warrior who could only be Batu's brother. They had the same face and build. Where Batu's hair was long, this man's was shaved on the sides, and the remainder flowed backward rakishly in the fashion of a horse's mane. He wore a long but neatly-kept mustache. A sword and an ax hung from his belt along with…a severed wolf tail.

Unsmiling, Batu dismounted and stalked toward his brother, hand resting on the hilt of his sword. The brother stepped forward to receive him, but both stopped short, leaving a sword-length between them as they sized each other up. Briga's gray whickered in protest as her grip on the reins unconsciously tightened. After a tense moment, both men broke into smiles and embraced each other by the elbows. The mood among the two groups eased considerably.

Gansükh smiled. It was always uncertain how the khan and his older brother would receive one another. Swinging down from the saddle, he greeted a few of the guards opposite him, old friends he didn't see often enough. Everyone had dismounted, except the she-wolf, who sat looking haughty atop the gray gelding. Bayanaa hovered near her patiently, and Gansükh moved to join him.

"Sartaq, it is good to see you," Batu boomed out. "I trust your journey went well?"

"Quite well," Sartaq confirmed, clapping his brother on the shoulder. "We have captured many treasures," he began, eyes turning to take in the foreigner atop the gray horse. "As have you, it seems."

Batu grunted, sliding his arm across his brother's shoulders and guiding him toward the woman.

"Who are her people?"

"She is from somewhere far west of the Danu. I do not know her people, but I captured her at a battle near the Rowanar village. She was a fighter," he added conspiratorially.

Sartaq examined her openly, judging her qualities with a practiced eye. "A female fighter? How will you ransom her?"

Batu shook his head, smiling mischievously. "I will not. She is too valuable."

The khan's brother looked her over again, jaw set doubtfully.

"She is a shaman of her people," Batu whispered to him. "And *our* gods favor her, as well."

Sartaq looked at him sharply, surprised. The woman didn't look at any of them, but stared at the far end of the clearing. Her attention was focused far beyond, that much was clear. Leaving his brother's side, Sartaq circled her slowly, noting her gray-blue eyes and reddish gold hair, revising his earlier assessment. Something about her haughty demeanor made him want to break her of it.

"How do you know, brother?"

"I know," Batu answered simply.

Sartaq eyed him dubiously and completed his circuit, coming to stand beside her. "Make a gift of her to me," he suggested without framing it as a true question.

One hand drifted to her thigh, testing the muscle there. She snapped her attention to him sharply with a look in her eyes that held a clear threat. Sartaq withdrew his hand, startled. She spoke then, her gaze shifting between the brothers. Silence descended upon the clearing as all eyes were trained on her, uncomprehending.

The slave Dagmer stepped up nervously, drawing the men's attention.

"My lady says she's had a vision. The god of the red tree visited her in the night and showed her a great city ringed by stone."

Silence reigned for a time as the men digested this statement.

"I took her to the tree yesterday," Gansükh offered, breaking the silence, "to seek the god's favor upon our armies."

Sartaq's eyes narrowed slightly, and he asked through Dagmer for her to continue.

"Batu's stallion stood on a riverbank outside a stone city with a raven perched on its back."

Batu stilled, watching her closely. Sartaq stared up at her, clearly disbelieving. "What was the god called?"

The woman shook her head. "The god cannot speak to tell me his name, therefore he has none. But he's left me a mark of his favor."

Without ceremony, Briga removed one of her bracers and lifted her sleeve. A series of large red dots like healing bruises marred her wrist in the shape of an animal's mouth. Sartaq reached for her arm to examine it, but a jingle of bells stopped him short. His own shaman stood at the side of the clearing, detached from the crowd, and looking on silently. *It was true then*, Gansükh realized. *Sartaq's shaman confirms it.* The khan's brother withdrew his arm slowly.

"I think the gods wish me to keep her, brother," Batu stated in answer to his brother's earlier suggestion. His eyes were fixed on the raven's feathers tied in her hair. *A raven on my horse...*

Chapter 7

They'd remained encamped for several days now, and Briga had fallen into something of a routine. Batu had not touched her since the prophesy she'd delivered in Sartaq's camp, but she nevertheless shared the furs with him at night. If anything, he was a little tense in her presence. But at least it provided her with slightly more freedom to wander the grounds when she pleased.

Each morning she saw he was dressed and fed, then made her way out into a clearing to greet the dawn. Dagmer sometimes accompanied her, sometimes not, but one of her personal guards was always present. Near mid-morning she would seek out the slave girl for lessons on the language and culture of her captors. This would often last for several hours, and they usually found themselves watching a group of warriors drilling by the end of their session. Despite her slowly improving language skills, Joren and Baby Bird had little interest in speaking with her. Something had changed the day they met with Batu's brother. The two guards were no more aloof than they'd been before, but the nature of it had changed somehow. She couldn't quite define the difference, but it was there all the same. Which was why she was startled when Joren laid a hand on her shoulder, interrupting her observation of a group of fighters engaged in a wrestling match.

"Seer, Batu Khan calls you."

Raising her eyebrows in mild surprise, she turned and strode in the direction of Batu's *ger*, and Joren fell into step beside her. Dagmer trailed behind, translating the more difficult bits of conversation for them.

"Is something wrong?"

He shook his head, which she knew to be his sign for indecision. "Stranger," he said simply, as if the meaning should be obvious.

Briga fell silent for the remainder of the walk. Batu's men were arranged before his tent in a semi-circle when she arrived, indicating that he was preparing for a formal reception of some sort. Briga supposed he would want her looking as savage as possible, playing her own small role in the strange customs of their diplomacy, and pushed into the tent quietly. Batu and one of his generals, a man she now knew to be called Khuyag, were seated at the table in quiet discussion. They looked up at her entrance, but she could read neither man's expression.

With their unspoken consent, she put on her bracers and charcoal paint. She always wore the leather jerkin and belt now, as a matter of custom, and as a place to hang her fighting knife. Batu and Khuyag were speaking quietly, and she made no effort to interfere, instead heading to wait outside with the others, but Batu stopped her with a gesture. Evidently he wanted her to wait inside.

She sat awkwardly near the two horselords, unwilling to break their quiet. Mercifully, it wasn't long before they heard a commotion outside. Batu did not react to it initially. His jaw was set. Clearly he intended whomever was out there to wait. Calmly he looked to Briga and gestured to a pot of milk tea warming by the fire. At times like this she wondered if this was how the women of his people were expected to behave, or if he was merely making a point of her obedience in front of the general. Nevertheless, she complied. She scooped and poured with the ladle, stirring the tea as she'd seen one of the serving women do, then poured a bowl each for Batu and Khuyag, and one for herself. They sipped the hot, salty liquid in silence, listening to the growing irritation of the stranger outside. *A waiting game,* she realized, wondering who this stranger might be to warrant such treatment. The khan drank at leisure, but once he'd finished the tea, he set it down, stood, and led General Khuyag out of the tent. Briga adjusted the wolfskin across her shoulders and followed the nomads out.

The area in front of the khan's tent was kept respectfully clear for just such occasions as this. In the center of the space stood a foreigner. Briga recognized him as a Magyun, and his presence was a surprise. She had become so accustomed to the nomad dress that his colorful tunic and hose seemed almost comical. The stranger wore a fur cloak draped over one shoulder and fastened with an ornate gold chain. His was not the rough hide Briga wore, but a neat and expensive-looking tailored thing. He had a small riding party with him, all waiting outside the semi-circle's boundary. The stranger's eyes rested on her fearsome visage with no small shock, but Batu commanded his attention.

"Who are you?"

The stranger thrust out his jaw proudly. "I am Jozsef Horvat, envoy of King Bela the Strong."

"Jozsef Horvat," Batu repeated slowly in the man's own language. "Envoy of King Bela."

He paused, watching the man with an air of mild interest. "Welcome."

He spread his hands graciously, and with a look, indicated for a servant to bring the stranger some of the milk tea.

Jozsef grunted. "Why was I kept waiting?"

Khuyag spoke up then, his voice a mild growl, grating against the foreign language. "You have come here for diplomacy, yes? It would be wise to address the khan with more respect."

Jozsef blinked, but to his credit, his confidence only wavered for a moment. Briga supposed he must have thought he was addressing a lesser noble.

"Khan Batu, my apologies. I a-am, ah, weary from travel," he simpered, accepting the tea finally from a servant.

"Weary from dragging around the weight of his importance," Khuyag observed in the Drev'an tongue, eliciting a few chuckles from the warriors nearest him.

If the nobleman was annoyed, he disguised it with a sip of the tea, controlling his features with an effort at the saltiness and unfamiliar taste.

"Why are you here, Jozsef Horvat?" Batu asked directly.

"King Bela requests you remove your armies from his lands and refrain from further violence against the good people of his kingdom."

Batu translated for his men, who laughed openly at this suggestion.

"What does he offer me in return?" Batu replied to the envoy, his disposition mild.

"He will give you ten thousand pounds of gold."

Batu regarded him with amusement. "Ten thousand...that is quite a sum. But I do not desire his gold."

"Silver then."

"I do not desire his silver."

Jozsef was fractionally off-balance but tried again. "Perhaps he can make you a gift of land—"

"I desire much more than his land," Batu interrupted, suddenly serious. He took a few steps toward the enemy, as if to speak in confidence.

Jozsef cleared his throat uncomfortably. "If you would allow an audience with the king, perhaps—"

"There will be no negotiations." Batu hadn't raised his voice, but the quiet finality of his statement carried to everyone in the clearing.

"King Bela will surrender unconditionally."

"Outrageous!" Jozsef sputtered.

"In return for obedience and loyalty," Batu continued as if nothing were amiss, "I will offer a degree of freedom. You will pay for the right to trade or travel within my territory. You may honor whichever gods you wish. But you will be subject to Drev'an law. *My* law."

Jozsef blinked several times in rapid succession, but Briga looked to the khan. She could infer enough of what was happening by the Magyun's body language despite her lack of ability to speak their language.

"Khan Batu, if you will speak with the king—"

Batu looked at him sharply, finally settling the full weight of his cold and calculating gaze on the envoy. "Tell your king if he does not surrender to me, I will kill everyone within his city walls. He *will* swear fealty and allegiance to me. This is the price to buy the lives of his subjects."

The envoy paled visibly and opened his mouth to respond, but wisely shut it again. There was nothing more to be gained here. Instead, he half-bowed to the khan and handed his tea back to a servant. Batu allowed him to retreat a few steps toward his waiting horse, watching him darkly.

"Envoy Jozsef," he called out, almost as an afterthought.

Jozsef froze with a hand on his horse's reins.

"Before you leave, perhaps you can answer a question. I have a most curious mystery on my hands."

Batu looked to his open palms as if the mystery in question could in fact be seen there. Then he clasped his hands before himself casually.

"It involves my brother."

The envoy watched him, face shifting from an expression of alarm to one of guarded curiosity.

"You see, over the past few weeks, he has sent six of his own envoys to seek audience with your King Bela, but none of them have returned, and my brother worries for his men. I wonder what has become of them?"

Jozsef appeared puzzled and shook his head slowly.

"Khan Batu, I—"

Batu cut him off with a gesture and began stalking slowly toward him.

"Perhaps they were attacked on the road, or have fallen ill," he waved this idea off, dismissing it. "We have discussed many possibilities, but none of them make sense. How could all six of them be attacked, or fall ill, or had a horse go lame?"

He stopped before Jozsef, meeting his eyes coldly. "No. I think perhaps they are now prisoners of the king."

Briga had missed Batu's signal, but his men sprang into action at once. Hands seized bridles and pulled men from the horses' backs. Five members of Jozsef's riding party were killed outright, their throats cut before they could react. Only a young squire was left unharmed, though he was held to a warrior's chest with a sword across his young neck. Jozsef merely stared in wide-eyed shock. Batu leaned in, speaking quietly.

"King Bela must be taught that I will not tolerate insubordination from my subjects."

Grabbing the terrified man by the back of the neck, Batu threw him roughly to the ground. A curved sword had appeared in his hands as if by magic, and it flashed in the late afternoon sun, cleanly severing Jozsef's head from his body. Grim faced, Batu turned away to clean his sword, indicating with a curt nod that the boy was to be brought to him.

The lad struggled mightily, but the sharp crack of a hilt against the side of his head put an abrupt end to his resistance. One of the warriors had taken Jozsef's head and was tying it to the tail of a horse.

Batu leaned in close, forcing the boy's panicked eyes to focus on him. "Do you understand what I have said?"

The boy blinked and nodded.

"I will kill everyone. That is a promise. Tell your king."

He turned his back on the boy and strode purposefully back to the *ger*. His eyes landed on Briga for a moment, glittering dangerously, and he placed a hand on her arm as he passed.

General Khuyag moved to her side, leaving Batu alone for a moment. Silently they watched as the riderless horses were led away to join the nomad herds. The boy was badly shaken and had to be lifted onto the remaining horse, the reins tied to his hands. One of the warriors smacked it on the haunch with the flat of his blade, and the mount lurched into a run, rear legs kicking as the grisly token of Jozsef's head bounced against its flanks. She could feel Khuyag watching her for a reaction and kept her face carefully blank. After a moment she excused herself to go speak to the gods, then turned and wandered off into the trees, uncertain of her feelings regarding the incident.

Chapter 8

There were so few of them left. Eamon had not moved from his tent since the battle. He'd been badly wounded, a large gash marring the side of his face, which was tightly bandaged. Cathbad and Amergin had done all they could to encourage healing, but their chieftain lay sleeping, wracked with shivering no matter how many blankets they piled on him. Two druids were absent. Owen was dead, Briga had been taken prisoner, and her skills as a healer were badly missed. As was her person. Two more warriors had died of their wounds in the days since the fighting. It was just too much for the two remaining druids to keep up with, given their limited supplies. Her skills might have been able to save them. But the gods rarely conformed to the plans of men, so they would have to make do without her.

Amergin emerged from the trees quietly, eyes flitting about their small camp by reflex, searching to be sure everyone was still there. Though not a warrior himself, he'd competently filled the void of leadership during Eamon's prolonged recovery. Cathbad eyed him speculatively, his question phrased in the silent manner of the druids. Amergin shook his head and came to sit beside the chief druid.

"She's alive, that is all I can say for certain. Her pattern is…distorted somehow. It's like trying to look through water."

Cathbad nodded slowly, prodding the fire before him with a long stick. "And the others?"

"I think they are also alive."

Cathbad understood. It was exceptionally difficult to feel out those not gifted or trained in the druid senses, even for one as skilled as Amergin. They could do nothing to help you find them, to lead you to their individual threads.

"We have difficult times ahead of us," he offered unnecessarily. That truth was plain to see.

"These horsemen seek territory. We must learn all we can about them. Have they enemies? Where are they from? And how far will they reach?"

Amergin nodded, agreeing. Too much was yet unknown. Behind them, Eamon groaned and stirred beneath his blankets. Amergin turned to check on him, his hands producing a waterskin and raising it gently to the chieftain's lips. Eamon accepted only a mouthful, one blue eye struggling open beneath a tangle of lime-washed hair.

"My lord?"

It was the first time they were sure he was awake since the battle. Eamon attempted to speak but managed only an ineffectual gravelly sound. Amergin immediately tipped him more water, which was readily taken.

"Not too much. Slowly."

"W…what happened?"

His speech was thick with disuse and slightly muffled by the bindings, but for all that it was a glorious sound after the days of silence.

"We were attacked. At Rowanar, lord," Amergin explained quietly.

"Who?" he asked, struggling to sit up, but Amergin gently restrained him.

"Strangers. A great army of horselords. I have never seen their like."

Eamon stared at him for a moment, then rolled his eye around the camp, taking in what numbers he could see.

"How many of us remain?"

"You must rest, my lord," Amergin stated after a pause. "We will speak of these things after you heal more."

That was all the answer Eamon needed. He paled, a stricken look evident in one clear eye. With a sigh of resignation, he laid back and gave himself to unconsciousness. Amergin saw to his comfort, then turned to rejoin Cathbad in silence.

The older man had been listening, but his attention was now focused across the fire, on something at the far side of the clearing. Amergin followed his gaze, and with a start he recognized a pair of yellow eyes and pricked ears regarding him from the brush.

"What is that?"

It was a wolf, and a large one, sitting on its haunches. Cathbad was smiling. On one side a dark stain formed a runic symbol against the silver fur.

"It is a good omen."

***

It had been more than a week since the incident with King Bela's envoy, and tension within the camp was rising steadily. The men were quieter as they began to prepare for upcoming battle, more focused on their daily drills. Briga and Dagmer had noticed the increasing sincerity with which they took the field, the diminishing smiles and banter. Bela's forces had entered a few small skirmishes with Batu and Sartaq's men, mainly the scouting parties who had been sent out to determine the best approach to the city. The majority of these meetings had ended in a draw, as the enemy sought only to harass and disrupt these scouting endeavors. But one skirmish to the south had been larger, and the nomad force had been routed.

The leader of this force had been one of Batu's generals, the one Briga had noted for his wispy mustache. The general was called Burd, and he was mightily incensed by the defeat. The attack had been wholly unexpected, and he'd been caught while traversing a narrow ravine. This restricting terrain had given the lighter and faster nomad warriors inadequate space to maneuver. The jagged cliff walls had further stymied the archers and rendered them ineffective.

Batu was equally incensed. Losses were expected in a campaign of this size, but he couldn't afford them in such small and inconsequential meetings. Worse, the nomads had been numerically superior. The Magyuns had chosen the terrain well. More importantly, Batu could ill-afford the boost of morale and spirit the defenders would now enjoy.

Briga sat along one wall of Batu's *ger*, silently observing as he berated his generals. Khuyag was watching Burd, who appeared to be holding his temper only with a great deal of effort. She had never seen Batu angry and marveled at the complete change in demeanor that came over him. At length he broke off into a weighty silence, pacing before the fire, and gradually, gradually calming a bit.

Beside Khuyag, the khan's brother Sartaq sat back and favored Batu with a schemer's smile. At length, he finally broke the silence.

"Brother, perhaps we can turn these failures into an advantage."

Batu looked over his shoulder at him, face set in a stone mask, but his eyes flashed with interest.

"My scouts have heard there is discontent among Bela's forces. His people think him weak and too fearful to attack."

Sartaq paused, assessing his brother for a reaction. Batu urged him on with a nod, withholding judgment for the moment.

"We can use this…if we 'lose' more battles."

Two of the generals stood in protest, Burd being one of them, but Batu silenced them all with a gesture.

"I am certain the commander has a plan," he breathed, his voice tight with impatient control. "Let us hear it."

"If we lose small battles, they will become overconfident and lose their discipline," Sartaq stated simply. "If Bela is truly as weak as they say, his generals can be provoked to act on their own to protect the city. Especially if they think victory is certain and they can clear the horde from their dooryard. They will over-commit their defenders…and then we will strike."

Batu nodded slowly, considering. He returned to the table, bending to examine the map his scouts had produced. Finally he straightened, nodding once.

"I like this plan." He paused, cold eyes searching the faces of the men assembled. "But what do our generals think?"

The men were silent for a moment, thinking, but ultimately they nodded in assent.

"Sartaq is a fox in man's skin," commented one of them dryly. "How will this be done?"

"Sartaq and I will take men to attack the bridge. If we control that, we control their flow of supplies and men, and therefore control the siege. Now that there are no supplies to come overland from Rowanar…" He paused, tossing a glance to Briga for the briefest of moments.

"General Burd, General Khuyag, and General Tseren, you will take your men south of the city and 'lose' battles. Commander Sartaq, send some of your generals north. Contain the defenders. Lose some battles, but do not allow them to cross this ridge." He paused to tap a terrain feature with his finger. "They must not be able to reinforce the bridge."

"This is an insult, Batu Khan, I will not lose to these weak-kneed stone-dwellers!"

"It is not an insult Burd." Batu didn't bother to point out that Burd had already lost to them once. "I have given you the most difficult of tasks, one that requires cunning and skill. Any man can lose, but the enemy must not discover they have been deceived in their victories. They must believe their fighters and their strategy to be superior. You must be even more cunning than Commander Sartaq."

Mollified by this testament to his skill, Burd fell silent and resumed his seat.

"Then I am honored, Batu Khan. I will not fail you," he finally responded, nodding humbly.

"Nor will I," added Khuyag, equally heartened.

The khan smiled then and looked at each man in turn. "Then it is decided. Before winter, we will have conquered the city and secured the steppe."

The men cheered this bold claim and lifted their drinks in salute. Batu clapped his brother on the shoulder proudly as the others stood and filtered out.

"It is a good strategy, brother. It will succeed," Sartaq confided quietly.

"Yes, it will. Take your meal with me tonight; we must seek the gods' favor."

Sartaq nodded and then he, too, left the khan's tent to prepare his men. With everyone gone, Batu sank wearily onto a stool and rested his forehead in one hand.

Briga watched for a moment, fascinated by the sudden and complete transformation of confident warlord into ordinary man. Wordless, she left her place by the wall and moved to stand behind him. She placed her hands lightly on his shoulders and worked strong fingers against the knots of tension she found there.

Batu stiffened at her initial touch, as if he had forgotten she was there, then gradually relaxed under her hands. With one hand she swept his hair aside, exposing the back of his neck to her attentions.

"When do you attack?" she asked quietly.

She hadn't understood the whole discussion but recognized they were developing a battle plan.

"Soon. Tomorrow, perhaps."

After a few moments, he reached up and laid his hands on top of hers, stilling them.

"Have the gods visited you again?"

"No."

He sighed briefly. "It is my fault. I should not have forced you."

"What do you mean?"

He glanced back over his shoulder at her. "It is said sometimes the gods only speak to the pure, especially among women. I have sullied you. Is it not so?"

Briga frowned, considering. No such superstition existed among her people. In fact, in times past, it was said that the high priest was given a maiden for an entire year before the summer feast. If he got her with child, it was supposed to be a sign of good crops in the coming year. Surely he wouldn't forfeit his ability to speak with the gods for such a thing? Then again, none of the druids she knew had been with a partner. Who could say for certain?

"I don't know," she answered finally. "These gods are strange to me. Perhaps it's only that."

He grunted, but released her hands. Briga ran her fingers through his hair, gently untangling it. Receiving no objection, she gathered it back and began ordering it into a thick plait.

"What is this?" he asked with a note of amusement.

"The warriors of my people wear their hair this way for battle."

"Do they? I did not notice."

She smiled but said nothing. It wasn't Eamon's face she was thinking of, but the man who must have been her father, his bright hair tied back in an elaborate series of plaits. Only the odd glimpse of him remained, flickering in her memory, but she was strangely certain of it. No, Eamon's people preferred a lime-wash paste combed into their hair, which they wore loose.

When she was finished, she started to untie the braid, but he stopped her. Using a discarded leather binding, he secured the braid himself.

"In my father's time, warriors bound their hair this way as well."

Briga smiled. The plait suited him.

"Tonight I will make an offering to the gods. If they won't speak, perhaps they will listen."

He caught her hand and rubbed his thumb across her knuckles. His eyes searched her face, studying her. After a moment he said something quietly, but the words were beyond her grasp of the language. She had a prickly sense he was speaking more to himself than to her. He dropped her hand suddenly and began rolling up one of the maps, demeanor shifting in an instant.

"My brother will eat here tonight. He will bring his shaman to meet you."

She nodded quietly and flung the wolfskin around her shoulders before setting out to find Dagmer.

***

"Why is Batu at war with the Magyuns?" she asked sometime later.

She'd found the girl after a minor search and now walked side by side with her along the outskirts of the camp. Both Joren and Baby Bird trailed a few paces behind.

"Bad blood," the girl offered, considering. "The horse people aren't from this place. They live far to the east. The Magyun kingdom is wide, and some of its people live along the borders near the Drev'an. In the beginning, there was trade. The horse people have no grain, and only felt and silk for cloth."

"What changed?" Briga prompted when the slave girl fell silent.

Dagmer shrugged. "I'm not certain. Ambition, perhaps. The Magyun weren't content with their borders. They tried first to convert, and then to invade the horse people. There was much killing."

Briga paused in her tracks, turning to study the girl openly.

"How long have you been with them?"

The girl hesitated before answering, her features tightly controlled. "They took me last winter."

"Where do you come from?"

"From the north," she replied tersely, waving a dismissive hand in the general direction of north. Clearly this wasn't something she wished to discuss. "Who are your people, my lady?"

Briga smiled wryly in her turn. "We are Velkcic."

Dagmer eyed her strangely, then slowly nodded. There was something odd and unreadable in her gaze. Feeling suddenly uneasy under the slave's scrutiny, Briga turned to scan the nearby trees as if by reflex. But of course there was no sign of Eamon or Cathbad hiding in the shadows there. Why should there be?

They had been walking for some time and were beginning to circle back toward Batu's tent. The watch fire outside was lit, but unattended, and Briga gathered the ends of her robes to sit. Dagmer followed suit, but she had to motion for Joren to join them. Using the slave as a translator, she asked for ale and four cups.

"Tomorrow may bring battle. Warriors should drink the night before battle. For courage."

Joren snorted, accepting the ale from Baby Bird.

"What?" Briga demanded.

"He doesn't think you will fight," Dagmer explained.

Briga eyed him curiously. "Your women don't fight?"

"No."

It was true, she hadn't seen any women in the camp, except for slaves and servants. And herself.

"Well, I am not one of your women. And I do fight. Pour the ale."

Joren eyed her for a moment, defiant, but he ultimately complied. Likely he didn't want her to complain of his reticence to Batu. She accepted a cup with a pointed smile. They all sipped in tense, if neutral, silence.

"I have made up names for you," she volunteered after a time, "but I wish to know. Your people, the horselords, what are they called?"

Joren regarded her warily as parts of her question were translated. "Drev'an," he answered simply.

"And you," she challenged with a tiny half-grin. "How are you called?"

Baby Bird sipped his ale, watching quietly.

"I am Gansükh."

Briga understood without Dagmer's aid. "Gansükh...it suits you. I've been calling you Joren."

"Zhoor-en," he repeated, rolling his tongue around the foreign-sounding name with the ghost of a grin.

"What does it mean?" Dagmer asked.

Briga shook her head. "It's only a name."

Dagmer pulled a face. "Gansükh means 'steel axe.' All names should have meaning. What do you call him?" she indicated the younger guard.

"I call him Baby Bird."

Dagmer stared at her for a second, then broke into laughter before translating. Baby Bird looked utterly confused but simply asked, "Why?"

"Your hair," Briga explained, gesturing vaguely.

Joren—Gansükh—began laughing loudly as he noted the comparison. Baby Bird himself smiled broadly with amusement, one hand attempting to smooth down the hair in question into a less birdlike appearance.

"My name is Bayanaa!" he protested good-naturedly.

Gansükh, still laughing, held up his cup in silent salute to her humor. They all met his gesture and enjoyed a healthy swallow. Dagmer broke the new silence by asking Gansükh a question. They exchanged words, the guard eyeing Briga once or twice before the slave translated.

"He knows your name but calls you she-wolf."

To everyone's surprise, Briga laughed at that and enjoyed another sip of ale.

"You aren't offended, my lady?"

"No," Briga responded, shaking her head. "I have a history with wolves. The clan who found me called themselves people of the wolf. It's a very fitting name."

Gansükh smiled thinly as the slave translated, uncertain how to process this information. Finally he nodded and led them in another round of toasts. She sensed more than saw his curiosity lingering. He probably wanted to know more about her but was hesitant to ask. It was Bayanaa who finally spoke up.

"The men we took you from…they were not your people?"

Briga hesitated. They'd taken her into their clan, but they were not her blood. She wasn't sure if she could explain.

"No," she answered finally with a small shake of her head.

"Were you their slave?" He gestured to Dagmer to illustrate his point.

"No," she answered sharply, lifting her chin unconsciously. "No. I…lost my people," she explained haltingly, her discomfort evident. "The others welcomed me into their clan."

It was a good deal more complicated than that, but Briga had no wish to explain it further. The two Drev'an accepted this quietly and abandoned the line of inquiry. Dagmer looked at her curiously but said nothing.

Chapter 9

It had been days since Eamon had woken briefly and learned of his clan's fate. He hadn't stirred since. If he was aware of anyone, he gave no sign of it, only laying there, unresponsive, staring sightlessly upward. He had begun shivering, and his skin was hot with fever. Cathbad could do nothing more than try to make him comfortable. He sponged a cool cloth against the chieftain's forehead, murmuring softly. A few of the warriors had drifted in and out to check on him, but seeing their distress at his condition, Cathbad had determined it was best to keep them all away. At least for the time being.

He'd busied himself with preparing another concoction for Eamon when a low, rumbling growl sounded from just outside the door. The berry-stained wolf hadn't left them, and had taken upon itself the task of guarding their small camp these past days. Cathbad poked his head out of the opening to see what was the matter. Beside the door the wolf had risen to its feet, hackles raised and growling at something across the clearing. At Cathbad's appearance, the wolf quieted and looked at him. Apparently satisfied the chief druid could handle whatever was happening, it huffed once, then turned and loped silently into the brush.

Frowning, Cathbad watched the far side of the clearing. At first only silence dwelt there, but gradually he began to discern the small snaps and pops of twigs and branches being trod upon, then the clink and jangle of metal. A few of the warriors resting in the area noticed the sounds as well, and a hush stole over the camp. Hands reached for weapons out of instinct. Cathbad himself checked the knife sheathed at his hip. They could hear voices now, speaking lowly in a foreign tongue. It was a small party, most likely scouts on horseback. Cathbad's blood chilled.

If the horselords had found them again… He glanced over his shoulder to check on Eamon. The chieftain was just as he'd left him, no worse, no better.

"What's happening?" Amergin asked quietly, emerging from behind the chieftain's tent.

He'd been searching for food with two other men and must have just returned. Cathbad shook his head, uncertain of the answer, and unwilling to speak. Scowling, Amergin drew his sword and strode across the clearing.

"Stop!" Cathbad hissed at him, but Amergin only waved him off.

He wasn't foolish enough to invite attack, but he wanted to investigate the strangers for himself. The clan warriors watched him and exchanged glances. They stood or crouched, some drawing weapons, preparing themselves for whatever would happen. One of their horses called out, excited by the proximity of the strangers' mounts. No one flinched. They all knew, in these situations, it was only a matter of time before the horses betrayed their location.

On the other side of the trees the voices called to one another, and the riders halted. There was a hiss of metal as weapons were drawn, and Amergin felt his hand tighten around the hilt of his own blade. A single rider broke from the party and rode in their direction. Near Amergin, a chestnut horse emerged from the trees, ridden by a blond man in strange ring metal armor. He wore no helmet, and his sword remained sheathed on the saddle. The stranger reined to a halt just past the tree line, surveying the small camp of survivors with evident surprise. Whatever he had expected to find, this wasn't it.

Cathbad felt a certain tightness in his chest ease, realizing whoever this man was, he wasn't one of the horse people. The stranger took in the state of the warriors around him with a practiced eye, noting the naked blade in Amergin's hand, and the tension in the fighters arranged behind him. His green gaze settled on Cathbad briefly, assessing his role, before returning to Amergin once more.

"Ki vagyte?" he asked, hand resting casually on the hilt of his sheathed sword.

Eamon's men exchanged glances at the unfamiliar words. This wasn't a tribe they had encountered before.

"Can anyone understand him?" Amergin asked without turning his attention from the stranger. "Cathbad?"

The stranger's eyebrows lifted once more in surprise.

"You're Velkcic?" he asked with a heavy accent.

"You speak our language?" Amergin returned, equally surprised.

"A little," the stranger confirmed with a nod. "What are you doing here, so far from home?"

"We were attacked at Rowanar." That was all the information Amergin was willing to volunteer at the moment.

The stranger grunted and nodded, a gesture that conveyed understanding and sympathy, and he ran a hand over his trimmed beard out of reflex. His eyes traveled the clearing once more, as if seeing it in a new light. His green eyes rested on Cathbad at the mouth of the chieftain's tent and lingered a moment.

"You are too injured to travel," he guessed. "Your losses must have been severe."

"We aren't too injured to defend ourselves," the warrior-druid warned quietly.

"But so few…" The stranger smiled thinly and cast a pointed look down at Amergin. He leaned back in the saddle then, easing the tension somewhat. "Be calm, friend. I represent no threat. Who attacked you?"

"They were horse people. We've never seen their like before."

The stranger's expression shifted in a manner Amergin couldn't interpret. "You survived battle with the horselords?"

The warrior-druid only stared at him. "Not all of us."

There was a shout from the stranger's comrades, which he returned. While Amergin couldn't understand the words, the tone was casual enough. He sheathed his sword. Behind him, he heard a few of Eamon's warriors doing the same.

"You need aid." Again, not a question. "It's not safe to stay here with so few, capable though they may be."

Amergin watched him quietly, suspicious, but attempted to keep all traces of emotion out of his face.

"We are returning to the king's city. Will you join us?"

Amergin turned then to look around the men in the clearing, finally resting his gaze on Cathbad. A silent question. A silent answer. The chief druid retreated into the tent to tend to Eamon. The younger druid returned his gaze to the stranger and nodded.

"Our chieftain is badly injured. We must prepare the wagon to move him and pack our few supplies."

"What's your name?"

"Amergin."

"Amergin," the stranger repeated. "I am called Ambrus. My men will help you prepare, if you'll allow them."

Amergin tensed for a moment, clearly concerned about some hidden motive on the part of the strangers.

"Your men outnumber mine three to one," Ambrus pointed out gently. "You are not in danger."

The druid flushed, embarrassed by his suspicion, and accepted the offer. "What you do for us is a kindness. The gods will remember."

"There is not enough kindness in the world, my friend. How well I know." He extended his hand then, a sign of trust and friendship.

Amergin stepped forward, and they gripped each other by the wrist, then the druid turned to face Eamon's men once more.

"We are going with this man to the city of his king. There we'll be safe. We will heal and decide what to do next. Go and prepare."

***

Near dusk, Sartaq returned to the khan's tent with his shaman in tow. The brothers embraced warmly and seated themselves at the small table. Briga was becoming familiar with some of Batu's expectations of her by now and crossed the tent to fetch them bowls of hot milk tea. One of the servants had brewed it earlier and showed her how to properly stir and pour the beverage. Mindful of the instruction, she swirled the ladle through the bowl, pouring it three times from a height before filling a silver bowl for the khan's guest. But before she could serve it, the shaman stopped her with a word, hand outstretched as if to reach her from across the room. Puzzled, she froze, glancing at the khan briefly for instruction. The shaman spoke in a peculiar voice, impossible to determine whether the person hidden beneath the broad hat was male or female.

"The first cup is for the gods."

Briga's gaze dropped automatically to the cup in her hands. This was a ritual she hadn't yet observed.

"How?"

The shaman flicked a hand subtly, but Briga caught the direction to follow, and reverently carried the bowl outside.

"Tengri," the shaman breathed, indicating the sky with a gesture once they were both outside.

Briga closed her eyes, reaching out with her druid senses, searching for a Pattern. She could feel…something…if she concentrated. It was faint, indistinct, but there. Acting on instinct, she sprinkled some of the milk tea skyward. The shaman nodded approvingly and led her in a circle around the *ger*, sunwise. She splashed out a bit of the milk at each of the cardinal points at the shaman's gentle direction, listening as the shaman chanted a blessing. When they re-entered the tent, Batu and Sartaq regarded her with twin expressions. They seemed mildly pleased, but were otherwise unreadable.

Feeling slightly uneasy, she collected a clean bowl and served Sartaq with freshly poured milk tea. The khan's brother accepted wordlessly, his eyes searching her face for the briefest of moments. Unwilling to hold his gaze, she turned away to serve Batu, surprised by a sudden flare of anger within her. Frowning slightly, she pushed the feeling to the back of her mind and served Batu his bowl.

A crude map of the city was spread on the table between them. It was hand drawn and adorned with short notes in key places. She realized his spies must have done this. How long had they been in the city?

"We will begin moving tomorrow. Carefully. They must not be warned of our advance. Better to give our diversions in the south enough time."

Sartaq nodded, agreeing. "They gathered their men and set off shortly after the council broke. A force that size would have been noticed quickly."

While the men strategized, Briga poured a bowl for herself, and for the shaman. She absorbed what she could of the conversation and seated herself beside Sartaq's cleric.

"This bridge is critical," Sartaq observed, tapping the drawing decisively. "What do your spies say?"

"It is fortified, wood and stone."

Sartaq nodded, assessing. "And the river is flooded. We shall see, but I think it is too deep to ford."

Briga was staring into the fire, her attention half on the dancing flames, and half on the brothers. The milk tea sat forgotten in her hands until the shaman nudged it with a bony finger.

"What do you see?"

Briga's gaze sharpened slightly, but the flames were roiling, indistinct.

"Only fire," she admitted uncertainly after a pause.

The shaman made a noise, watching her.

Further discussion was interrupted by the entrance of a serving woman bearing roast meat. Rising, Briga accepted a tray and set it before Batu and Sartaq. A separate portion was allocated for her and the shaman. In addition they were each given a bowl of broth and noodles.

The meat wasn't one Briga could identify, though it was delicious. She licked grease from her fingers hungrily, washing it down with the broth. Absorbed as she was in her own meal, she only now noticed the shaman was not eating.

"Are you not hungry?"

The shaman shifted slightly, the shells in his—her?—hair clinking in an unsettling way.

"I never eat before battle."

"My people feast before battle," Briga observed neutrally, "even the priests."

The shaman turned to look at her, face hidden beneath the darkness of a wide-brimmed ceremonial hat, and screened behind what might be either braided hair or rope. It was impossible to tell which, and more impossible to penetrate the shadows enveloping that face. It was as if those hidden eyes pierced right through her. Briga found this person to be somewhat unsettling and resisted the impulse to shift away.

"Yes," the shaman began in that strange, genderless voice, "in their great wooden...constructions."

Briga frowned but said nothing. Eamon's people usually feasted outside. There was no dwelling large enough to accommodate everyone.

"They hold a great hunt," she pressed on, shouldering aside her unease, "and bring back a boar or sometimes an elk for the village. Hunting prepares the spirit for battle."

The shaman stared at her, silent. At that opportune moment, Dagmer entered carrying a covered clay pot.

"And the druids offer sacrifice to the gods for victory."

She accepted the clay pot solemnly, watching as Dagmer retreated to the shadows beside the door. Shells clicked softly as the shaman leaned over and lifted the lid to the pot. Inside was a stoat. A white stoat. Briga smiled to herself.

"We should go to the tree."

The shaman shook his head slightly.

"No, I will summon them here."

"Wait—"

"Drink this." The shaman produced a small vial of some milky, opaque substance from somewhere on his person and held it out to Briga. "For protection."

Briga stared at the vial for a moment. The shaman gently urged her to take it, finally pressing it into her hand. He waited while she unstopped the container and examined its contents. It smelled faintly sweet, but there was something ominous about the liquid. The shaman gently nudged her hand up toward her face, calmly insistent. She closed her eyes, but her own gods offered her no warning or guidance. Gathering courage, she tipped the vial into her mouth and swallowed.

"Good. Let us begin."

Briga frowned. Cathbad had taught her to worship the gods in their own places. It was dangerous to call them away from their seats of power. But the shaman was already up and moving toward the fire. Perhaps the horsemen's gods were as nomadic as their people? As she watched, the priest sprinkled a handful of herbs and sweet grasses on the fire, causing a thick and fragrant smoke to rise and slowly fill the *ger*. He removed a painted drum and striker that had been slung across his back. Briga hadn't noticed it before among the strangeness of shamanic attire, but was startled by how much the drum resembled the bodhran of her people.

Unlike the Velkcic, the shaman held the drum up in front of his face, beating it rhythmically with a curved striker. The beat started slowly, like the beating of a heart, and gradually increased. The shaman punctuated this tattoo with sharp, precise movements, jerking his attention this way and that. The pounding was becoming more insistent now, and the shaman began to chant. It was nothing but a wordless, throaty sound at first. Then he began to dance; long, sweeping turns led by the ever-pounding drum. A flurry of cloth strips swung like the wings of a bird, swirling and spreading the smoke among them.

Briga was suddenly dizzy, watching those wings and breathing the smoke. The room was growing dimmer, as if the fire were hoarding all the light for itself. She was choking on the sweet-smoky air. She gasped as it filled her lungs, blurring her vision while also somehow buoying her, holding her up. The shaman was moving with unnatural fluidity, singing now in a voice she had never heard. Or maybe she had, once, in a dream. Her mind seemed to be just as hazy as the room.

She wasn't aware of standing, nor of the cautious steps that carried her body to the fire. She was floating through the smoke, feeling disconnected, drunk, but she felt assured it was always this way. The whole world had felt this way from its first moment. The whole world was this room. The stoat was in her hand, and she regarded it silently. A blade was in her other hand. And everywhere the sound of tinkling shells surrounded her, that insistent heartbeat, the low drone of an otherworldly voice shimmering in the air and resonating in her chest, pulsing through her limbs. Her gaze drifted to the stoat held carefully in her hand. The drum matched its frantic heartbeat; she could feel it in her hand. No, its heartbeat was the drum, resonating out of the tiny chest, up her arm, through the dim, smoky air.

The words came to her unbidden, beseeching the horse goddess, the gods of war and battle, of the oak and the sky and the water to look with favor on these strange and unfamiliar warriors.

"Accept this humble sacrifice," she concluded, unaware of having matched the shaman's chanting cadence.

She drew her dagger fast down the animal's belly. The creature squealed madly, fighting the inevitable as its gut-rope slid out to hang grotesquely, its blood coursing through her fingers and into the fire, where the drops flared and sizzled. She held the screeching creature up, its blood dripping now on her face, onto her mouth, painting her hand and arm. The struggling slowed. She was holding a bowl, collecting the last of the blood as the flow diminished and finally ceased. She was dizzy. Unbalanced. Her skin didn't quite fit. The drum had slowed, but was still hammering, her own heartbeat now. Her heart was beating so loudly it shook the room. Sound and sight and scent mingled into a single, hazy tapestry, the senses indistinguishable from one another.

She knew what to do, moved by wordless suggestion. It could have been Cathbad, or the god in the red tree. Or in the fire, or any of a hundred nameless things, which possessed her flesh and whispered what she must do. She was moving again, the bowl in her hands, holding it out now to Sartaq. He was pale, staring at her, plainly uncertain. His eyes were unfocused. The shaman had followed her and was dancing menacingly beside the warriors. Briga dipped her fingers in the blood and drew them gently down his face, caressing brow, eye, cheek, lips, and chin in their turn.

She moved as if in a trance, panting slightly and watching him closely. Too closely. She leaned forward to taste his mouth, but a slight movement drew her attention sharply to Batu. She was standing before him, vision hazy from the smoke. He reached into her bowl, anointing himself. He never looked away. There was something terrible in his eyes, something lurking, waiting. It was instinct. She was pulling him forward, hands fisted in his robes as if she could hold the terrible thing at bay. The smoke tingled on her naked breasts, on her belly. She was astride him on the furs, moving in rhythm to her pounding heart, the pounding drum, aware only of the weight of his hands on her hips and the urgency to pass on to him the stoat's fighting spirit, its blood, its very life-essence flowing through her.

"Aid the horse lord," she whispered feverishly, "and his men."

A wave was building within her in time to the ceaseless, urgent drumming. Building as she moved against something unstoppable, finally crashing with a force that shook her whole body and left her collapsed and panting on his chest. His heart hammered beneath her cheek. Neither of them moved.

Gradually, the heady feeling eased. His breathing and her heart slowed. His hand was tangled in her hair. The drumming had ceased. The smoke was still present, but it was clearing. The shaman stood poised beside the fire, watching her, waiting. Sartaq still stood, dazed, beside the table, watching her distantly, but she was certain his gaze was somewhere far beyond them.

"Tengri," she murmured to the shaman, who regarded her silently for a moment, head cocked to one side in wordless appraisal.

But finally he turned, nodding respectfully, shells clicking as he departed with the bowl. Sartaq followed, still entranced. Dagmer slipped out soundlessly behind them, forgotten.

Outside, Gansükh had seen the blood bowl in the shaman's hands and stood urgently, mirroring one of Sartaq's guards, who stared open-mouthed at the blood on his master's face. Dagmer placed a quelling hand on the guard's shoulder.

"It's all right. The shaman would not do him harm."

All the men outside the tent had been somewhat distressed by the drums and chanting that had gone on for so long, that scream, but Gansükh looked at the departing shaman with a peculiar mix of outrage and concern, and gathered his weapons to follow.

"She is all right too," Dagmer told Gansükh quietly, guessing the source of his concern. "They appealed to the gods for their blessing."

He looked at her sharply, but the severity of his look faded to concern once more as she averted her gaze.

Chapter 10

Briga awoke sometime in the predawn. Gray light shone through the smoke hole in the ceiling. The fire had gone out. She was naked, and mildly surprised at that discovery, but she lay still, curled against Batu's side, her head resting in the hollow of his shoulder. She hadn't slept well. Her dreams had been troubled by images of fire, blood, birds, and lightning. Batu must have been awake, for his hand reached over to smooth the hair back from her brow. She looked at him, but his eyes were closed, reluctant to abandon the peace of sleep. Watching him, she was struck by the calmness of his features, and felt an indistinct flutter of emotion. It wasn't affection, not quite. She was still a captive here, despite her liberties. Nor was it loyalty, though strangely she did feel some small measure of that. It was a vague sense of connection, undefined for the time being.

Whatever spirit had possessed her the night before, it was still present. She could feel her blood as if it were made of smoored embers. It burned and tingled through her veins, not unpleasantly, and she turned her attention from Batu to this curious sensation. The exploration was short-lived, however, as Batu stirred and came fully awake with a deep drawing of breath.

The camp had a generally subdued, expectant air about it. There was less jocularity around the fires as the warriors prepared for the serious business of battle. The prevalent attitude was not anxiety or concern, but quiet confidence. These were men certain of their success as a matter of course. Briga and Batu dressed in silence. She laced him into his armor efficiently and settled onto the furs in order to arrange her hair in a warrior's plaits. Her paint today was black once again, and she applied it to each eyelid and across the bridge of her nose in a shallow 'V', then extending outward onto her temples. One curved snake-fang descended on her cheek from each eye. In leather bracers, her thick leather vest, and the wolfskin around her shoulders, she felt rather fierce. Batu was eyeing her approvingly. He lifted one long, tawny braid, examining it between his fingers. The plait she had laid into his hair was still intact, she noticed.

"You will need this," he said simply, letting the braid slip through his fingers as he held something out to her in his other hand.

It was the twin to her other fighting knife, and she accepted it gladly. She withdrew the blade from its scabbard. It had been sharpened and oiled. Not bothering to mask her joy, she smiled at him broadly.

"Thank you."

With both blades in their places at her waist, she followed him outside to assemble his men.

She rode beside Batu today, the khan flanked on either side by the she-wolf and his brother Sartaq. Gansükh eyed all three of them from his place a horse length behind, assessing. He didn't like the mystery of what had happened in the khan's tent last night and was irritated that the slave Dagmer would not speak of it. The blood had been part of a sacrifice, he'd figured that much. Rumors were already circulating that the she-wolf had called down a blessing from her gods to grant them victory.

But why? These are not her people.

Yet Sartaq's shaman drifted near the trio, and to his eye, had a subtle sort of kinship with the she-wolf. No, how was she called? He could not remember.

"You're staring."

Gansükh jerked his attention to the side, where Bayanaa was watching him disapprovingly. Making no effort to respond, he shifted his gaze to the forest around them instead, watchful.

The column was impossibly long, and impossibly quiet for so many men and horses. They rode five to ten abreast, widely dispersed, picking their way through spindly trees. The branches were not yet bare, but the leaves had lost their color and were drying to a dull brown. The ground was spongy, absorbing the crunch of fallen detritus under the horses' hooves. Somewhere to the left was the wide, fast river that separated the column from the Magyun city. The river was still too far away to hear or smell, but their course would eventually converge with and parallel it. It would take some time still.

For now, all eyes in the column were engaged, seeking out scouts or signs of their foe. Overhead, Sartaq's hunting eagle flew in wide, lazy circles. Sartaq wouldn't allow it to fly long, or it could give away their position prematurely, but the beast was hungry and hunting. As if on cue, the eagle folded its wings and dove away, intent on some prey.

They had ridden all day with no sign of the enemy—or anyone else, for that matter. When the khan finally signaled a halt for the night, the warriors grimly dismounted and began to prepare their make-shift camp. There would be no cookfires tonight, not with their position still unknown to the enemy,

Unlike the previous camp setups, there would be no *gers* tonight, either. All that had been left at their previous site, with a guard force, and many of the slaves. Some slaves had been brought along, however, and Briga noticed them leading strings of riderless horses, seeking out various warriors. She realized suddenly that each warrior had several personal mounts. *Of course they would,* she thought to herself. In battle, a warrior was wise to have spare weapons, replacements. For a culture that lived from the back of a horse, of course they would need spares. Just in case.

Quietly, she watched the warriors seek out dry and suitable pieces of ground to make their beds for the evening. They tied their horses nearby, as a rule, instead of leaving them in loose herds like the larger camps. Nearby, Batu was staking his own string of horses. Uncoiling a long lead rope from her saddle,

Briga tied one end to the bridle, and led her handsome gray to be tied with the rest of Batu's animals.

He laughed quietly, taking the rope from her.

"Like this." He began untying the rope from the bridle.

With ease born of long practice, he fashioned a rope harness around the horse's head and tied the loose end to the string. With the horse secure, he removed the bit and let the bridle hang around the horse's neck, reins looped up safely out of the way.

"Better." He nodded.

"Better," she agreed, realizing the gray would be much more comfortable this way.

Following his example, she removed the saddle and blanket from her mount, and followed him a short distance away. The saddle would be her pillow tonight, that much was clear. Gansükh, Bayanaa, Dagmer, and Batu's guards chose their own places close by. They were never far from Batu and Briga as a rule.

"It will be cold tonight," Gansükh commented absently.

He was right. They had ridden until dusk, and there was a chill in the air tonight. Briga was glad for the wolfskin and adjusted it around her shoulders. Above them the sky was clear, promising both Tengri's favor and crisp air. Dagmer and two other slaves appeared with bowls of fermented milk and dried meat. Briga accepted hers gratefully. The alcohol warmed her bones and took the chill out of the night air. No one seemed much inclined to talk, instead drifting off to sleep.

Batu held out an arm to her, and she settled in, curled against his side, heedless of their armor and weapons. He spread a horse blanket over them both to hold their body heat. Within moments, she'd drifted off, more or less comfortable.

Much later, Briga sat bolt upright, woken suddenly from sleep. The night was dark and moonless, but she could see the indistinct shapes of sleeping bodies around her. She looked around wildly but saw no threat that would have caused her to wake. Batu placed a restraining hand on her arm. He had sensed it, too. Gradually, she became aware that several of the Drev'an were awake, listening. She took a deep breath to control her racing heart and tried to reach out with her druid senses for the source of their unease.

She need not have bothered.

The night's stillness was subtly disturbed by the creak of a bowstring, followed by the distinct twang of an arrow being loosed. The shooter wasn't close, and the arrow didn't appear to be traveling toward the camp. No, this was likely one of the sentries firing. Moments later, soft feet could be heard running toward them. Bayanaa and Gansükh swiftly roused and intercepted the visitor. He was a runner sent back from the sentry post with news.

"Batu Khan, we have met a party of scouts."

"How many?"

"Six. To the northeast. They stumbled within range of the sentries."

Batu swore under his breath. He had hoped for two more nights at least before they were detected.

"Capture all of them," Batu ordered. "They must be silenced and blindfolded. Let none escape."

The messenger nodded and dashed off. Sartaq watched his brother curiously. "You should kill them."

"If I kill them, they will be missed, and the city will know our position. It is too soon to reveal this."

He paused to think, irritation palpable, his mind almost visibly churning through ideas. Though it was dark, Briga was certain she could see the small muscle bunching in his jaw.

"I do not see how we can prevent compromise, but perhaps we can delay it?" Sartaq suggested.

The idea clearly resonated with Batu.

"Yes," he agreed. "We can lessen the impact."

He paused to look around the circle, gaze settling on one of his more senior warriors.

"How many men do you have?" he asked the warrior.

"Two hundred, my lord."

Batu nodded thoughtfully. "Take twice that. Gather all your men quickly and take control of the prisoners. March them south and west. Do not take a straight path. When that star sets," he paused, pointing to a prominent beacon, "create an opportunity for them to escape. Not all of them need to be successful." He paused again with a meaningful look to the captain, who nodded grimly.

"They will flee back to the city. They must not stumble across us a second time. Make a wide arc to rejoin us. Now go, swiftly."

The captain bowed and ran off. Sartaq eyed his brother shrewdly.

"They will underestimate our numbers," Sartaq observed with approval.

Batu nodded. "With luck they will not realize our direction of travel, either. Which will protect our target from gaining reinforcements for a little longer. We only need to buy a few days. Now we must move. We need to distance ourselves from this position. Rouse the camp…quietly."

And so they moved, slowly but steadily, under the moonless sky. Briga was exhausted and found herself dozing off in the saddle, only to jerk herself awake each time she lost her balance.

They rode all night, stopping finally just before dawn to rest and sleep for a few scant hours. The ride hadn't been fast; in fact they had moved a bit slower than normal due to the extra vigilance needed. After a few hours of this, the group was too tired to ride on without the risk of preventable mistakes. Briga climbed down gratefully and settled on a soft patch of ground. She pulled the horse blanket up over her face and fell promptly asleep.

Sometime around midday she was woken by a hand on her shoulder. Pulling the blanket from her face, she blinked up at the hand's owner to find Gansükh crouched over her. He was holding a bowl of something and offered it to her. She sat up stiffly to accept it, willing herself to wake up fully.

"Eat."

She nodded and greedily drank the bowl of cold broth and noodles.

"Thank you."

Gansükh grunted and took the empty bowl from her, then moved off to check on Bayanaa and ready his horse. Some of the warriors were moving as stiffly as her, but before long, everyone was up and mounted once more. Briga took her place beside Batu, and the formation moved out.

***

Hours passed uneventfully as they picked their way over cold, soggy ground. Sometime in the late afternoon, the captain cautiously rejoined the main body with his men. The captain had ridden to the front of the column to give Batu and Sartaq his report. He looked tired but rode alongside his commanders and spoke steadily.

"Three of them escaped. I do not think the third man will survive."

Batu nodded, satisfied, but Briga could see his mind churning behind a stoic mask.

"Any casualties?" he finally asked.

"Two wounded, but they will heal."

Batu was silent for several more moments, but finally thanked and dismissed the captain.

"What's wrong?" asked Sartaq quietly.

Batu shook his head, uncertain. "Perhaps nothing. We will know soon if this deception was successful."

Sartaq's eagle stirred on his arm and looked skyward. It made a small sound, not quite a scream, but certainly some kind of alert. The small group looked up in time to see another eagle knifing through the thinning canopy before settling into a wide arc above the column. Bayanaa removed some kind of leather ball on a long tether from where it had been coiled up behind his saddle. He rode away from the group by a few paces and swung the thing in a wide circle at his side. The eagle spotted this and turned toward it. Bayanaa swung it twice more, then released the tail, sending it nearly straight up. The eagle tucked its wings and dove, talons extended fiercely. It caught the leather device and flew it straight into the ground. The leather firmly trapped beneath its talons, it tore at the hide with its sharp beak.

Bayanaa dismounted and drew on a heavy leather gauntlet. He then gathered up the end of the leather and began winding it back up as he approached the eagle. A piece of meat had been hidden inside the ball, which the raptor had finally extracted. The bird barely acknowledged Bayanaa as he approached, remaining focused on its meal. A tube lay situated along the eagle's back, held in place by some kind of harness. Bayanaa extracted a roll of parchment from the tube and wordlessly carried it to Batu.

The khan unrolled and read the parchment while Bayanaa tended to the eagle. One corner of his mouth twisted downward, and Briga stared at the message as though by sheer force of will she could read and understand it. The others watched the khan patiently.

"King Bela has recalled his forces to the city."

Chapter 11

Amergin had never been to a settlement like this before. It dwarfed Eamon's camp, and even the nearby villages. He'd seen buildings made of stone before, but these were different. Most of the buildings were wood, but there were clusters of stone edifices packed close together. Everything felt cramped, even the wooden structures. Buildings shared walls with their neighbors, there was little or no space between the houses, and few if any even had a garden. And then there was the smell. He didn't see how this place could be good for healing, but there wasn't much choice. The soldier he had befriended had secured a barn for them near the city wall. It was slightly less crowded here, but at least the structure was large enough to house what was left of the clan together.

Cathbad was busy seeing to Eamon's comfort. The old druid and several men had found clean straw and piled it up in one of the empty stalls. Eamon would at least be dry there, if not entirely clean. Amergin felt restless and uncertain. He needed to do something. Search for Briga again, perhaps? There had been no more sense of her after the last time Cathbad had tried to reach her. With a sigh he picked up a pot of water and carried it to Eamon's stall. Cathbad took it from him with a smile and dipped a ladle.

"How is he?"

"Better," Cathbad confirmed, "now that we have stopped moving him for a bit."

Amergin nodded, surveying the chieftain for himself. The bandage still obscured half his face, but the edges of the wound were beginning to scab over. That was a good sign. Yesterday his fever had broken and showed no sign of return.

"Cathbad, I would like to go out. Perhaps see what I can learn."

The chief druid nodded. He understood. Druid or not, he too had once been a young man and could remember the need to do something, anything, in times such as these. It was the need to feel useful.

"Go, then. Bring back some fresh meat."

Amergin inclined his head gratefully, and with a last look at Eamon, let himself out. The city around him assaulted his nostrils, but there was nothing to be done for it. Wrapping his cloak a little tighter around his shoulders, he set off toward the market. That was always a safe bet for gaining information.

There were a fair number of people milling about the makeshift stalls, but the air held a subtle note of tension in it somehow. He'd tried speaking with some of the merchants, but neither he nor the locals had enough words in common to discuss anything but the price of their goods. Resignedly, he finally gave up trying to communicate and focused instead on obtaining supplies. In the end, he wound up with a basket full of fruit and vegetables, two loaves of bread, a large fish, and a milk-goat.

Still feeling a bit restless, he decided to take the long way home. Weaving his way out toward the city wall, he noticed most of the houses here were wood or sported only a facade of stone here and there. Marveling, he wondered what the reason for this might be? The price of materials? Status? Or were these structures simply older? It was impossible to guess. They all had thatched roofs; at least that was something familiar. Amergin was already imagining how the clan could earn some little wages repairing thatch, should they stay long enough for that to become necessary. Amergin and Cathbad had agreed that they should leave as soon as possible. Their hosts were Magyuns and seemed to be preparing for conflict of some kind. Neither druid wished to be thrust into another man's war. They'd tasted enough of that at Rowanar. And besides, the Magyuns were

114

longtime allies of the Emorians, whom all true Velkcic tribes despised.

Amergin wandered the path that ran along the stone city wall, allowing his thoughts to wander. He kept thinking he could sense vague hints of Briga's pattern, but they evaporated when he tried to concentrate on her. *Why is that?* he wondered. His attention was drawn reluctantly back to the present by some sort of disturbance taking place ahead. Magyun soldiers were clustered around the closed southern gate, intent on something at the center of their group. Drawing closer, he noticed his friend Ambrus hovering at the edge of the cluster. Tugging on the goat's lead, he made his way toward the soldiers.

"Ambrus," he called out to catch his friend's attention.

Ambrus turned, and Amergin felt a flicker of unease at the look on his face. Ambrus stepped away from the group and waved the druid closer.

"What's wrong?" Amergin asked, attempting to peer through the cluster of bodies. He was taller than most of them, but it made no difference.

"It's a scouting party. They ran into trouble last night—"

Ambrus was interrupted by a sob of pain from the center of the cluster. Amergin could smell blood. Without thinking, he shoved the basket and the goat's lead rope into Ambrus' hands and shouldered his way through the cluster. There were three men at the center, all looking as if they'd had a rough time of it. But the third man...

Ignoring shouts of protest and shrugging off restraining hands, he dropped to his knees beside the third man. His hands instinctively probed the wound, assessing its seriousness. He'd sustained many wounds, but the worst was a deep slash high in his side. A froth of bubbles and a steady ooze matched the rate of his shallow breathing. Behind him Ambrus addressed the other soldiers, probably explaining that he was a healer. A dozen pairs of fearful eyes rested on him. He felt the blood drain from his own face as he visually examined the wound, and realization dawned. His gaze locked onto Ambrus uncertainly.

"I can make him…more comfortable."

Ambrus only stared at him for several moments. A look of pure anguish flickered across his face for an instant, then gradually set into a mask of grim acceptance. None of the other soldiers seemed able to understand Velkcic, but they understood Ambrus' expression all too well. One of the injured man's friends moved swiftly and sat at his side, speaking to him quietly. Amergin supposed he was telling his comrade everything would be all right, this foreign healer would take away the pain. He should just relax…

The man was shaking now, but it wasn't from fear. His friend nodded to the druid. Amergin dug into his pouch to produce a bottle of laudanum. In small doses, the opiate was a mild sedative and helped ease pain. Amergin fed him the entire bottle. The man grabbed his friend's hand as a new spasm of pain shivered through him and whimpered pitifully. It was only a few more moments before the laudanum started to take effect, and the man sighed, staring up at his friend, who smiled comfortingly through his tears.

It didn't take long. Gradually the man's breathing eased, and his eyes fluttered open and shut. Finally, he slipped into sleep. His body went limp, and his hand slipped out of his friend's grasp to fall upon his chest. The friend covered it with his own hand and bowed his head. Amergin looked down as well, allowing the soldier a moment of grief. Then he slowly, reverently rested his hand on the dead man's brow to help guide the spirit out of its mortal shell.

"What happened?" he asked Ambrus quietly, after a silence.

"They were on a patrol last night and stumbled across a small army of horselords. They were taken prisoner, but managed to escape before they could be brought to the slave ranks. It seems three were killed during the escape."

Amergin's blood inexplicably turned to ice in his veins.

"Was there a woman with them? With the horselords, I mean. A slave woman, perhaps?"

Ambrus stared at him, puzzled by the strain in his voice, then asked the remaining scouts what they had seen.

"They were hooded for most of the time, but they didn't notice any women."

The tiny spark of hope that had flared in his chest was just as suddenly extinguished. Ambrus frowned, listening to the survivors.

"What is it?" Amergin prompted.

"There is a large army to the south of the city. The scouts think the group was moving to reinforce them."

Amergin's blood turned to ice once more. "Will they attack the city?"

"They may try," Ambrus conceded, "but they're disorganized and have poor tactics. They won't get far."

Every hair on the druid's body seemed to be standing on end. He had fought these men once, and while he was no tactician, what he'd seen of their tactics had been far from poor. Nodding absently, he took his supplies back from Ambrus, and turned to go. Cathbad needed to know about this.

***

Khuyag was concerned. He and the other generals crouched atop a low ridge, carefully observing a mass of enemy forces encamped on the other side of the valley. They were between him and the river, which meant they had crossed somewhere. Thanks to terrain and their clumsy horses, the main bridge was a day or two's ride to the north. It seemed too much of a coincidence that such a force would have ridden around the long way just to make this show of force. Khuyag would have seen their approach. He knew from reports that the water was swift. The Magyuns wouldn't have been so foolish as to try swimming their horses, not so close to the Drev'an camp below the ridge, within full sight of the valley. Such a course would have been foolish in the extreme. The horsemen hadn't bothered to conceal their presence. They had moved hastily after departing the main camp, and as expected, the Magyun scouts had discovered them within a day. No, there had to be another bridge. One Batu Khan was not aware of. They would need to locate it quickly.

"This would have been better in the winter," Burd grumbled. "At least then the river would be frozen, and we could ride over it to take the city."

Khuyag grunted—there was validity to his claim. Using frozen rivers as roads was a favorite trick of the Drev'an horde.

"But in winter they would already have harvested their crops. They could withstand a siege. Now, the fields are still full and ripe. We will starve them out."

Burd nodded quietly, acknowledging the point. He was only impatient for action and a chance to redeem himself, Khuyag knew.

"How long until they work up the nerve to attack?" Burd wondered aloud.

Khuyag wondered the same thing. They'd been camped here for three days with no response from the opposing force.

"Perhaps it is time to give them a demonstration of our…prowess. Drill the men."

Burd smiled grimly, understanding what sort of demonstration was required.

***

Amergin had developed a habit. Daily, he would take a long walk around the city. Eventually he'd stop and gather supplies, but he was more interested in gauging the attitude of the city's inhabitants. Today, Cathbad had joined him. The chief druid wanted specific herbs to help with Eamon's healing and his own meditation. Amergin could easily gather these items, but Cathbad wanted to stretch his legs. Truthfully, Amergin was glad for his company. The old priest had been holding constant vigil at Eamon's side, and the stress was beginning to show on his face. It was better for him to take in some fresh air and get his mind off their troubles for a change.

Around them, the city's people carried on as usual. There was still a slight tension in the air, but no worse than it had been for the past several days. The druids walked along the city wall, preferring the slightly fresher air and the slightly less crowded streets.

"How long before Eamon is well enough to travel, do you think?"

Cathbad sighed, his gaze dropping to examine the weeds that grew along the base of the wall. Amergin mentally kicked himself. He was supposed to be taking Cathbad's mind *off* such matters.

"I am not certain. He still gets dizzy when he sits up for too long."

"It seems like he should be healing faster."

Cathbad nodded wordlessly. He thought so too, but was at a loss for how to help speed the process.

The pair walked on in silence, each exploring their own thoughts. They rounded a corner. Amergin had been about to ask about Briga when they were both startled by a loud, frantic neighing and crashing from the stables ahead. It was an army stable, but no soldiers appeared to be standing guard. Exchanging curious looks, the druids made their way toward the sound. There was a single horse inside; clearly all the others had been removed for their own safety. Several boards lining the horse's stall were cracked. It had been kicking at the walls. The

119

beast stood stock still as they approached, ears erect and swiveled in their direction, nostrils flared wide.

"Cathbad," Amergin began, and the horse spooked violently at his voice.

It screamed and reared up, heavy hooves pawing at the air dangerously. The whites of its eyes were showing—a clear sign of panic.

But Cathbad had a special talent for animals. The old druid raised his hands and murmured soothing words in the old tongue, attempting to placate the beast. The gelding dropped its head and kicked the wall with its back feet. Cathbad took another slow step forward, still chanting quietly. The horse's panicked screams diminished to an agitated whickering, and it tossed its head and pawed the ground. The old druid fell silent and waited, hands still spread wide.

Gradually, the horse calmed. It was still tense, but it had stopped tossing its head and stood quietly, if a bit stiffly. Very slowly, Cathbad reached out and laid his hand on the creature's nose. The horse balked slightly but finally allowed it, breathing fast and heavy through wide nostrils.

"Shhhh, mo chroi, it's all right now."

Amergin looked on calmly as the chief druid worked his gift. He knew there was nothing he could do to help. The beast was far too traumatized. There was a vague crackling sensation in the air, similar to what's sometimes felt before a lightning storm. Amergin closed his eyes and silently prayed with the old priest.

The horse was calming. Its breathing slowed to a normal cadence, and its body relaxed somewhat. Cathbad ran his hands over the beast, along its neck, down each foreleg, down its back and rear legs, but he paused by the tail. The horse's flesh shivered and twitched along its withers and flanks. It stomped one foot, and Cathbad returned to the head, repeating the sequence. He completed the ritual twice more until he could touch its tail without the riotous twitching. Finally he rested both palms on the beast's forehead, chanting softly.

"That's amazing," a voice breathed from the entrance behind them.

The horse yanked its head up and danced sideways away from the men, but its earlier violence was gone.

Amergin turned to face his Magyun friend, features carefully kept neutral at the intrusion.

"How did you do that?"

Cathbad gave the creature a pitying look as Amergin answered for him.

"Cathbad has a way with animals."

"That horse was completely mad not an hour ago."

"Mad with terror," Cathbad offered. "He has been through a terrible ordeal."

Whatever the old druid had seen, he clearly did not wish to share the knowledge in front of Ambrus. For his part, Ambrus only nodded, not volunteering any information, either.

"I was afraid we'd have to put him down."

"He is calmer now," Cathbad cautioned, "but he may never be fit to ride again."

Ambrus nodded again, solemn. His gaze sank for a moment before fixing on the younger druid.

"I've been looking for you, Amergin."

The younger druid looked at him but said nothing, waiting for Ambrus to continue.

"Your clan...you said you were in Rowanar, yes?"

"Yes," he answered, uncomfortable.

"So you've seen the Drev'an up close?"

"The horse people…is that what they're called?" He was evading, and Ambrus knew it.

"Walk with me. I would like to know what you have seen."

Amergin nodded and folded his hands behind his back as he walked with the Magyun. Silently he wondered if Ambrus just wanted to get away from the horse, or if he had a destination planned. Cathbad trailed a few paces behind.

"How was it at Rowanar?" Ambrus finally asked after they'd walked a bit in silence.

Amergin paused uncomfortably. "I'm not a soldier…" And he didn't particularly wish to recall the details of that awful day.

"I know, Amergin, I know. I only ask because they are camped south of the city, as you know. I'm certain they would attack if they could, and I don't believe they can, but I wish to understand their tactics."

Unwillingly, Amergin was drawn back into the memory of that terrible day. Of the flashing swords and axes, the arrows and blood. Briga atop her horse charging recklessly into the fray with her daggers brandished like a savage. He shook himself, not wanting to remember more.

Ambrus endured his silence for a time, eyeing his friend out of the corner of his eye.

"Our troops are growing restless," he finally said to break the silence. "Yesterday we saw the horsemen drilling. They couldn't even get through an entire drill sequence before the formation dissolved into squabbles and fist fights. They have no discipline."

What Amergin had seen on the battlefield seemed to contradict that statement, but he was no soldier. It wasn't his place to speculate.

"The officers had a difficult task getting their men back into order." After a moment, he added, "King Bela still withholds the order to attack."

Ambrus hadn't meant to say that, Amergin was certain. The sudden silence was confirmation enough. So was the note of scorn with which it had been spoken. The druid eyed him discreetly, deciding if he should say anything. Curiosity finally won out over discretion.

"You think he is wrong?"

"I think we must disband them quickly, or they will camp on our doorstep all winter."

Amergin was surprised. "All winter?"

"It's a long way back to their lands. Why risk their animals when they can raid our fields and our merchants? No, we must make battle a poor option so they go away."

"Your king knows this?"

Ambrus fixed his friend with a long, penetrating stare, evaluating.

"The king knows best," he said finally.

Amergin nodded and the trio walked on without further conversation.

"We cannot risk staying here much longer," Cathbad warned in the silent language of the druids.

Amergin nodded to himself. Eamon needed to heal, or they would be forced to carry him.

"Three days," he responded wordlessly.

"Amergin…" the Magyun questioned, glancing sidelong at the priest. But whatever it was the man wanted to ask, he seemed unable to voice the question. Amergin didn't press the matter.

Chapter 12

Briga lay on her belly on the cold ground, scarcely daring to breathe. Gansükh was pressed up along her side on his belly as well, both of them attempting to share a concealed position atop a low ridgeline. From here they could see the river, the stone bridge, and the guard towers. It was a small miracle Batu's forces had been able to travel another few days and creep this close without being detected. Men could stay quiet, but they could advance no further without the enemy noticing the sound of their horses.

Gansükh scanned the river. They would not attempt to cross so close to the bridge, but if the Magyuns could cross, Batu would want to know about it. The river here was deep with a fast current. The banks angled sharply up from the water, too steep for a horse to manage. Perhaps not too steep for a man, if he could somehow manage the current.

"I don't think they can swim," Briga murmured.

Gansükh looked at her, surprised. She simply pointed to the distant figures patrolling the bridge. It was difficult to make out details at this distance, but she could tell the soldiers all wore heavy metal armor. It glinted occasionally. Gansükh nodded. So their enemy would not be swimming across. They had seen enough. Squeezing her shoulder as a sign, they wriggled backward off the crest of the ridge, and down onto lower ground that would mask their presence from the soldiers on the bridge, so long as they remained silent.

Attacking the bridge would be fairly straightforward. It was a stone structure with waist-high walls, and the roof was covered by thatch and wooden slats. A gatehouse with a tower stood at each end, with a much larger structure on the far end. Gansükh thought it might be an armory. The city was perhaps another thousand meters away from the river. Its walls didn't extend to the gatehouse, so any reinforcements from there would be vulnerable to Batu's archers as they crossed the open terrain between the two structures. The danger would come as the Drev'an tried to take the second tower, the one at the far end of the bridge. They had no other way to cross the river, so they would have to rely on what men were on the bridge itself. The bridge was wide enough to accommodate two wagons side by side, but this was still close quarters for swords—even the shorter, curved blades of the Drev'an.

When they returned, they were met by Bayanaa, who had another eagle perched on his gauntleted fist. Batu was already reading the tiny message.

"Do the Magyuns use birds as messengers?" she wondered quietly to Gansükh as they approached.

Batu was grinning as he handed the paper over to Sartaq, hovering nearby.

"They have finally drawn a line in the sand. General Burd sent his forces forward to test the Magyun defenses. He was 'routed', it seems."

"It is not enough," cautioned Sartaq. "We need them to fully attack."

"They will."

"Defending their line is not the same as an open attack," Sartaq pressed.

Annoyance rippled across Batu's face, but he maintained his confident stance. "You are right, brother. But they will attack. When our men return to our line to test the defenders again and again, they will lose patience with Bela and attack. Have patience. You will see.

"Now," he said, and turned to face Briga and Gansükh, "tell me about the bridge."

***

That evening Briga lay on her back, staring up at the stars through thinning trees. Her head was pillowed on Batu's shoulder, his arm around her. Gansükh was close by her other side. As they'd neared the Magyun lines, he had crept closer and closer to her and the khan, as if he could shield them by proximity alone. She smiled at him thinly. Gansükh, ever the protector. Bayanaa and Dagmer were nearby as well, curled together for shared warmth. Briga sighed, returning her gaze to the sky once more. *When did this begin to feel normal? This closeness with the people who captured you? This sense of peculiar...kinship?*

Why are you helping them, Briga?

The thought arose unbidden, and she frowned into the night.

You're a prisoner still, why are you helping them?

She recalled an earlier vision from Cathbad, urging to her to cooperate, to obey the whims of the gods. But did that order extend to collusion? Unsettled, she turned onto her side and attempted to clear her mind. She stared at Gansükh sleeping beside her and had a sudden flash of memory, back to the first time she had encountered him. When he came into the *ger*, leering, and dragged her before the khan. But he'd never been truly rough with her. Not like Batu. She realized dimly that she could escape into the night. Right now. She could get up, creep into the woods under the pretense of relieving herself, and walk to the bridge. They would gladly accept a Drev'an prisoner, especially one who knew the khan. She could warn the Magyuns of what waited on their doorstep. If she desired.

Moving quietly, she sat up, careful not to disturb Batu. He stirred, but didn't awaken. Carefully she stood and pressed her daggers against her sides so they wouldn't clink and betray her. Slowly she picked her way through the sleeping bodies, mindful of each step. It seemed to take half the night before she finally reached the edge of the makeshift camp. The sentry didn't challenge her as she slipped into the woods, but she could feel his eyes following her. She ventured out as far as she dared. It would not do for the sentry to call to her and raise the alarm.

She finally stopped amid a small circle of trees and sank slowly to her knees. Her palms settled against the cold earth, fingers splayed loosely. With a slow, deep breath she closed her eyes and reached, stretching her senses out in all directions. The world suddenly shifted, and it was as if she could almost see the web of threads around her that formed a great Pattern so vast she would never fully grasp its weave. So many threads, all thrumming with life, but indistinct. She gasped, marveling, fighting to breathe, to stay in this strange plane. Every thought was an effort. Silently she called out to Cathbad, to Eamon, to anyone from his clan, sifting carefully through the innumerable strands wending this way and that. She'd never seen them before, not truly.

"Cathbad," she whispered, beseeching the most powerful of Eamon's druids for help.

The threads were maddeningly silent. It took so much effort to stay here. Physically straining, she poured all her concentration into the search, *willing* the threads to appear. Her whole body was tense with the effort and quivering with fatigue as she sorted, searched.

"I need your help," she gasped, forcing herself to keep looking, to breathe.

The strain was unbearable, but there, she thought she saw a glimmer in the distance, a single shimmering light hopelessly intertwined among the riotous threads. Shaking, she stretched her senses toward it, weaving between the other threads, trying to reach it. It was so far, and she was moving so slowly. The light flickered, faded.

"No," she panted, fighting to slow her breathing, to regain control.

But the strand was dimming, receding into the Pattern. By an effort of sheer will, she surged forward. Pain lanced through her, pulling her back, pulling her down.

"Cathbad!"

A sudden need lanced through her, a strong, insistent mental pull toward the city. Without understanding it, she knew she had to get there as quickly and as bloodlessly as possible. She could feel it. And that meant helping the Drev'an. They now had a common cause. The Pattern released its hold on her without warning, and she collapsed forward onto the ground, shaking uncontrollably, teeth gritted so hard her jaw ached. Her body pressed into the ground, suddenly heavy. Some distant part of her mind registered that the weight wasn't hers, but something laying on top of her, crushing her into the ground. She hadn't collapsed, she had been tackled. Wildly she forced her senses back into her body to regain control of herself. A rough hand clamped firmly over her mouth.

"Be silent!" the weight demanded harshly against her ear.

There was a rustling nearby, the sounds of men moving stealthily in the night. Magyuns, she was almost certain of it. Magyuns coming to investigate the noise.

"Damn it," the weight growled as he caught sight of two scouts moving in the distance. Now he would have to deal with them.

Glancing over his shoulder, he shot a look to the sentry to stay put. The man nodded but kept a firm grip on his bow, crouching out of sight. The weight lifted, and rough hands hauled her upright. One hand clamped across her mouth again. The second drew one of her daggers and held it across her throat, pressing her against a hard, familiar body.

"Move," Gansükh growled and marched her deeper into the forest.

The two shapes marking the Magyun scouts froze, watching. Gansükh didn't walk her far, just out of hearing distance of the camp. Without warning, he threw her roughly to the ground.

"Whore," he growled. "I should kill you right here."

Briga landed hard on her side, knocking the wind out of her. She stared up at her protector, wide-eyed. He was speaking in the Magyun tongue.

"But first," he leered, "it would be such a pity to let you go to waste."

To her horror, he fell on her, hands fumbling at her lacings. She groped blindly for the remaining dagger at her waist, but Gansükh caught her wrist. The look in his eye was deeply apologetic, and deadly serious. Suddenly she understood. The Magyun scouts couldn't be allowed to live. It was her fault they had found this edge of the camp, drawn by her calls for Cathbad. And now they must be lured closer to be dealt with. Gansükh was giving them a damsel in distress, or a whore for the taking, whichever they chose to see. She released the dagger, playing along. Gansükh lifted the hem of her tunic but left her breeks intact. She struggled and fought, even with the dagger across her throat.

"Stop!" rasped a voice not far to their right.

So they had opted to save the damsel. Gansükh didn't hesitate. He leapt off Briga and hit the man square in the chest, burying her dagger in his neck to the hilt. The second scout had drawn a sword and slashed at the horselord, but Gansükh dropped and hooked his heel behind the other man, sweeping his leg out from under him. The horselord's own blade sang as he drew it, stabbing downward and making short work of the second man. A third flew out of the night and crashed into

Gansükh, knocking him forward. Briga was on her feet, dagger in hand to help her protector.

Someone grabbed her from behind and dragged her back. To safety, perhaps, but she whirled and jammed her knife between his ribs. The stranger stared at her in utter shock. Ripping her blade free, she kicked him in the stomach. He stumbled back and landed hard on his tailbone. Falling forward with the momentum from her kick, she landed crouched over his chest and slashed his throat. The man clawed at her face, then at his own neck, but it was over quickly. She grabbed the ax he'd been carrying and stood quickly, searching for the next threat.

There was a snarl behind her, and she whirled to face a large silver wolf, its muzzle stained with blood. Gansükh was getting to his feet behind it. Not his blood, she realized. The wolf focused on something beyond her and flashed past. She could hear someone running, the wolf snarling in pursuit. Then silence.

The violence was over almost as soon as it had started. Briga glanced around, assuring herself they were alone now. Shaking, she sank to her knees. All the unshed tears of the past weeks burst forth in an unexpected torrent, and she sank until her forehead touched the ground, boneless. She wept for the losses, for the dimmed thread, for everything she had truly parted with that terrible day outside Rowanar. Gansükh hovered nearby, terrified to touch her.

"What is wrong?" he breathed fearfully. "Are you hurt?"

When she didn't respond, he edged closer, crouching, and laid a tentative hand on her shoulder. She turned to him, and he gathered her up in his arms awkwardly. Briga cried into his chest, allowing the pent up emotions to flow out of her in a tide.

The wolf howled distantly, circling back toward the city. She listened, and knew. She had seen the stain of berry juice on the wolf's flank and knew where it had come from. She had to get into the city, quickly and bloodlessly. She could feel the draw of it in her very bones, stronger now than before.

"It was only one man," Gansükh whispered as she calmed, mistaking the source of her distress.

"No," she replied. "It is a whole city."

His hands slid to her shoulders, pushing her back so he could look at her. He frowned, examining her face.

"What are you doing out here?" There was an accusatory note in his voice.

"I just needed to be alone. To pray…" she sounded defeated. The tone was uncharacteristic of her, and his frown deepened.

"Who is Cathbad?" he finally asked, somewhat gently.

Briga paled.

"Your…husband?"

She stared at him, wide-eyed for a long moment.

"He was my master. The high priest," she amended, aware of the sensitivity the Drev'an held regarding slavery or anything that sounded like it.

Gansükh stiffened, wariness and anger flickering across his features for the briefest of moments.

"You have been in contact with him?"

"No," she admitted. "that's not within my abilities."

He stared at her for another long minute as he tried to decide how to feel about this revelation. Sighing, he got to his feet and pulled her up as well. He cleaned the blade he had borrowed and returned it to her.

"Come, we must go back now."

Nodding, she sheathed the knives and tucked the confiscated ax into her belt. It was hers now by right. Gansükh gripped her by the elbow and led her quietly back into camp.

***

Gansükh lay awake, staring at the she-wolf and Batu Khan. He was troubled by what he had learned tonight. Could all shaman contact one another that way, or only her people? Was she even telling the truth? He had never seen her so resigned, and that in itself was troubling. The encounter had left him with more questions than answers. He turned his face away and caught Bayanaa watching him quietly, Dagmer curled up against his back. He nodded reassurance to the younger guard and closed his eyes. The questions could wait. For a little while, anyway.

Chapter 13

"Your friend is hiding something from you, Amergin."

They were seated before a carefully constructed hearth fire in the center of the barn. Excess straw had been cleared away to prevent fire. The stable would be a deathtrap if fire ever broke out, so they were always cautious.

"Of course he is. He doesn't fully trust us."

Amergin stirred the pot of stew bubbling between them. The warriors watched them, willing the meat to be ready.

"And," he paused, tasting the broth carefully, "we aren't Magyuns."

"We are not," Cathbad agreed, "but we are in their city, and while we are here, their interests are our own."

The younger druid ladled out a modest helping into a wooden bowl and signaled one of the warriors.

"Rorik, take this to Eamon."

A redheaded warrior roused himself and took the bowl, handing over a roughly-hewn vessel of his own in return. He would receive the first helping after the chieftain.

"Is it the horse?" Amergin asked quietly, spooning more stew into Rorik's bowl as the others approached.

Cathbad nodded. "Not only that. I sense there are larger forces at work."

Amergin frowned but said nothing as he doled out stew to his hungry clansmen. He eyed bandages and movement as they neared, appraising. At least they seemed to be healing much faster than their lord. But there were so few of them now…

"I want you to befriend Ambrus," Cathbad said suddenly. The chief druid's attention was fixed steadily on the younger priest.

Amergin furrowed his brow, returning the gaze. "I am his friend."

Cathbad's face registered incredulity, and he favored Amergin with a look the younger man hadn't seen in many years. It was clearly patronizing.

"He is not your friend, Amergin, he is using you. I want you to establish trust and rapport on a personal level. Maybe then we will learn some truths about the situation here."

Amergin was silent as he ladled a bowl for the chief druid and himself. Cathbad was right, he knew it, but surely the seeds of actual friendship had been sown. The man had had no reason to offer them aid and protection when he'd stumbled across them after Rowanar. He had a kind soul beneath the soldier's armor.

"Cathbad," Amergin began cautiously, "what did you see with the horse?"

"His rider had been killed. Something was tied into his tail that frightened him badly. The images were…confused."

Amergin nodded his understanding and frowned. Perhaps he would convince Ambrus to tell the story.

***

"Parchment," Khuyag ordered.

A servant scrambled through the makeshift command tent to find ink, quill, and paper for his general.

"It is absurd to celebrate our loss," General Burd commented, though he was smiling thinly.

They were all streaked with blood and dirt from the day's battle. After days of demonstrating poor discipline and taunting the Magyun defenders, their enemy had finally decided to attack. Their fighting skills were marginal, and the Drev'an soldiery had performed their assigned role well. They'd fought sloppily, careful to avoid losses as they ceded ground. After a concentrated charge by the Magyuns had penetrated the Drev'an front lines, the nomads had broken and fled, chased back beyond the ridgeline.

If the generals were worried about how the men would take to their new role as actors, they need not have been concerned. The men were unseemly joyous, having apparently enjoyed their task. The camp held an air of victory rather than defeat. Burd was right, though. They would need to be subdued before reports of this strange behavior made it back to the Magyun warlords.

Finally, a pot of ink was set before General Khuyag, along with the other needed items. He began writing his report at once.

"Did any of our scouts make it to the river?"

"I still have a team out, but I do not think so."

"We need to find the bridge. I am certain that is how they crossed, a temporary construction of some kind."

"What if it is a new stone bridge?" one of Sartaq's generals suggested.

Khuyag looked up from his report to fix the man with a solemn stare. Another fortified bridge this far south could devastate their plans.

"Let us hope it is not. Send our best scouts to hunt for the crossing point, wherever it may be."

The general nodded and stepped away. There was nothing more to discuss. The plan had been successful, but now they needed to contain the men and prepare for the next battle.

The presence of a possible second bridge changed things. Khuyag's theater was no longer purely one of deception. They would need to find it and control it. But they'd have to await word from Batu Khan. Smiling, Burd clapped him on the shoulder in a gesture of reassurance.

"I will see to the men."

Khuyag watched the general depart, musing that the man had turned out to be such a good right-hand, despite his temper. He would make a note of that to the khan as well.

***

Briga lay on her belly beside Batu. It was the same ridgeline she'd scouted previously with Gansükh. Sartaq lay beside his brother. Gansükh and the other guards lay by their ankles, ready to pull their charges down to safety on the backside of the slope if necessary. Behind them waited thousands of dismounted nomads, utterly silent. They would attack at nightfall, when darkness would shroud their approach. Batu was taking advantage of the dwindling light to conduct one last reconnaissance. He hated to fight dismounted, she could see it in the set of his jaw, but there was no room on the bridge for so many horses.

Batu had received an eagle earlier telling of Khuyag's success. The Magyuns had been lured into battle seemingly against orders and had driven back the nomad raiders. If word had spread to the defenders on the bridge, they would likely be celebrating…and perhaps lax in their watch.

Yet Briga felt uneasy. She had finally fallen into a fitful sleep last night, though it came with effort. Her dreams had been troubled, cloudy. She awoke with a feeling of dread, whether from the dream or Batu's reaction to what she'd revealed to Gansükh, she couldn't be certain. Batu had said nothing. He did

137

not even comment on the blood that flecked her leathers, though he raised an eyebrow once he noticed it. Perhaps Gansükh hadn't told him what had happened after all. The terse warrior had been especially guarded with her today, almost as if he expected some kind of betrayal. Batu glared at her questioningly, and she realized she had been staring.

"What is wrong?" he whispered.

She frowned but shook her head. He squeezed her arm reassuringly and returned his attention to the bridge.

They lay for some time, watching, until darkness finally claimed the land. With it, a fog was rising.

"Good," Batu breathed, noticing. "Tengri aids us."

Briga looked at him, uncertain.

"He has sent the clouds to mask our forces from the Magyuns."

She couldn't claim to know Tengri or his will, but the mist left a cold prickle on the back of her neck. Somewhere a wolf sounded its lonely call. There was no answering howl.

"Come, it is time."

The trio slithered off the hill, and their guards fell into step behind them. Briga was strangely reassured by the presence of Gansükh and Bayanaa hovering close, watchful. The generals clustered around their commanders at a gesture from the khan, who then nodded to Sartaq.

"Tonight we take the bridge," he stated in hushed but confident tones.

The simple statement was met with hisses of approval, and he pressed on.

"General Mor, take your best men and clear the road of sentries. Quietly."

Carefully and concisely, he went on, explaining the plan and the role each general was expected to fulfill. The warriors nodded their understanding. A spark of confidence and enthusiasm had been ignited and spread among the men until it was almost a palpable thing. Having received their orders, the generals strode off to govern their men.

Mor was already moving at the head of thirty or so men. They were lightly armored, but heavily armed, and set off on their task with quiet confidence. After granting the advance guard several minutes to work their way forward, Batu himself stepped onto the road to lead his army into battle. Briga surveyed the ranks of Drev'an before her. Unlike the Magyuns, their armor was made from plates of bone sewn into tough, cured leather. Some bore metal grommets, some not. It wasn't as sturdy as the Magyun's metal plating, but it was much lighter. The nomad warriors wore bronze helmets adorned with more of the leather-and-bone plating falling to protect their neck and shoulders. Each helmet was plumed with a lock of black horsehair. Briga herself wore no helmet as she moved to Batu's side, her two guards close on her heels. With Briga to his left and Sartaq to his right, Batu signaled to advance.

***

Ambrus leaned on his spear and stared out into the night, but it was plain to see his attention was miles away. One of his fellow soldiers noticed and edged up to him quietly. When Ambrus failed to react, the man kicked Ambrus' spear out from under him, sending him stumbling to catch his balance. The soldiers erupted into raucous laughter. Scowling, he swatted at the prankster with the butt of his spear.

"Ambrus! You should be minding your watch, not brooding over some woman!" one of the guards chided good-naturedly.

Ambrus smiled himself and laughed. A certain woman had been on his mind, briefly, though at the moment he was more concerned about what was happening to the south. The king was angry. Against his orders, two of the commanders had grown impatient and attacked the gathering nomad force. The invaders had been defeated at every meeting, yet they wouldn't be driven off. Why?

"What's her name, Ambrus?" asked one of the younger men in accented Magyun.

"She's your mother, Caleb, now hush."

More laughter as the soldiers found amusement at Caleb's expense this time, and Ambrus found himself smiling with them. But there was a brief, discordant note to their revelry. Something out of place, somehow. Ambrus frowned and squinted into the night.

"Did you hear that?" he asked the man nearest him.

"Hear what?"

Ignoring the laughter, he concentrated on the darkness beyond the gatehouse for anything that might have alerted him. His attentiveness must have been catching, as the others gradually quieted and peered out into the night for themselves. The mist obscured almost everything beyond the initial line of trees, so they would have to rely on their hearing for anything amiss. Faintly, Ambrus heard the distant clinking of armor from the soldiers at the far end of the bridge. That end—the side closer to the city—boasted an armory and barracks, but the sounds weren't quite what he thought he'd heard. They were too normal. After a few tense moments, their captain shifted, breaking the silence.

"Ambrus, I think—"

"Shh!" Ambrus silenced him with a gesture.

He had definitely heard it this time. A faint, hissing whisper sounded out in the forest, then a gurgling choke, almost like a rabbit caught in the coils of a snake. More of the soldiers heard it this time, and all eyes turned to the trees.

"Was it an animal?" someone whispered.

The captain grunted his doubt. "Jakob, Caleb, go and check."

The two men gathered up their spears and quivers and made to go. There was a meaty thud, and the captain staggered backward, a black-fletched arrow sprouting impossibly from his neck. Bewildered, he clutched at it while his men looked on in stunned silence. A second arrow lodged in the wooden window frame beside Ambrus' head, startling him into action.

"Archers!" he called out and raced for the stairs, heedless of the captain's still-falling body.

There was a signal fire atop the gatehouse, and he must light it.

"Caleb, with me," he called for the boy to follow.

The others were hastily fastening armor and nocking their bows. Four more arrows sailed into the guardhouse, but only one struck a defender. A terrible cry issued from the woods, unmistakably signaling the nomad charge. Arrows poured through the open portal, and men rushed to shield themselves behind the heavy oaken gatehouse doors. They leaned their weight against them to force them shut. Nomads were running from the trees now, racing to beat the door. The soldiers strained and shoved. The hinges were rusty with disuse, and the wood at the bottom was swollen with damp from the river, but it grudgingly gave way. The doors swung shut just as a wave of Drev'an reached it and threw themselves against its bulk. The door shuddered beneath their force. Defenders fought to maintain their footing, holding the door with their shoulders until thick wooden braces could be propped into place. Some of the archers had moved to flank the gatehouse and were firing into the windows. Their arrows ricocheted chaotically in the small space.

Atop the gatehouse, Caleb and Ambrus were firing down at the invaders, ducking below the ramparts with every wave of returned fire. In his haste Ambrus had forgotten to bring a

141

torch, and he cursed as he discovered the one normally kept here was conspicuously absent. Now they were effectively pinned by enemy archers and stone-throwers, alone with two vats of oil and a host of spare quivers.

"Jakob, the door!" he called down the stairs.

"It's nearly braced!" came the answer amid the din of men throwing themselves against the barrier.

"I need a torch!"

"Give me a few minutes and you shall have it!"

The warriors must have noticed that the door had been reinforced, for the thudding of their bodies had slowed, and the archers had retreated a few paces to seek better angles of fire. Below, Ambrus could hear his own men scrambling into their positions. Surely the far end of the bridge was likewise preparing, they would have heard the attack and the shouting. Maybe their signal fire was now lit to warn the city. Ambrus dared a glance over the rampart at the retreating archers. It seemed as if they were taking a moment to assess their next move. He knew it was a stalemate that couldn't last.

Batu watched from the edge of the clearing as the massive oaken doors groaned laboriously closed. The men hurled themselves against the doors, but they wouldn't budge. Already the captains were calling their men back to secure better positions. Wordlessly the khan gestured to his brother. Sartaq turned and nodded to the man behind him, who darted off to his preassigned task. Briga stood at Batu's left side, observing as stoically as she could. She glanced to Batu, but his attention was fixed firmly on the gatehouse.

Sartaq's general was quick about his task, returning up the road before a phalanx of men carrying a rough-hewn battering ram. Warriors cleared a path as they approached, closing ranks again in their wake. They made it halfway to the gatehouse before the defenders could make them out in the misty dark.

There was a cry from atop the gatehouse, and a hail of night-arrows poured into the phalanx.

"Shields!" Briga called out before she could stop herself. "Shield wall!"

Batu and Gansükh regarded her with twin looks of puzzlement. The soldiers seemed to understand, however, and several dashed forward to protect the ram-bearers as best they could. The archers renewed their fire, trying to kill or at least pin down the defenders. Atop the gatehouse, a fire flared to life, followed quickly by fire-arrows. Below, rhythmic thudding of the ram against the doors punctuated the still air.

Caleb had managed to scuttle to the stairwell and had returned with a fresh quiver and a torch. The defenders held their fire during the lull to preserve their arrows, but that changed once they spotted the battering ram.

"Ram!" he cried out in warning to the men below.

The Magyun archers loosed their deadly rain upon the ram-bearers, felling nearly third of them with the first volley. Ambrus had been about to cast his torch into the smaller vat of oil, which served as a signal fire, when a female voice rang out from the trees and froze him in place.

He thought for the briefest of moments of Amergin and his strange questions regarding a woman with the raiders; surely this couldn't be the same one? He'd only paused for the span of a heartbeat, but an arrow sailed past him, and he lit the oil. More of the soldiers were arriving upstairs now, and they dipped their arrowheads into the flaming vat before firing.

More of the nomads rushed to replace fallen kinsmen on the ram, and others held their shields over their comrades. If the ram reached the doors, they would eventually fall. He knew it.

"Ambrus!" A messenger dispatched from the far side of the bridge stood tensely at the top of the stairs. "They said your captain was slain. What news, Ambrus?"

143

"We're under attack," was the simple reply.

"How many?"

"I can't tell in the dark. A few hundred at least. We will hold the gatehouse as long as we can, but tell the garrison to prepare."

The soldier nodded crisply and dashed off again. Ambrus turned back to survey his situation, mouth set in a grim line. Below, the steady thud of the ram sounded and rattled up through the stones. The door itself would likely shatter before the braces failed, but how long would that take?

"Caleb! How many men are downstairs holding the door?"

"Two dozen, perhaps." The young soldier paused in his firing just long enough to call over his shoulder.

Ambrus nodded, thinking. There were perhaps another dozen or so up here on the watch deck.

"Caleb, tell them to fall back onto the bridge. Beware of archers. Once the door fails, they must retreat to the armory. We'll stop the invaders there. You will go with them."

"What about you?"

"I will protect your retreat. Fear not," he clapped a hand on the younger man's shoulder, having noticed his flash of panic, "I have no plans to die here."

Uncertain, Caleb nevertheless accepted his tasking and dashed down the stairs to prepare the men. The sides of the bridge were mostly open to admit fresh air. They would have to be quick when it was time to run.

Briga watched the attack with growing impatience. The defenders were firing less frequently, but with much more precision now as the ram battered away. No doubt they were trying to conserve their arrows. The door was beginning to splinter, but not quickly enough.

"The door is braced," she commented to Batu, who nodded agreement. "If we could draw the defenders away, I could fit through the window and dislodge the brace."

Batu examined the window critically. It was narrow, designed for archers and observation. Too narrow for a man to climb through, but Briga in her leather armor was likely thin enough.

"No, Batu Khan," Gansükh interjected, correctly reading the khan's intentions. "It is too…dangerous."

Briga looked at her guardian sharply, but he refused to meet her gaze. He did not trust her after the other night. Her safety was not the cause of his objection.

"Batu," she tried again, softening her voice and laying a hand on his arm. "The Magyuns must know they cannot hold. Look at how their archers have slowed their fire. The longer it takes to break the door, the more time they have to plan and prepare a defense."

There was a sudden, loud crack as the ram splintered part of the door.

"It looks like we will be through the doors soon, anyway."

Grinning in anticipation, Batu strode boldly from the trees. Briga and Sartaq flanked him, though their attention was on the door as it cracked and splintered around the ram's point of impact. They would have a man-sized hole in a matter of minutes, and Briga was anxious to attack. Men hacked and pulled at the splinters between blows of the ram, finally exposing a small hole. One more swing widened the hole to the size of a man's head, and a multitude of hands tore at the opening, tearing it wider.

The first man drew his blade and shoved his way through the opening. A defender killed him neatly with an arrow through the hole. More hands pulled his body away as they continued to rip at the door. A second man managed to get his shield though the hole and squeezed through after it. Two others followed quickly, using the first man and his shield to protect their entry. Within seconds they could hear the clash of steel as the first of the Drev'an met the blades of their foe.

Impatient, Briga felt she could wait no longer and broke into a trot, weaving and shouldering her way to the splintered door.

"Breeg!" Batu called out and snatched for her arm, but she was too quick.

She didn't look back. All her attention was on the door. Another three men had been killed or wounded trying to enter, but four more had made it through. She drew one of her daggers. Without hesitation, she forced herself up to the door and scrambled through, long knife up and ready to fight. She caught a glimpse of the Magyuns running back across the bridge, a small contingent remaining behind to hold the invaders at bay. She barely noticed the arrows or the swinging blades as she danced to the wooden supports that braced the door. Placing her shoulder beneath the brace, she shoved with all her might, trying to force the beam away from the door. It wouldn't budge. Briga looked down and realized it was set against a small stone lip to prevent slipping.

Someone grabbed her arm, but she twisted away. A large body crashed into the side of the support, sliding it a few inches across the ground. Struck by inspiration, she kicked with all her might. On the third kick, the brace fell away suddenly, and she stumbled forward. Catching herself gracelessly, she set her sights on the second beam. Dislodging that would free one of the doors. As she delivered her first kick, a sword flashed out at her, and she twisted sideways to avoid it. She met the second swing with both of her daggers and stumbled to get both feet back under her. The man shoved, and she twisted under his sword arm, her dagger scraping his armor in the process. He staggered forward from his own momentum, and she plunged the second dagger into his side, hoping for a gap in his armor. The man fell forward, and she delivered another solid blow to the door brace. The man spun to his knees, arcing his sword toward her as her

146

third kick dislodged the brace, and a flood of Drev'an bodies poured through the suddenly open door.

Briga was knocked forward by the living wave and slammed against the stone wall. Another body pinned her in place, crushing against her in the chaos of noise and men. Two hands braced themselves against the wall, bracketing her, and she turned to see a familiar form attempting to protect her from the crush of men. Sartaq stood over her. The shaved sides of his head reflected the torchlight, and blood flecked his face. He had lost or discarded his helmet somewhere. She froze momentarily at the savage look on his face, struck by an undefined memory. Batu stood at his shoulder, urging his warriors on. A second later Gansükh shoved through the crowd, with Bayanaa on his heels. He pulled Sartaq away to give Briga space, now that the rush was more controlled.

A storm of arrows slammed into the attacking Drev'an, felling one in five men with the first volley. And the second. The bridge was a killing field. Sartaq saw this and ordered archers to fan out along the near back to suppress the enemy archers.

The last line of Magyun archers was slowly retreating from their overrun gatehouse, providing as much cover for their fleeing comrades as they could. One of them called out, and Briga thought she heard an answering shout from above. Her eyes drifted to the ceiling, and she caught the sheen of dripping liquid through a square hole. An enemy soldier flew down the stairs and tossed a burning torch into the room as he sprinted through the melee onto the bridge. Briga reacted before her mind could actively process what was happening. She shoved Batu and grabbed Sartaq by the arm, herding them toward the stairs.

"Oil!" she warned as the torch landed and lit a pool of oil that had been poured through the murder-hole in the ceiling.

The flames spread in an instant, igniting oil that had pooled on the floor and soaked into the nomads' clothes. Briga led her small band up the stairs as warriors fled the pyre, some alight and screaming. Fire engulfed the room in a matter of moments, cutting off the Drev'an who had moved onto the bridge from the reserves outside. Isolated, Magyun arrows slammed into the group relentlessly.

Briga and Batu peered down the stairs into the inferno as Gansükh and Sartaq leaned over the rampart to call commands. Bayanaa and two other warriors who had escaped up the stairs were gathering arrows that were still in good condition.

"We can't wait for this to burn out."

Everyone agreed quietly. Already Sartaq was ordering men forward with buckets of dirt to create a path through the burning oil. They passed the buckets hand-to-hand, heedless of stray arrows from the far shore in their effort to smother the flames.

The warriors on the bridge were suffering mightily, but they weren't yet defeated. A few brave souls were advancing behind their shields, determined to catch the retreating fighters ahead of them. It was only a matter of minutes before the oil had been smothered enough to permit additional warriors through, though it felt like hours. At last enough men had gotten through to reinforce their brothers on the bridge, and they pushed forward en masse. Sartaq clapped his brother on the shoulder, then dashed down the stairs to lead the assault.

"How long before they send reinforcements?" Briga asked.

The battle might have lasted minutes, or hours—she could no longer tell. In response, Batu turned to look at the distant city wall, hidden in the darkness.

"No fires yet," he said almost to himself.

"Batu." She touched his arm to gain his attention.

In the tower at the other end of the bridge, a defender was pointing at them and yelling something. Not taking any chances, Batu expertly nocked an arrow, drew, and fired. The stricken enemy fell backward, out of sight.

148

"Batu Khan, we can cross the roofing."

All eyes turned to Bayanaa, who had managed to climb over the rampart and down onto the timber-and-thatch roof of the bridge itself.

"We will be too exposed," one of the warriors protested.

"Not if we move carefully and stay low," he countered and tested the beams beneath him for strength. "It seems sturdy enough."

Below, a handful of warriors had grown impatient for their turn to get onto the bridge and had attempted to swim. They were swept away by the current as soon as they left the shore. Nodding his agreement, Batu himself climbed over the ramparts and down to join Bayanaa on the roofing. Briga hesitated for only a moment; Gansükh was at her heels as always. The thatch was spongy in places, particularly in the open spaces between support beams. They would have to go carefully, indeed. But Bayanaa was right, it seemed strong enough to hold them.

The group crawled on all fours, mindful of their footing, and listening to the battle below. The lead forces had caught up with some of the trailing defenders, and the fighting in such close quarters was fierce. Drev'an knocked wounded enemies from the bridge if they were near enough to the edge. Those in the center were simply trampled.

Halfway across, the roof supports became much less stable. They bowed and flexed beneath the unfamiliar weight of the raiders, but held, though their group was forced to slow considerably. The roar of the fighting below them was deafening. Batu glanced up to scout for any sign that reinforcements might be coming from the city. As he turned to survey the group behind him, an arrow pinged off the back of his helmet. The glance backward had saved him. Simultaneously, another arrow buried itself inches from Briga's hand, and she flinched sideways reflexively. Gansükh and Bayanaa were already rising to their knees, bows drawn to return fire, and they loosed into the night as two more arrows whistled harmlessly by. Briga dropped to her stomach and scuttled forward as quickly as she dared. They were being silhouetted by the signal fire behind them, she realized with a cold chill.

"Batu! Get down!" she called urgently, even as she registered an odd swaying beneath her.

Glancing backward, she realized with horror what had tipped the defenders off. Dozens of Drev'an warriors had spotted their khan in his unusual tactic and were following. The timber was struggling to support their combined weight. Trapped between the advancing warriors and the archers, she lurched forward. A rotted support gave way beneath her hand suddenly, and she crashed headlong through the thatching. A hand at her sword belt arrested her fall. It took her a moment to realize what had happened, and she flashed a grateful smile at Gansükh. And then she was weightless again, falling through empty air beside her guardian as the support gave way beneath them both.

Briga didn't have enough time even to scream before crashing onto the swarming mass of warriors below her. A shoulder caught her in the side, driving the air from her lungs, and several men stumbled beneath her. And then she was flat on her back, gasping as she stared up through the forest of bodies. Warriors pressed forward, stumbling over her, stepping on her, kicking her. She couldn't breathe. Like a vision, the slender form of Bayanaa slipped through the crowd and crouched above her, pulling her to her feet. Dazed, she stumbled upward and shook her head to clear it. Batu and Gansükh were lost from her sight. Pressed forward by the wave of attackers, she could do nothing to help them, though she scanned the crowd around her continuously. Bits of straw drifted down from above, knocked loose by the scrambling warriors. Perhaps Batu and the others were still up there.

Blinking rapidly, she realized she had fallen among the front ranks of the Drev'an. The mass was semi-controlled by a commanding voice just a few ranks ahead.

"Sartaq," she breathed, and Bayanaa nodded tensely beside her. "Come on."

Bayanaa led the way, and they shouldered through the crowd to stand beside him.

Chapter 14

Ambrus had run like never before to get behind his retreating archers. He had successfully lit the oil trap, which would certainly enrage the attackers further. It wasn't likely to kill enough of them to make a difference, though it did provide the needed distraction for his men to cross the bridge to the relative safety of the barracks. With luck, one of the horselord commanders would be caught on the bridge to be dispatched by the archers.

Caleb was at the far gatehouse, watching for Ambrus. His relief was palpable as the older soldier sprinted inside, then immediately turned around to check on the retreating archers. Only a handful remained, and they were on the verge of being overrun.

"Ambrus!" a voice called from upstairs.

Ambrus answered the call and trotted up the stone stairwell. At the top, he could see Captain Tamas pointing out across the bridge, directing his archers. A black-fletched arrow struck him high in the chest, above the edge of his armor, and the man fell backward. Ambrus lunged forward to catch him, preventing a tumble down the stairs.

Tamas swore and grabbed at the arrow shaft, but Ambrus stopped him.

"No, don't remove it, you'll bleed too much."

The captain growled but left the arrow alone. Ambrus righted him slowly, carefully.

"They're crossing the top of the bridge."

Ambrus swore. "They're nearly to the gatehouse here. We have to stop them."

The captain gurgled, worrying Ambrus with the sound, then croaked out the name of his lieutenant. It was decided, then. The lieutenant would defend the top of the bridge, while the captain, aided by Ambrus, would see to the main defenses.

"Ambrus!" It was Caleb this time, a panicky note to his voice.

The captain clutched at the bloody shaft of the arrow and accepted Ambrus' assistance down the rest of the stairs. Neither man needed Caleb to explain; they could see clearly enough. A wall of Drev'an filled the bridge from edge to edge, and for the entire length of it. The front ranks were advancing slowly, menacingly. They were perhaps only twenty-five meters from the defenders now.

"Crossbows!" the captain called out.

Swiftly, crossbowmen advanced and formed a double line at the mouth of the gatehouse. A large man at the center of the foreign mass raised his sword. Ambrus felt his heart skip, spotting a feral-looking woman standing at his side. She wasn't one of them, he could tell even in the misty dark. Her skin was fair. Her hair—by the gods, she looked like she was wreathed in fire. The torchlight limned red-blonde hair and set it ablaze beside the dark, helmeted mass around her. The man with the sword wore no helmet, but his hair was a black strip down the middle of his head. In another heartbeat, his sword arm swung forward, and he called the charge. The woman and the men around her surged forward, weapons brandished, while a line of archers loosed into the Magyun crossbowmen.

Ambrus drew his sword impossibly slow as the crossbowmen returned fire. Short, stout quarrels tore through the invaders, wreaking havoc at such short range. At least half the enemy line went down with the first salvo. Even shields were no protection at this range. Bringing his sword ponderously up to a ready position, he watched the woman drive on. She took an arrow through her left shoulder and staggered with the force of the impact. She looked at her injury for a moment, then her face twisted into a mask of fury, and she plunged forward. She threw herself onto a crossbowman, driving a dagger into his belly. When it would not dislodge easily, she left it, slicing at a second man as she reached for the ax at her belt. Another arrow grazed her leg, but she barely seemed to notice. Ambrus watched as she cut through another crossbowman, and then her terrible eyes locked on his.

***

Forward, forward. It was the only thought in her mind. Once Sartaq had called the charge, she had slipped into a feeling not unlike the one she sometimes had when communing with the gods. Her limbs moved of their own accord, set on the task before her. Her shoulder and her leg throbbed, but it was only an inconvenience.

*The golden-haired Magyun…the one who'd set fire to the gatehouse…*she was certain it was him. Drawn like a moth to flame, she raised her ax and lunged at him. He met her swing with his sword, and a slash with her remaining dagger sent him dancing backward. She pressed forward, slashing and swinging to keep him off balance. Another fighter came to his aid, and she cut him down with only two swings. The blond man cried out in rage and surged forward, taking full advantage of her wounded leg and shoulder. She stumbled on her bad leg, forcing her to block a swing of his sword with her left hand and dagger. The wounded shoulder was too weak, and his sword bit into her side, just below the arm. She cried out, pain and rage flooding her senses, filling her.

***

Ambrus could only spare a quick glance for Caleb, who lay curled on his side from the woman's strike. Any thoughts of mercy fled him, and he jabbed to force her to retreat. When she stumbled on her injured leg, he swung for her injured shoulder.

His blade met only light resistance, and he was rewarded with a satisfying bite into flesh at her side. He raised his blade again for a killing blow, but she kicked his leg out from under him. Another pair of fighters crashed into them both, sending them to the ground. She recovered first and leapt on top of him, holding her dagger to his throat. She raised her ax, and there was a sudden *whoosh* from above. They both gasped as all the air vanished for a moment, and cast their vision upward. Flames engulfed the thatching all at once, and screams filled the air as the invaders atop the bridge tried to escape.

"Batu," she breathed, then shifted her gaze aggressively down to Ambrus.

Thinking quickly, he grabbed the arrow shaft protruding from her shoulder and pulled her forward, off balance. He slammed the hilt of his sword into her head and sent her crashing limply sideways. Her unconsciousness afforded him a few precious seconds to survey the battle around him. Blades clashed and blood sprayed in the stifling air, obscured now by smoke as well as mist. Burning thatch rained down on the invaders, forcing some to retreat.

Withering volleys from a reforming line of crossbowmen were taking a heavy toll on those who remained. Glancing down again, Ambrus decided to capture this woman rather than kill her. He wanted answers. He bent to grab the back of her collar with his free hand, but a flash of metal glinted beside him, and he whirled to block by instinct. He was met by a huge horselord wielding a curved blade two-handed and with murder in his eyes. With a fury he drove Ambrus back from the prone woman, and another warrior dashed in to collect her.

"She comes with me!" Ambrus demanded, renewing his attack.

He called for the soldiers around him to form ranks. This battle needed to end, quickly. The woman swayed to her feet with help from the second warrior, still clutching her ax in one hand. The second warrior was pulling her back, but she refused to go. Her eyes locked once more on Ambrus, and the hate he saw there chilled him to the marrow. She slashed clumsily at him as the big warrior attacked again and grinned as her blade grazed Ambrus' leg. But her strength had fled, and she collapsed into the second warrior once more, who scooped her up in his arms and retreated with her down the bridge, covered by the large fighter.

"Archers!" Ambrus called, turning. "Those three. Alive!"

The archers who heard him turned and targeted the trio. Even the big one had turned to run now. The smaller man took an arrow to the leg and fell against the side of the bridge, spilling his charge onto the waist-high stone wall. She slid, grabbing for the edge, but lacked the strength to hold on. In the span of a breath she rolled over the edge and disappeared into the cold, dark water. With a cry of rage, the large warrior sheathed his blade and dove after her. Ambrus stared, dumbfounded at this turn of events.

Around him the defenders were regaining control of the bridge. Crossbowmen were driving back the last of the invaders who were now taking heavy tolls. The bridge was left carpeted with the dead and injured.

The dead. Ambrus remembered suddenly and spun on his heel to search for young Caleb. The young man was exactly as he'd left him, curled on his side. Still. Ambrus knelt beside him and hesitantly laid a hand on the boy's shoulder. He was still warm…and trembling. Gingerly he turned Caleb over to inspect his wounds. An ugly crease marred the armor on his stomach, but the real damage came from a cut to the shoulder, which bled freely. Moving quickly, Ambrus unbuckled his friend's armor and pulled off his shirt. The armor was tossed aside, but the shirt served as a temporary bandage to slow the bleeding.

"Caleb, can you hear me?"

The young man was shaking and kept his eyes squeezed shut but managed a tiny nod.

"You need a healer. I'll take you to my friend Amergin, but you need to stay awake, all right? Hold this. Don't let go."

He snatched the youth's sword from where it had fallen and pressed it into his hand.

The boy managed a nod again, then curled back around himself.

"It'll be all right," Ambrus reassured him, patting his good shoulder gently.

Glancing up, he spotted two other young soldiers milling about uncertainly and gestured them over.

"There is an old barn near the south gate. Do you know it?"

"Where the foreigners are staying," one guessed.

Ambrus nodded. "Take him there. They have a healer. Go carefully."

The barracks had its own surgeons, but they would be busy for some time, by the looks of things. Better this man be seen by someone he trusted. As the two gently shepherded Caleb away, Ambrus turned to survey the area again.

"Captain Tamas!" he called out amid the rapidly dwindling sounds of battle.

The barracks were now a hive of activity. Archers continued firing to drive back the last of the invaders. Others were shoring up defensive positions. More were collecting the injured and dead to move them out of the main corridor.

"Captain Tamas!" he repeated, finally sheathing his sword.

There was a groan from somewhere behind him. Ambrus turned and spotted the captain slumped against the wall. He was pale and clutched at the base of the arrow still embedded in his flesh. The bleeding had slowed, but he was barely conscious.

157

"I need a healer!" he called out and crouched at the captain's side.

"Mess...senger..." he managed to croak out, eyes shut against the pain.

"Messenger!" Ambrus called out impatiently.

After a few maddeningly long moments, a young, blood-streaked soldier answered the summons.

"Go to th...the king..." Tamas breathed, with effort. "Tell him...tell..."

"Tell him the Drev'an have attacked," Ambrus finished grimly.

***

Cathbad jolted awake in a cold sweat. His gaze flickered around the room, trying to determine what had awoken him. The fire glowed in the center of the space, banked low for the night, and benign. Behind him, Eamon breathed steadily. A quick headcount revealed all present. The night around them was silent. Heavy, almost. All seemed to be right, but there was a subtle, insistent *tugging* deep in his bones.

Moving as quietly as he could, he got up and wrapped a cloak around his shoulders before shuffling over to the fire. Retrieving a precious few stems of sweet herbs, he scattered them into the fire, wafting the sweet smoke into his face. He needed to meditate, and the herbs helped him sink into that realm of altered vision. With a groan he seated himself and closed his eyes. But he didn't reach into the Pattern as the sweet scent of the herbs floated around him. Instead, he cast his senses out, searching for anything amiss, anything that might have pulled him from sleep.

Amergin was awake as well. He watched Cathbad silently at the fire, but didn't join him. It was the silence, he realized, that bothered him. The silence was too deep, as if the world held its breath. Troubled, he quietly strode to the door and peered out into the misty night. The thin fog produced a strange, muffling effect, but through it he began to hear sounds. They were subtle at first, far-away creaks and clanks masked by the darkness. He recognized them, however, as the sounds of soldiers moving about. Amergin frowned. He'd never noticed such activity at night before. There was sometimes light activity he assumed to be some kind of shift change, but this was bigger. He could almost make out voices, and then he heard the squeal of hinges protesting as the southern gate swung closed, and more soldiers hurried past.

Amergin didn't bother going out to investigate. There was only one explanation. Grimly, he stepped back inside and closed the door. He would have to wake the others soon, but first he wanted a moment with the chief druid. Cathbad was still cross-legged before the fire, and his eyes tracked the younger druid as he approached.

"The city is preparing for siege," he announced quietly. "The gates are shut."

Cathbad only nodded, his eyes red-rimmed from smoke. If only they had been given one more day, they could have gotten Eamon up and been on their way.

"I saw Briga," the chief druid rasped.

Amergin felt his blood go still.

"Is she near?"

Another nod. "Or she was. Her thread blazed so bright, Amergin. So bright, but it faded."

"What do you mean?"

Cathbad only shook his head, uncertain and concerned. "I cannot see it anymore."

Amergin's blood chilled at that. Pointedly he reminded himself that it meant nothing. She'd been hidden from them all this time; surely this was more of the same.

"I have never seen an individual burn like that."

The younger druid shifted uncomfortably. "I will wake the warriors. We must prepare.'

"Has the city been attacked?"

Amergin shook his head. "I'm not quite certain. If not, then an attack must be imminent."

Cathbad nodded again but returned his gaze to the fire distractedly. In another moment the uneasy peace was disturbed by frantic knocking at the door. The two exchanged a glance, wondering if it had already begun.

Chapter 15

It was dark as night in the dungeons. There were no windows, no torches, save one carried by the occasional patrolling guard. But not tonight. Tonight there were guards. Tonight there were torches. Several torches, illuminating the paths of several guards. And…soldiers?

Interesting…

He did not receive visitors. Even the guards barely spoke to him, except to slide food under the slot in the door. Or to question him. It had been a long while since anyone had bothered to question him. Sometimes he wondered if anyone besides the cook and the guard who fed him remembered he was even here. He hated the silence the most. Endless hours of dark monotony that stretched on until he no longer counted the days.

But not today. Today there was…activity. Something was happening outside this prison, something important. The guards and soldiers didn't speak of it, but their very presence was evidence enough. That, and the way they moved. There was a certain anxiety to it.

How long had it been? Years? Decades? …or only months? He was no longer certain. Time ceased to have any meaning. But in all that time, he had never seen activity like this. Yes, something important was happening. Maybe the king had died. Or maybe the city was under attack? He smiled at the possibilities. Asking would do no good. In fact, it might remind them to keep away. He would be patient. He would wait and watch and listen. And he would pray to his gods in the meantime. Cruel they may be, but faith was eventually rewarded.

A spark of light gleamed in the crack below the door. He drank it in greedily, absorbing what meager details he could. He could see two pairs of boots illuminated in the sliver of light as they tramped by.

At the far end of the hall, someone was talking. The words echoed and crashed into themselves in the stone corridor enough that he couldn't make them out. Something about raiders. Something about a gate. The king's name. And then they were gone, the light fading as they continued down the hall, leaving him in darkness.

Chapter 16

The gray light of dawn broke weak and watery over the Drev'an camp. The night's fog had persisted and cast a pallor over the warriors who had retreated to lick their wounds. Batu sat scowling in the direction of the bridge as a healer tended to minor scrapes and burns on his hands. Within his line of sight, soldiers were retrieving one rock apiece from the pile they'd made before the battle. Batu's eyes flicked to it, silently noting the slow rate at which it diminished. That was how they measured their losses. The rocks remaining represented the warriors who had not returned. The pile was still much larger than it should be. It was the mist. The accursed mist. He'd thought it was a gift from the gods, a blessing. Had she tried to warn him? He couldn't remember. He wasn't sure how long he stared at the rocks, but eventually Sartaq wandered into his line of sight. Reluctantly, his attention cut to his brother.

Sartaq crunched into the space his brother had claimed, eyes raking over the minor wounds he sported.

"Two of my generals and their men hold the near end of the bridge."

It wasn't enough, but at least it was a foothold. The night's battle would not be a total loss, then. But the khan said nothing. Nor did his gaze stray from some distant point now that his attention had settled on it again. Two hundred men. Batu was certain that many at least had fallen. Likely more. He didn't flinch at the sounds of the injured as they were treated nearby. He barely heard them.

"Batu," Sartaq ventured, seeking the khan's attention.

Two more men passed through the area, a dead nomad slung between them. Batu's eyes tracked them distantly. Sartaq too turned to watch their progress. Then he stepped closer to the khan and crouched.

"Brother," he tried again, more gently.

There was a hardness in Batu's eyes as they rested once more on his brother. He waited for the healer to finish dabbing the burns on his arm with some salve, and then shook her off. A dismissal.

"Tengri was not with us."

Sartaq remained quiet, waiting.

"It is only a test of our will. Nothing more. Make your preparations." The khan paused and cast a meaningful gaze on his brother. "They *do not* retake the bridge."

Sartaq grinned thinly, but nodded and stood to prepare the siege engines. As he turned to walk away, Batu halted him with a question.

"Where is she?"

The grin faded from the commander's face as he leveled a stony gaze at Batu. His eyes flickered to the lines of casualties awaiting treatment and back again. He shook his head. They both knew the she-wolf was not among the wounded. Not yet, anyway, though more were trickling in. Batu clenched his teeth, jaw muscles tightening. He said nothing. The words were plain enough without speech.

***

Cold. That was his first thought. He was cold. Freezing, actually. There was something wet and slimy under his cheek. Shivering, Gansükh opened his eyes. He was on the riverbank, calves still submerged in the cold water. How had he gotten here? He squeezed his eyes shut trying to remember. The battle on the bridge… He sat up quickly, remembering with sudden clarity where he was. Bayanaa had taken an arrow and stumbled. Then time seemed to slow as the she-wolf fell so slowly over the edge. He had jumped into the icy water after her without pausing to think. The weight of his armor had pulled at him, and it was a fight to keep his head above the rushing water. Better than the Magyuns, though. Their heavy metal armor had dragged them straight to the bottom. He'd spotted Briga being swept downstream and—

"Breeg!" he breathed, looking around frantically.

He did not see her. Numb fingers pulled him free of the water, and he hauled himself onto numb feet, immediately falling again onto hands and knees.

"Breeg!" he tried again hoarsely.

He dared not call for her too loudly, even if his raw throat would have complied. He had no idea where he was, if an enemy might be near enough to hear him. Only the sounds of rushing water and his own harsh breathing greeted him.

"Gods," he cursed, curling one hand into a fist.

As if in answer, a small sound floated to him over the rush of the water. His head snapped up, searching. There, a tuft of wet fur shifted in the light breeze. It was her wolf pelt. She had partially washed up on the bank just a little upstream from him. Her perch on the bank was precarious. Ignoring the cold and his numb legs, he scrambled to his feet and lurched toward her unsteadily. She lay face-up on the bank, her waist and legs still drifting in the current. The ax was still in her hand, but her breathing was ragged, and gods, she was so pale. Blood seeped from her side, her temple, her shoulder. He grabbed the collar of her leather jerkin and hauled her up the bank, away from the water.

"Breeg, open your eyes."

Her lips were tinged with blue. She wasn't shivering. She was too cold for shivering. It would kill her if he did nothing.

165

How long had they been in the water? He pulled her into his lap and rubbed her arms, offering what little warmth he could. It was still dark out, and he knew it wouldn't be enough. He would have to risk a fire. He pulled her closer into his chest, one hand rubbing her arm and back, while the other cast about for any dry wood within reach. Carefully he laid her down and scooped dry leaves and twigs into a pile, then pushed numbly to his feet to gather larger sticks. He only needed enough to get the fire started for now. Thankfully the little bag of his prized possessions was still secured at his hip, and he withdrew a flint and striker. It took a few attempts before the kindling caught, but he carefully coaxed the flame to life. Within a few minutes, the fire was hot and burning stably.

Gansükh pried the ax from her hand and tucked it into his belt for safekeeping, then pulled her closer to the fire and into his lap once more. Uncertainly he removed her sodden cloak and rubbed at her arms and back again to help warm her. Her wounds would need tending soon, but before anything else, they both needed the fire's warmth. Cradling her to his chest, he rested his chin on top of her head and closed his eyes. Just for a moment.

He awoke sometime later to her shivering. The fire was nearly out. Her shaking was a good sign, though, it meant she was thawing out from her time in the river. Neither of them were out of danger from the cold yet, however.

"Joren…"

He looked down at her, but her eyes remained closed. Gansükh tossed a handful of nearby twigs onto the fire, then gently laid her down so he could gather more substantial pieces of wood. More this time.

He glanced up as he walked. The sky was slowly beginning to lighten. Dawn would find them in an hour or two, and then he could figure out how far downriver they had been swept. The wood this close to the river was damp, and he was forced to wander farther into the woods. His thoughts turned to Bayanaa and his arrow wound. Had he gotten off the bridge? Gods, had he fallen into the river, too? Gansükh pushed back a pang of fear as he stooped to gather dry timber. Those thoughts would have to wait. They would do no good right now. When he'd gathered all he could carry, he returned to the dying fire. The sight greeting him froze him in place.

***

By morning, the barn showed every indication of having been converted into an infirmary. The two soldiers who had barged in last night with the young dying man slung between them had evidently been satisfied by the way Amergin and Cathbad had responded to the situation, as they returned with more wounded. Nearly two dozen men lay in rows along the barn floor. Eamon's warriors had spent the better part of the night fetching supplies and fresh straw. Their warriors' eyes appraised each injury, and Amergin was careful to mark their expressions. He had learned to read much in those fleeting gazes. They could spot a fatal wound at a glance. The types of wounds would also reveal some information about the battle in a language common only to soldiers. He would speak with them later.

Amergin checked the color and temperature of yet another casualty before standing and wiping his hands on his breeches. In a small pen, the goat bleated. She hadn't yet been milked. It had already been a long morning, and the sun had barely risen. He looked to Cathbad. The old druid was crouched over a grievously injured soldier. His hand rested on the soldier's brow, and Amergin knew he was helping the soul escape its shell. Amergin bowed his head and mouthed a quick blessing. The men had been in various states of injury when they arrived. Those who could walk were sent away after they'd been treated. While happy to help, neither druid wished to lodge additional mouths in their barn beyond those in dire need. The space was already crowded and was the one place Eamon's surviving clansmen had felt was theirs. Hospitality was important to the Velkcic, but so was having a space to claim as their own.

A few hours after first light, Ambrus finally appeared at the barn. There was a hollowness to him, as if some task was the only thing that kept him moving. Amergin took one look at him and was instantly at the soldier's side. He led the Magyun to an empty seat near the stalls and handed him a cup of warm, thin broth. The soldier's eyes traveled the room, taking in the men.

"Drink," Amergin urged gently.

Ambrus obeyed mechanically, draining half the bowl in one draught.

"I'm sorry Amergin, I didn't know they would send so many."

The druid nodded and took his bowl to refill it. He badly wanted to ask exactly what happened but could tell by the set of Ambrus' shoulders that now wasn't the right moment. Ambrus sipped once at the fresh broth and stared into his bowl. Amergin waited quietly, sensing that his friend wanted to speak, but on his own terms. After a few prolonged moments of comfortable silence, Amergin stood to check on the wounded and give Ambrus some time to reflect.

"Wait," Ambrus rasped and caught his friend by the arm.

"Where is…" His eyes swept the room again, searching.

Amergin sank back onto his seat. He realized suddenly that Ambrus had only sent one man here to him. It was that first boy. It had to be. Amergin's silence reflected fear on Ambrus' face, and the soldier shook his head slowly.

"No," Amergin began, "he is alive."

The tension drained out of Ambrus in a great wave, his shoulders slumping with relief.

"The bleeding has stopped. I don't know if it was enough, Ambrus."

The words were quiet, measured, but they caused Ambrus to look up sharply.

"The wound was very deep," Amergin went on gently. "He may still bleed inside. I cleaned the wound myself but…time will tell."

Ambrus looked at him for a moment, then nodded as if he'd expected this answer. Accepting the news, he sipped at the broth absently. He was exhausted, but Amergin could tell he wasn't yet ready to rest. He could almost see the thoughts churning in the soldier's mind.

"You should have that looked at," Amergin prompted, eyeing the cut and dried blood on his leg.

Ambrus looked down and touched the torn fabric. He had almost forgotten about the wound. She had caught him below the bottom edge of his chainmail skirt.

"It can wait. I'd like to see Caleb," he added hesitantly.

"He needs to rest," Amergin insisted gently.

"Then I won't wake him."

Amergin set his jaw, but the look in Ambrus' eyes silenced what he'd been about to say. There was a frightening hollowness that seethed, a deep wound there. One a druid couldn't heal. Finally, he sighed.

"Very well. But only for a few minutes."

Moving carefully among the rows of wounded men, Amergin led the warrior to a clean straw pallet near the back. One of the Velkcic warriors had loaned their cloak as a blanket for him. The boy was impossibly pale, and sweat beaded his brow. An ugly red gash peeked out from beneath the edge of a linen bandage, marring his shoulder where it joined his neck. His armor had been removed and neatly stacked by the wall. What remained of his shirt was soaked in dark blood. Looking at him, Ambrus' hands curled slowly into fists. Amergin clasped his shoulder, silently urging calm. When he felt the tension start to ebb, he stepped away to give the man a moment alone. Cathbad was watching him from across the room, and the younger druid picked his way to him, stopping here and there to check a bandage or a temperature.

"His brother?" Cathbad guessed.

"He didn't say."

They watched as Ambrus stiffly lowered himself to the ground to sit at Caleb's side. He held his soup bowl absently, watching the boy's face, speaking in tones too low to hear.

"Any more news?" the younger man asked.

"It was the horselords, that much we know. They control at least one end of the bridge."

Amergin nodded, absorbing this. "I don't think we will be leaving anytime soon."

Cathbad was silent.

"A siege," Amergin huffed, disbelieving. "Surely they can't wait out there all winter?"

"No." Cathbad eyed him gravely. "I fear they will not."

"We need to inventory our supplies," Amergin began, steeling himself to the task at hand, "and determine how long we can make them last."

"The city will have some provisions set aside, surely."

"The men may have to fight. The men may *want* to fight, actually."

"They are free men," Cathbad advised. "Fighting for the city does not mean they will abandon us. Or Eamon. We shall walk that path when we must. For now, we must prepare and tend to these wounded."

Across the room Ambrus had fallen silent, simply staring at the boy.

"I had better see to him," the younger druid commented, not liking the tone of that scene.

Cathbad nodded and handed over some fresh bandages and a poultice. Threading his way through the room once more, Amergin made an indirect path to the Magyun and his friend. Quietly he set down the supplies and left again to fetch a milking stool.

"Here," he commanded quietly, setting the stool behind Ambrus and pulling him up by one arm.

Ambrus complied, settling himself on the stool. The soup bowl still dangled from his hand, forgotten. Gently Amergin took it from him and set it aside. He settled into a crouch beside the warrior and began to examine and clean the cut on his leg.

"That bitch. I'll kill her."

Frowning, Amergin paused to look at his friend, but the warrior was focused on something far away indeed.

"She did this."

"A woman hurt your friend?"

"Him, me, all of them."

His frown deepening, Amergin moved to check the warrior's temperature. Ambrus merely scowled at him.

"I didn't know their women fought," Amergin commented, applying a poultice to the cut. At least it had been clean, no ragged edges to contend with.

"She wasn't Drev'an."

"No?"

"No."

Amergin took his time measuring out a strip of clean linen to bandage the Magyun's leg. "How can you be sure? She was fighting for them."

"Because she was pale skinned. Like us."

For a moment, the druid paused and allowed himself to wonder. *Can it be...? No, certainly not. She was a prisoner*, he reminded himself.

"I will kill her," Ambrus vowed with quiet certainty.

Chapter 17

Yellow eyes stared at him from across the weak fire. It was a wolf. It lay curled beside Briga, head resting protectively on her chest. It was the *same* wolf, he was almost certain. The same one that had saved him the other night. The same one she had summoned that day in the woods.

Gansükh froze in place, sensing the malice with which it regarded him. It watched him, alert. He stepped forward, and a low, rumbling growl issued from the beast's throat. Gansükh froze again. Surely the creature didn't intend to eat her? Not after what they had just survived? But it must have been drawn by the scent of blood. Moving slowly, he withdrew one stick from the bundle he had gathered and eased toward the fire. When the wolf didn't object, he carefully added the stick to the blaze. In a few moments he added a second branch segment. And a third. Wolves feared fire. This was clearly no ordinary beast, but perhaps... A stick popped in the fire, and the wolf tensed, baring its gleaming fangs at him.

"Are you hungry?" he asked calmly, remembering the first time he had seen the creature. Briga had wanted to feed it.

One shaggy ear twitched, but the tension did not fade. Slowly lowering himself to a crouch, Gansükh set the sticks down and watched as calmly as he could. Moving cautiously, he reached for the leather bag tied at his hip, hoping a bit of dried meat or fish remained there after his trip into the river.

The sound of another cracking stick issued through the space, but it didn't come from the fire. Gansükh and the wolf both swiveled their attention in the direction of the noise. Something was out there. The wolf half rose into a crouch, fangs exposed in a silent snarl. Gansükh grasped the hilt of his sword, loosening it in its water-tightened scabbard. Another snap, closer this time, followed by the creak of a bowstring. Gansükh drew his blade, the metal singing roughly. The wolf was gone. Vanished. He would worry about that later. There were two men out there. He could distinguish their footsteps. If the archer didn't kill him, he could handle two men. He rocked into a half-crouch, edging closer to Briga. They knew where he was, no point in moving away from the fire now.

"Show yourself," he growled in the Magyun tongue.

The men stopped for a moment, then one laughed and came forward.

"We could see your fire form the ridgeline," the stranger taunted. In Drev'an.

Surprised, Gansükh straightened and allowed the tip of his sword to fall.

"What are you doing out here?" the stranger went on. "Deserting?"

"You are one of Khuyag's men," Gansükh commented, calmly assessing the scout. "Come into the light. Do you recognize her?"

Gansükh gestured with his blade at the supine and shivering form of Batu's she-wolf. The warrior stared, his bowstring creaking again as it lost tension.

"I thought you might. How close is your camp? She needs a healer."

"Just over the ridge."

Gansükh nodded and sheathed his sword, then carefully gathered the woman up and lifted her in his arms.

"Lead us there. Batu Khan has attacked the bridge. I will tell you about it on the way."

"Exactly what part of my order was unclear, Captain?" Batu snapped irritably.

The warrior before him bristled and dared a glance at Commander Sartaq for support. Sartaq lounged in a makeshift seat, face impassive as he watched. Batu was furious, much more so than he allowed himself to show. Only Sartaq and perhaps a few of the khan's closest generals might know what truly transpired behind the carefully guarded mask he wore. It had to be because of the defeat. That, or this captain was foolish beyond measure. No one would have dared to challenge the khan in a public setting like this before, even indirectly.

"You said no prisoners, my lord," the captain repeated roughly.

"And now I am telling you to bring me the survivors."

The warrior opened his mouth to speak again, but Batu cut him off, "*Now*, Captain!"

The captain gritted his teeth but bowed stiffly and stalked off. Sartaq eyed his brother silently.

"Davaa," the khan barked, meeting his brother's gaze coldly.

A woman stepped forward, clearly uneasy. She was dark-haired, but her flesh was paler than the rest of the Drev'an. Her eyes were green, downcast before the khan, hands clasped protectively before her.

"Yes, my lord."

She wore the clothing of a Magyun peasant, but spoke near perfect Drev'an. Sartaq eyed her impassively, noting and disregarding the uncomfortable shifting of a few of his men. He knew what she was.

"How much grain do they have set aside for a siege?"

She thought for a moment, those green eyes flashing around the circle of men, strangely calm despite her nervous stance.

"They have not brought in this year's harvest yet. They have perhaps two months stored within the walls, maybe longer if they adjust the rations."

"Any other reserves?"

"Dried meat at each of the barracks. Not much. There will be stores below the castle as well, where it is cool. King Bela likely will not share that."

Batu nodded. "Water?"

"One well in the southern market. Two more nearer the castle. Most draw from the river."

"You said they have not brought in the harvest."

"No, my lord, not to the city."

"But they have gathered their fields?"

"Yes, lord. After the attack at Rowanar, they rushed to gather what they could. It was a bit early, but some of the landowners were concerned that the Rowanar taxes would not be received this year. Much of the remaining grain has been threshed but has not been transported."

"Now that we are at their doorstep, they will try to gather what they can, and quickly," Sartaq intoned, "if they hope to outlast us."

Batu nodded, agreeing.

"Where are the largest fields?"

"I am not certain, my lord."

"Very well. How—" he bit off the next words as the crunch of dead leaves sounded nearby.

The captain was returning. They could hear him leading a string of prisoners. A look of profound irritation flickered across the khan's face as they filtered into view. His stormy gaze settled on Davaa for an instant. She nodded subtly, setting her jaw, and allowed her own gaze to linger on the prisoners. Swiftly, Batu brought the back of his hand up and struck her across the face, knocking her to the ground and opening a cut on her lip. Leisurely Sartaq pushed away from his seat and withdrew a knife. The first of the prisoners lurched forward, having seen what was happening, but was quickly restrained by a guard.

"Please…" she begged in the Magyun tongue as Sartaq loomed over her.

Brandishing the knife, he grabbed her by one arm and yanked her to her feet, pulling her back against himself in a crushing hold. The knife came to her throat, a clear message to the captured soldiers. Their resistance would have consequences.

Batu nodded once to the captain, who forced the men to their knees before him. Some watched Batu with fear. Some watched Sartaq and the Magyun woman with rage. All of them listened.

"I do not take prisoners," Batu began in Magyun, pacing slowly. "Extra mouths to feed, extra men to guard…I do not need them. But I could perhaps use *this* one."

Those Drev'an who spoke Magyun laughed darkly as their khan indicated the woman. Grinning malevolently, Sartaq scented the side of her neck, savoring her discomfort. The thumb of his knife-hand wiped the blood from the corner of her mouth, and he tasted it. Locking his gaze onto one of the prisoners, he pressed his lips to her ear and whispered words no one else could hear. She squirmed away, her face an open display of fear and disgust.

"Stop this," one of the prisoners pleaded.

Batu stopped pacing and looked at the man who had spoken.

"Do you know who I am?"

The man did not tear his attention away from the woman. Sartaq met his gaze, grinning a challenge.

"I am your new khan. Your king."

"King Bela—" began another, but one of the captain's men cut the prisoner down before he could speak another word.

The staring man, the one who'd spoken up first, finally wrenched his gaze away from Davaa and stared dumbly at his slain comrade.

"King Bela is already defeated. He cannot withstand a siege. I am your liege now, and as such, your lives belong to me. To do with as I see fit."

Batu paced over to this brother and took the girl's chin in his hand, examining her as one might examine a new horse, though he addressed the kneeling men.

"My advisors think I should kill you. Are they right?"

"Go to hell, you coward."

A guard's sword sang as it cut through the air, but Batu stopped it with a look. He then turned the full weight of his gaze on the man who had spoken, a man in his early thirties, and clearly no stranger to combat.

"Coward?" Batu questioned. "Perhaps you need a lesson in fear yourself. Alas, I lack the time to teach you properly, and my men have taken a liking to this woman. We shall have to improvise, then."

He nodded to the man's guard, the one who had almost cut him down a moment ago. The guard hauled the prisoner up and walked him a few paces in front of the rest. Withdrawing a knife in place of his sword, he took hold of the man's hands and cut the rope binding his wrists. He then slashed deep and cleanly across one newly bare wrist and let the man go. Blood welled, and the man grasped his wound instinctively, gasping in shock.

"My horses might break a leg trampling you, and I lack the time to let you die of a belly wound," Batu explained apologetically. "I hope you understand."

Already the man was growing pale. Fear shone plainly in his eyes as the blood pulsed between his fingers.

"A pity," Batu went on. "I look at this man and I see a strong back, a strong sword arm, and battle experience. But now he is a useless corpse. Well, nearly useless."

Batu paused and smiled conspiratorially at his men. The man had torn a strip of fabric from his shirt and was feebly attempting to bind the wound.

"This is cowardice," Batu explained, his tone harsh as he gestured at the prisoner. "The fear of death."

One heavy boot planted itself on the man's back and kicked him forward. The dying man lay sprawled on the half-frozen ground, clutching his ruined wrist to his chest while his eyes began to flutter. Batu crouched near him and spoke softly.

"I will hack your corpse to pieces and fling them back into the city for your loved to find. Would you like that?"

The man stifled a choked sob. The blood was beginning to slow. Whatever the other prisoners might have been thinking, they wisely remained silent. Sartaq noted that fear had replaced anger on many of their faces. The girl had stopped struggling, so he adjusted his grip to provoke her, sliding a rough hand across her ribs.

Batu sighed and stood, abandoning the dying man.

"You." He indicated one of the younger, more frightened-looking prisoners.

Singled out, the boy paled considerably but said nothing.

"What is your name?"

"J-Jamin, sir."

"Lord," one of the Magyun-speaking guards corrected with a growl.

"Lord! J-Jamin, my lord," he stammered.

"Do you have a family, Jamin?"

The boy looked up sharply, frozen.

"A woman? Children?" Batu prompted gently.

"Yes…my lord."

"Would you like to see them again, Jamin?"

"Alive?"

Batu smiled and stifled a laugh. "Yes, alive."

"Yes, my lord, I would."

"What if I offered you that chance?"

Jamin blinked, uncertain. His gaze traveled to his comrades, to the dying man, and back to the raiding khan, weighing his options. "What would I have to do?"

"I told you I have no need for prisoners, and is true. While I do have a use for corpses, I would have killed you already if that was my desire." Batu kicked the wounded man's leg with disgust, then turned and looked at each prisoner in turn, evaluating.

"You have seen our savagery, but I am your khan, and you must see compassion as well. We are not the monsters your Bela paints us to be. But he has committed a grave transgression which could not be ignored. Your king has dragged everyone into his war. His…not yours. I warned him to surrender the city

180

or I would kill everyone within his walls." He paused and looked at Jamin kindly. "But you are not within the walls, are you?"

The prisoners dared to glance at each other, confused.

"The city will fall," he went on. "I control all avenues of trade. There will be no more food entering those gates. The longer this siege continues, the more my innocent new subjects will starve, suffer, and die. All for the arrogance of their defeated king. You are soldiers. You have known hunger, cold. Is that how you want your woman to die, Jamin? Or as an old woman, warm in her bed?"

Jamin shuddered, growing still paler.

"The city need not be taken in blood," Batu added gently, "so long as it can be taken quickly."

Defeated, Jamin hung his head and nodded.

"Jamin…" one of the others breathed.

"No, he's right," another admitted, sounding profoundly tired. "The sooner this is over, the cleaner it will be. Think of your wives. Do you want a bunch of Drev'an marauding through the streets, drunk on the wine of prolonged siege?"

One by one, their gazes dropped to the ground, and Batu smiled in triumph. More would follow, but he only needed one. He nodded to the guard to help the man stand.

"One word of warning, Jamin. There is no greater crime in my empire than disloyalty to your khan. If you attempt to deceive or betray me, the penalty is death. Obey this simple rule, and you will live a long and comfortable life."

Jamin remained tight-lipped but nodded understanding. In the end, three more pledged the khan their oath. The others were slain. The survivors stood huddled together, rubbing their wrists uncertainly.

"My khan?" Sartaq prompted, still holding the girl.

"Eh? Oh. Take her away." He waved them off dismissively.

"Lord Batu…" Jamin said hesitantly, staring at the girl again. "Please, don't…hurt her."

Batu mentally cursed his brother. He wasn't finished questioning her. If they hadn't been reminded of her presence, it might have been avoided. He should have sent them away earlier. This was an unnecessary inconvenience. But perhaps it was another opportunity to gain their cooperation.

"Commander," Batu said formally, not wishing to identify his brother, "she is to be…treated gently."

That was the best he could do. He followed the order with a meaningful glare. Sartaq affected an indignant glance at his brother, then at the foreigners, then sheathed his knife and led her away more respectfully.

"Now," Batu sighed, turning back to the group. "Your first task. Where do you gather your winter crops?"

Chapter 18

Dagmer crouched comfortably on her haunches, examining the short blade in her hand. She was dressed in one of Bayanaa's spare fighting tunics and her own leather leggings. It was more comfortable to wear than the cut and weight of a woman's tunic. She was bloodied, her hair unbound in a wind-blown curtain. Beside her, Bayanaa reclined against a tree, his leg wrapped tightly. She poked at a small fire to stoke its warmth.

"You were fighting?" he asked, eyeing her clothes and her general appearance.

She shook her head, absently fingering the blade in her hands.

"Give me some water."

There was already a cup sitting nearby. She nudged it into his hand, and he drank gratefully.

"Why are you dressed like that?" he asked after a moment.

"I was helping to retrieve the dead."

Bayanaa looked at her sharply but said nothing. The gravity seemed so unnatural on his features. For a moment she was back there. Back in the clearing before dawn when they had started to bring in the wounded. The dead were taken elsewhere. She'd stood uneasily, searching the faces for anyone familiar, listening for any information on how the fight was progressing.

By then they had taken the gatehouse and were beginning to advance across the bridge. Then, information turned into a disordered maelstrom of truth and fiction. The one truth she could discern was that the fight had turned bloody. She could hear the roar of it, accompanied by the eerie glow of distant fires. Large ones. She couldn't say when the battle had ended. She ceased to be aware of its noise as she and the others focused on treating the wounded, focusing on the cleaning, binding, stitching, but not cutting. Never the cutting. That was for other hands than hers.

Sometime near dawn she had spotted Bayanaa, pale and patiently waiting against a tree. His eyes were closed, and the broken haft of an arrow jutted awkwardly from his leg. Dagmer felt her blood chill but didn't go to him. Instead she found the closest surgeon and sent him to remove the arrow barb. She scanned the area quickly, searching for Gansükh or Briga. They would be nearby, waiting for Bayanaa, she was sure. But they weren't there. Nor were they among the wounded. A few of the men she questioned had seen them on the bridge, near the front, but none knew what had happened to them.

Killed or captured, she'd thought grimly.

By mid-morning she had been able to leave her duties as nurse, and she wandered among the wounded, searching for Briga or her protector. Bayanaa was still leaning against the tree, bandaged and asleep. No one had seen the she-wolf among the dead, nor Gansükh, either.

When one of the captains announced a small party would be permitted on the bridge to collect their dead, she had volunteered. She felt filthy and constricted in her tunic and had quickly rifled through Bayanaa's pack for a spare, hoping he wouldn't mind. Then she'd joined the others on the bridge.

It was difficult work, hauling the dead away. Occasionally they came across someone badly wounded and had to determine whether he could be healed or if he should be put out of his misery. Enemy soldiers had to be ignored, living or dead. Once she had tried to tend to one, and the defenders at the far gatehouse shouted something and aimed their weapons at her. She had backed off immediately with a placating gesture and resumed her work. She'd been mindful of those soldiers the whole time, in their wary hostility. Closer to their end, younger warriors were collecting their own dead and wounded. The two parties settled into a mutual awareness, each eyeing the other as wild dogs might over disputed territory, each hesitant to directly challenge the other.

They had just crossed the center point of the bridge when she found it. She recognized it at a glance. A long, bloodied knife lay abandoned in the carnage, glinting coldly in the overcast light of day. A fighting knife. *Briga's* fighting knife. Glancing about carefully, she'd hidden it within the loose tunic top. And though she had searched for the rest of the time they'd been allowed on the bridge, she couldn't find its mate, nor did she find Briga herself or Gansükh among the dead. They had vanished, or been taken prisoner, perhaps, though there had been no reports...

At length, her party had been called away. They needed to rest, and by unspoken custom, it was time to allow the Magyuns to collect their own dead. She trudged after the others, heedless of her surroundings until they reached the main body once again, and the ranks of wounded. Having no task to set her mind on, and wanting to rest, she had sought out Bayanaa, still resting against his tree, and settled down near him.

"Why did you do that?" he questioned, snapping her back to the present.

But she couldn't remember the question and glanced down at Briga's knife again. Bayanaa followed her gaze. She could feel him tense suddenly.

"She wasn't on the bridge," Dagmer volunteered. "Neither was he."

"He? Batu?"

She met his eyes sharply, easily reading his anxiety. "Batu Khan is fine. He suffered minor wounds only. I was talking about Gansükh."

185

"Gansükh…" His eyes clouded as if he was trying to remember.

"I haven't been able to find any sign of them. Except for this." She paused and looked at the knife again. "What—"

Bayanaa gasped suddenly and grabbed her knife hand by reflex. "Oh, gods, the river. I was shot, and she fell. *I dropped her into the river.*"

The look of anguish on his face was heartbreaking.

Bayanaa had refused to rest after that, despite Dagmer's repeated pleas as his nurse to stop and allow his leg to heal. His blood had soaked through two bandages as he limped around the camp uselessly. The khan had refused to see him. More accurately, the khan's brother had refused him an audience, stating that his lord brother was busy seeing to other matters, and he should try back in the evening. No amount of protest would change his mind, not even mentioning that he had a report on what had happened to the she-wolf. Sartaq had asked for the information himself, and Bayanaa had reluctantly given it. Sartaq had accepted the news grimly and assured him he would inform the khan. He'd then looked meaningfully at Bayanaa's leg and suggested he rest until Batu summoned him.

***

"What did she say?" General Khuyag and General Burd looked on carefully as one of the healers tended to her wounds.

Her arrival in camp had been eventful. The two scouts who escorted them had recognized her, but not the kheshig who had carried her from the river, mistaking him for a low-ranking soldier. When they'd attempted to bar his audience with General Khuyag, he'd threatened to kill them if anyone tried to touch her. Swords had been drawn and curses uttered until one of Khuyag's men, recognizing Gansükh, stepped in to order the fighters away. Khuyag was sent for at once, as well as the healer. He easily read the exhaustion in Gansükh's face, but the warrior would never admit to it. Khuyag, at once noting the depth and location of her wounds, had ordered cloth walls erected to protect her from onlookers.

She was pale, far too pale for even her kind, and the slash at her side was oozing dark blood slowly. Two guards had spread a clean cloak or a skin on the ground, and Gansükh finally set her down. At once Khuyag had ordered broth and ayrak brought for him to restore his strength.

The healer arrived as the last cloth wall was strung and set to work immediately. At Gansükh's insistence, they didn't cut away her clothes or leathers, but carefully peeled them off and set them aside.

She had muttered something as the healer began probing the slash under her arm, and all eyes turned to Gansükh, but he shook his head. A servant arrived, offering restoratives to the kheshig, who accepted stoically.

General Burd had blustered in a few moments later, furious that he hadn't been sent for formally.

"Ah, General Burd," Khuyag began smoothly, motioning the other general over beside him. "I am glad someone told you. There was no time for formality," he added apologetically.

But Burd was already sobered at her condition. She lay half exposed as the healer flushed the wound carefully. She whimpered piteously, a few breathy words escaping her pale lips.

"What did she say?"

Gansükh shook his head again, though he recognized the name she had spoken. "Will she survive?"

The healer cast a look at his general, who nodded.

"She has lost a lot of blood. Perhaps too much. But I will sew the cut, and perhaps her will is strong enough to overcome this."

"And her head?" Gansükh prompted calmly.

The healer's eye flicked to the purple flesh at her temple. "Let us first worry about this cut; it is the most serious."

Carefully, the healer stitched the slash wound, then applied a poultice of some kind, and wrapped a bandage around her entire chest to further bind the wound. For good measure, he fashioned a sling and secured her arm to her chest as well, so she wouldn't tear the stitching.

Her leg and head were similarly treated, the healer cautioning that he was a warrior first and a healer by necessity. But the man seemed competent enough.

"How soon can she be moved?"

The warrior-healer shook his head uncertainly. "That is up to her."

Gansükh nodded. She would survive, his experienced eyes told him that much at least. Word would need to be sent to Batu.

"General Burd," he prompted, aware of this general's sensitives. "Do you have a messenger eagle?"

Burd nodded, understanding at once. "Two left that can find the khan's camp."

"We will add news of her condition to our report," Khuyag added.

"Report?"

"Ah, yes, there is another bridge."

For the next several hours, Gansükh and the two generals traded news from the past evening. Khuyag had sent a scouting party to get behind the Magyun camp if they could. He suspected there might be another bridge in the area. That would explain how the force had arrived so quickly and without discernable approach. Their position on this side of the river seemed pointless. Unless...the council of generals had concluded they were protecting a crossing point of some kind, and had granted scouts to his effort to find it. Gansükh listened carefully, driving the talons of fatigue from his mind. He still had many questions, but they were interrupted by the arrival of a scout. The warrior was admitted to their makeshift tent and politely avoided staring at the injured woman. He carried an eagle on a gauntleted fist, a dead bird caught possessively in its talons.

"What do you have there?" Burd prompted curiously.

"I saw the Magyuns release a messenger bird from the southern walls. I set my eagle on it. She was supposed to capture it," he added sheepishly.

The eagle looked at the generals defiantly and resumed feeding on its prize. Khuyag smiled. Burd kept his face carefully neutral.

"Did they see your eagle strike?"

The scout nodded, contrite. "Most likely."

"What was the message?"

The scout held out a small metal tube in one hand, which Burd accepted. He extracted the tiny rolled paper and began reading as the scout explained to the rest of them.

"My Magyun is not the best, but I believe they are asking for help."

"So they are," Burd commented as he read, finally allowing himself a small smile. "From Emoria."

"Priests?" Gansükh blinked, astonished.

"Fighting priests," Khuyag clarified, plainly amused. "I believe I have heard them called 'knights'."

"Knights," Gansükh repeated, regaining his composure. The word seemed vaguely familiar, but he couldn't quite place it.

189

"Perhaps they will try to pray us away from the city," Burd said with a sneer.

The scout waited patiently, favoring his bird with a thin smile and ruffling the feathers at her crest. The raptor hissed, but there was no force behind it, and she returned to plucking the feathers from her prize.

"We should mention this in the report," Khuyag commented, and Burd nodded agreement. "This is likely not the first or only carrier-bird they have flown."

"My lord?" the scout prompted politely.

Burd looked at him. "You have done well. Return to your post. Batu Khan will know of your actions here."

The scout nodded but kept his face impassive. "And if there are more messages flown?"

Burd cast a look at Khuyag, weighing the options.

"Let them go for now," Khuyag suggested. "Your eagle has no mind for strategy."

He smiled, admiring the creature as she tore relentlessly at her meal. "But note how many they send and the direction they fly," he added after a moment.

The scout bowed and excused himself, loose feathers strewn in his wake. When they were alone again, just the two generals, Gansükh, and the sleeping form of Briga, Burd turned to Khuyag and allowed some of his stoicism to slip. Beneath, he wore a look of concern. He'd recognized Khuyag's earlier amusement for what it was. For while Burd's mask was angry stoicism, Khuyag's had always been levity.

"You are worried about these priests?"

"The Emorian knights are no meek priests," Khuyag explained. "They are fighters. Fanatics. But they have no nearby garrisons, and none of these Westerners war in the winter. I am

190

concerned, though. How many others have they asked for help? How soon might we have an enemy at our backs?"

Chapter 19

It had been three days since the Drev'an attacked. Three days of uncertainty and growing restlessness within the city walls before King Bela called a special council of soldiers and advisors. Ambrus had been among the audience, sullen, but wearing clean clothing for a change. The boy Caleb hadn't survived the night. Amergin was right, he had lost too much blood to internal wounds. Ambrus hadn't been there when the boy passed. Amergin told him the next morning. Ambrus had merely stared, uncomprehending, then walked away without a word. Caleb's father would never forgive him. The boy hadn't even been holding a blade when he died. Ambrus hadn't been back since and felt badly for it. After all, he liked Amergin well enough, for a priest. And anyway, it wasn't his fault about Caleb. It was *hers*.

"We must have a plan for the food, Your Grace," one of the king's advisors urged as patiently as he could.

The tone of his voice pulled Ambrus back to the present, and he willed himself to focus.

"But how long can we expect a siege to last?" another questioned, sparking a fresh murmur of voices.

"It's three weeks until the first snow. We should assume they will be here at least that long."

Bela held up a hand for silence, looking for all the world like a man suffering from a tremendous headache. The courtiers gradually stilled, allowing silence to descend on the room.

"Lord Heinrich," he called out in a voice tight with leashed irritation, "what's the status of the fall harvest?"

A man stepped into the center of the chamber wearing a fashionable tunic of rich red and blue. Ambrus had never had occasion to meet the minister of tribute, whose job it was to store and account for agricultural taxes, but there was a coldness about the man that prickled at his senses.

"The southern and eastern tributes were being gathered during the attack, Your Grace. The grain fields have mostly been culled, and the bundles set to dry."

"The eastern fields are grain, yes?"

Heinrich nodded.

"What about the south?"

"Corn, mostly. Some additional grains."

"And the gathered grains, these were left in the fields?"

"No, sire." Heinrich smiled thinly, pleased with his foresight. "We have winter storehouses near the fields to protect them from damp. There's also a small guard force. The farmers carried what they could, despite their haste, but thankfully most of the grain was already in storage."

"You didn't mention the west."

Heinrich blanched for a moment and averted his gaze, gathering himself. "The…ah…incident at Rowanar, Your Grace."

The king scowled but said nothing. The horsemen had completely destroyed their storehouses to the west and decimated entire villages. They could expect no help from that direction. After a few moments, he nodded curtly.

"So now we must figure out how to move these stores past the Drev'an and into the city." He flickered a gaze over the lords assembled before settling on Heinrich once more. "What of the garrisons to the north?"

Heinrich shifted uncomfortably and shot a glance to a lord adorned in russet and gold. It was this man, Lord Olechs, who cleared his throat and spoke up.

"You ordered them returned, sire."

Bela's irritation was palpable now, causing Olechs to cringe. Beside Ambrus, General Larsson spoke up, coming to the lord's aid.

"There is still a small force to the north, Your Grace, and another far south, guarding the trade routes to the Southern Sea."

"How long would it take them to get here?"

"Perhaps a month, if they move quickly. Longer if the snows come early."

"They may be on the move already, sire, I sent a bird to Emoria," Olechs added hopefully.

It was the wrong thing to say. Bela's attention snapped to him in a cold fury.

"You did what?"

"I thought—"

"Who told you to think?"

The lord cringed but pressed on bravely.

"We'll need help, sire, to break a siege."

"Help." The king sneered. "Do you think me weak, Lord Olechs?"

Yes...Ambrus thought to himself, disgusted as he always was with court behavior. Larsson shot him a sharp glance, silently warning him to keep emotion out of his face.

"Of course not, sire, I—"

"Those…*pagans* hold the bridge," the king growled, abruptly changing the subject, his eyes darting around the space before resting on Ambrus.

"Or one end of it, anyway. Until we recapture the bridge, it's useless to us. But so, too, they must tie up a significant portion of their force to hold their end. I am told there's another, smaller Drev'an army to the south."

"Lord Rybus holds them at bay, Your Grace," Larsson answered the lingering question. "The foot bridge is secure."

"Additionally," Heinrich interjected, "small bands of women have been allowed unmolested travel. They've been hand gathering what they can, discretely of course, and never too close to the enemy. Surely scouts must have seen them, but no horsemen have tried to interfere."

"Lord Larsson?" the king glanced to his general, seeking his opinion.

"It's true, sire. Very small groups. True also that they've suffered no harassment, but I do not endorse such risk."

"Your caution is noted. However we may require what meager supplies they can obtain. How did you come by this information, Lord Heinrich?"

Heinrich cleared his throat impulsively. To Ambrus, he seemed uncomfortable. "I have my…sources, Your Grace."

"I see." The king most certainly *did* see. Heinrich's love for women was widely known. "She can be trusted?"

"Perhaps we should discuss this in private, Highness."

"Very well."

The Drev'an were allowing unprotected women to roam near the city? But why? It made no sense. They should have made for easy capture. Ambrus had been mulling over the various implications of the conversation when a sudden weighted silence pricked at him. The king was glaring directly at him.

"My lord?"

Bela made an exasperated sound and turned back to Lord Larsson.

"Why do you bring this...reaver before me?"

"This *reaver*," answered Larsson, intentionally stressing the word, "is one of your soldiers. I thought you should like to meet the man who saved the bridge from total capture."

The king had the good grace to allow his stern face to lighten for a moment, and he examined the blond-haired warrior with new interest.

"You?"

"Not alone, Your Grace."

The king eyed him a moment longer. Ambrus had the distinct impression the king was coming to terms with something distasteful, but forced himself to remain calm, collected. Neutral.

"My thanks, then," the king managed with a polite nod.

"Sir Ambrus found survivors from Rowanar," General Larsson added casually, "and escorted them here."

This caught the king's attention. Ambrus saw his gaze sharpen slightly. "Did he now..."

"They are Velkcic, sire," Ambrus volunteered.

"Pah. More foreigners."

"They were some of the few to survive combat with the Drev'an. Open combat," he added tightly, torn between duty and dislike.

"My kingdom doesn't need assistance to defeat this plague of…of…scavengers. I am grateful for your service, but under Lord Larsson, you and your fellow soldiers are entirely capable of breaking their lines. God will protect us."

Ambrus bit off a remark about which god might be protecting them and kept his silence. In truth, the king's dismissal had shocked him. After all, Ambrus himself was a foreigner. Larsson cast him a sideways look, another warning.

The council didn't last long after that. Decisions were made to begin food rationing, and guards would be placed by each of the wells to enforce order. And to protect the water, though the king was certain no Magyun would do such a thing as poison wells. Guard routines were adjusted, and the king ordered birds flown to the returning northern garrison, though not to the south. Not yet. They weren't likely to arrive before the snows anyway, and if the trade routes were threatened, they'd be in much worse trouble come spring.

"If the king doesn't wish to speak to the Velkcic, so be it," he whispered to the general, "but perhaps you will."

The courtiers were filing out now. All but Heinrich and Larsson, who remained behind to discuss this mysterious source, which was probably nothing more than some waif he'd taken a liking to. Larsson nodded and gestured him out as well. He bristled for a moment at the dismissal, then, thinking better of it, turned and left. Some of the courtiers lingered in the reception hall, socializing or criticizing, it was impossible to tell which. There was a scattering of ladies present as well, waiting for their men. Glancing around idly, he wondered if one of them might be Heinrich's woman.

It was bright out. Brighter than such a somber day had any right to be. Larsson would be a few minutes, and Ambrus knew he wouldn't be expected to wait for the general. He should really go and right things with Amergin…but not yet. He was in a foul mood, and the brightness of the day gave him a perfect idea about where to vent his various irritations.

Rusty hinges squeaked as two guards muscled the door open. The hinges had once been kept oiled, but had been intentionally neglected in recent years. Ambrus wrinkled his nose in distaste. It always stank down here. One of the guards carried a torch for him, lighting the way down staircases and through winding passageways until at last they reached the corridor he sought. A second guard stepped forward to open the cell, producing an iron ring of keys far less numerous than one might expect for a dungeon.

The guard rapped loudly on the door twice, but no sound came from within, except for a soft scraping. Grumbling quietly, the guard unlocked the door and swung it open. Weak light flickered partway into the small room, revealing a pair of filthy bare feet, and the bottom edge of ragged breeches. The owner of these items sat against the wall. Ambrus nodded slightly, and the guard with the torch thrust the light into the doorway. The prisoner blinked and shielded his eyes with a dirty hand.

"You," he grated, voice sounding weak even to his own ears.

But Ambrus merely stared at him. It was one of the other guards who finally spoke.

"What have you done with your boots?"

The other hand he'd been leaning on moved suddenly, whipping a cracked boot at the guards, but hunger had stolen his strength. The boot clanged off the open door impotently, and none of them so much as flinched.

"Keep that up, and we'll take them away," Ambrus chided coldly.

The prisoner cursed in his own tongue, knowing full well Ambrus could understand him, but the blond soldier would not be baited. Instead he watched the prisoner for a few moments. Casually he withdrew a perfectly ripe apple from a bag at his waist and examined it for blemishes.

"You shouldn't be so rude to those who offer you shelter," Ambrus admonished him in Magyun.

The prisoner scoffed.

"Or a meal."

Ambrus noted how those ice-blue eyes flickered to the apple in his hand. He'd always loved fresh apples. He waited another moment, then took a large, juicy bite. The two men locked gazes, challenging. Finally the prisoner looked away, and Ambrus tossed him the apple. The prisoner caught it, but what dignity survived would not allow him to eat in front of *this* man. No matter his hunger.

"It's a shame they keep you in such…uncomfortable conditions," Ambrus continued quietly. "It need not be this way."

The prisoner only looked at him, shifting slightly to lean back against the wall. His face wasn't quite hostile, but it was close enough to suit Ambrus. The blond man smiled thinly and shook his head.

"Suit yourself."

Ambrus nodded to the guards and stepped out of the cell. The guards took the prisoner's boots when they left to join him in the hallway. The soldier waited as they closed and locked the cell door again. After a pause, he took a hunk of cheese and stale bread from the guard who'd been carrying the prisoner's meal. Cheese was a luxury, he knew. Eyeing the distance from the small opening at the bottom of the door, Ambrus set the victuals on the floor—a hand's breadth beyond what he knew the prisoner could reach—then turned on his heel to leave.

"Think about it, Siggi," he advised in the prisoner's native language.

Chapter 20

There was a great haze over the world, that was her first coherent awareness. Nothing was clear. It was as if she were hearing and seeing from underwater. Someone touched a cool cloth to her forehead; that seemed real enough. The sensation was chased moments later by pain, which crackled in her head, lanced through her shoulder, her side, and burned at her leg. It was as if her entire left side was submerged in fire. She must have grimaced because the cloth was removed, taking its coolness with it. Someone was speaking, but they seemed so far away.

There was a delicate clinking sound. Shells…shells tumbling in the waves. So she was underwater after all, a child caught in the surf. Something rough touched her mouth, and a trickle of water flowed in. She coughed, panicked at the thought of drowning in the surf. No…she wasn't supposed to drown. They were supposed to find her and drag her from the ocean, but now it was all wrong, and she would drown before her story began and—

With a gasp Briga surged upright and coughed to purge the water from her lungs, but it wasn't there. There was no salt on her lips, only clean moisture. She wasn't a child, but an adult beneath the clear blue sky, and as she registered the faces staring back at her, familiar but from the wrong time, pain exploded in her head. She clutched at it and slumped sideways, drawn into a comforting chest while hands smoothed back her hair. Someone pulled the corner of a wet rag from her lips, and she was dimly aware they had been using this method to help her drink.

"You should not move so quickly," a voice soothed, genderless and strange.

Why would she need help to drink? Where was she? *When* was she? Suddenly she realized she could only move one arm. Panicking again, she pulled back and tried to force her left arm to respond, but she was rewarded only with another sickening explosion of stars behind her eyes.

"Shhh…" the voice soothed. "It is alright. Calm down."

"My arm," she whimpered, hating herself for the pathetic tone of her voice, but unable to control it.

Other voices murmured, and she was dimly aware they were speaking another language. Drev'an. They were speaking Drev'an, and she needed to as well. But the voice didn't translate. Another answered first in her native tongue.

"You were injured, my lady. Badly. You'll recover, but they bound your arm to help you heal more quickly."

It took a moment, but this voice she was able to place. "Dagmer?"

The thrall smiled and touched Briga's leg reassuringly. She looked at the slave girl, having difficulty bringing her into focus.

"Your vision will clear," the first voice resumed in Drev'an. "Be patient."

"Broth," added a male voice. Batu.

He was sitting nearby, watching her with an odd mix of emotions on his usually taciturn face. There were others beside him, but she paid them no heed for the moment.

"Where am I?" she asked him.

"Khuyag's camp," he responded quietly.

"Khuyag?" She frowned as another face swam into focus beside the khan.

"You have been with us for several days. I have no healers," he shrugged apologetically, "but your wounds should mend well enough."

"Your injuries were too severe to risk travel," another voice chimed in. Joren. Gansükh. "Besides, you are heavier than you look."

Her protector smiled thinly, as if joking didn't come easily to him. She sensed it was something else, though. The others laughed lightly. The clicking sound issued again, and she realized it *was* in fact shells. She was still half-slumped against the owner of the shells, and she peered curiously into the shadowed face of Sartaq's shaman.

"You're a woman," she realized aloud, solving the private mystery.

The shaman shifted to set Briga more upright. The sound she issued might have been a laugh, or it might not.

"I was, once," the shaman replied cryptically.

There was a shuffling at the door as someone brought a bowl of warm broth at Batu's request. She realized they were in a sort of makeshift tent. Blankets were lashed to poles, forming a rough, roofless structure. Dagmer brought the broth to her and attempted to tip some into Briga's mouth, but Briga refused, taking the bowl in her good hand and sipping it slowly. Memories gradually returned, though fragmented, as the broth warmed her bones and soothed stiff muscles. The shaman chanted something and sprinkled some crumbled herb into her broth.

"I take it we didn't capture the bridge," she commented blandly.

And so the story was told again. The events on the bridge, how Gansükh had dove into the river to save her. The hurdle-bridge here at the south end of the city, and the small force of defenders Khuyag and Burd had encircled and captured. She was light-headed from the effort it took to stay upright and concentrate on their words. The bowl of broth had been refilled twice, but the shaman would allow no more.

"I looked for any sign of you on the bridge," Dagmer explained, shadows of worry still lingering on her face. "I found only this."

The slave girl pressed something into Briga's good hand, and she looked down, trying to focus. It was a knife. *Her* fighting knife, cleaned and sharpened and oiled. She grasped the hilt reverently, then set it in her lap to squeeze the thrall's shoulder affectionately.

"Thank you," she said sincerely.

The girl smiled, pleased with herself.

"What happened to your ax?"

"When I pulled her from the river, it was still clutched in her hand," Gansükh interjected, sounding amused.

Dagmer looked at her sharply, a peculiar look in her eyes. But there was also a glimmer of fierce pride.

"She-wolf indeed!" Khuyag laughed, recalling the first word he'd said of her all those months ago and sparking a chorus of comradely laughter.

Batu only smiled, drawing her attention quietly.

"The fire," Briga prompted, looking at him with frank curiosity. "How did you escape the fire?"

Batu shrugged. "I climbed through the hole you and Gansükh fell through."

"Our khan is too modest," Gansükh corrected. "When the fire came, he shot at the fire-starters and killed them both. Then, quick as a stoat, he dropped through the hole and began fighting.

Everyone else above the bridge was badly burned, but Tengri was with the khan. He has hardly a scratch."

"…a stoat?" she repeated, suddenly dazed.

The shaman placed a hand on her shoulder, steadying her. "You must rest now."

Briga nodded her assent and allowed herself to be guided down to the furs that served as her sleeping pallet. She glanced around at the faces assembled, puzzled at their expressions. Dagmer smiled faintly at her. Burd and Khuyag looked on in silence. Gansükh was jovial, but there was an edge beneath his countenance she couldn't quite place. Batu…Batu's face remained expressionless, but there was something alive and threatening in his eyes. Unsettled, she allowed unconsciousness to claim her.

***

The balm of sleep only held for a few restful hours. When she awoke again, it was still light out, though the light was fading. Briga kept her eyes closed, allowing her senses to expand and examine her surroundings. There was the nearby crackle of fire. Her head ached. Her shoulder throbbed and itched beneath the binding. She could hear voices beyond the rustle of the makeshift tent but didn't care to make out their words. She could smell the poultice on her wounds, the musk from the furs, acrid smoke laced with a familiar herb…and a person. He smelled of horses and leather and sweat. Cautiously she opened her eyes and sought out Batu. He lounged nearby, watching her. Her vision was still hazy, but she could tell by his demeanor that they were alone inside the cloth walls. The khan watched her in silence for a moment, then held out his bowl of ayrak, the fermented mare's milk. With a grimace she fought to sit up while he made no move to assist, and finally accepted the bowl.

"Ayrak is good for strength."

She nodded once and raised the bowl to her lips.

"Tell me," he began calmly, "did you know the attack would fail?"

Alarm flooded through her instantly, and she took another sip from the bowl to pause and regain her composure.

"I told you once, my visions are rarely clear," she offered, "until they've already occurred."

He frowned, watching her, but seemed to accept this as he took the bowl from her. "You did not like the mist. I should have listened to you."

There was something in his tone. It was subtle, but foreign enough that her hazy vision snapped to his face.

"How do you feel?" he asked after a moment.

"I...hurt," she concluded.

In truth, she was frightened for her bound arm and for her unfocused vision.

"You will heal," he offered quietly. "In time."

He sipped again at the bowl of fermented mare's milk, eyes never leaving hers as he casually weighed how much remained.

"Will you still be able to talk to the gods?" he asked after an uncomfortable silence.

"Yes," she breathed, trusting, but not understanding the source of her confidence.

"Good. Drink this, you must rest."

Batu produced a packet of herbs and crumbled them into the remaining ayrak, then pressed the bowl to her lips. She obeyed, savoring the warm, fuzzy feeling of the alcohol and the medicine. The khan touched her forehead gently and waited with her for sleep to come. Just as the sonorous effect was carrying off, he had one final question. She heard it in the briefest flicker of clarity.

"Who is Eamon?"

***

Gansükh and Dagmer sat before a small fire that had been lit near Briga's makeshift tent. The fire's keeper and Briga's self-appointed guardian prior to the khan's arrival was a man called Jinghim. He sat to one side of the fire, while the kheshig and thrall sat opposite. Gansükh had been thrilled to learn that while Bayanaa was unable to ride due to his injury, he was well, and expected to recover quickly. Bayanaa had stayed back with Sartaq to intercept the eagles and discreetly monitor the khan's brother in his absence.

"How is he?" Gansükh asked quietly. He didn't know Jinghim and wished to keep their conversation at least semi-private.

"Angry," Dagmer responded just as quietly. "His leg will heal, but he feels he has failed in his duty."

"He got to her first. And he was the one who tried to carry her off the bridge."

"He didn't go into the river after her. Or you," she pointed out with a shrug.

Gansükh bit off a retort, understanding Bayanaa's position. But it couldn't be helped. Battle is chaos, and he was injured. But he was right, he did fail her.

"How are you?" she asked, changing the subject slightly and spitting him on a piercing blue gaze.

"Tired," he admitted, but that was all he would allow.

She eyed him critically and said nothing. Dagmer could tell there was something on his mind, but knew pressing him would do no good. He would tell her, or not, in his own time. She merely nodded, silently accepting the answer.

"It's a small miracle you weren't injured," she said instead.

206

"Or drowned," he agreed seriously, thinking of the Magyun soldiers in their heavy mail and armor. "Tengri was with me."

"At night?" She smiled teasingly. "Perhaps it was one of the she-wolf's gods."

"Luck is luck," Gansükh commented with a thin smile. The wolf surfaced unbidden in his memory. "And favor is favor. Do you know her gods?"

Dagmer eyed him strangely. It was a look he had noted on her several times recently, but he couldn't quite guess its meaning.

"I know her gods," she answered.

"Is one of them a wolf?"

Her strange look resolved to one of satisfaction. And puzzlement. *Here is what's on his mind*, she thought.

"A wolf?" She paused, considering. "No, I don't think so."

Gansükh grunted, then nodded as if expecting this answer. The two of them watched the fire, lapsing into comfortable silence.

"When she woke up…" Gansükh began after a time. "I do not know the tongue of the Velkcic, but I can recognize it."

He paused, fixing her with a serious look, causing the flesh on the back of her neck to prickle. But she waited for a question.

"What language were you two speaking?"

Dagmer smiled, but before she could respond, Batu strode out of the makeshift tent, interrupting them.

"She is asleep again."

"That is good, master," Dagmer offered, noting his perturbed expression. "Did she take the herbs?"

Batu nodded curtly, gaze landing on Gansükh.

"Walk with me," he ordered, and Gansükh obeyed.

Chapter 21

"No, no rabbits. None today."

Amergin sighed. It was the third stall he'd tried, and so far everyone seemed to be hoarding meat. Even butter from the nanny goat would not entice them, though he knew eventually it would. He hoped that would occur before he was forced to slaughter the poor beastie.

The day wasn't entirely wasted. He had managed to acquire some potatoes, onions, and two loaves of fresh bread, plus hay and forage for the goat. What they needed, however, was medicinal herbs. With a slight sigh, he tucked the wrapped slab of butter back into his sack and quickly adjusted the other items inside so as not to crush the bread. The market was crowded today, and the crowd moved and jostled one another impatiently. Therefore it was no great surprise when someone was eventually knocked to the ground in the crowd's oblivious haste.

It was unexpected, however, that the person would fall right in front of him. She was carrying a shallow basket full of apples, which subsequently flew in all directions. Those around her jumped to claim an apple or two and disappear into the crowd, and it was *this* that spurred Amergin into action. Druid he may be, but he could fight and was no small figure, either. Growling an oath, he sprang forward and grabbed those near enough who were trying to steal the scattered apples. His posture and foreignness were enough to scare the immediate crowd back a step, and a timid few even offered their stolen fruit back to the girl warily. Amergin had never considered himself an intimidating man but he pressed his advantage to help the woman recover most of her produce.

"Are you all right?" he asked in rough Magyun and laid a tentative hand on her elbow to help her up.

"Yes, just clumsy." She sighed in irritation.

She gathered the rest of the fruit back into her basket and allowed Amergin to help her. She smiled up at him. It was a tired expression, but the druid was struck by her eyes. They were the most unexpectedly striking shade of green, flecked with bits of amber. Amergin had never seen anything like it. He didn't realize he was staring until she blushed and gently extracted her arm from his grip. Impulsively, Amergin coughed and recovered himself.

"Thank you," she offered hesitantly. "I thought I would lose them all."

He waved away her gratitude. "Folk will turn greedy under a siege."

"Siege or no, folk *are* greedy."

"Where did you find such lovely apples?"

She might have thought he was trying to win her favor, but Amergin was genuinely curious. Those with fruit seemed to be hoarding it, for it was a rare sight in the market lately.

"In the orchard, of course."

"The orchard?"

They had started walking slowly. She carried the basket on the side closest to him to protect it from the crowd. Amergin glanced around curiously. He hadn't explored the whole city yet, but no one had mentioned an orchard.

"Beyond the south gate," she explained, noting his confusion. "Where are you from?"

"I am Velkcic. My home is west of Rowanar, though it's surely gone now."

210

"Gone?"

The druid said nothing, and they ambled on in silence for a moment.

"Velkcic," she repeated slowly. "There is a healer here who is Velkcic, I have heard."

"I am he. Well, one of the healers," he smiled modestly. "Amergin."

The green-eyed woman glanced up at him with a smile. "You have done us a great service, Amergin. Thank you."

"It's the will of the gods." He shrugged, uncomfortable with the praise. "Any man with a healer's skill would do the same."

They'd reached the edge of the market by now but were still walking slowly, in no apparent rush to be anywhere.

"Take this," she ordered, pushing the basket of apples toward him.

"I couldn't possibly accept that."

"Pssh. I will get more tomorrow. Our healer must be thanked."

"Lady, I—"

"You can take them now, or I will bring them to you later," she insisted. "It would be easy enough to find the foreign healers in this city."

Uncomfortably, he accepted. "This isn't necessary, but thank you."

She patted his cheek affectionately, and Amergin was appalled to feel his skin flame beneath her touch.

"I am permitted outside the gates to gather what I can, at least while the Drev'an remain on the far side of the river."

"By yourself?" Amergin was shocked.

211

She only laughed at him. "Of course not, but only women may go."

"You're very brave," he complimented her earnestly.

"If you need medicines, come and see me," she went on as if he hadn't spoken.

"How do I find you?"

"At the market, of course. We have a stall selling bread and cheese. Ask for Dianna."

And with that she turned away and disappeared into the chaos of the milling crowd. Amergin watched after her, feeling stunned. He wasn't sure how long he stood there looking foolish until a hand landed on his shoulder and snapped him back to the present.

"If you're not going to eat them all at once, you should dry them."

Startled and sheepish at having been caught staring like a moonstruck calf, he snapped his head around to catch sight of his moody Magyun friend.

"Ambrus?"

"The apples," the soldier clarified jovially. "And you'd best get them home before the entire city hears of this treasure. Are you all right?"

"I wasn't sure if I would ever see you again." That wasn't a lie; they hadn't parted on good terms after Caleb's death.

Ambrus had the grace to look wounded at that remark, and Amergin could feel the hand on his shoulder stiffen for a moment before falling away.

"I owe you an apology," the soldier finally said.

The druid smiled thinly in acknowledgement. "Grief does strange things to a man."

212

Ambrus nodded, then eyed the supplies his friend was carrying. "Need a hand with that?"

"No, but you're right. I should take it home."

Home, he thought with sudden unease. What had become of their lands? Ambrus fell into step beside the druid, and they walked in comfortable silence until they were well away from the market.

"So," Ambrus began, "who is she?"

"She?" Amergin glanced sheepishly at his friend but feigned innocence.

"The woman you were staring at in the market?"

Amergin laughed. "It isn't what you think."

"Oh no?" Ambrus appraised him with a knowing eye.

"…her name is Dianna," the druid said finally. "But really—"

"Dianna," the warrior repeated. "Lovely name. So tell me about her."

"She's a vendor…that's all I know."

"I know you don't have the coin for so many fresh apples. Have you done her some…service, perhaps?"

The warrior really was enjoying himself too much, Amergin noted. "Please, Ambrus, I only helped the girl."

"Helped her?" The warrior asked, amused.

"She was knocked down by the crowd, and they tried to steal her fruit."

"That was kind of you," Ambrus commented honestly. Crowds sometimes turned violent under a siege, especially when squabbling over food.

Amergin shrugged modestly. "They were afraid of me," he said, uncomfortable again.

Ambrus eyed the healer critically. He could have been a warrior, and *had* been at least once, he reminded himself, at Rowanar.

"You're a big enough man," he replied thinly, noting Amergin's unease.

But the druid shook his head. "I'm not Magyun."

That stopped Ambrus in his tracks, and he grabbed Amergin by the arm to stop him as well.

"You and Cathbad are a welcome blessing to these people. The city can be unkind to foreigners, but don't be discouraged."

"Cathbad and I." Amergin nodded. "Just us?"

Ambrus grimaced briefly. "I didn't mean it like that. The two of you are skilled healers. Folk know that. They so rarely have access to skilled healers, not right here in their dooryard."

The druid began walking again, and Ambrus fell into step beside him. Amergin handed him an apple, then bit into one himself.

"Since you bring up the others…I think some of them will wish to fight. They feel useless, languishing in the barn all day."

"Can they speak Magyun?"

"No. But they could learn enough to get by."

Ambrus paused, considering. "I'll keep an ear to the ground for where they might be able to help."

"For an unkind city, you're a good man, Ambrus."

The warrior laughed, but his tone fell a few shades short of levity. "I'm not from the city."

"No?" Amergin was surprised. The big man seemed to fit naturally into this place of stone and civilization, though his blond hair was distinctive.

"No," he said simply, then changed the subject after a breath. "How's Eamon faring?"

"Better." Amergin nodded. "He sits up now and tells us the pain behind his eyes is less."

"Will he recover fully?"

"I don't understand why he hasn't recovered already. We pray and flatter the gods, but nothing seems to speed his healing."

"The gods can be unkind, but they have their reasons, I suppose."

There was a sudden, subtle *tug* on his senses, his druid senses, that stopped Amergin cold. Frowning, he turned to look east. Beside him, Ambrus had stopped as well, and was staring in vaguely the same direction with a look of concern.

"What is it?" Amergin asked.

"Trouble," was all his companion said.

Moments later they heard a shout of alarm from the ramparts.

"Go home, friend, I'll send word."

***

When Briga awoke, she was more clear-headed than she'd been before, though she still felt groggy, and wondered what had awoken her. The sky was dim. She couldn't tell if it was morning or night. Someone had changed her dressings for clean ones. Her tunic was missing, she realized, recognizing the feel of pelts against her bare skin.

"You're awake, my lady?" Dagmer was just entering through the makeshift doorway. "I cleaned your tunic," she offered, indicating the bundle she carried.

"How long was I asleep?"

"This time? The better part of a day, perhaps. It's nearly nighttime. Are you hungry?"

Briga frowned, certain something had awoken her. Her gaze drifted to the west, toward the city, and she thought she could feel a fading familiar prickle on her senses, as if someone was searching for her Pattern. Had she been dreaming?

"Mistress?" Dagmer prompted gently, crouching at her side with a look of concern.

"I'm all right," she said and tore her gaze from the west, allowing the ghost of sensation to fade.

Dagmer helped her sit and carefully worked the clean tunic over her uninjured shoulder, leaving it loosely draped over her bound arm.

"The shaman says you're healing well," the slave girl offered, uncomfortable with Briga's silence.

"Where is my wolfskin, Dagmer?"

The thrall blinked at her, then recovered herself. "Here by the fire. I laid it out to dry."

"Bring it to me."

The girl obeyed and helped the she-wolf drape the short cloak around her shoulders.

"Now help me stand," she ordered, "I wish to walk."

Dagmer opened her mouth to protest, but immediately thought better of it, and moved to Briga's side. Briga's injured leg was stiff, but bore her weight with only a mild ache. She was pleased to note that her vision had cleared, and only a mild dizziness still affected her. She hoped it would fade after a few moments. The ground was cool and crisp. She relished the feel of it for a moment, then allowed Dagmer to slip her feet into her fleece-lined boots. Briga smiled as the slave girl strapped a sword belt around her waist and handed her the recovered fighting knife.

"We'll find the other one," she stated confidently.

Briga laughed. "One knife for one working arm seems fitting for now, doesn't it?"

Dagmer smiled, uncertain, but happy to see Briga's spirit returning. The she-wolf walked stiffly to the door. She seemed stable enough, but Dagmer hovered at her left side, ready to assist. The evening air outside the makeshift walls was cool, and Briga dared a deep breath. Gansükh was crouched beside another small fire close to the door and looked at her stoically. *Faithful Gansükh.* She smiled. Opposite him, another man crouched and looked at her with open curiosity.

Briga glanced skyward at the first of the evening stars, picked one at random, and set off slowly in that direction.

"Where are you going?" Gansükh hissed.

"She wants to walk," Dagmer replied calmly.

He could tell by the look on the she-wolf's face that arguing would achieve nothing. So with a growl, he rose to follow. She walked vaguely toward the northeast, where the crest of their ridge rose higher into the darkening sky.

"Where is Bayanaa?" she asked the slave girl.

"He remained at the northern camp, my lady."

"But he's my assigned protector?" she asked, though she already knew.

Dagmer eyed her with concern. Briga knew full well the two kheshig were her assigned protectors, even if she didn't know why. "Your kheshig, lady...yes..."

"Then shouldn't he be here?"

Dagmer frowned, trying to determine if mere curiosity prompted this line of questioning, or if there was another motive.

"He was injured on the bridge. Do you remember? He couldn't sit a horse yet when the khan received news of you."

True enough, though not the whole truth. Briga looked at the thrall expressionlessly for a moment, and Dagmer had the unsettling feeling the priestess could read her thoughts.

"Is that his replacement?"

They had paused in a small clearing to take a moment's rest. Gansükh hovered nearby, though out of earshot for their low conversation. Dagmer looked back to see another warrior following discreetly. He remained several paces behind Gansükh. It was the same warrior who'd shared the small fire with Gansükh. She laughed briefly, once.

"No, my lady. Bayanaa is still part of your kheshig."

"Why does he follow us?"

For a moment she had a fearful memory of the warrior who had tried to molest her in the early days, though she noted Gansükh hadn't driven him off.

Dagmer smiled, amused. "He's declared himself your protector. There must always be at least two kheshig by custom."

"He's part of the kheshig?"

"No. That is a special honor. Only the khan can appoint new protectors into that rank. The kheshig are very special."

"Then why—"

"That one hasn't left your side since he learned of your presence here."

Briga watched him, puzzled. Noting her attention, Gansükh followed her gaze. He scowled but said nothing.

"He annoys Gansükh," she commented.

"Everything annoys Gansükh." Dagmer laughed. "If he isn't fighting, he looks to fight."

"What's that one's name?"

"Jinghim."

"Jinghim," she called without preamble.

The warrior approached with quiet confidence, then inclined his head respectfully when he neared Briga. Gansükh rested a hand on the hilt of his sword, though his stance remained casual enough.

"Dagmer tells me you have offered your protection."

"I have." His voice was coarsened by years of yelling.

"Why?"

"As thanks."

"Thanks?"

"You do not remember..." he began and shifted on his feet uncomfortably, but then he smiled. "My horse fell into a pit of spikes when we crossed the Danu."

She blinked in surprise, then eyed the man once more. "That was you?"

"My leg is good as new, thanks to you. Not even a limp!"

"I am glad to hear it! But really, you were very lucky. None of the spikes pierced anything vital."

"Luckier you were there. They would have left me otherwise. To escape on my own, or to die."

"Jinghim—" she began uncertainly, but he cut her off.

"So I will watch over you and your slave while you are here."

Briga watched him for a moment, evaluating. She was uncertain how to handle this situation. With the Velkcic, it would have been simple, but Drev'an custom was still sometimes foreign to her. There was a stubborn set to his jaw, suggesting refusal might not be an option.

"The lady is grateful for your services," Dagmer broke in confidently. "One of her kheshig is wounded and couldn't come to her here. Gansükh would welcome your assistance, but you must not get in his way."

"Of course." Jinghim bowed respectfully, the ghost of a smile coloring his features.

Sensing dismissal, he turned and resumed his place, trailing Gansükh. Briga turned as well, continuing a slow ascent up the gentle slope of the ridge.

"Was that wise?"

Dagmer shrugged. "Khuyag would have sent him away days ago if he thought it inappropriate."

She nodded, considering.

"Thank you," she said finally.

Dagmer grinned and gave a short, breathy laugh. "Of course, my lady."

Night was rapidly descending. Briga seemed content to stand and watch the stars appear as the sky darkened. Gansükh eyed the forest around them irritably, but this close to the camp, they would be safe enough. It was a clear night, and the air had a bite to it. The cold made her wounds ache. She was turning to leave when something caught her eye. From this height, she could make out a haze low and to the northeast. The haze blotted out the few rising stars and seemed vaguely underlit.

"What's that?"

Dagmer squinted and followed her gaze. "It looks like fire."

"It is fire." Drawn by their attention, Gansükh stepped closer to see what they were looking at. "The khan's brother is burning the fields."

A wasteland of burned and withered crops. That was part of her vision. Her head throbbed worse than any of her wounds.

Chapter 22

"But why?"

The question was plaintive, disbelieving, and was met with stunned silence. Ambrus didn't see who asked, but it might as well have been the king himself. Everyone was thinking the same thing.

"To send a message," he responded quietly.

General Larsson didn't often permit him to speak in council, but they had agreed on this point.

"They burned the crops to prove to us they don't need them. They think the siege will end quickly."

Someone scoffed but said nothing in response.

"So much waste," a priest lamented, sounding tired.

The council was small, much smaller than normal. The usual retainers who followed their lords like puppies had been excluded. Except for Ambrus, all present were high lords, responsible for some function or another. The king did not want this news to become public knowledge. Not yet. Not until he had a plan. That gave them little enough time—Ambrus knew this type of news would spread like fire in dry rushes.

"We'll make them pay," the king vowed quietly, subdued. "And when we've broken the siege, their horseflesh will see us through the winter."

A flicker of anger rippled through the room.

"The women can still forage," Heinrich added hopefully.

"The women cannot feed an entire city!" Ambrus snapped.

He disliked them moving freely beyond the walls. They couldn't feed a city...but one could feed a druid, he realized slowly, and wondered again at Amergin's mystery woman. Larsson shot him a warning look before taking half a step in front of Ambrus.

But the king looked at Heinrich thoughtfully. "How many women venture beyond the walls?"

"Not many, Your Grace. Seven perhaps? Ten?"

"Find out."

The high lord bowed in acknowledgement, ignoring Ambrus completely.

"General Larsson," the king prompted, and the general stiffened. "Tell us of these heathens. How many are there?"

"None of the scouts have returned, but based on what we saw of their movements here, perhaps four thousand."

The crowd began murmuring quietly, but the king silenced them with a gesture. "The forest won't sustain such a host through winter, and they've burned extra food."

Larsson waited for a question.

"So they must attack or retreat."

"Yes, Your Highness."

"Lord Olechs." The king beckoned to him.

Olechs flinched slightly but squared his shoulders and stepped forward.

"Have you received word from the Northern garrison?"

"No, my lord."

"Emoria?"

"No, lord."

The king stared at him silently, and the high lord found it difficult not to squirm beneath the weight of that gaze.

"Send word north. Recall the garrison immediately. They must approach from the east. We will trap the bastards at the river."

***

Bayanaa scowled at the note in his hand. He'd been in a foul mood for days. While his leg had healed enough to sit a horse, he couldn't ride aggressively without the wound tearing open to ooze bright blood. He had learned this while attempting to ride after Sartaq as he went to burn the crop fields. He'd warned the commander that his brother wouldn't be pleased, but Sartaq had brushed him off as easily as shooing away a fly. Scowling, Bayanaa had stalked for his horse, determined to observe this activity, but the cursed wound had torn open. Both the pain and the threat of blood loss were too great to ignore.

Instead, he'd limped back to the old deer thicket he had claimed as quarters and rebound the wound. The only use Sartaq seemed to have for him was with the eagles. Which was fine. As Bayanaa had no real purpose in the camp presently, he could wander and observe at will.

He'd written to inform the khan of Sartaq's crop destruction, knowing he risked retaliation if the commander found out. But Bayanaa was responsible for flying the eagles, so the risk was easily taken.

That had been yesterday. Batu Khan's reply had come today, but the note held no mention of the crop burning. It was casually written. The she-wolf was well enough to sit a horse at the walk, and they'd be returning north. He also mentioned the besieged Magyuns had flown more messenger birds north.

Why north? Bayanaa wondered, *when their allies lay to the south?* The eagle shook her head impatiently and adjusted her grip on his heavy gauntlet. Bayanaa clicked at her and tucked the message away to gently scratch her head with his finger. She preened under his touch, settling, and was rewarded with a piece of raw meat before he slipped a leather mask over her eyes. The bird secured, Bayanaa pulled out the message and read it through again, searching for any hidden meaning. Nothing seemed obvious. Scowling once more, he headed leisurely in the general direction of Sartaq's tent.

He'd only taken a few steps when a scream sounded overhead, startling him and the eagle perched on his arm. Cursing, he tightened his hold on the eagle's jesses and spun to look up. Another eagle was circling, but there was something sluggish and off about its wingbeats. The bird was exhausted.

Cursing again, Bayanaa looked around for a safe place to rest the bird already on his arm, who screeched in agitation and beat her wings. Above, the strange bird dipped one wing, descending lazily into the treetops. Looking around hastily, he spotted a group of captured Magyun soldiers preparing trees for siege engine construction.

"You!" he called out sharply, gesturing at one and not really caring whether his words were understood. "Here!"

The man looked around nervously, but the display of irritation on Bayanaa's face was clear enough. Bayanaa threw a spare glove at the man as he scuttled over, then thrust the agitated bird onto his arm and shoved her jesses into his fist.

"If you lose her, I will kill you."

Without pausing, he turned back to the strange bird and withdrew his lure. He need not have bothered. The eagle clipped a branch in its erratic descent, which sent it tumbling gracelessly to the ground.

Swearing, he jogged to the bird. It kicked half-heartedly, trying to right itself, but one wing seemed pinned. He approached cautiously, fishing a spare hood from his pouch. The bird was strange. Its mottled plumage was mostly white, with dark gray edges on the underside of its wings, and all gray on top. It rolled one steel-gray eye at him over a large, heavy beak. *Winter colors, perhaps?* It was clearly not a golden eagle, or anything that lived on the steppe, and therefore not Drev'an. A message tube of boiled leather was affixed to one leg, indicating clearly that someone had trained this raptor to fly on command.

Bayanaa spoke soothingly, attempting to calm the bird. It watched him, open-mouthed and panting around distressed-sounding screeches. The feathers around its head rose and bristled. Moving smoothly, Bayanaa approached with his gauntleted hand extended. The bird thrashed, struggling to free its wing. Fearing that the raptor would injure itself, Bayanaa reached out swiftly to grab its legs. The bird hissed and screamed, but its claws couldn't penetrate the thick leather of his glove. Behind him, the Magyun swore as his golden eagle hissed, but Bayanaa couldn't afford to divert his attention. Deftly he maneuvered a hood over the gray-and-white bird's large beak and slipped it securely over the bird's eyes. The eagle screeched once more, then finally began to calm. Bayanaa crooned softly to it, urging calm, and stole a glance over his shoulder.

The Magyun was white faced but kept hold of the golden eagle's jesses. Her wings were flared in agitation, but she'd stopped calling, and was beginning to settle as well. Within a few moments, both birds had calmed enough to be handled. Bayanaa lifted the strange eagle carefully, noting its general condition. This bird was smaller than the Drev'an bird, but it was heavier, and quite strong. He noted grimly that its wing hadn't been pinned, it was broken, probably from its tumble to the ground. Blood flecked the gray and white feathers of the broken wing. A gentle and cursory probe revealed it had taken an arrow neatly through the wing. That would explain the erratic flight. But where had it come from? The message tube was empty. The eagle settled on his glove, broken wing trailing awkwardly. Steps away, his golden had calmed as well, and the Magyun was slowly adjusting to having the big raptor on his arm. The Drev'an sneered. *Do these people not know how to handle a bird?*

226

"She can smell your fear," he jeered at the Magyun.

The man regarded him with a look of mixed puzzlement and distress.

Bayanaa shook his head. "Come with me."

The prisoner fell into tentative step behind the Drev'an warrior, divining that he was to follow. The falconer wended his way back to the deer thicket he'd claimed for lodging and indicated a thick branch for the prisoner to offload the golden eagle.

"Her name is Khutga," he explained quietly as he transferred the winter eagle to another thick branch.

"Knife," he clarified in the Magyun tongue. "She is my favorite."

"You speak my language?" the man asked, astonished.

"No."

Gently he extended the winter bird's wing to examine the injury and crooned soothingly as he switched back to Drev'an. "If you survive, I will call you Irbis."

The arrow puncture was a neat wound and would heal cleanly with time. The break, however, would need splinting. The heavy beak swung for his hand as he touched a particularly tender spot, and he withdrew hastily.

"What is this slave doing here?"

Bayanaa turned to see one of Sartaq's kheshig, Ganbataar, regarding the Magyun with a look of open hostility.

"I needed him to carry a bird," Bayanaa responded, waving off his presence.

"You are too weak to carry an eagle?" Ganbataar asked, a subtle note of challenge in his voice.

Refusing to take the bait, Bayanaa gestured wordlessly to the gray and white eagle he was working on.

"What is that?" the other asked, dropping all pretense.

Bayanaa eyed the slave before responding. He could not assume the man had no Drev'an, nor did he trust him. "Go back to your work," he ordered in Magyun.

The slave glanced between the two warriors for a moment before finally daring to walk between them and take his leave. Bayanaa watched him go. Finally he returned his attention to the other kheshig.

"I do not know."

"Is she one of ours?"

"No. She has been trained, but I have never seen an eagle like that before."

They both stared at the bird for a moment, quietly musing.

"Why are you here, Ganbataar?"

The other kheshig sighed and rubbed at some stiffness in his neck. "Commander Sartaq is looking for you."

Bayanaa nodded. "He heard the eagles. Yes, I have a message for him from the khan. He and the she-wolf are returning."

"She must be recovering, then," Ganbataar nodded, "that is good."

The big warrior hesitated, then added quietly, "Anything about the crops?"

Bayanaa turned to look at him fully, willing his face into neutrality. "The khan does not share his thoughts, or his plans, with the kheshig."

Ganbataar's face hardened, but he nodded. Once. Without another word, the two set out to deliver the khan's message.

***

Briga awoke to the strange sensation of something soft and light scuttling through her hair. She opened her eyes slowly, reaching out with her senses to identify what the presence might be. It was early morning. The sky was filled with the gray light of pre-dawn. The small, carefully-tended fire crackled to her left, smelling pleasantly of dung. To her right, Batu reclined against his saddle, fingers twining idly through her hair, gaze fixed on something far off. She studied him, wondering at the contemplation clearly written on his features.

"How many days has it been since the bridge?" he finally asked in a low, tired voice.

His eyes remained fixed on distant thoughts, and she realized the question wasn't meant for her.

"How many days…and not a single sign from the gods. There are storms far to the north, but here? Nothing."

"They aren't ours to command," she offered gently.

"Tengri has shown me nothing. Every day is the same, every night."

"Perhaps he waits."

The fingers stiffened in her hair but didn't cause her pain.

"We linger too long. I must take the bridge."

"Why? So long as you hold this end, the Magyuns cannot leave."

He looked at her then, tearing his gaze away from that other sight. "So long as we only hold part of the bridge, a large portion of my men must stay there as well. Men I might use elsewhere."

"Attacking across the bridge again is foolish."

Batu grunted agreement and allowed silence to settle.

"You are well enough to ride?" he asked, after a time.

"I think so."

"Good. We leave today."

Their departure from camp had been efficient. Generals Khuyag and Burd both came to see them off and to wish Briga speedy recovery. They all had a hot breakfast together before Briga was given a fresh bandage and the makeshift tent was dismantled. Sartaq's shaman had changed the bandage personally.

"These wounds will heal," she'd said, watching Briga with an uncomfortably intense stare.

Briga nodded and accepted a small bundle that was pressed into her hands. The shaman was unnaturally still, eyes narrowing as she seemed to notice something in Briga's expression.

"You knew it would happen," she breathed softly with no hint of a question in her odd, genderless voice.

Briga frowned even as the small hairs on the back of her neck pricked up in warning. "Knew what would happen?"

"All of it," she breathed, sounding faintly…amused? "And you did it anyway."

Unconsciously, Briga pulled back half a step. "I don't understand."

"No," the shaman agreed, "you do not."

***

Something about that interaction had troubled Briga greatly. She kept replaying the words in her mind, examining them for meaning.

"Are you in pain?"

Dagmer had ridden up quietly, looking concerned. Batu cast a glance over his shoulder at the question, but kept his mount moving at an easy pace.

"Pain?" Briga looked up. The sun was shining, fully risen and revealing that they were well into the morning now.

"You seem distracted."

"I am." She nodded confirmation.

The slave girl nudged her horse a little closer. "What's wrong?"

"Something the shaman said," she confided, lowering her voice.

Dagmer's features darkened into something akin to anger, and she glanced quickly at the nearest riders. Gansükh was hovering close, as always, with Jinghim trailing near behind him. The self-appointed guard had argued that some of Khuyag and Burd's men should escort the khan and his party back to the main camp. The ride would take no more than a day, now that they controlled this side of the river, but there was no guarantee the way was clear of enemy scouts. If one recognized the khan, they might risk death to kill or capture him. Of course Batu had brought guards of his own, but Khuyag couldn't begrudge the man wanting to protect his lord...or the she-wolf.

At the look on Dagmer's face, both Drev'an guards fell back a few paces to give the women some privacy.

"What did she say to you?"

"She said I knew it would happen."

"Knew what would happen?"

Briga shook her head. "I don't know. Batu asked me if there was an ill-omen before the bridge. I'm not sure."

Dagmer fell silent for a moment, thinking. "Mistress, I'm no druid. No seer. I have no…" she stumbled for a moment, searching for the Drev'an word, "dreams."

Briga continued to stare between her horse's ears. She was listening, but her thoughts were elsewhere.

"But you have."

She flicked a quick glance to the thrall.

"Did you dream of the bridge?"

Briga frowned, thinking. Had she seen a bridge in her visions? She closed her eyes, attempting to recall her visions in their original clarity. There had been a wolf swimming, but that didn't seem to hold meaning. Not only was she unaware of what the wolf represented, the water it crossed was much larger than a river. There had been streaks of fire in the sky. Fire-arrows, perhaps? The streaks didn't seem like arrows, but interpretation was always difficult. There had been a wasteland of crops...

"The crops!" she gasped. "The vision warned me he would burn the crops."

Batu had been half listening and regarded her stoically. "Why does that matter?"

"I don't know," she growled, frustration coloring her tone. She was not at all certain this was what the shaman had meant. "Why did you burn them?"

"Sartaq burned them."

"But you ordered it."

"I ordered him to put the harvest out of the Magyun's reach," he snapped, irritated at being questioned.

To his far side, one of his own personal guards shifted at the khan's agitation.

"Mistress," the slave girl interjected, "why does it matter? The shaman said *you* did something. I don't think she meant the harvest."

Briga sighed and shook her head. Dagmer was probably right. Unless something she'd done had led to the conflagration, but what was the greater import? She didn't know. The shaman had seemed certain she knew. So what did it mean?

Her horse tossed his head in annoyance, and she relaxed her grip on the reins. Her wounds ached dully. It was after midday; they'd been picking their way through the dying forest for hours now. The sky was clear and crisp, the first sunny day they had enjoyed since she awoke from her injuries, and she looked up to take in the sight of it and clear her mind.

Perhaps it was an omen. Tengri was the Drev'an god of the wide blue sky and clear days were said to be a mark of favor. There was a glint of reflected light at the corner of her vision, and she looked at it by reflex. Far to her left, the river burbled and glittered in the sun. The water had a strange motion to it, and the hair on the back of her neck began to stand up. With a sudden jerk of the reins, she moved her horse toward it. There was a ripple of protest and surprise from the guards, but Dagmer, Gansükh, and Jinghim flanked her smoothly.

"What is it?" Batu asked, noting the intensity of her gaze.

"The river," she relied in an odd, flat tone.

Batu raised a hand to halt the column while his she-wolf went to investigate. After a score of cautious paces, the river came into view through a screen of thinning trees. While the current was still undeniably fast, the water looked different here. Less smooth. Several logs had piled up, forming a small, unstable jam that stretched across the river's width and...withheld some of the flow. Her eyes traveled to the far bank, and her blood froze.

"Batu Khan," she called over her shoulder in the same flat tone, without tearing away her gaze. "This is where we cross."

233

For far beyond the far bank stood the great stone wall of the Magyun city. And on the bank itself, the exact spot where she had envisioned a raven perched on the khan's horse.

Chapter 23

The army had mobilized far more swiftly than she would have ever thought possible. By nightfall, the first contingents of the great horde had arrived from the north. A sizeable force was left to hold the bridge and keep the Magyuns' attention. Each man remaining lit extra fires at dusk so there'd be no visual indication anyone had departed the camp. When they arrived, Briga was once again shocked at the silence such a mass of men and horses were able to achieve.

Sartaq rode at the head of the near-silent column, flanked by his guards. He halted well back from the river and signaled the men to dismount. They would wait while the generals discussed the plan, and their distance prevented any warning sounds from drifting across the river to betray their position.

"Brother." Batu grinned tepidly as the commander approached.

"What have you found?"

"A ford. Or what could become a ford."

Quietly, the brothers crept forward to observe the potential crossing point. The sky was clear, and they risked some sharp-eyed scout spotting them in the starlight, but Batu knew they had very little time to pull off his scheme. He wanted to take advantage of the crossing, should it prove viable, before the Magyuns noticed the jam and sent troops to clear it.

"There," he breathed, indicating the tiny dam.

The surface texture Briga had noticed was a result of shallower water flowing over a rocky bottom. If more debris was added to the jam, the shallow area would become shallower still.

Sartaq nodded, and the small group withdrew a safe distance from the river.

"The Magyuns know this river. They will know it is shallower here. Maybe not shallow enough to cross," one of the generals put in, "but if they see what we are doing?"

Batu nodded agreement. "We must move quickly. Tonight."

Sartaq regarded his brother with surprise but did not dispute him.

"Once across, we must assault the bridge. Take it before they can send reinforcements. We will trap them in their stone city."

"What then? Lay siege all winter?" another general questioned.

"They cannot withstand a siege," Sartaq commented.

"Neither can we."

"One thing at a time," the khan intoned calmly. "I promised the city before winter. Perhaps we will be a little late on this promise, but before the snows melt, we will dine in that fool Bela's castle."

The general seemed dubious but didn't argue.

"Commander," the khan resumed formally, "return north. Prepare the men for battle. You will know the signal."

Sartaq grunted acknowledgement and nodded. The contingent of men who had ridden south would remain here and follow the khan. Only the commander's blood riders would accompany him.

"Good luck, brother."

Sartaq flashed a grin before departing. Batu then turned his attention to the two remaining generals and outlined his plan. It was simple, really. Their men must go slightly upriver and add to the debris with anything they could. They would fell trees further back in the woods and carry them to the river. Silently. When the ford was shallow enough, they'd all cross.

***

"What's that?"

The younger soldier grinned up at Ambrus at the question. He had a scar across his cheek from the fighting previously, and the raw, pink flesh stretched grotesquely.

"I call it the prize room." He grinned again around the answer.

Behind the younger man was a storage alcove packed with an assortment of weapons laid out in no particular order. Ambrus scowled, his gaze sweeping across the blood-stained arrows, bows, and blades of every length. There was even an ax or two of familiar design.

"We've been salvaging them from the bridge," he continued blithely.

"The horselords allowed this?"

"Oh, no!" The soldier laughed. "But they've allowed us to clear the debris. It's an easy enough thing to remove some weapon or another with an armload of burnt thatch or wood. Of course, we've gone about as far as they will allow, so there'll probably be no more additions to the collection. Unless they are foolish enough to attack again."

Ambrus grunted at the suggestion, leaving his meaning open to interpretation, and slipped into the small space. There might be something to learn from the construction of their weapons. And if they should attack again, these wouldn't be readily at hand for the enemy. Perhaps this salvage wasn't entirely a bad idea.

He crouched as some instinct drew his attention to one pile of blades in particular. It was not an instinct he particularly understood, but he'd learned to trust it over the years.

"I saw you fight last time," the soldier went on, more serious.

Ambrus only grunted acknowledgement and picked through the assortment of blades with mild interest.

"We were lucky to have you here."

"I am a warrior." Ambrus shrugged. "If not here, I'd be fighting somewhere else."

"Perhaps for the horsemen?" the soldier asked, his tone playful, but there was a shade of sincerity there.

"No. Not for them."

He noticed the way Ambrus slightly stiffened. The man grunted, an approximation of Ambrus himself, and nodded as if satisfied with some private thought. "You should take one."

Ambrus half smiled at the suggestion as his fingers closed around the hilt of a finely crafted Kithian blade. Simple, expertly balanced on an ivory hilt, it was a beautiful weapon.

"From my homeland," he explained to the watching soldier.

"Maybe it's a sign from your gods," the man replied. "You should keep it."

Ambrus nodded, turning the blade in his hands and tracing the small inlaid sigil with his thumb before thrusting it through his belt and rising to his feet. He rested a grateful hand on the man's shoulder a brief moment before turning to look out across the bridge.

"What are our friends up to this dark hour?"

"The same thing every night." the soldier sighed. "They stare at us; we stare at them. Everyone waits."

He paused, checking the position of the stars. "They might begin singing soon."

"Singing?"

"Yes, probably insults to our mothers and wives. Who can tell?"

Ambrus chuckled, remembering war camps of his own. "No sign of siege engines?"

"None we can see. Though we sometimes hear what might be sounds of building."

The blond warrior nodded. "Where's your captain?"

"This time of night, he's probably in the tower."

Ambrus nodded again and excused himself with another word of thanks for the dagger. On the way to the tower, he passed a warrior from Amergin's clan. The man was big, nearly as large as Ambrus himself, and nodded gruffly in recognition. The lime paste was beginning to grow out of his hair, leaving a dark band at his scalp.

"What are you doing here?"

The Velk shrugged and replied in heavily accented Magyun, "I am a warrior. What else to do?"

Ambrus laughed in understanding. "Are you alone?"

"No, Finbar and Rorik are here."

"And the others?"

"Guard Eamon and the druids."

"That's good."

In the courtyard below, a horse called out in the night. Both men looked out at it by habit. The horse was just visible at the edge of the torchlight. Something about the horse prickled at his senses. One glance at the Velkcic warrior beside him confirmed something was wrong. The Velk was frowning as well and met his gaze. Unsettled, Ambrus looked to the horse again, this time evaluating its stance. In an instant he realized the horse wasn't looking across the river or back toward the city, but rather was focused downriver.

"He smells something," the Velk grumbled.

"A wolf maybe?"

The other man shrugged, unconvinced, but evidently unconcerned. Indeed, a wolf howled somewhere in the distance. Ambrus touched the hilt of his new dagger for luck and shook off the feeling.

"Keep a weather eye open, brother. I'll bring some dried meat to the barn tomorrow."

They clasped arms, wrist to wrist in the warrior fashion, and the Velkcic warrior flashed him a grin.

Ambrus found the captain of the watch a few minutes later, exactly where he expected to find him. The captain was a man named Braxus, whom Ambrus knew as a fellow foreigner. Braxus was Emorian and had cut his teeth in a legion before opting to serve a tour in Magyuna. Ambrus liked him despite all that.

"How goes the watch?" Ambrus intruded on the captain without bothering to announce himself.

"That's the trouble with these foreign troops." Braxus said to a sergeant beside him. "No manners or protocol."

"None whatsoever," Ambrus agreed with a grin.

The captain laughed and clasped wrists with the blond warrior. "What brings you out here in the small hours, Ambrus?"

"General Larsson thought you might need some adult supervision." He smiled good-naturedly but cut his eyes to the sergeant for the briefest moment.

"Then perhaps he shouldn't have sent out a mere puppy." The Emorian flashed a toothy grin in return and focused his attention back on the sergeant. "Thank you, Davitt, that will be all."

The sergeant looked from Ambrus to Braxus and back again before saluting both of them crisply and departing the room.

"What's wrong?" the captain asked, dropping all pretense after the sergeant had left.

"Another cut in rations." Ambrus sighed, sobering as well.

"Another one?"

"There's no consensus on how long the siege will last."

"But we're on half rations already. The army fights on its stomach, you know that."

Ambrus nodded. "Meat for those on watch. It's the best we could do. And there's a new order in the city. The peasants may not slaughter any female animals. The males will be culled and the meat dried so they are not a burden to feed. But milk, cheese, and eggs will be collected as long as the animal can produce it."

Braxus clenched his jaw and looked out over the ramparts to the far side of the river.

"This is madness. They won't sit there all winter."

"No, they won't," Ambrus agreed.

"What would you do?"

Ambrus knew he meant to seek an opinion of the enemy mindset. "If I didn't want to wait for a spring campaign? I would find a way to cross."

Braxus nodded. "There are potential crossing points both up and downriver when the water starts to calm again. Yet they haven't decamped to find them."

"Which means they intend to take the bridge." Ambrus paused for a moment, thinking. "How would you do it?"

"Hah. I'd wait for the spring campaign. I wouldn't camp all winter unless I knew I had enough food and fodder, and even then, the risk is hardly worth it."

A sudden clamor arose from the far side of the river, and Ambrus spun, hand on the hilt of his sword. Braxus stayed him with a gesture.

"It's only the singing."

"Ah," the blond man commented noncommittally as he straightened. "I see."

"Not every night, but they like to howl that noise after dinner hours, and now before dawn as well. Perhaps to keep us awake."

Laughter drifted across the water between verses, and Ambrus blew out a breath.

"You're tense," Braxus observed, studying his friend with the shrewdness of a battlefield commander. "You didn't come out here before dawn to talk to me about rations. Why are you here?"

"Just a feeling," Ambrus confided quietly. "I couldn't sleep."

"A woman would help with that problem," the captain commented slyly, "though I hear your kind prefer to lay with dogs."

Ambrus looked at Braxus sharply. "Bears. Dogs don't have enough fight."

"Kith savages," he scoffed good-naturedly.

"Emorian milk-sop," Ambrus retorted.

Braxus raised an eyebrow and turned to look fully on the blond fighter. Below, the horse called again. "You *are* worried."

"It's just a feeling." Ambrus insisted, but Braxus noted the way his hand still rested on his sword.

"I take it you've had these feelings before?"

"What fighting man hasn't?"

At his tone, Braxus allowed all vestiges of good-natured rivalry to fall away and grabbed Ambrus by the shoulder, as a commander to his subordinate.

"Tell me what troubles you, Ambrus. These Magyuns might not understand what it is to be a warrior, but I do."

"I'm not certain," he sighed, relenting. "Something's not right; something is going to happen. I feel it in my bones."

Braxus nodded soberly, understanding all too well what his fried was experiencing. It was a warrior's intuition.

"What are you going to do with that cache of recovered weapons?" Ambrus asked, changing the subject abruptly.

Braxus smiled and opened his mouth to respond, but a curious sound floated up from the darkness below. It sounded almost like...

"Did you hear that?"

Both men stared into the gloom of the courtyard but heard nothing. Braxus laughed softly.

"Your instincts must be getting to me Ambrus."

This time the sound wasn't so subtle. A man cried out and was abruptly silenced. Seconds later another soldier raised the alarm, and the sound of steel being drawn filled the garrison.

"What's happening?" Ambrus asked, drawing his own long blade.

He crossed the small room swiftly and looked out onto the empty bridge. At the far gatehouse, Drev'an warriors sang around their fires, unconcerned with the Magyun end of the bridge.

"There's no one on the bridge," he reported automatically.

Below, they could hear steel clashing with steel and additional warning shouts. Braxus drew a gladius with deliberate ease. His voice was calm, but his face was puzzled.

"I think these bastards have crossed the river somehow."

Ambrus gaped at him for a moment, then checked the empty bridge again. By now the general alarm had been raised, and soldiers were rushing forward to the sound of fighting. In the courtyard a small fire blazed where someone had tossed a torch into the dry straw. A horse screamed and skittered sideways away from the fire. Braxus was already moving to the door, and Ambrus rushed to follow him.

"Davitt!" he roared, muscling his way through the soldiers to reach the fighting.

"Captain!" came the answering call at the end of the hallway.

Braxus bulled his way to the sergeant with Ambrus in tow. "Report."

"The horselords have attacked" he barked, panic edging his voice.

"I can see that; where did they come from? How many?"

"They came from this side of the river," he reported, half disbelieving his own words. "They were inside the gatehouse before anyone knew they were here."

"Did they cross under the bridge?" Ambrus asked urgently.

The sergeant shook his head, uncertain. Ambrus met the captain's eyes in a silent message, then turned and called out to the men below, "Secure the bridge!"

Men would be forming battle lines already, but they needed direction. Gritting his teeth, he turned to lead the defenders on the bridge, but Braxus stopped him.

"No, you need to take this news to the city!"

"How, Braxus? We're surrounded, and if the bridge falls, warning will do us little good."

He shook off the captain's grip and bounded down the stairs. Below was chaos. The gatehouse was aswarm with fighting men.

"Close the gate!" Braxus screamed from somewhere, but there was no chance of that now.

Fighting spilled out into the courtyard as the invading Drev'an sought to overrun the defenders. Ambrus couldn't get to the bridge without fighting his way through the gatehouse—a prospect that would take entirely too long. Archers had climbed to the top of the guard tower and were firing down into the courtyard ineffectually. Perhaps the added chaos would be in their favor.

Ambrus ducked to the side and raised his sword as a blade flashed past his shoulder. His answering stroke caught the Drev'an in his throat. He kicked the man to free his sword, and the heavy body tumbled backward down the stairs. Ambrus knew he could not get caught in the fighting here or he would never escape it. Retreating a step up the staircase, he pushed his way to the wall. A sword slashed across his ankle, causing him to stumble. He was saved only by the iron strips he'd sewn into his boots as an old trick from the shield wall and kicked with his other foot into the attacker's face with a satisfying crunch. Scrambling to his feet, he hauled himself up to a narrow window and squeezed himself through. It was a tight fit, and his armor momentarily wedged in the opening as his shoulders came partway through. Cursing, he wrested himself free, and held on to the wooden eaves, sword still dangling from one hand.

There was no way to scramble onto the roof, and a drop to the ground below in armor would break his legs. But the stone facing of the building was rough, and his boots found some purchase where stones were joined with mortar. Cautiously he crabbed along the wall, toes seeking any grip, while his hands carefully traversed the wooden eaves. He cursed again as a black-fletched arrow smacked into the wall beside him. A Drev'an archer stood at the waterline, evidently ready to pick off any defenders who might try to escape.

The night was clear and moonless, probably the only thing that marred the archer's aim. A second arrow bounced off the stones, and Ambrus crawled along as quickly as he dared. At last he reached the place where the gatehouse wall met the stairway, and he surged up onto the wooden roof of the shorter building. Moving quickly, he stabbed his blade between two roof-planks and pried them apart as another arrow embedded itself close to his foot. Holding his sword awkwardly, he dropped into the opening and hung there above the room to get his bearings.

He was in the open chamber outside the armory. On one end was the bridge, on the other a receiving area connected by a double-wide archway to accommodate wagons. In the open space beyond the arch, the fighting was fierce. A line of men five deep stood in the archway, protecting the bridge defenders from the attacking Drev'an.

Ambrus dropped carefully to the stone floor, knees barking in protest at the impact, but without injury. The fighting at the entrance seemed to be contained, so he turned his attention to the bridge. The Magyuns had been asleep when the alarm was raised, and some were still buckling into their armor.

"Crossbows!" he ordered, rushing to organize a defense.

If the Drev'an were intelligent, they'd take advantage of the chaos to attack across the bridge. Ambrus hoped to prevent that.

"First rank here!" he shouted, indicating their line-up point. "Shield your crossbowmen."

"You," he called out to another group finishing with their greaves, "check under the bridge. Make sure none have come that way."

He'd noted that the water seemed high and was worried they might have risked climbing beneath the structure. An arrow sang past, and Ambrus merely turned to regard its source at the far end of the bridge. The Drev'an war machine was ready now. A line of archers stretched out along either bank in support of the forces on the bridge. There was an unknown quantity at their backs, but one enemy force large enough to hold their ground within the barracks. Ambrus knew at that moment the bridge was lost. They would not survive.

"Sir?" a soldier beside him prompted, frightened.

Ambrus set his jaw. "Load quarrels!"

A chorus of creaks and clicks added their noise to the tumult as two score crossbows were loaded and drawn. With a deafening roar, the Drev'an horde thundered across the bridge. There was no thatch to burn now. No shielding mist. Just the cold starlight of a moonless sky.

"Hold!" he screamed as they crossed the mid-point of the bridge. "Hold!"

Arrows flew at the Magyun defenders, but the first rank, the shield rank, performed well. A shield rose unexpectedly before him as another warrior moved in to protect him. He recognized the man as one of the Velkcic, Rorik. He nodded once and noted that the Drev'an had crossed two thirds of the span.

"Loose!" he bellowed, swinging his blade forward for emphasis.

The first row of crossbowmen fired, their short, stout bolts punching unsightly holes through the raiders and felling most of their front line.

"Loose!" he called again, as the second line stepped up to loose their bolts as well. "Reload!"

The fallen Drev'an were enough of an obstacle to slow their brethren, but that impossible sea of humanity surged forward. One crossbowman fell to an enemy archer, and a shield-man immediately snatched up his weapon to take his place.

"Fire!" he called, freeing the archers to select their own targets and quickly reload without further command.

Ambrus stepped back from the line, checking on the waiting swordsmen behind him. This would be a close-quarters fight. Cursing savagely, he sheathed his sword in favor of a shorter blade. Not the new dagger, it couldn't be trusted in battle until tested, though he touched its hilt for luck. The first of the Drev'an forces had reached the line of crossbowmen, dissolving their ordered ranks with hacking swings of their blades. The crossbowmen retreated, opening paths for their own swordsmen to surge forward and engage. The projectiles from their archers were significantly lessened, now that the forces were merged in fighting, and Rorik lowered his shield to fight. Ambrus left him, sprinting to the line of defenders in the archway.

"Forward men, forward!" he urged them.

If he didn't create more space for the men defending the bridge to swing their blades, they would all be cut down like lambs.

As one, the mass of defenders roared and shoved a step forward, then another, forcing the disorganized Drev'an ranks back into the entryway of the gatehouse. The fighting there had spilled into the courtyard and the adjoining stairwells, thinning the room as the invading force began to spread throughout the garrison. The floor was slick with blood, but the defenders braced against one another and managed to keep their footing. Ambrus checked over his shoulder to gauge the status of the bridge. The defenders there were slowly being driven backward into the room under the onslaught of countless Drev'an pressing them. Half a dozen swordsmen had fallen, and their line was moving in toward the center as its flanks took the worst of the assault. They wouldn't hold much longer; he needed to find a better position for the soldiers to regroup and attempt to retake the gatehouse.

"Ambrus!" a voice bellowed from across the room.

Carefully Ambrus climbed onto a footer supporting rough stone columns on either side of the archway to see over the fighting. The captain was bloodied, but he'd fought across the space to secure the barracks area. Ambrus could move his small band of forces there to regroup, but they must maintain the outer doorway, or they'd be trapped in the barracks with nowhere to escape.

"The portcullis!" Braxus yelled, having caught Ambrus' attention.

His gaze flickered to the main entrance, where the heavy iron portcullis was still fully raised. The control wheel was above the gatehouse, protected by the guard tower. To get there, he would have to fight back up the stairs, or else climb the outside walls again and hope to avoid the archers.

There was a roar of victory elsewhere in the garrison, and Ambrus frowned at the stairwell.

"Braxus!" he called desperately. "We can't hold!"

A sword flashed out at him, and he ducked backward off the column. Behind him, the line of defenders he'd left at the bridge were in danger of being overrun. The straw in the courtyard was fully aflame now, and terrified horses screamed and pulled at their stays. If they stayed here, they'd be killed to the last man. If they retreated, they would surrender the bridge, but they might be able to regroup and recapture the gatehouse.

Ambrus decided then and there that holding one end of the bridge was tactically no better than ceding that ground entirely. Either way, the Magyuns had lost the use of the roadway for supplies. Better to spare the lives of these men for a future fight that might make a difference.

"Men! Fall back to the barracks! Secure the barracks and the doorway!"

A handful of the crossbowmen and swordsmen held their positions, fighting fiercely.

"Fall back together, do it now!"

Rorik, understanding, grabbed the man beside him by the back of his armor and dragged him along as he stepped backward. Reluctantly the remainder of the line fell into place, giving ground in as controlled a manner as possible until they were nearly back-to-back with the swordsmen defending the archway. The two lines, packed into a dense, elongated circle, defended from every side as they slowly advanced toward the barracks. Rorik swore as steel found his unprotected face, but the injury only seemed to inspire him to more savagery. He surged before the line, cutting down the Drev'an who'd wounded him, and two others as well, before the circle reformed to either side of him.

Braxus had seen what was happening and organized his men into a line of advance that began to move toward Ambrus' circle. The onslaught of Drev'an blades slowed as they realized it was only a matter of time now before all defenders had been overcome, and they fought only to keep the defenders from retaking ceded ground. Those Drev'an caught between Braxus and Ambrus were swiftly dispatched as the two forces met near the center of the room.

Ambrus took quick stock of the situation, sweeping his gaze over the mass of defenders and appraising the situation at the main doorway, the stairwell, and the bridge. He could see perhaps sixty men left to defend the gatehouse. The bridge was lost, and Drev'an fighters had free movement at the stairs. He could see no invaders beyond the main gate, but he was certain there'd be a reserve force outside. A small Magyun reserve force stood in the doorway of the barracks, prepared to fight, while others dragged the badly wounded into the barracks itself. Breathing heavily, Braxus came to Ambrus' side, scowling at the standoff that was forming between his Magyuns and the Drev'an. Mustering as much bravado as he could, Ambrus flashed half a grin at the captain.

"What now?"

Something dripped on his shoulder, and he looked up. They could hear fighting above them, indicating others had survived and were fighting to hold their ground and the portcullis control wheel.

"If they control the tower, they'll close the gate and trap us inside."

Braxus nodded in silent agreement, having turned his attention upward as well. Ambrus could almost see his mind feverishly churning, working through options.

"The garrison is lost, Braxus," he growled quietly but firmly. "Save your men before they are lost, too."

The captain shook his head slowly, but whatever he'd been about to say was swallowed by a sudden and familiar *whoosh*, followed a heartbeat later by a defiant Drev'an roar.

"Christ," Braxus muttered, drawing a sharp and quizzical look from Ambrus.

A heartbeat later, the timber roof above the barracks roared into flame. The Drev'an were smiling strangely at the defenders, and Ambrus took his gaze from them only for a moment to assess the burning ceiling, wondering how it had caught so quickly.

"Oil," he realized suddenly, looking at the spot on his shoulder.

The Drev'an facing them took a slight step backward.

"Oil!" Ambrus warned, dragging Braxus backward toward the barracks and out from beneath the murder-holes.

Mere seconds later someone tipped over a barrel of oil into the hole, raining it down on the open hall below. This was followed by a torch, and suddenly the room was a blazing inferno. Ambrus shielded his eyes by reflex, keenly aware that he'd used this exact tactic on the invaders at the far end of the bridge. They were laughing now, cutting down or driving back any men who tried to escape the pyre. Their only escape was the main entry now, and that was surely a trap, but they had to try.

Braxus had the same thought and began shoving men toward the opening. The screaming and the smoke had a disorienting effect, and Ambrus stumbled in the direction he thought was the entryway. Men were aflame, the floor was aflame, and everywhere was burning chaos. The heat seared his throat, but he grabbed the man beside him.

"The wounded," he rasped, but already some were being carried or dragged by their fellows.

There was a hand on his back, shoving. "Go, damn you, go!"

Some of the horses had broken free in their panic and charged blindly out into the night. He stumbled on a still-burning corpse, but another hand reached out from the smoke to steady him and pull him forward. A horse shouldered past them both as they stumbled outside. Ambrus blinked the smoke from his eyes to find a suitable rally point, and then he saw the archers. A cold fist gripped his spine. It was a trap after all; the Drev'an intended to kill them to the last man. Streaks of fire cut through the thinning smoke as flaming arrows sought their targets.

Screaming in fury, Ambrus brandished his sword and rushed the line of archers, not caring how much ground lay between him and them. He knew he could survive thirty paces with an arrow in his chest if it meant killing them.

Strong hands seized him, restrained him, drew him back. He thrashed wildly to escape, but someone punched him across the jaw. Not hard enough to cause damage, but more than enough to draw him back from the brink of battle madness.

"Ambrus, get to the city," Braxus rasped as Rorik shoved the reins of a panicked horse into his hands.

"I'll be right behind you," he promised when the blond warrior hesitated.

Rorik didn't give him a chance to respond. He shoved Ambrus up onto the horse's back, then smacked its rump with the flat of his blade. The animal surged forward, acting on pure instinct. It was all Ambrus could do to hold on. Arrows sang past him, but miraculously none hit him or his beast. Behind him the survivors were running toward the city, hoping to get out of archery range and into relative safety.

The horse danced sideways, and he looked forward again, clinging to its mane desperately. On the next hill, perhaps a hundred meters from the garrison, stood a line of three horsemen, seven more waiting a pace behind. They were dimly lit by the fire blazing behind him, but he would recognize that face anywhere. In the center of the line, mounted placidly, sat the woman he'd fought on the bridge. For a moment his heart stopped, and time slowed. She stared at him coolly, face expressionless as she watched him. Beside her a warrior he recognized drew his bow, and in that instant, he knew this arrow wouldn't miss. Her cold blue eyes narrowed on him for a heartbeat, and one corner of her mouth lifted in a wry grin. Then she raised her hand, calling off her archer without breaking eye contact.

Ambrus couldn't have hauled the horse around if he tried, and the idea didn't even occur to him as he rode past, staring at her in mingled shock and frigid rage. Then his heart resumed beating, and the horse careened on toward the city, leaving the Drev'an and the fires behind.

***

"Why did you spare him?" Gansükh growled, though his tone was more puzzled than angry.

Briga watched the retreating figure for several silent moments before answering. She'd recognized him, the blond warrior from the bridge who had set fire to the gatehouse and nearly killed her. Oh yes, she recognized him. It felt oddly satisfying that he'd nearly been burned alive as she, too, had almost suffered. Fitting that his men should be subjected to the same unexpected fury. There was a peculiar balance to it.

She hadn't known he would be there, of course, but when he came flying over the hill, the very blood in her veins seemed to freeze as she recognized him. He looked like a god of battle on the panicked horse, streaked and spattered as he was by ash and blood, his face distorted by rage. His green eyes were fierce and clear, and when she saw the flicker of recognition in them, she was certain this was not the moment he was meant to die. She felt compelled to spare him in her very marrow. The message could be no clearer if the gods had appeared to stay Gansükh's hand themselves.

Batu was watching her narrowly, waiting for an answer to Gansükh's question. Mentally she shed the mysterious tendrils of the Pattern and adopted a stoic mien. With a cool glance at Batu, she regarded Gansükh blandly.

"There must always be one survivor to tell the tale."

Gansükh frowned, eyeing her with a strange expression. She turned to face him more fully, allowing real anger to show on her face.

254

"That was the warrior I faced on the bridge. I will kill him myself."

Chapter 24

In the end there were eighteen survivors. All but four were heavily wounded, but the druids expected them to live. Ambrus stood in the open doorway of the barn staring out into the gray morning as the first flakes of snow were beginning to fall. Beside him, Amergin wiped the blood from his hands with a semi-clean rag. He kept his attention on his hands. Ambrus watched the falling snow, shoulders stiff with anger. When the druid remained silent, Ambrus glanced over and the anger seeped out of him, no matter how he wanted to hold it near, and he sighed briefly.

"I'm sorry, Amergin, I didn't intend to turn you into a full-time hospital."

The druid smiled benignly as he folded the rag. They were both acutely aware of how few patients lined the floor of the Velkcic's barn. Ambrus had managed to escape the fight essentially unscathed; the survivors strewn across the floor sported more substantial wounds. The blond warrior was watching him, concern edging his features.

"And...I'm sorry...about your kinsmen."

Amergin went still for a moment, attention fixed on the rag. Then he nodded once, the movement slight.

"They died as warriors."

Ambrus nodded agreement and spared a glance for the lightly falling snow "How is Rorik?"

"He'll survive. The eye is ruined, but he will live to fight again."

"I shouldn't have let them work outside the gates."

Amergin held up a hand for silence. When the warrior looked over, the druid was smiling faintly, a sad but secret smile.

"You are a warrior, Ambrus; would you have been content waiting within the walls?"

As Ambrus had ridden out during the night, they both knew the answer to that question, and a slight pang of annoyance rippled through the warrior.

"When this is over, we will wake them properly. I'm certain Eamon will order funeral games in honor of all our fallen."

His smile turned wistful as he realized there would be no one left for the sport, but Ambrus was looking at him curiously.

"Games?"

Amergin laughed and laid an affectionate hand on his friend's shoulder. "Oh, there's nothing so grand as a good death, my friend."

"Amergin!"

Dianna dashed around the corner, her face a mask of concern as she ran to the barn and caught herself with both hands on his chest.

"Is it true?"

Amergin shifted awkwardly to intercept the girl, drawing an amused grin from Ambrus.

"Is it true the bridge has fallen? Have the horselords crossed the river?"

"Slow down, mo chroi," he soothed. "It is true. I'm afraid you will not be allowed to venture outside the gates for some time."

Her hands dropped for a moment, but then she stepped backward and gathered her dignity about herself like a shawl as she seemed to suddenly notice Ambrus.

"I had heard there was fighting, but I hoped…well, I brought this to help."

From beneath her cloak she withdrew a sizeable bundle of healer's herbs and two bottles of poppy-milk. Still amused, Ambrus' eyes narrowed a fraction at the gift.

Amergin laughed softly. "Where'd you get this? By now I thought we must surely have every medicine in the city."

"I have my sources," she chided with a sidelong, suspicious glance at Ambrus.

"He is a friend," Amergin commented, noting her look.

She nodded once, but an edge of wariness clung to her. "What happens now?"

"Now," Ambrus interjected, "the siege begins in earnest. See to your sources, my lady. They may need to see you through the winter."

She nodded and stepped back, eyes lingering on Amergin for a moment. Before she could turn to walk away, Ambrus posed another question in a casual tone, as if it had suddenly occurred to him.

"Amergin tells me you're one of the women who went out to gather what crops you could."

She nodded slowly, waiting.

"Very brave," he complimented with a regal bow of his head. "Bring your friends next time you stop by, I should like to talk with you about these excursions."

Her brow creased in irritation or anxiety. "We had the king's permission."

"Oh, of course, of course!" He put up a hand soothingly. "I only meant I'd like to know what you saw of the Drev'an. What you observed might help provide insight into their plans."

She paused, then nodded in acceptance, and with a final glance at Amergin, took her leave. The two of them watched her go. When she was out of sight, Ambrus sighed lightly and flicked his attention back to the druid.

"She looks lovely with the snowflakes in her hair."

"She does," Amergin agreed, sounding distracted.

"You're besotted."

That drew Amergin's attention, and he looked over indignantly. "I certainly am not."

Ambrus merely laughed. It felt good to laugh.

"What was that about? Talking to them about the Drev'an?"

"We need more information regarding their intentions. I think it might help."

Amergin was watching him closely and shook his head. "You don't trust her."

"I don't trust anyone," he answered honestly.

Amergin was silent a moment, then nodded once. Ambrus sighed.

"Amergin, I've known you long enough now to recognize the cut of your cloak. You are not just anyone, my friend."

The druid smiled thinly, but accepted the offering. Ambrus glanced over his shoulder as someone in the barn moaned pitifully, his earlier good mood having completely vanished now.

"What happened? At the bridge?" Amergin asked quietly.

"I need a mug of ale."

Amergin extended a welcoming hand back into the barn, then followed the warrior inside. Minutes later they were seated in a relatively clear area of the room. In the stalls nearby, Eamon was awake and sitting upright, talking to his warriors. His gaze rested heavily on Ambrus for a moment, then returned to his men. Cathbad was attending to the wounded, but seemed unconcerned with Amergin's absence. Warrior and druid sat on either side of the fire with a mug of ale in hand, and for a time they sipped in companionable silence.

"She survived," Ambrus finally said after a time, venom edging his tone. "I saw her fall into the river, yet somehow she survived."

"Into the river?"

"After she…killed Caleb, I ran a sword through her. Two of those savages carried her off, but I saw her fall into the river."

Amergin sipped at his ale, waiting. When Ambrus remained silent, he prompted him.

"Last time you were here, you swore to kill her." He waited. "So you must have sensed then she would survive."

Ambrus' brows knitted together in frustration. "She spared my life. Last night. She killed everyone else in that garrison, but let me go. Why?"

Amergin frowned, considering. The relative silence was broken as a form announced itself with a loud rap in the doorway.

"Ambrus!"

Every conscious head swiveled in the stranger's direction as he called loudly. The man had grace enough to flinch and look ashamed at disturbing the peace.

"Sorry," Ambrus mumbled to his friend, then raised a hand to wave at the figure. The stranger limped over painfully and helped himself to a seat by the fire.

"I'm glad to see you alive, Braxus."

The warrior grunted a laugh and patted his wounded leg. A deep cut marred his thigh, blood crusting in a thick trail down to his ankle. It had been crudely bound.

"Barely," he finally acknowledged. "I heard you started a hospital."

"Amergin and Cathbad are skilled healers. I sent my worst cases to them, but it seems to have taken on a life of its own."

Ambrus indicated his friend and noted with quiet surprise that though the druid smiled placidly, his eyes were cold and flat. *Is the hospital really such a sore subject?* Cathbad, ever attentive, drifted to the fire as if drawn by the scent of fresh blood.

"Skilled indeed." Braxus turned to indicate the druids. "Rumor has it you are more skilled than most garrison healers."

If Cathbad felt any of Amergin's reticence, he was more adept at masking it. "By the look of your wounds, it is good you have come to examine the rumors for yourself," the chief druid surmised.

In addition to the gashed leg, Braxus was holding his non-sword hand close to his chest. By the smell, it was badly burned. Flash burns and scratches marred one side of his face.

"Your Magyun is improving, Cathbad."

The chief druid nodded in thanks, then gently took Braxus' wrist to examine the damage. Most of Eamon's warriors filtered out of the barn, evidently done with their discussion.

"You should have come sooner," Amergin commented tightly as he eyed the gashed leg. "That cut is serious."

"He had to give his report first."

Like Ambrus, Braxus had ridden directly for General Larsson. The soldiers on the city gate could see the fighting once the garrison went up in flames, but it all happened so fast, they had no chance to respond or offer aid. Someone had evidently sent word to Larsson, as the general was on his way to the gates when Ambrus nearly ran him down with his panicked horse. The general managed to dodge aside and grab the animal's bridle, slewing the horse around in the narrow street. One look at the blond man's face told him everything.

Ambrus shook himself from the memory when he realized there was a flutter of activity happening around him. Amergin was returning with a small wooden box.

"No," Braxus was saying.

"Your leg must be stitched. I can't do it properly with you sitting up," the younger healer explained irritably.

"Do as they ask, captain," Ambrus offered. "They'll have you back on your feet in no time."

"There are still defenses to organize," the Emorian protested.

"If you don't get that leg treated, you won't be defending anything. General Larsson will understand."

Braxus set his jaw for a moment, considering.

"I'll go speak with him now. Join me after your treatment?"

Ambrus eyed Amergin at that last question, seeking approval. The druid nodded curtly, once. A fresh stab of pain from one of his wounds convinced Braxus he would be wise to submit and nodded as well. Grunting, he stood and followed Cathbad to a clean, makeshift cot, with Amergin trailing behind.

Ambrus sighed and drained the last of the ale in his hand. As he stood to leave, he felt eyes upon him, and glanced up to find Eamon watching him. The chieftain's gaze was impassive, cold. Uncertain what was expected of him, Ambrus inclined his head respectfully for a moment, then stepped back and turned to leave. He could feel the weight of that unsettling gaze following him all the way to the door.

***

Batu watched the city, a faint smile curling his lips as he stood amid lightly falling snow. He had established his new headquarters on the Magyun side of the river, slightly to the south of the captured bridge. At dawn, he'd taken the black banner from his standard-bearer and rode to the top of a low knoll. Without dismounting, he speared the banner into the ground, claiming it, and called for his tents to be brought forward.

It was an impressive sight, the khan riding forward alone to stake his claim in full view of the city walls. They were far out of archery range, but that did not diminish the feat. Briga followed his gaze to the wall, watching the tiny figures peering over the ramparts, all of them too small to identify. Briefly she wondered if *he* was there, the blond warrior from the bridge, staring back at her. Feeling eyes upon her, she looked to her left to find Batu watching her, his face unreadable. She'd been scowling and schooled her face back into an expression of neutrality. A muscle feathered in his jaw, and Batu glanced skyward. It had been overcast all day, flakes of snow fluttering down in fitful drafts, but the outline of the sun had been visible through the clouds. The khan nodded, assured of Tengri's favor, and rested the weight of his gaze upon Briga once more.

"What happens now?" she asked before he could pose his own question.

"Now we wait. They are helpless behind their walls."

"How long?"

"Patience," he chided gently, raising a hand to pluck a snowflake from her hair and adjust the wolfskin around her shoulders. "This will not last all winter. If they do not surrender, I will persuade them."

263

She had been about to respond when Sartaq rode up to his brother and dismounted. The two warriors flanking him followed suit, but remained a respectful distance away, near Batu's own guards. The commander was as happy as Briga had ever seen him, though he kept his emotions loosely subdued. The two brothers embraced at the elbows in the Drev'an fashion. Gone was the tension of their first meeting all those weeks ago. Briga cast a brief, wry smile in Gansükh's direction, and he idly scowled at her seeming lack of composure. Stepping back, Sartaq glanced around briefly in surprise.

"The tents are not here yet?"

"I have ordered them brought up, but no."

A flicker of irritation flitted across Sartaq's features, and he shot a glance at one of his warriors. "Orus will see to it."

Batu waved a hand dismissively, evidently unconcerned with the delay. At a nod from his commander, Orus mounted anyway and spurred away to see to the logistical tail.

"Is there somewhere we can talk?"

"Here is fine."

Sartaq eyed Briga for a moment, then seemed to remember she'd been accepted into the khan's inner circle, and nodded, but lowered his voice.

"General Khuyag and General Burd remain south of the city. They will remain there until we have reason to move them. They report that the force the Magyuns believe to be holding them at bay has received several birds. Khuyag believes they will have orders to move soon."

"I expect they will want to compromise our crossing point before revealing their own."

Sartaq nodded. "Indeed. The scouts were told to prepare, but nothing else."

"That charade has already lasted longer than anticipated. So be it."

"I have ordered half the northern body across the river. Two of my generals will camp well north of the bridge to watch for Magyun allies or reinforcements. The rest will camp along the river surrounding the gatehouse in either direction."

"Good," Batu murmured, glancing back to the bridge and noting the mass of warriors gradually organizing themselves.

"The other half is across the river, guarding the prisoners and the engines."

Batu nodded once more, pleased. "We will give them tonight to decide if they wish to challenge us. Tomorrow, bring the engines forward."

Briga listened, but only halfheartedly. Her attention was elsewhere, distracted by a feeling she couldn't quite name.

***

By dusk, the tents had all been assembled. These were not the large felt *gers* of an army at rest, but smaller constructions of wood and cloth, meant to keep out the elements and little else. Batu's, larger than the rest but without adornment, sat perched near the top of the small knoll. Sartaq had set up his tent somewhat nearby rather than moving to the captured garrison. A fire had been lit outside Batu's tent, and Briga sat, talking and enjoying its warmth with Dagmer and Gansükh. The sound of a galloping horse drew their attention, and Briga looked up to see a palomino weaving recklessly between the tents and small fires. She knew that horse. A moment later, Bayanaa reined to a hard stop beside the little group, who were all rising to their feet. He was incredulous, starting at them, breath coming a bit shallow until Dagmer smiled up at him and laid a gentle hand on his leg.

"Alive…" he managed, not quite believing it.

Gansükh nodded, his expression hovering somewhere between concern and relief. In another heartbeat, Bayanaa had swung from his horse, wincing at a sharp pain in his leg, and looking over Gansükh from head to foot. Then his face broke into a broad grin, and he embraced Gansükh as a brother.

"You are not hurt?"

"No," Gansükh confirmed, smiling faintly. "Dagmer told me about your leg."

Bayanaa waved it off, stepping back. "It is good to see you, brother; how did you survive?"

Without waiting for a response, he turned to look at Briga, and paled at the sight of her, eyes resting on her left shoulder. He stared at her for a long moment, lips parted as if to speak, but no sound would come. With a faint tremor, he glanced quickly to Dagmer before lowering himself to kneel before the she-wolf, forehead pressed to the bare earth.

"I have failed you," he breathed quietly.

Briga blinked down at him in surprise, then glanced to Dagmer and Gansükh, then down at Bayanaa again.

"Bayanaa...if not for you, I wouldn't have gotten off that bridge."

"I will accept your punishment," he went on as if she hadn't spoken.

"Stop that," she demanded, crouching down and grabbing his shoulder with her unbound hand.

He flinched away, staring fixedly down at the ground.

"Bayanaa, get up this instant," she ordered, irritation edging her words as she straightened.

He hesitated for a moment but finally obeyed. She studied his face, surprised to see grief and shame there.

"Look at me," she instructed.

Reluctantly, his eyes rose to meet her gaze.

"Bayanaa, you saved me. You and Gansükh. Without you, I wouldn't be alive now."

He blanched at that, gaze falling to her left shoulder again. "But your arm...you will never swing a sword again."

"My arm will heal just fine. And in the meantime, I prefer to fight with my right hand."

His eyes shot to hers again, blinking in utter confusion. He glanced to Gansükh, who had assumed a stone-faced mask again and would not meet his gaze. Briga's attention flickered to Dagmer, drawn by some small motion, and she realized the girl was struggling not to laugh. Shocked understanding settled at once, and her attention snapped back to Bayanaa.

"You thought I lost the arm?"

He blanched again, and she realized with her arm bound to her chest and hidden beneath the draped wolfskin, that was indeed how it must look. She burst out laughing then, only deepening his confusion before drawing the cloak from her shoulders to reveal the bandaging. Dagmer laughed as well, and Gansükh merely cracked a smile as Bayanaa stared at the bound but intact arm.

"You are all right?"

"You should have strung him along a little longer, my lady," Gansükh offered good naturedly.

She smiled at him for a moment, wondering if that was the first time he'd addressed her by that title.

"Fine, Bayanaa, or I will be when I'm healed."

He smiled in relief and grasped her uninjured arm.

"Even so," Gansükh interjected soberly, "he did lose you over the side of the bridge. That was a failure of his duty and must be punished."

Bayanaa nodded soberly, agreeing.

"No," Briga returned.

"You must, mistress," Dagmer confirmed gently. "It's a matter of honor."

"My honor *is* satisfied," she insisted.

"It is not a question of *your* honor, lady."

Briga was silent for a few moments, considering.

"You are kheshig," she finally began in a calm voice. "I know what that means. What it is."

She paused for several more moments, allowing old memories to well up to the forefront of her mind where she could examine and dwell on them for a moment. When she began again, there was an edge of hardness in her voice, a glint of it in her eyes.

"It must have been an insult for kheshig to be assigned as mere guards to an injured foreign captive."

Both men flinched slightly at the hint of venom in her words. Her stony gaze flickered to Gansükh for the briefest moment before resettling on the lowered head of Bayanaa.

"It was an honor to fulfill the wishes of the khan—" Bayanaa began in a conciliatory tone, but he was quickly cut off.

"Silence when your lady speaks," she hissed, all traces of Briga erased in the presence of the she-wolf, "and don't presume to hide the truth from me; I can see it plainly."

She waited a few moments more, allowing a peculiar sense of anger to stiffen her spine.

"When you were first assigned to me, you resented it. Resented *me*."

It soon became clear she was waiting for a response, and Bayanaa steeled himself for what was coming.

"Yes," he answered simply, flatly.

"Both of you did." She did not look at Gansükh.

"Yes."

"Until you realized I was shaman."

"...yes."

"Do you still resent serving a foreigner?"

Bayanaa hesitated, his face betraying some emotion for a moment that Briga couldn't identify.

"I do not think of you as a foreigner," he responded quietly.

Briga paused again, watching him. She recognized the chance to finally gain answers to some of her questions. Why her? What was she to them? What happens after they take the city? She was tempted to ask, but the questions seemed like a betrayal of the thin trust they were forming. Bayanaa was baring his soul, calmly and honestly. She couldn't take advantage. She had demonstrated she was aware of their motives, and for now that was enough.

"Can I trust you, Bayanaa?"

"It is my duty to protect you."

"That's not what I asked."

She paused again. She hated this cruelty but could sense he craved it, needed it after punishing himself for so long.

"I was unconscious when you picked me up. Tell me...how did I end up in the river?"

269

"I ran too close to the side. The middle was packed, impassable. I was shot through the leg by an arrow and fell."

"A kheshig protects their charge with their life, do they not?"

"Yes, my lady."

"And yet you are alive while I nearly died. Had it not been for Gansükh, I would have."

"Yes…my lady." Pain touched his voice now. Pain and regret.

She sighed heavily, weighing her options. "Gansükh. What is the normal punishment for this failure?"

"Loss of a hand," he replied unemotionally.

"Without a hand, he could no longer be kheshig."

"That is correct, my lady."

She shook her head. "No, that won't do. I suppose I could take a finger from each hand…"

Bayanaa stiffened, but to his credit gave no other indication of distress.

"No…I have a more fitting punishment in mind."

Her gaze rested heavily on Bayanaa now, pitiless. "You will give me your oath. You will serve me loyally as kheshig until death or I release you."

Bayanaa looked up at her sharply and he could have sworn his heart stopped beating.

"I have sworn my oath to the khan," he breathed, an edge of fear touching his voice. Even Gansükh was wide eyed.

"Your failure demands punishment. Your life as a kheshig belongs to me, and this is what I have decided fitting."

He merely blinked at her in shock. "But the khan…I cannot…"

"I'll explain it to Batu," she finally offered. "He will not punish you further for this."

He watched her another moment, then finally bowed his head once more. "I…I swear it."

She turned a hard stare on Gansükh. "You as well."

"What?"

"As I recall, I fought alone on the bridge without my protector Gansükh and was gravely injured. You failed to protect me, as well."

Bayanaa looked to Gansükh, but the larger man simply stared at her. His absence was explainable by their fall through the rotted thatch. She was testing him. Gansükh said nothing, merely watching her with grudging respect in his eyes. Respect and…pride, she realized.

"I swear it," he said simply.

Chapter 25

Darkness fell, and the camp showed no signs of tiring. Batu himself was smiling uncharacteristically as he made the rounds among his men. Sartaq watched him, smiling faintly from the doorway of his tent. Laughter drew his attention to the nearby fire, where Batu's foreign shaman and her kheshig sat, sharing cups of ayrak. He recognized the smaller of the two, the eagle-hunter who'd been convalescing in his camp while Batu raced south to attend to his…pet. The man appeared to be in much better spirits now. Batu had been stopped again by another group of warriors, and someone handed him a mhorin khuur—the horse-headed fiddle. Batu accepted after a modest protest, and another warrior moved to offer the khan his seat.

After testing the strings, the khan launched into a lively tune, drawing enthusiastic singing from the men around their small fire, and several more groups in the area as well. Another musician joined him shortly, and even Sartaq found himself quietly humming the familiar lyrics.

"Ayrak?"

A serving woman stood before him, attempting to look demure as she clutched her pail of fermented milk. Sartaq nodded once, watching her, but didn't move from his position to accept it. She poured delicately, then boldly met his eyes as she offered him the bowl. He smiled with one side of his mouth, but still didn't move. Cutting her eyes uncertainly to his guards, she took a tentative step closer, then another. Orus moved suddenly, startling her and causing her to spill the commander's drink. Swearing, she threw what was left of the drink and the bowl itself at him for frightening her. Orus blinked in surprise, and Sartaq himself bellowed in laughter at the spectacle. He laid a gently restraining hand on her arm before she could throw the entire pail at him.

"You will have to forgive him. Orus likes to scare pretty young women," he apologized, still laughing.

"It is the only way he can get attention from a woman!" Ganbataar chimed in from Sartaq's other side. Orus laughed himself, but shot a look to Ganbataar. The woman was still glaring at Orus, but allowed herself to be calmed.

"Here, pour me a bowl," Sartaq continued, somewhat less jovially, and produced his own silver drinking bowl.

Mollified, the woman recovered her charm and dripped her ladle into the ayrak. "Yes, Commander."

He smiled at her over the rim of his bowl, but the warmth didn't quite reach his eyes. The woman took her leave, swaying her hips more than was necessary as she went. Ganbataar huffed a laugh again, and Sartaq's gaze drifted back to his brother. He found the she-wolf watching him strangely. There was something unsettling about her, something vaguely familiar about those foreign blue-gray eyes. Shoving the feeling aside, he nodded once at her and took a sip from his bowl. She mirrored him, then after another moment cut her gaze back to Batu.

Sartaq frowned slightly. Orus was watching after the serving woman making her rounds, but Ganbataar noticed and followed the commander's gaze. He said nothing, but Sartaq was aware of the question lingering there.

"I am tired," Sartaq grunted. "No disturbances tonight."

The two kheshig nodded and waited for Sartaq to enter his tent before seating themselves at the fire. Ganbataar glanced at the foreign shaman once more, attempting to puzzle out the meaning of his commander's expression. She seemed to be fitting in well with the Drev'an. Gansükh respected her, which carried no small weight. Perhaps Sartaq was suspicious that she might influence the khan. Further rumination was interrupted by Orus playfully shoving his shoulder.

"Why so serious, tonight is for celebrating!"

"Tonight is a good night for the Magyuns to counterattack," Ganbataar grumbled.

Orus nodded soberly at that. "Perhaps. But we have a chance to enjoy ayrak, and so we should."

"You just want another chance at that woman."

"Tonight is a night to enjoy a woman as well." He winked.

Ganbataar laughed at that, for Orus was right, after all.

Sartaq stepped into the relative darkness of his field tent and sighed heavily, allowing all his masks to drop now that he was alone. He ran a hand over the ridge of hair down the center of his head, examining the cup of ayrak. And froze. He *was not* alone.

"I thought you would stay out there all night." a feminine voice purred from the shadows beside him, drawing a thin smile to his lips.

"How long have you been in here?"

"Long enough to be sure your guards are unaware of my presence."

"Huh. You are too pretty to be an assassin."

Sartaq smiled through his teeth, but made a mental note of their oversight. Still relaxed, he fell into his furs with a grunt.

"Careful, you will spill your ayrak."

Sartaq chuckled quietly and looked into his drink before downing some of it. Smiling faintly, the woman sidled over to him in three steps, and sank to her knees between his legs.

Without comment, she began to untie the lacings at the top of his boot and slid it off.

"What news have you brought me?" he asked, watching her.

"Commander Sartaq," she mocked in a low voice as she turned to his other boot, "only interested in business and spy whisperings. Have you forgotten how to entice a woman?"

Her voice was light, but there was a note of chiding in it. Sartaq laughed lightly, but he fingered the knife at his belt.

"I was disappointed you did not come to me last time. You were so pretty with my blade at your throat."

"The prisoners," was her only reply, accompanied by a slight shrug, her green eyes sparkling in the dimness.

Sartaq leaned on his elbows in the furs, waiting.

"Yes, I have news," she finally sighed and rolled her eyes.

Sartaq grunted approval and held out his cup to her. Davaa slid her hands up his thighs not-so-innocently as she leaned in to take the cup. He withheld it from her with a teasing smile and was rewarded by a playful slap on his chest armor.

"They do not have enough food to last the winter."

"That is not news," he chided, but allowed her to take the cup.

"No," she agreed, annoyed at the interruption, "but if you care to know how bad it is getting, there is an edict that no female animals are to be killed. The males, however…it is thought this will keep them in milk a while longer."

Sartaq nodded as if expecting this information. "Defenses?"

"The same as before. They have engines, but nothing to throw. They are making as many arrows and quarrels as they can."

"How did you get out?"

She paused to look at him with a cat's smile, picking at the bindings on his armor. "It is not a way open to you, beloved."

She would let him interpret that as he chose. The sally port she'd found was all but forgotten, but wasn't useful for admitting an armored Drev'an warrior. She could barely squeeze through without her cloak.

Sartaq was quiet a moment, then traced a thumb lightly under her chin to lift her gaze. "Have you found him?"

"No." She shook her head. "Lord Heinrich never speaks to me of foreigners."

His grip tightened for a moment.

"There are Emorians in the soldiery. And a Kithlander."

That got Sartaq's attention, though he tried to mask his interest. But Davaa noted it and tucked the information away for later. She would have to learn more about the Kith.

"Keep trying," he finally said, allowing a smile to creep back onto his face.

"I detest Heinrich," she said, preening and sitting up a little straighter. "He sweats like a pig and pants like a dog."

Sartaq smoothed back her hair soothingly. Batu's woman might be a horse for breaking, but Davaa was a hawk. Hawks can't be broken, only persuaded for a time. He sank deeper into the furs and pulled her up over him.

"Then let me make you forget him for a while."

Davaa smiled pleasantly, sinking down to accept a kiss from the commander. He proceeded to clear her memory of fat, sweating Heinrich.

***

Dawn found Briga on the edge of camp. She'd risen without waking Batu and picked her way through the low mist to a point beyond the last tents as the Drev'an behind her slept off the previous night's revelry. The Magyun in the sleeping city before her clung to their dreaming. Only the guards, Drev'an and Magyun alike, watched her. She wore her shaman paint and her hair unbound. In her good hand she carried a firebrand. She had come to greet the dawn. How long had it been since she'd last performed this ritual? Laying with Batu in the night, she had realized her sense of the others, of the Pattern, was fading. Had they given up searching for her, or had she forsaken the gods?

She moved beyond the Drev'an camp far enough to raise suspicion from the guards. Another few paces, and they'd likely come after her. She was well out of archery range from the Magyun, and therefore out of danger, but also out of range of their help should she decide to flee now. There was no reason the Magyun city would shelter her now, not after they'd heard of her presence on the bridge.

Her senses still pulled dully toward the city. Whatever was calling her there was waiting.

With a sigh she closed her eyes, cleared her mind, and focused on her breathing. Gradually her senses recognized the crackle and heat of the firebrand, then a peculiar shimmer as the sun's rim touched the far horizon. With the dawn she was filled with a sudden serenity, and she lifted the torch.

***

"You called for me?"

Ambrus took one step into the relative gloom of General Larsson's chambers, brushing a wool cloak over one shoulder. There were other men there as well, and a few eyed him as he entered. Braxus was there, seated to rest his injured leg, and he smiled wryly before returning his attention to the general.

"Now that we're all here," Larsson began, nodding once to Ambrus but ignoring the question, "Mikelos, tell them your report."

Mikelos was not a captain, but he'd been head of the watch at the north gate. He stood wide-eyed near the general's desk, and Ambrus couldn't decide if the man was more unnerved by whatever he had seen, or because he was in the presence of so many officers.

"Go on," one of the captains urged gently, probably the soldier's superior.

"Witchcraft," he stammered before summoning more courage into his voice. "Pagan witchcraft."

A few of the more seasoned warriors exchanged skeptical glances, but no one said anything, waiting for the rest of the report.

The man's captain stepped in for a moment to guide the conversation. "They have siege engines."

Mikelos cleared his throat and picked up the thread, "They appeared this morning. A woman in paint and skins danced for hours, weaving a spell in fire, and she thickened the mist. Then the engines arrived."

"What sort of engines?" Ambrus chimed in.

"Great wooden ones, my lord, and all wheeled."

The captain clapped Mikelos on the shoulder and took over. "Towers, ladders most likely. And something that looks like it might be a catapult, but there's no sign of anything to launch from them."

"They've been building," someone commented, sounding annoyed. "We reported that days ago."

"Why catapults?" another asked. "There aren't many large rocks in the area to throw at us, not with lasting effect."

278

"There are trees," Braxus offered. "Thick enough stumps could cause damage behind the walls.

"They can't range beyond the city wall from the river."

"No, they can't," Larsson agreed, "but if they've built scaling towers, they have a plan."

Larsson paused, glancing down in thought.

"Watch captains…place your sharpest-eyed men on the towers. If they move the engines, or collect rocks or wood for those catapults, I want to know about it. Braxus, send word north. Find out how close our reinforcements are. Any why has Rybus not moved?"

"There is still an army camped to the south."

"Ah, yes," he commented dryly, remembering. "It's time he dealt with them. Guarding the foot hurdle gains us nothing now."

"General," Ambrus interjected, drawing a few eyes, "I'm concerned that the southern barbarian force hasn't done anything."

General Larsson scowled, more at what Ambrus was suggesting than at bring interrupted. One or two of his captains misunderstood, but the general raised a hand for silence.

"Speak your mind, Ambrus."

"Why haven't they moved? If the barbarians fear an attack on their rear or flank, why not move that force up to protect the bridge? This stalemate with Rybus makes no sense."

There were some grunts at that, and nods from others who shared his misgivings.

"Best to attack. Wipe out the force and be done with it," Braxus offered grimly.

Larsson nodded. "Agreed."

**

"They're terrified of you," Dagmer commented with a slightly wicked grin.

The thrall was cleaning and rebinding Briga's wounds. Her dance this morning had strained the stitches in her side, but they'd held.

"Who is?" Briga's voice was somewhat detached, as if she were still in a trance.

She had danced for hours, weaving her spells, her dawn greeting in streaks of fire through the misty morning light. And she'd continued long after the firebrand had burned out. Batu and Sartaq had watched in fascination from the crest of a small rise, but neither dared approach. Sartaq's shaman watched curiously, then wandered off to complete her own rituals. More and more faces appeared above the distant ramparts, as fascinated and as unnerved as the Drev'an.

Eventually Batu and his brother went to monitor the arrival of the siege gear, leaving Dagmer and the two kheshig to watch over Briga and her strange ritual. Gansükh had tried to stop her at one point, fearing she could not stop, but she'd waved the torch at him to drive him back. Only Dagmer had eventually gotten through to her, chanting lowly in a strange language.

"All of them," the slave girl finally answered. "These stitches can come out soon."

"Why should they fear me?"

"Because you're a shaman," she replied with a shrug. "They fear your magic."

"Magic," Briga scoffed disdainfully.

"What did you see?" Dagmer interrupted. "In your vision?"

Briga glanced away absently, her eyes tracing the flight of a few small birds across the sky. "Streaks of fire."

"From the torch?"

"No."

Dagmer frowned. "Fire arrows?"

"Streaks of fire," Briga repeated, her eyes following the birds' paths back into the Magyun city.

An eagle screamed overhead, drawing their attention and breaking the tension that was seething around them. Bayanaa pulled on a heavy leather glove and went to lure and catch the bird.

"I saw a ritual like that once," Dagmer commented, helping Briga shrug back into her robes, and fastening the ties at her right shoulder, "when I was young."

Briga eyed her interestedly. "Did your people have druids?"

"No. They said they were of the ancient races. Druids aren't the only priests who worship the gods in the old way. Just...different gods."

Briga's skin rippled with gooseflesh.

"It is for the khan," Bayanaa announced, soothing the eagle on his arm.

The message was from General Khuyag, confirming that the Magyun forces were still contained. General Burd had spent the last two nights in their camp, ensuring the captured soldiers were bound and cooperating. Furthermore, the Magyun commander had received a bird from the city. Its message ordered him to wipe out the Drev'an forces, then destroy the hurdle bridge. Burd had donned the Magyun commander's own uniform himself and led a small band to destroy the bridge. They hadn't drawn any undue attention from the guards at the south gate.

"Commander," the khan called out.

Sartaq stepped forward obediently.

"We will have more…guests soon. See to their comfort."

Sartaq nodded, and with a malevolent half-smirk, called out two of his generals to make preparations. They saluted and headed off to their task.

"As for the rest of you," his tone fell as he eyed the assemblage, "the men are getting soft, sitting around for so long with no one to fight."

He paused and glanced to his brother with a half grin of his own. "Let us show these city-dwellers what real horselords look like."

"What does he mean?" Briga whispered to Gansükh.

"It means, mistress, you will need another horse."

Chapter 26

News spread quickly through the camp, almost a palpable thing, as the warriors polished armor and saddles and weapons. Gansükh sat beside Briga, enjoying their midday meal as he worked on his own tack. The horse heads ornamenting either end of his bit gleamed in the weak, watery sunlight burning through the mist, but he continued to polish everything. Briga looked on in curious silence.

"Are you hoping we blind the 'Magyuns'?" she finally asked.

Gansükh did not bother to look up from his task. "Clean tack makes obedient horses."

Briga raised her eyebrows, but he cut her off before she could say anything.

"Warriors must keep their blades clean, sharp, and oiled, or they will not survive many battles. To a Drev'an, the horse is another weapon."

She decided to keep her mouth shut and instead turned her attention to Dagmer, who was oiling her leather armor.

"How is your shoulder?" Gansükh asked.

"Better," she affirmed, "even after this morning."

"Bind your side tightly if you wish to participate in the drills."

Her arm had been left out of the sling after she'd ended up removing it herself during the dawn greeting, and she rolled her shoulder experimentally. The flesh beneath her arm, where the blond warrior's blade had bitten into her, was tight but no longer stiff. The constant ache had dulled in recent days. She doubted she could lift a shield yet, but there were other drills.

Hoofbeats resounded in the earth. They were numerous, but gentle, and she knew from the feel that the beasts were walking. Bayanaa appeared between the tents, leading a string of six horses. Her gray was in the lead, and he whickered softly as he recognized her.

Around them other warriors were leading horses to their own tents, or guiding them to the clearing before the camp. The horses were as excited as their men, and some danced eagerly in the relatively tight confines between tents. An occasional shout indicated someone's failed attempt to calm a keyed-up mount nearby.

"Come, Lady, let's get you dressed," Dagmer offered, rising.

Bayanaa tied the horses to the string tether and would soon begin to saddle them as Dagmer led her into Batu's tent. The khan was inside, polishing his own bridle until the silver ornaments glowed in the dim light. He barely looked up as Briga shrugged out of her robes, letting the top hang down around her waist so Dagmer could apply additional binding to her wound.

"You will ride?" Batu asked, glancing at her.

"I've drilled with the men before, have I not?"

Batu paused, watching her, his expression unreadable. "This is different."

She narrowed her eyes at him, assessing his tone. "Are you riding?"

"Of course."

"Then so shall I."

"This is *different*," he intoned again. Not a warning, not quite.

Dagmer wisely remained silent, pulling yet another binding over the first two for added pressure and support. She knew what the she-wolf would likely do.

"How?" Briga finally asked.

"These are skills all Drev'an learn before we can walk."

She waited for more, eyes fixed on him expectantly.

"And it is a display for the Magyuns even more than drills for the men."

"Are you forbidding me?"

"No. You should be there, at my side. Train, practice with weapons, but only watch the horse-work."

His eyes drifted to her wound, buried under layers of supportive bandaging, and she understood. If she were to get hurt or fall from her horse before the men, before the Magyuns, her reputation would be tarnished. She nodded her understanding, meeting his gaze as she shrugged back into the robes. Dagmer helped her into the leather jerkin and bracers. Briga loosened her knife in its sheath, absently fingering the twin, empty scabbard with her injured arm. The thrall pointedly looked away from the empty sheath and handed Briga her ax. The she-wolf smiled thinly, accepting it, and tucked it through her wide leather belt.

"And your paint," Batu ordered, standing from his work.

Dagmer went to fetch it obediently, but when she returned, Batu took the bowl from her with a grin. He dipped his thumb into the paint and drew a thick line under each eye, right at her lash line, and extending slightly up onto her temples.

"You have been in two battles with me now, and came away from both badly wounded."

She scowled, but he smiled in amusement. His thumb gently touched her lips, drawing two lines down her chin and onto the column of her throat.

"Some war drills would do you good."

Outside, Bayanaa and Gansükh had finished saddling the horses. Batu carried his tack to his own stallion and readied the creature himself. Briga approached her gray gelding with a warm smile she reserved especially for the beast. The horse tossed his head once, both ears swiveling to her eagerly.

"Hello, Singer," she crooned in Velkcic, stroking the animal's velvet nose.

Gansükh eyed her curiously but said nothing, instead adjusting the bridle of his white horse and a chestnut gelding tied next to it.

"Who's is this?" she asked in Drev'an, eyeing a white gelding with a gray mane tied beside Singer.

"That is your second horse," Gansükh explained.

Briga frowned. "Second?"

"In case your gray is wounded."

"But I don't have a second horse," she reasoned.

"All Drev'an have a second mount. Or more," Batu interrupted, leading his black stallion with a tight rein.

Briga blinked at the unfamiliar horse, then at the pair of chestnuts tied beside her kheshig's mounts.

"They all need exercise," Batu went on, not allowing her time to ask a question.

She thought back to the herds of riderless horses she'd seen all those months ago in the marching column. They must have been all the spare mounts.

"You would not go into battle with only one weapon," Gansükh offered. "Nor with only one horse."

She considered for a moment before nodding and offering the back of her hand to the unfamiliar animal. The horse sniffed, then reached for her playfully with his muscular top lip. She laughed and petted his nose.

"Dagmer," she called, and the thrall stepped up obediently. "You'll take him today. You could use some training too, I think."

Briga winked as the girl smiled at her and nodded. Bayanaa and Gansükh exchanged a look but said nothing. Batu led the group through the tents to the clearing beyond, where his men were already assembling. They couldn't all drill at once, there were far too many of them to remain outside the range of the Magyun archers, so some had tethered their horses and began setting up wooden targets. Batu swung astride his big stallion, handing off his second horse to one of his personal guards.

The stallion was ready to work and danced excitedly, testing the khan's ability to control him. He unslung a bow from where it hung at his knee along the saddle and kicked his horse into a gallop. Man and beast alike cleared a path as the warhorse charged through, some trying to chase after him despite the tight reins of their riders.

Grinning madly, Batu sprinted the length of the assembled horselords, then turned his beast in a sharp display of agility and raced the other direction. He dropped the reins as he neared the targets and drew two arrows from his quiver, nocking the first in a single, fleet motion. The stallion charged on, ears pinned back against its head, knowing exactly what was expected of him. He approached a target and loosed, striking nearly dead center. He turned in the saddle as he passed, nocking, drawing, and loosing the second arrow in the span of a single breath. This struck near to the first, eliciting a cheer from the men, and Batu raised his bow briefly in acknowledgement. The signal given, a horde of riders raced to the end of the line to practice their own shots. Briga looked on, impressed. Hardly any of the riders missed, though not all of them attempted the double shot Batu had managed.

"Can you draw a bow?" Gansükh asked, his eyes drifting to her injured shoulder.

"I don't know," she responded, holding out a hand.

Gansükh passed his own to her, watching carefully as she attempted to draw.

"It hurts." She winced and allowed the string to go loose.

"Your ax then," he decided, nodding. "Join the line and graze the target with your ax. Do not try to throw it yet."

"Batu said no horse work."

He looked at her as if to ask *since when do you obey his commands?* Bayanaa laughed softly.

"Raise your left arm as if holding a shield. You can practice riding with your knees."

One side of her mouth twisted up in a grin. "Very well, master Gansükh. Dagmer will ride, as well."

Dagmer looked between them, uncertain. Even Bayanaa kept a leash on his mirth, waiting for Gansükh to react.

"Her people are warriors. I'd like for her to sharpen her skills, too."

Dagmer blinked once, watching Briga with a peculiar look shadowing her eyes. "How do you know that?"

"I can sense it," the she-wolf replied simply.

Gansükh stared hard at her, then finally nodded and handed the thrall his bow. "Only aim. No arrows."

Both women grinned, and there was a dark edge to Briga's expression that made Gansükh slightly uneasy. After tossing a mischievous glance to the thrall, Briga dug her heels into Singer's sides, and they lurched into a run, Dagmer close on her rear. Gansükh cursed and raced after them with Bayanaa.

Briga worked herself into the closest line easily and drew the ax. Gansükh rode close by her left flank, assessing and coaching her technique. For the first pass, she held the reins high in her left hand, mimicking carrying a shield. She wanted to get a feel for her horse before trying the drill completely without reins. Singer was a smooth streak of gray beneath her, his rhythm fluid enough that she kept her seat easily. As they approached the target, she raised her "shield" into position, and fixed her eyes on the spot she intended to hit. The ax swung cleanly, barely grazing the face of the target stump, if an inch further forward than she wanted.

After two more passes, she was content to let the reins sit loose across the back of her horse's neck while she leaned in to take her strike. After five passes, Gansükh dropped back to practice his own drills, satisfied that she could handle the horse well enough for his liking. She caught Batu watching her at one point, though he didn't look displeased. Instead he gestured for her to accompany him. She rode to where he waited, using the opportunity to practice steering her horse with her knees. Finally taking up the reins again, she pulled to a stop before him.

"Good," he said mildly.

She had the impression he couldn't decide whether to be angry with her for disobeying, but he grudgingly acknowledged her progress nonetheless. She nodded in thanks, fluidly sliding the ax back into her belt. He took his time assessing her posture, the way she sat in the saddle.

"Steady," he crooned, though to the horse or to her, Briga couldn't be sure.

She waited quietly as he circled her, assessing.

"You are learning to ride as a true Drev'an," he commented beneath the ghost of a smile, "but if you insist on doing this, you need better balance."

"Balance?" She blinked at him. Had she not spent the last thirty minutes or so riding hands-free?

The khan only grunted and held out a hand for her ax. Frowning slightly, she withdrew the weapon and handed it to him handle first. Batu took it and tested its balance as he looked it over before flipping it end over end in his palm.

"Drev'an youth learn to ride before they learn to walk," he commented, repeating himself. Briga only waited.

With a casual flick of the hand, he tossed it into the dirt five feet away.

"Pick it up."

Annoyed, Briga nudged her horse forward and stopped beside the downed ax. But when she kicked a foot out of the stirrups, he halted her.

"No," he repeated as she met his gaze, then he turned to scan the group of onlookers they'd drawn.

"You," he indicated with a nod to a young Drev'an astride a chestnut gelding with a tall, white sock and an off-center streak up its nose.

The youth nodded and adjusted his foot in the stirrups. He walked his horse forward, and without bothering to stop, leaned all the way to the ground to sweep up the ax. He'd come out of the saddle, completely hanging on somehow by his opposite foot, still in its stirrup, hooking onto the cantle.

"How did you do that?" she asked him frankly as he returned the ax to the khan.

"Again," the khan instructed, tossing the ax and indicating another fighter.

This one, aiming to impress his lord, approached at the trot, pausing to smile up at the she-wolf as he picked up the ax. Batu smiled, but *tutt*ed as if disappointed as he eyed the gathering riders.

"Is this the best we can do to impress the shaman?" he asked them. "Who can do better?"

The clamor drew yet more attention, and Batu signaled to clear a space. He selected two riders this time and threw the ax. Both charged after it in an all-out gallop, shoving each other to make room. One, dodging a shove, took a handful of mane and leaned over with his back to the horse's side, boots latched onto the saddle above him perilously. His friend tried to pry his fingers from the mane, but the inverted rider scooped up the ax in his free hand, smoothly reversed it as he sat up, and struck the other rider on the shoulder with its handle.

The watching riders erupted in a cheer. Briga watched, mesmerized by their skill, as the winner rode in a small victory circle with her ax held high before returning it to the khan, who returned it to her.

"You are an extension of your horse, and he is an extension of you."

She nodded, awed, and slid the ax back into her belt. The warriors were already clearing space to add this to their practice.

"Balance," he commented with a smirk.

"That'll be difficult with an injured shoulder," she huffed.

"There are other skills you can work on that will not be so taxing to your injury."

She nodded, still watching after the boisterous group.

"Get your second mount, and we will practice somewhere less crowded."

***

Ambrus scowled as he stalked through the city streets without purpose. He'd been up on the ramparts all day watching the horselords drill. The soldiers were unnerved, and Ambrus and their captains had their hands full reminding them that horses were no good for scaling stone walls. But the veterans among them silently noted how the Drev'an warriors did not appear to be suffering the effects of rationing, as they were. To look at them, one would think they had no food shortage whatsoever. And in fact, they might have plenty of meat and milk to see them through the winter, if need be, but the Drev'an had no intention of waiting outside the walls for that long.

Ambrus, no stranger to fighting himself, had been impressed with their skill on horseback. But without horses, they seemed as any other enemy. Grumbling these appeasements to himself, he rounded a corner and spied Amergin at the end of the alleyway with a woman pressed close to him. She spotted Ambrus soon after he entered the alley, and her eyes flashed in recognition. Amergin turned to follow her gaze, then immediately flushed red when he found Ambrus watching him with a bemused smirk. As he neared, the woman turned to go, allowing her fingers to trail lightly across his chest and arm.

"The lovely Dianna is well, I presume?" Ambrus asked casually as he watched her disappear down the street.

In reply, Amergin merely held up a small round of cheese and a small bag of oats.

"Oats?"

"For Clíath. The nanny-goat."

Ambrus looked as if he was about to make a highly inappropriate jest, but thought better of it.

"I didn't realize you priests were permitted to…dally," he commented instead.

To which Amergin immediately changed color again as his entire face bloomed red.

"I am a druid," he corrected, flustered, "and I'm not *dallying* with her."

Ambrus eyed him starkly, as if to say the gifts and blushing were evidence to the contrary. Composing himself by sheer willpower, the druid stepped away from the wall, expecting his friend to walk with him. Ambrus obliged.

"What brings you to me today?"

"I seek your wise council."

Amergin looked over mildly, expecting further mockery, but sobered when he noticed Ambrus wore a serious expression. Schooling his features into neutrality, he waited.

"What do your gods tell you of the siege?"

"I haven't prayed over it," Amergin answered honestly.

It was Ambrus' turn to be surprised. "You haven't?"

"Why should I? Our clan is here, there's no changing that, and our sister is still missing We've spent our energy searching for her."

In truth, both he and Cathbad were losing faith they would ever see Briga again. Her thread had dimmed and become indistinct over the last weeks.

"What does your god say?"

Ambrus scowled. "I told you, I am not Magyun."

Amergin raised his hands placatingly.

"My gods watch. They rarely speak."

Amergin noted that his friend reflexively touched the iron hilt of his sword. He was about to ask Ambrus about his origins when Eamon suddenly appeared in the street before them, his piecing green eyes fixed on Ambrus.

"Eamon!" Amergin breathed in surprise and reached out to take his chieftain by the shoulders.

This was the first time he'd ventured outside the barn since he was brought here.

"I am all right," he reassured the druid in Velkcic. "Go and see to Cathbad. I would talk with your friend."

Still recovering from the surprise, Amergin nodded and stepped back.

"Ambrus," he said, switching back to the Magyun tongue. "I'll seek an omen for you tonight."

Ambrus nodded his head in thanks, shoving aside thoughts of how *his* gods would react to such a thing. He then turned his attention to Eamon, having understood that the chieftain wished to speak with him. He eyed Eamon appraisingly. The Velk was nearly as tall as he was, with golden hair a few shades darker than his own. And while he was thin from so much time spent recovering, Ambrus could see that he normally carried a warrior's muscled body. But it was the gold torc shining at his neck that caught his attention. For his own people used a torc to distinguish nobility, and he knew its sight well. By reflex, he nodded his head respectfully.

"Chieftain…I'm glad to see you well," he offered in halting Velkcic.

One side of the chieftain's mouth curled up in a grin, stretching the red lines of his still-healing scars.

"Amergin has done well to trust you," Eamon offered in passable Magyun. "Thank you for sheltering my clan.

Ambrus nodded again. He'd offered them sanctuary as a means of learning more about the Drev'an, but from that small action, he'd found a friend and offered the city valuable healers. And placed them in further danger.

"Would you…take me to the wall? I would look upon these horselords again."

And so it was that Ambrus once again found himself on the ramparts, watching the Drev'an war display beyond. The chieftain remained stoic as he observed the war games, but Ambrus could see that his mind was turning feverishly behind his calm demeanor.

"It's been like this all day," Ambrus offered, to break the silence.

Eamon nodded once but said nothing. Ambrus caught his attention drifting to the torc again. The chieftain was a fairly young man, perhaps just a bit older than himself, but the weight of leadership appeared to sit heavily on him.

"Who is that?" he asked suddenly.

Ambrus followed his gaze to the distant war camp, where a group of archers had broken off from their training and were gathering around three riders. The figures were too distant to pick out any identifying features, but Ambrus recognized the armor of the rider astride a spirited black stallion.

"I think that's their leader."

Whatever the distant warlord had said raised a cheer from the men. The rider beside him commanded a stallion of his own, this one a roan. With a visible arrogance, he lifted a shield on one arm. His horse reared up and pivoted on its back feet before charging toward the city.

"And that?" Eamon queried.

Ambrus squinted at the lone rider. The man wore no armor or helmet. His hair was shorn into a long mane down the middle of his head.

"One of their generals," he guessed.

If the man kept riding, he'd be within archery range in seconds. Ambrus noted the creak of bowstrings as the rider drew into range. One archer fired. The rider was near the limits of the Magyun bows, but still close enough to catch the arrow on his shield. He reined to a stop then, his horse sliding to a halt. Ambrus recognized him now. He'd been on the bridge, at the forefront of the first attack. His horse screamed in rage and reared. Patting the stallion on the neck, he laughed and dismounted. Another arrow streaked at him, but flew wide.

"Hold!" Ambrus ordered. Wasting arrows on a lone rider would serve no purpose. Not unless the warlord himself was so foolish as to approach.

The warrior held out his arms, inviting another shot, then laughed and taunted them in his own tongue when none came. Shaking his head in disgust, he turned back to his horse and untied something from his saddle. With a casual arrogance, he tossed the bag on the ground. There was a weight to whatever it contained, and a hint of metal gleamed at the opening. The warrior paused to look up at the wall and its idle line of archers, then with a smirk he drew aside his robes to expose himself before urinating on the object in full view of the men on the wall. Ambrus felt his fists clench.

"Archer," he growled, making eye contact with a man he recognized as a superior shot. "Kill that man."

Without hesitation the archer drew and loosed. Without breaking his stance, the Drev'an snatched the arrow from midair with his bare hand. Cheers erupted from the war camp, which the rider acknowledged by casually raising the arrow as he finished. Two more archers loosed, but they both missed. As casually as he'd come, the horselord remounted his battle-mad stallion and trotted back to the camp.

"What was in the sack?" Eamon wondered aloud.

Nothing good, Ambrus was certain. But before he could say as much, his eye was drawn to another motion in the camp. The war leader was swinging his sword to clear a path as the third rider rose to stand on her gray horse. The horse danced, but she maintained her balance, turning it to walk out of the circle. It soon became clear that she stood on the back of not one, but two gray horses who remained impressively close together. With a flick of the reins, they took up a trot toward Sartaq, then eased into a run. Her balance was impressive, as was her control of the horses. When she reached the returning warrior on his roan stallion, she wheeled carefully and looked back over her shoulder, directly at Ambrus. Ambrus felt his blood go hot and cold all at once. He was tempted to employ the archers again, but she was well out of range. As their gazes locked, she reined to a sudden stop. There, atop the impatient horses in her paint and leathers and furs in the fading afternoon light, still as death, she cut an intimidating figure. And she knew exactly what effect she was having on them, he was certain of it.

Her eyes flitted upward as a bird flew overhead. The bird had a message tube tied to one leg. She watched it curiously, tracking its progress. From the war camp, a Drev'an eagle screamed into flight, focused intently on the messenger. The bird, sensing this new threat, redoubled its efforts to reach the city. The eagle stooped, but the bird had already reached its aviary. Someone threw a rock, breaking the eagle's dive, and it gracelessly veered upward and away, searching for any trace of its quarry. When Ambrus looked to the hated woman again, she was staring at the eagle. The warrior on the roan horse was returning to her position, all traces of arrogant mirth absent from his face now. He reined up at her side and said something. She shook her head, but didn't look away from the eagle. He grabbed for her ankle. Suddenly angry, she shook loose and kicked at his shoulder, then flicked her horses into an easy run back to the camp. Ambrus found himself watching after her with a narrowed gaze, wondering at what he'd just seen. Beside him, Eamon was pale.

"Eamon, are you all right?"

"Too much time on my feet," he mumbled, waving off the attention.

Now that the Drev'an were at a safe distance, one of the captains dispatched a small party to investigate the soiled token left beyond the wall.

"I'll see myself back," Eamon offered with a wry smile, noting Ambrus' interest. "You have duties to attend."

"Are you certain?"

Eamon merely clapped him on the shoulder and turned to go. Ambrus weighed his options. He should report his observations to General Larsson. There was a good chance the bird carried a message pertinent to the city's defense. He was curious about the bag the horselord had left, but it was unlikely to contain anything of significance. Nearing the camp, the woman dropped onto one horse's back, leading the other by the reins. Scowling once more, he turned to seek out the general.

***

Carefully but purposefully, Bayanaa and Gansükh rode at either side of Briga's horses, guiding her around the throng of lingering warriors to a place well clear of the khan's tent. Dagmer was waiting to receive them.

"You did well," she said, beaming as she helped Briga dismount.

Gansükh shared a look with Bayanaa, then abandoned the trio to see to some task of his own.

"Are you all right?" Dagmer asked, studying the she-wolf.

"That bird," Briga responded. "Something's coming."

***

The khan was furious. He'd cheered the display along with his men, but quietly left orders with the kheshig that

Commander Sartaq was to report to his tent immediately. He took a breath, schooling his face into a mask of neutrality. When the commander finally arrived, Batu smiled and clapped him on the shoulder before dismissing both of their guards.

"Well done," he crooned, sincerely appreciating the display of bravado, "but next time, maybe not so close, yes?"

Sartaq laughed and patted the arrow now thrust through his waist sash.

"This army could fight without its commander, but not so effectively," he warned, his voice cooling a few degrees to emphasize a more subtle message.

Sartaq eyed his brother, but said nothing. Instead he crossed his arms and waited for Batu to get to the point. The khan obliged him. Without warning, he drew back and punched his brother across the jaw. Outside, steel whispered at the throats of scabbards, but the kheshig wouldn't interfere unless called for. Sartaq took half a step to maintain his balance, then touched his jaw. And laughed.

"Do not touch her again. Never in front of the men," the khan growled, rubbing his knuckles, "and never in front of me."

Sartaq looked at him, incredulous. "This is about the *woman?*"

Batu didn't bother to respond, he only watched his brother with a hard expression.

"I thought she was going to make a run for the city," Sartaq elaborated, still incredulous. "You should be thanking me."

Batu huffed a laugh and shook his head once, now turning to pour them both a bowl of ayrak. "Why should she flee? Her life is here now."

"Brother," Sartaq warned, "you really think a few months with the khan would make her forget her people?"

"Those are not her people. And as far as they are concerned, she is one of us. Have you forgotten already that she fought on the bridge, as well? They would kill her as surely as they would kill you, given the chance."

Sartaq accepted a bowl from his brother and drank irritably.

"Then why did she linger?" the commander growled.

Batu shrugged. "Perhaps she saw an omen in that messenger bird. I will ask her."

Sartaq tossed his brother a pointed look but said nothing.

"She does not know," Batu explained and finished his bowl, then changed the subject. "Why did you burn the crops?"

"You are like a woman, little brother, worrying over every little thing."

"We do not have enough food to last the winter, Sartaq; we could have used them."

"I thought we should send a message that would crush their spirits."

The brothers glared at one another for a moment. The khan was their undisputed leader, but the commander was the focal point of the army. Each knew they couldn't push the other too far for fear of destabilizing the army, and each held that knowledge to their advantage.

"Besides," Sartaq went on airily, "I did not burn everything."

Batu snorted in concession. "Next time tell me in advance."

The commander raised his bowl in mock salute.

"Are the machines in position?"

"As soon as darkness falls."

"Then I leave it to you, brother."

300

***

"Eamon," Ambrus breathed at seeing the chieftain appear in the door.

He'd been waiting impatiently for the lord to return and was dismayed at his pallid color. Cathbad was already preparing a seat for him, leaving the younger druid to guide him inside to the fire.

"Are you all right?"

Eamon stayed the question with a gesture and briefly surveyed what was left of his clan before allowing the druids to usher him to a seat.

"What did you see?" one of the Velkcic warriors asked.

The chieftain sighed heavily. "The only chance this city has of breaking the siege is if the horde runs out of food before they do. If it comes to fighting, the trained soldiers are outnumbered."

"What do we do?" another of them asked.

"There's nothing we *can* do," Eamon admitted. "Only wait, and hope to defend ourselves when the city falls."

The Velkcic survivors met this news with a range of expressions. Some were grim-faced, some disheartened. Some were angry.

"Why did you bring us here, Amergin?" one of the latter demanded.

"Amergin," the chieftain cut in with a hard edge to his voice, "did the best he could to lead you all to safety during my illness. He could not have known this would happen. I would have done the same."

"It is in our Pattern," Cathbad offered in a neutral if somewhat weary tone.

"Will we ever see our homes again?"

This question was from Oisean, the youngest of the survivors, who'd left a new wife in their village. It seemed a lifetime ago.

"My visions are not clear, but many will survive this city and its ordeal."

That news sparked a ripple of relief and hope. Amergin noted the chief druid hadn't said, "all."

"Go and rest, brothers," Eamon chimed in again with a little more forced cheer. "Keep your sword arms strong, for we will fight again."

He smiled knowingly at those who'd chosen to take a turn on the wall, augmenting the Magyun soldiers.

"Fetch your mead cups; tonight each man receives a full measure."

That was the surest way to rouse the men from their gloom, and a mild cheer broke from them at this unexpected indulgence. Amergin watched the chieftain. Though Eamon smiled, it didn't quite reach his eyes. Noting his attention, Eamon clapped a comforting hand on his shoulder as the warriors broke to seek their cups.

"Cathbad, come and speak with me. Amergin will look after the men for a while."

Amergin nodded, understanding the dismissal, and turned to go, but Eamon held him back.

"Take my ration. You've earned it."

This time the lord's smile was genuine, and Amergin responded in kind, leaving the chieftain and his chief druid to their consultation.

***

Ambrus was furious. He was tired of this city, and being trapped here only chafed him further. And at the hands of those horse-loving whoresons, no less. His meeting with General Larsson had gone well into the evening, and he stalked now through the darkened city with the restless rage of a tethered beast.

They'd been interrupted shortly after his arrival in the general's quarters by Braxus. The Emorian had been informed by the captain of the watch that the object left by the Drev'an rider had been an intact Magyun helmet. Inside the helmet was the severed head of Lord Rybus. The message had not been lost on any of them—their reserve force to the south had been defeated. They were all furious. There'd been no indications of a battle having taken place at all.

"Perhaps the force is still intact, but leaderless?" Braxus had suggested, but they all knew that to be unlikely.

They'd been strategizing over how to inform the king and the rest of the council when more news arrived. The bird they'd received was from the northern outpost. The force had been marching south these weeks to rescue the city, and would be within striking distance as soon as the following night. It was a stroke of pure luck. While the force was relatively small, just two hundred men, it had the element of surprise. If they could attack the Drev'an rear, they could inflict disproportionate damage and interdict their supply route. However, the original plan called for support from Lord Rybus' force in the south, and that was now almost certainly destroyed. None of the seasoned veterans in the room felt the ploy would succeed, but there was no way now to notify the northern commander of the change. Perhaps they could do enough damage to force the horselords to rethink their ability to linger throughout the winter.

After hours of debate, they opted to allow the attack to proceed, and would prepare a force to ride from the city as an aid and a distraction once they struck. Larsson had left to notify the king, leaving Braxus and Ambrus to their own devices. Ambrus had quietly taken leave of his friend, needing to pace and work off the anger he was feeling. What he wouldn't give to have a woman right now.

As he paced, his mind wandered. He imagined turning a corner to find *her* standing alone in the darkened street, with that infuriating look on her face. He imagined stalking up to her, taking her by the throat, slamming her into the stone wall, and—

A motion off to his left caught his attention and wrested him back to the present. Ambrus stopped dead in his tracks, alert to his warrior senses. Something moved again, and he turned to look. It was a...woman, he realized with a start. This one pulled a hood up to hide not tawny hair, but dark. She was exiting Lord Heinrich's quarters. The sight of her caused a ripple of unease to settle in his gut. Was this the paramour he had mentioned so often in court? Their unwitting spy?

"You, there," he called out.

Startled, she whirled to face him. For a moment she looked familiar, and he narrowed his gaze in an attempt to place her. In the next moment there was a strange whirring sound, followed by a splintering crack as something crashed into the wooden structure beside him.

He ducked instinctively, and the woman dashed off in terror. A skinny cow bayed in protest. After a moment it became clear nothing else was going to happen, and Ambrus slowly rose to examine the source of the noise. As he drew closer, a woman started screaming on the next street over. He felt the small hairs on the back of his neck stand up. The scream was soon joined by others scattered loosely in the area. Ambrus sifted uncertainly through the splintered wood until he found what had caused it. There, partially covered by a broken slat, was a severed human arm.

Chapter 27

The onslaught continued off and on throughout the night. The dismembered corpses could only be those of Rybus' men; there were too many to be merely prisoners taken from the bridge, or from scouting missions. Worse, one of the festering tokens had landed squarely in the well near the market. The nearby inhabitants had found it at first light, but there was no telling how long it had been there. The water was surly contaminated and wouldn't be safe to drink for some time.

"When is the garrison due here?" King Bela questioned furiously.

"Perhaps tonight," General Larsson offered. "Maybe two nights at the latest."

"Can we get word to them?"

Larsson hesitated. "We have one bird, my lord, but even if it can find them on the move as they are, it would give away their position."

"If it's not snatched from the sky by the damned eagles," Lord Heinrich added sourly.

"My lord," Larsson began again, eyeing those in the chamber meaningfully.

Scowling, the king nodded once and dismissed all but the small council. Ambrus shot a glance to the general, who shook his head, indicating that he should stay.

In a matter of moments the hall had been cleared of all except the king, General Larsson, Lord Heinrich, and three other ministers. And Ambrus.

"Forgive me, my lord, but I fear we have a traitor in the court."

The king's eyebrows shot up in surprise, the expression mirrored on the faces of everyone there. Except Ambrus. The king followed his gaze, features hardening when he recognized the blond mercenary.

"Of course," Bela growled, incorrectly inferring the meaning behind his presence in the small council. "The pagan foreigner."

Ambrus bristled at that but waited patiently.

"You never should have taken him in."

"If I hadn't," Larsson answered smoothly, "he would be rotting in the dungeon with his kinsman, and we'd be none the wiser of this potential plot."

King Bela had the grace to look mildly rebuked and allowed his features to soften. Ambrus had stiffened again at the reference to Sitric as "his kinsman" but remained stoic. Patient. After a suitable pause, the king gestured magnanimously.

"Very well then. Enlighten us…?" He shot a questioning look to Larsson.

"Ambrus," the general supplied.

"Ambrus," Bela concluded with a nod.

"I've seen it before, my lord." Ambrus began in a calm, confident tone. "The Drev'an send in or recruit spies long before they attack."

"You are from the north lands," the king replied skeptically, "yet you're an expert on the Drev'an?"

"Their ambitions are wide-ranging," he replied tightly, anger evident despite the leash on his bearing—but this was not the time to reveal his true intent.

Recognizing a genuine, and favorable, animosity in this man toward their mutual enemy, the king relaxed slightly and gestured for Ambrus to continue.

"One such spy is in your dungeon," he began again, voice tight with control, "though not a spy against *your* city."

"I understand how a spy might be useful before their forces arrive, but the gates are closed. How would they communicate?"

"I don't know, my lord," Ambrus admitted.

Bela paused, watching him. The other council members held their silence, waiting as well.

"Why bring this information to me now?"

Ambrus caught the warning in his words. The implication was that Ambrus could have brought this up sooner...or withheld altogether.

"I didn't realize it might be happening until last night. And the Drev'an agents may still be within the city."

"Last night?"

"Yes, lord. The...*projectiles* seemed to be randomly aimed, but I suspect there were targets in mind."

Larsson nodded, encouraging him.

"The attacks were heaviest around the two water wells within reach of their siege engines. I suspect they were attempting to hasten the city's surrender by contaminating the water. They knew the location of the wells."

"That information could have been passed weeks ago."

"And probably was," Ambrus agreed.

"If spies are still within the city, would it not be easier to poison the wells directly?"

"Not if they are unable to move in and out of the city, and not without alerting us to their presence. But someone could have dropped a body into the well during the chaos. It's very unlikely their catapults would have hit such a small target without assistance."

"The spy would have had to know when the attack would take place."

"Exactly," Ambrus agreed with a glint in his eye. "This wasn't planned weeks ago."

The king frowned, finally having been led onto Ambrus' line of thinking.

"Who was the first to discover the…item in the well?"

"Your Grace," Lord Heinrich interrupted smoothly, "I don't mean to unravel this plot of spies, but the northern garrison is our immediate concern."

Bela nodded sagely. "All the more reason to keep knowledge of their advance contained."

Good luck with that, Ambrus thought to himself. *Half the garrison has already seen the message.*

"Lord Larsson, place a watch on the uncontaminated wells, and prepare your forces. When the northern garrison attacks, we must be ready to support them."

The general bowed his head respectfully. "Yes, Your Grace."

***

Amergin shook himself awake, deeply troubled by the vision he'd received in his dreams. Cathbad had been staring into the fire, seeking visions of his own, but looked over when the younger druid stirred.

"What is it?"

Amergin felt as if he'd been panting and drew in a steadying breath. "I don't know."

The chief druid merely watched him, waiting. Cathbad seemed to have aged in the last weeks, more quickly than the rest of them. His silver hair seemed thinner, his flesh looser. Amergin knew the chief druid had never stopped searching for Briga, and the strain appeared to be weighing on him.

"Perhaps…it's time to let her go," he suggested quietly, though the notion was a physical pain in his chest.

The creases in Cathbad's face deepened. "Did you see her?"

"No," Amergin admitted with a sigh. "I was seeking an omen."

"What did you see?"

The younger man hesitated, unsettled. "A wolf. A wolf carrying decaying flesh in its jaws."

Cathbad waved a hand dismissively.

"It's all this…" He gestured to the door, indicating the highly distasteful bombardment from the previous evening. "It's clouded my mind."

Cathbad frowned slightly but said nothing.

"Have *you* seen her?" Amergin pressed.

"No," he sighed heavily, "but I sense she is still out there."

Amergin eyed him curiously. "You believe she still lives?"

The lines in the old druid's face deepened even more. "I am certain of it. Though I fear we may no longer recognize her."

"What do you mean?"

The old druid didn't respond. He watched Amergin for a moment, as if considering how to craft the words, then cut his gaze briefly to Eamon, before tossing a handful of herbs on the fire and refocusing his gaze on the flames once more.

***

As the daylight began to fade, so too did the pain in Briga's head. Thanks to yesterday's dawn greetings and the afternoon of horse drills, her wounded shoulder ached terribly. Fearful that she might have torn her wound open, Dagmer and Sartaq's shaman had examined her in Batu's tent. The wound was intact, but inflamed. The shaman returned sometime later with a bowl of ayrak. No, not ayrak, Briga realized as she sipped, but some kind of potion. She recognized it faintly. She had tasted this before.

"It will help you sleep," the shaman promised in her strange voice.

As Briga lay among the furs with her head swimming, she realized she *did* recognize the potion. The shaman had drugged her with it the night she'd sacrificed the stoat and worked her own magic, the powerful and taboo magic of joining, of transferring life energy, upon Batu. Alarmed, she fought against the growing pull of sleep, but the shaman sensed her thoughts and laid a calming hand on her brow.

"No magic tonight," she soothed.

Briga need not have feared. She slept soundly through the night and didn't wake until well past dawn. The morning light brought with it a headache, as if she'd been up all night drinking ale. She spent the day curled up on herself while Dagmer, Gansükh, and Batu fussed over her in turns.

By the afternoon, Batu had sent the others away, opting to stay with her himself. In a rare display of tenderness, he cradled her head in his lap, absently smoothing her hair as he penned some correspondence or another. She dozed off and on. But now, finally, as the light was fading once more, her headache was fading as well. She lay now, watching him quietly.

310

"Feeling better?" he asked, catching sight of her attention.

She nodded. "What are you writing?"

"An account of our conquest."

He took a few moments to finish the passage he'd been working on, then rose to call for someone outside. A serving woman arrived shortly after and handed him a bowl, which he in turn offered to Briga. She eyed the milky liquid distrustfully.

"Milk tea," he clarified.

And so it was. None of the chalky taste of the shaman's potion, only the soothing warmth of hot, salty milk.

"Warlord," she mused uncertainly, "yet kind to me. Why?"

Batu watched her for a moment, considering. By way of answer, the khan moved to sit behind her and gently pulled her hair over one shoulder. He kissed the back of her neck briefly, then set to work loosening tight muscles in her neck and shoulders with strong fingers. She hummed in appreciation, allowing herself to be plied.

"Warrior or musician, I don't know which is more mysterious." She paused to sip at her tea, enjoying his attentions. "The musician perhaps. The warrior I understand, but I don't know that other Batu."

"War is art. Music is art," he reasoned, hands venturing only slightly lower on her back and easing the tension there.

"I enjoy hearing you play," she remarked lightly, voice falling to a near whisper. "It reminds me of home."

His fingers stalled for a brief moment. Leaning forward, Batu lightly nipped at a spot on the back of her neck, causing her body to arch away and gooseflesh to pebble her arms. He chuckled lowly.

"A woman's body is a lovely instrument. Shall I play for you?"

His breath against her skin as he spoke elicited another subtle response and another ripple of gooseflesh. She laughed despite herself. Perhaps it was the lingering effects of the potion, perhaps it was the lingering sense of affection, or loneliness, or just the tender attention, but Briga found herself turning to face the khan and allowing him to kiss her.

Outside, Gansükh had lasted all of ten minutes before rising irritably to pace. Bayanaa watched him with wry amusement, while Dagmer was clearly sympathetic. He was unsure which of them agitated him more.

"Brother, come sit, I will find us some ale," Bayanaa offered.

"I am fine."

"The khan is *fine*; he knows what he is doing. So does she, for that matter."

"Bayanaa," Dagmer whispered harshly and pinched him on the arm.

"You should worry less about the khan and more about keeping watch," Gansükh retorted sternly.

Bayanaa folded his arms but said nothing more. His flat glare spoke enough.

"Stay here then, I will patrol."

Dagmer and the smaller kheshig watched their companion stalk into the night. When he was out of sight, the thrall blew out a breath, drawing Bayanaa's attention.

"He is a fine mood tonight," the younger man commented dryly.

Dagmer blinked at him.

"Surely you noticed," Bayanaa continued, incredulous.

"Men," she responded in exasperation.

Around them the camp sounds were muted, though many of the men were still awake. Politely ignoring the sounds from the khan's tent, they focused instead on the distant steady sound of the river.

Beside her Bayanaa tensed suddenly, and the sound of a sword rasping free of its scabbard issued in the distance.

"What?" Dagmer questioned, alert.

The sounds behind them had stopped as well, as if the others had also heard the blade. Gansükh hurried back, sword glinting in the firelight.

"Bayanaa," his hissed, warning.

But the khan himself stepped out into the night, wrapping a belt around his unfastened robe. A moment later Briga appeared at his side, smoothing her hair.

"Fetch Commander Sartaq," he ordered, and Dagmer hurried off.

***

The Magyuns of the northern garrison had been carefully approaching the king's city for several nights now. They'd ridden hard at the first summons, but eventually had to slow their approach to a deliberate crawl in order to detect Drev'an scouts and avoid detection themselves. They knew the enemy had arrayed his forces to the east and north of the city, controlling the only standing bridge for miles in either direction. Lord Rybus held his force to the south, which would hopefully keep the invaders' attention drawn south and west. They had no information on what defenses might be at the Drev'an rear, other than a probable supply route leading back to a larger camp somewhere.

The supply base would be defended, but even if defeated, would not attrite the horselords quickly enough for the city to survive the winter. No, the only hope was to swing wide to the east. If their relatively small force could cross the river, they could conduct a simultaneous assault on both ends of the bridge, with the help of Lord Rybus, and support from the city itself.

Two scouts had made it all the way to the river undetected and had obtained useful information. The log jam that had rendered the river fordable to the invaders was still intact. There would be a watch post keeping an eye on it, certainly, but its position was unknown. More, a signal fire had been lit atop the city ramparts. There had been no prearranged meaning. With no obvious signs of danger, and with scouts reporting the Drev'an elements to be where they were expected, the northern garrison was forced to conclude the signal meant they were to proceed as planned, the city was prepared to support, and perhaps that Lord Rybus had begun to move up the eastern bank. And so it was decided, they would cross and prepare to attack.

The men dismounted, leaving their horses far enough away not to alert the Drev'an. For the next hour, they crept slowly and quietly through the frosty night, alert for sentries or any sign of trouble.

At last they reached the river and paused to assess. The makeshift dam was indeed intact, and even fortified in places. Likely the Drev'an intended to keep an escape route open in case they needed it. The bridge would be too narrow to withdraw in large numbers with any haste. Below the damn, the river was wide and still fast-flowing, but appeared to be only waist deep. The captain selected their best swimmer to test the crossing. He would carry across a length of rope to aide others against the current, if the water wasn't as shallow as it seemed.

The soldier silently slipped out of his armor and waded into the cold water. He stepped carefully, bracing himself against the current in case of unsteady footing. As he progressed, the water crept up past his knees, then to mid-thigh, then up to his belly, but no higher. The bottom was rocky, and he had to slow down, adding minutes to an already long crossing. All the while, archers stood ready in case of an ambush. Eventually the soldier made it across, proving the water would reach no higher than mid-torso on an average man, and crouched to survey that side of the river. He scouted for a few additional tense minutes before deciding the area was clear and tying off the rope to some spindly trees.

Their captain was a cautious man. Knowing their archers could barely range the swollen far bank, he opted to send half of them across in the first wave so they might have adequate defense if the Drev'an camp awoke to discover them. Knowing now that the water wasn't deep enough to drown a man, they would all cross in their armor to speed their reaction on the far side. The captain himself would cross with the first wave as well. After a few whispered commands, the first group of perhaps thirty men ventured out.

The captain sucked in a breath at the first shock of cold water climbing his legs, but he knew they'd be warm enough soon. Men around him stumbled on the rocky bottom, some opting to hold the guide rope, while others went without it. When the first group had gotten about a quarter of the way across, the next group of about thirty started themselves. Continuing in this fashion, nearly all the men would be in the water together at one point, but it was the fastest way to cross and minimize risk.

Everything was proceeding according to plan until the first group was perhaps two thirds of the way across. The captain had fallen slightly behind while visually surveying the far bank and feeling along the guide rope through the deepest part of the river, but when he checked again, he seemed to be short a few men. Frowning, he glanced behind for stragglers. The fastest of the second wave was catching up, making it difficult to keep track of individuals. Some sound from ahead caught his attention, and he turned again in time to see one of the archers stumble and slip beneath the surface. Too far away to help, the captain continued forward and watched for him to resurface. He did not. Nearby, another man fell and failed to reappear.

Three quarters of the way across, it seemed as if all around him, men were falling. Some resurfaced, sputtering, but very few. He was knocked off balance when a man grabbed him from behind, gasping. The captain had no time to draw his sword before recognizing the panicked face of a young swordsman. The youth had lost his helmet and chest plate to the river.

"A trap!" the youth gasped loudly. "There are deep pits—"

The captain nearly shoved him under again, desperate to silence his noise.

"Shh!" he urged, helping him up again.

"A trap," the soldier rasped again, quieter this time.

The captain looked around. *Surely not...* The river had a rocky bed, and what seemed like pits were likely only deep spots. Still, that would drown a man in armor. More rope was needed, urgently.

A different sound drew his attention forward again. One of the swordsmen had almost reached the far bank, but now staggered awkwardly. He fell sideways, but the captain clearly saw the arrow sprouting from his neck. With a creeping sense of horror, he looked up to see a line of five horsemen perched atop the low ridge beyond, just watching. A sixth rider to one end of the line was loading a second arrow.

"Ambush!" he cried out, abandoning stealth.

The majority of his force was in the deepest part of the river, unable to effectively return fire or seek cover. Those within the archer's range scrambled to the bank, over half succumbing to the deep spots and failing to rise. Those who made it across were met by a war party. He gritted his teeth. If they were going to die, they'd take some of the horselords with them.

***

Briga sat to one side of the khan, watching the men in the river impassively.

316

"Enough of them will make it across to bloody the nose of your war party, Commander Sartaq."

Sartaq grunted his agreement, unconcerned.

"How did you know they would cross here?" she asked Batu.

"I wanted them to cross here," he replied. "That is why we left the dam intact. The debris is too unstable to cross, but just below…"

He paused and looked sidelong at her. "Do you remember the boar pits?"

She blinked in surprise and looked at him. "Yes…"

He gestured to the river below, where the men stumbled and fell. "Magyun armor is heavy. It makes them slow in a fight…and useless in the water."

She shuddered, realizing the implications. What Batu did not tell her was that he'd had ample time to prepare. They had intercepted the birds sent between this force and the city that confirmed what his spy had reported. He knew their timing and approach. Allowing the final bird to "escape" back to the city during their horsemanship demonstrations had ensured the Magyun force would continue as planned. It also provided the leverage he needed for his next move.

Gansükh eyed the she-wolf carefully. There was a tense set to her shoulders, and her back was tight and straight. Something in her posture made him uneasy.

"You resort to traps now? I thought they were dishonorable."

The khan eyed her sharply. "You wanted me to end this quickly, did you not? War and hunting are not the same. If not for you, we would never have thought of such a thing."

He reached out to touch her cheek, and to Briga's credit, she didn't flinch.

***

Atop the ramparts, Ambrus slammed his fist against the stones. The attack was failing, and there was nothing they could do to support the garrison at the river, not without taking on the entire Drev'an force encamped around the bridge. A force attacking from the south gate wouldn't get there in time, either. At this rate, the attackers would all be dead before word would even reach the palace. This attempt to break the siege was over before it had begun. Frustrated, he turned away to stalk off into the night. If he were to stand any chance of surviving the city's eventual fall, he'd need to lay plans now.

By daylight it was all over. Remnants of the northern troop that had made it across the river fought for their lives, but the battle was short lived. The city's only hope now would be to somehow last until the spring thaw enabled Emorians or one of the distant Magyun outposts to ride to their rescue. It was a slim chance at best

Chapter 28

For the next two nights, the Drev'an expressed their displeasure with the attempted attack by mutilating the bodies of the dead and catapulting them into the city. One particularly vocal captive was launched still alive over the city walls, which ceased further protest by those fortunate enough to have been captured earlier. The damage was worse to the people's minds than to their homes. In addition to the sheer horror of severed body parts raining down throughout the night, the city folk had known the northern force was their only real remaining hope. The sound of weeping had ululated through the streets for hours. It had broken Amergin's heart to hear it. Unbidden thoughts of Dianna floated to the front of his mind, concerned for her safety and wellbeing. It was only with effort that he was able to free his thoughts of her to focus on his divinations.

Inexplicably, it was the sound of laughter that finally dragged him out of his druidic trance. Amergin blinked into the gloom. He and Cathbad were alone in the barn. The older druid was gaunt and haggard, still in the depths of his own trance. The siege was taking a hard toll on him. Concerned, Amergin stretched stiff limbs as he rose to his feet and crossed to the door. He blinked in the strong daylight, having grown too accustomed to the barn's dim interior. A trio of thin Magyuns wandered by, their eyes creased with laughter. The young druid stared, uncomprehending, at the seemingly out-of-place mirth. Puzzled, he stepped outside and ambled in the direction of a crowd that seemed to be gathering at the end of the street.

"Amergin."

He turned at the sound of his name to find Dianna advancing up the street in his direction.

319

"Dianna, I'm glad to see you are well."

She squeezed his arm affectionately as she reached him, though her smile was tired and strained.

"It was a long night." She waved away the concern evident on his face. "I hope this will be over soon."

"I fear it will be."

They both turned as someone laughed quietly nearby.

"Do you know what's happening?"

She shook her head, then linked her arm through his. "Perhaps we can find out together."

Smiling despite himself, Amergin led the way toward the distant crowd. Whatever was happening, it seemed to be concentrated along the more northern end of the city. They picked up snatches of conversation as they walked, though nothing that made much sense of the situation.

"Amergin!"

The druid looked up to find Rorik grinning down at him like a one-eyed fox. The warrior motioned for him to come join them up on the wall. Dropping Dianna's arm, he led the way up a makeshift ladder to find Eamon and all his surviving warriors clustered at the ramparts. Dianna followed, but kept her distance.

"So this is where you all went," he scolded softly, reverting to the Velkcic tongue. "What's happening?"

"Look," Rorik instructed and clapped him on the shoulder with one hand. The other stretched out to indicate something beyond the wall.

Below, the Drev'an force was dismounted and scattered in the fields. They seemed to be concentrated along the brush lines rather than out in the open, but those who ventured farther afield remained out of archery range. He scanned the river's edge for any sign of the previous skirmish, but a burst of laughter pulled his attention away again. A mixed group of soldiers and townsfolk were laughing and pointing over the wall. Amergin followed the line of their attention…and frowned. In the brush, a group of three Drev'an were jumping after a bird that seemed to be eluding them among the branches.

"What…?"

"They seem to have lost their tolerance for the Magyun messenger birds," Rorik explained with a clear undertone of mirth.

"So they're…catching them?"

"As far as we can tell," Rorik confirmed.

Puzzled, Amergin watched as bands of horsemen chased birds. Several eagles were aloft as well, plucking from the sky any smaller birds brave enough to try and outrun them or escape the Drev'an hunting in the trees.

"It would appear they didn't like being surprised at the river," Eamon commented evenly.

Unlike the warriors, the chieftain showed no hint of amusement as he watched the activity below. He wore the same pensive look Amergin had noted many times on Ambrus' face when he analyzed tactics. Some warrior's instinct, no doubt.

Drawn by a druid's instinct, Amergin moved casually to stand beside the chieftain.

"Where is Cathbad?" Eamon asked quietly.

"Still praying."

The word seemed woefully inadequate to describe the depth of trance the chief druid was in, but he knew Eamon would understand.

Eamon nodded to himself. "I'm worried about him."

Amergin felt a chill of dread at the words. He was worried, too, but could never say so. Instead he turned a cool and assessing gaze on his chieftain.

"He hasn't been the same since Briga was taken."

"No," Amergin agreed.

Eamon looked at him briefly before returning his attention to the distant Drev'an camp. An uncomfortable silence settled between them, which the druid finally broke.

"We…all miss her, my lord."

He patted Eamon's shoulder once, intending comfort. He knew of the mutual attraction between the young druid and their chieftain, but such a thing could never be.

"She is alive."

There was real conviction in Eamon's tone. He turned to look at Amergin then, his gaze like a palpable weight, and the druid found himself feeling slightly uneasy.

"I trust in Cathbad's visions, my lord."

Eamon was looking at him in the same way a wolf eyes a deer, coolly assessing. He'd heard the unspoken words. There was a fever-brightness to him in the chill air.

"I have seen her, Amergin."

The druid blinked, incredulous. Had Eamon's head not fully healed after all? Should he be up and moving around so much?

"I think you have seen her, too."

Amergin felt himself frowning now with real concern. He hadn't been able to feel more than a whisper of Briga's Pattern in all these long months.

"Amergin? What is wrong?"

A female voice and feather light touch on his arm drew his attention, and Eamon's as well.

"Is it the invaders?"

He remembered then. She did not speak his tongue and must have assumed the exchange between himself and his chieftain was more bad news.

"No, Dianna," he responded in Magyun and smiled reassuringly, patting her hand. "Just clan business."

Eamon was smiling faintly as he watched the exchange, but there was still something else at the edge of his expression.

"Ah," she began awkwardly. "I suppose I should be going, then."

"No, there is no need..."

But her attention had already strayed, her eyes glinting as she recognized someone in the crowd.

"Perhaps your handsome captain friend will have news. I will tell you what he says."

She winked and was gone before he could protest, and he noted with an unpleasant feeling that she was picking her way along the wall toward Ambrus in the distance.

"Well, well," Eamon commented after a few moments. "I thought it was *all* druids who were discouraged from earthly attachments, not just the women."

Amergin looked at him sharply, not appreciating the barb.

"She's not an *attachment*," he countered tightly.

"I can see that," the chieftain returned smugly.

"Come now, m'lord, Amergin wouldn't know the first thing about 'attachments'," jeered Kessan, another of the warriors, and they all burst into laughter at the insinuation.

323

Amergin felt himself flush red but was powerless to stop it.

"What would you know about it, Kessan boy-o?" Rorik cut in smoothly. "The only attaching you've done lately is to your own hand."

That brought fresh laughter, including from Kessan himself after an indignant moment, and Amergin threw a grateful look to Rorik.

"All right, all right," Eamon said soothingly to calm the men. "Amergin, help me down and let's go check on old Cathbad. The rest of you, watch them chase birds as long as you wish."

Amergin nodded obediently. He cast one last look over his shoulder toward Ambrus as Eamon swung onto the ladder. The blond warrior's face lit up with a predatory gleam as Dianna reached him. Turning away, Amergin felt a stab of…jealousy. The realization disturbed him.

***

His eyes fluttered open to a familiar but out-of-place sound. Slowly, his senses awoke from their daze and he registered the same cold, damp stone behind him. The same filthy stone beneath him. The same dank, chill air. Below the door was a slender strip of light, broken where someone stood beyond. His eyes narrowed. It was too early for his evening meal. It must be Ambrus then, back to torment him. A key grated in the lock as it turned, and the door squealed on its rusted hinges. Meager light spilled into the room from a lit sconce, and with it, a familiar smell.

"Lilac," he rasped as Ambrus watched him from the doorway.

Curiously, he was alone.

"Have you been with a woman, Ambrus?"

Ignoring the question, Ambrus stalked into the cell, leaving his torch in the hallway sconce.

"I can smell her on you." He grinned lazily. "I don't remember the last time I had a woman."

The sound of his boots scraped to a stop, and he stood staring down at the prisoner.

"Your betro—"

"Shut up," Ambrus finally snapped.

The prisoner had opened his mouth to retort, but shut it again as Ambrus tossed something at him. His reactions were slow, and it thumped into his chest before he could deflect. Belatedly his hands closed around the bundle, and he looked at it curiously. The thing in his hands smelled strongly of lilac. And beneath that, the faint scent of some roast fowl. Frowning in distrust, the prisoner turned his gaze once more to Ambrus.

"Do you remember how to pull an oar, Siggi?"

"What is this?"

Ambrus paused. "Eat, Siggi. I have to take whatever's left out with me."

Sitric cast him a hard glance that lasted the space of several heartbeats. Finally he sighed, pulled a bit of meat free from the wrapping of lilac leaves, and ate suspiciously.

Ambrus quirked a grin. "What good would it do to poison you now?"

Sitric scowled, but tore off more meat. It was hard to eat slowly. He was hungry, and he couldn't remember the last time they had given him meat. But he also knew his body was likely to reject such rich food, so he ate slowly and sparingly to improve his odds of keeping it down. His mind worked at this turn of events with interest. Clearly the lilac was meant to mask the smell of meat. Therefore this visit wasn't sanctioned by his masters. Something had changed, which meant whatever was happening in the city was significant.

"You could have brought meat sooner," he growled around a mouthful.

"Gather your strength, you whoreson," Ambrus growled back, but his tone lacked venom. "We need to think about leaving soon, and I'll be damned if I'm carrying you anywhere."

"Ah, Ambrus, you miss your chance to leave me behind for good."

The blond warrior was silent and faced the prisoner with a cold glare. His fingers found the hilt of the Kithian blade at his belt and absently fingered the sigil carved there. Ravn's sigil. No, he would be twice damned to leave this bastard behind to cause more trouble.

"There's still unfinished business between you and I."

Indeed there was. Ambrus had never shown any interest in freeing him previously, which meant whatever was happening, it was more dangerous to leave him behind. *But more dangerous to which of us?* he wondered. He'd seen that blond bastard touch the hilt of a new blade out of the side of his vision and recognized its construction. *Interesting...*

***

Briga sat staring at the ground outside Batu's tent. She hadn't been herself for several days now, instead quiet and withdrawn. It distressed Dagmer and her kheshig greatly to see her in such a state. Even Batu noticed, but kept his distance, focusing instead on seeing to his army. Quietly the thrall approached and sank onto the frosty ground beside her lady. Briga didn't look up, she merely sat there with her knees drawn up. Cautiously Dagmer touched her arm, hoping to break her attention.

"Will you tell me what's troubling you?"

"Something terrible is coming, Dagmer," she said in a low tone.

Gansükh and Bayanaa exchanged a brief look.

"What is it?"

Briga shook her head. "I don't know. But I can feel it."

"Mistress, it isn't good for you to dwell on these things."

The look she turned on Dagmer then was laced with a nameless grief. It chilled the slave's blood to see it.

"Please," she tried again, closing her fingers around Briga's arm, "let's go for a ride, just the four of us. We'll find a place away from the camp where you can pray."

The she-wolf laid an icy hand atop Dagmer's, her grip surprisingly strong.

"…I'm late," she finally confided, her voice barely above a whisper.

She did not dare flick her gaze over to Gansükh or Bayanaa. Dagmer felt her blood chill, but forced a smile to her face.

"Is that what's worrying you?" she asked in the same near whisper. "It happens to all women from time to time. You haven't felt ill?'

Briga shook her head. She felt young and vulnerable, and hated it.

"Fear not." Dagmer flashed her a comforting smile. In a louder voice, she called to Bayanaa, "My mistress is cold. I'm going to find her some warm broth. Please make her a fire."

Bayanaa nodded, scanning her face for any hidden clues or meaning, but Dagmer knew she betrayed none of her thoughts. Gansükh, happy to have something to do, set off to retrieve more wood. Bayanaa stood awkwardly as he watched the she-wolf, wondering if he should say anything.

"Death is a part of battle," he ventured gently, puzzled by her state. "Those Magyuns at the river died with honor."

Her gaze moved to him slowly, but she smiled a thin reassurance. "The death of our enemies is no concern to me."

"They are not likely to attack again. These stone dwellers do not war in the winter. Is that what troubles you?"

She frowned, uncertain, and searched her thoughts. Could the vague sense of threat be from more fighting? Perhaps the city wouldn't be so easily taken as she'd hoped. Or was the source of that faint but insistent *tug* on her senses in danger?

Bayanaa opened his mouth to speak again, but stopped as a firm hand touched his back. Dagmer gave him a look as she brushed past him and sat beside her mistress.

"Here," she began, offering a warm bowl of fragrant broth. "This will ease your mind."

Briga paused with the bowl raised to her lips, eyebrows raised questioningly.

"It's only broth, nothing more," Dagmer reassured her.

The she-wolf frowned but sipped quietly as she watched Gansükh build up a fire. Dagmer shot him a look, warning both males to keep their distance.

"Mistress," Dagmer began uncomfortably.

The tone of her voice cut through Briga's brooding and drew her full attention.

"You asked me once where I was from."

"I did," Briga recalled, realizing now that the question had never been answered.

"I'm from a place called Stonvik. Far to the north, on the coast. Have you heard of it?"

"No…"

"It's a Kith settlement."

"Who are the Kith?"

Dagmer regarded her strangely. Briga had seen this look from her several times before, but couldn't determine its meaning. The thrall's gaze dropped to her belt, to the fighting knife sheathed there.

"Where did you get your weapons, my lady?"

The change of topic startled her. She took a measured sip of broth before responding. "I've had them since I was a child, I suppose. I've always had them."

"I didn't know the Velkcic used weapons as girl-children."

"The Velkcic are born warriors," Briga confirmed, "but I had these before I came to the clan."

"Before?"

Briga paused. What had she just said?

"You weren't always Velkcic?" Dagmer pressed gently.

"No…before them, I…" she surprised herself by answering, grasping at half-remembered images that refused to form clearly in her mind. "They found me as a small child and took me in."

"You have no memory of the time before?"

Briga shook her head to clear it, agitated and uncertain. "Why are you asking me this?"

"I apologize, mistress, I was only trying to make idle talk. I didn't mean to upset you. It's just that your knives…they're Kithian. I was curious how you came to have them."

Kithian? As she had so many times before, her thumb rose up to idly stroke the familiar ivory hilt of her blade.

329

Chapter 29

"Sartaq!" Batu called out as he stalked through the camp.

Warriors were quick to clear his path. Sartaq looked up from where he'd been lounging outside his tent. Orus and Ganbataar stood as their khan approached. The commander did not. Batu eyed his brother expectantly, but Sartaq only shook his head in warning, then indicated a space beside himself for the khan to sit.

"I have a viper in there," Sartaq explained to his brother's harsh look.

It was a code they had established some time ago. Batu looked toward the tent flap with mild surprise and the barest ghost of a smile.

"In the daytime no less. It must be angry."

"Furious," Sartaq confirmed.

Batu lowered himself wearily, waiting as their kheshig fanned out to keep any curious ears at a comfortable distance.

"Is everything ready?" Batu asked, dropping his voice.

The commander nodded. "Signals have all been arranged." He cut his eyes to the tent briefly. "I will have details later."

"What does your shaman say?"

"She cannot predict the future, as your wolf can. But she is praying for favor."

There might have been a note of jealousy in his tone, but if Batu noticed, he let it go without remark. Sartaq merely shrugged.

"We will be ready at your command."

"It will be good to sleep in a warm palace soon," Batu growled through a feral smile.

"And then what?"

The khan looked at his brother sharply, but there was no challenge here. "The Surians have been testing my governors. I suppose I shall soon have to pay a visit."

"You will have to return home eventually," Sartaq counselled. "What will you do with the she-wolf?"

Batu eyed his brother suspiciously now. "Bring her with me, of course. She will join the other wives."

"She will not like that. Frankly I am surprised she has not tried to escape back to her people by now."

"Why should she escape?" Batu sighed, tired of having this argument yet again. "She is practically Drev'an now. Her loyalty is to me."

"Brother, her loyalty is to the gods."

"She has already had many opportunities. If she was going to run, she would have already."

Noting something in his voice, Sartaq sat up a little straighter in surprise. "Batu...do you actually care for this demoness?"

Batu glared but stubbornly refused to respond. For a moment, Sartaq was reminded of a much younger version of his little brother, before he'd been named heir. He tucked this bit of information away for later use. Instead, he leaned forward conspiratorially and lowered his voice further.

"Then you should know some of her people are in the city. I do not know if they are blood-kin, or merely from the same lands."

The khan regarded his brother with a flat expression, calculating. "The spies have told you this?"

What else had my *spy revealed to Sartaq that had been withheld from me? Did Briga also know this?* He stood abruptly.

"Prepare the men. Discreetly. I do not want the Magyuns to have any warning. You must be prepared to move quickly when the time comes. And tell the men, I want any non-Magyuns in the city taken alive."

Sartaq saluted formally, touching his fist to his chest, and bowed his head. The motion hid a tiny, satisfied smile.

***

Briga had been silent and withdrawn for most of the day. As dusk began to take hold, she started to act more like herself again.

"Gansükh," she called suddenly, a hard glint in her eyes.

The Drev'an stepped forward dutifully, waiting.

"We haven't trained today. I wish to fight."

Gansükh didn't so much as blink. Instead he nodded and rested a hand on the hilt of his curved blade. Unsettled by something in the she-wolf's demeanor, Dagmer took a step forward, but Bayanaa laid a restraining hand on her arm.

"What do you wish to drill?" Gansükh asked mildly.

"Not drill," she corrected, withdrawing her blade. Her *Kithian* blade. "Fight."

All the tension and fear building within her over the last few days had bubbled to the surface, demanding an outlet. She wanted to scream. This was the next best option.

333

"Here?"

But there was no more time for debate. Dagger drawn, she stalked toward him and aimed a sweeping cut at his belly. Gansükh avoided it easily, twisting his torso away.

"My lady, this is not—"

But she snarled and thrust the point at him, more than just a playful sparring cut. Startled at the *intent* behind her attack, Gansükh reflexively knocked her hand down with an open-palmed strike to the back of her wrist. Briga was ready for him and punched his jaw with her free hand. It was a left-handed blow, and lacked strength thanks to her continued recovery, but the force of it made him angry. This wasn't sparring, this was something else. Nearby, Dagmer and Bayanaa looked on in open-mouthed shock.

Gansükh held her gaze as he stepped back and slowly withdrew his blade. Whatever she needed him to be right now, he would oblige.

"Gansükh," Bayanaa warned quietly, but the older kheshig ignored him.

The nearest of the Drev'an warriors were beginning to gather, having noticed the nascent fight. Dagmer glanced around nervously, seeking the khan or his brother, but thankfully neither was nearby. The watching Drev'an were mostly confused. Some rested hands on the hilts of their own blades, uncertain whether to interfere. With a growl, Gansükh lunged with a vicious, upward curving arc of his blade. Briga twisted out of the way, knocking his weapon further along its trajectory with a slash of her own. Her wrist rolled around, laying her blade against his forearm. It glanced harmlessly off his leather armor, and he seized her wrist in the powerful grip of his free hand.

The crowd, taking their cue from Bayanaa, assumed the fight was a contest and began to cheer for one combatant or the other. Bayanaa and Dagmer both glanced around at the noise briefly before carefully monitoring the match for any needed intervention.

Briga twisted her wrist in an attempt to free it. Failing, she felt the direction of his swing change as he peeled her hand away, opening up her torso to attack. Growling, she darted forward and grabbed his sword hand in her free one to turn his swing, then followed up with a kick to his stomach for good measure. Gansükh was too strong for her to hold back. He turned his hips to absorb the kick and smacked her injured shoulder with the flat of his blade.

There were a few cheers in the gathering crowd, but neither of them noticed.

"Slow down and think before you strike. You are leaving yourself open."

The counsel was quiet, but she didn't receive it well. Instead she kicked again, this time aiming for the side of his knee. Her foot connected and stole his balance out from under him. He released her wrist as he fell to one knee, and she used the momentum to slam her dagger's hilt into the back of his neck. He grunted, catching himself on his hands. She stepped on his blade and drove her other knee into his face. Gansükh saw it coming and shifted to the side, then forward, throwing his weight into her hips. One hand grabbed her ankle and violently pulled it off his weapon and out from beneath her. She fought to keep her balance, pushing aside and away from him with her arms to prevent being taken to the ground and to distance him from his sword. The Drev'an cheered, recognizing one of their own wrestling techniques, and appreciating her agility.

The kheshig didn't let go, despite being disarmed now, nor did she release her straight-armed grip on his shoulders. If he threw her to the ground, the fight would be over. They grappled for a moment, Briga unable to reverse the grip on her dagger in order to use it, and Gansükh unable to retrieve his sword. She saw too late that he'd maneuvered her closer to the downed weapon, and fast as a snake, he released his hold on her ankle to retrieve it. Using her grip, she hauled him forward, hoping to throw off his balance just enough that she'd be able to roll to the side and put a little distance between them. Gansükh allowed the break, watching her carefully as he settled back into stance. He'd seen grief and rage in her eyes warring for primacy and finally understood.

Briga rolled up into a low crouch and flipped her dagger into a reverse grip. Baring her teeth, she slashed at him. He blocked easily. Twice. Three times.

"Careless," he taunted. It was time to end this before things got out of hand.

He swung wide, leaving her an opening at his exposed side. Pivoting, she turned to deliver a back swing, aiming the point of her dagger for a space between his ribs. In slow motion, he pivoted with her, sweeping his leg into the back of her knees. In a heartbeat he was crouched over her, blade to her throat. She wasn't ready to yield. Briga had managed to bring her dagger up as she fell and braced it with both hands to protect her throat. She kicked with a knee, hoping to create enough space to wiggle free. Instead he allowed part of his weight to settle on her, pinning her.

"Stop, it is over," he growled quietly to her.

She was lost to some battle madness, and he was unsure what to do now. Around him the Drev'an were disappointed that the fight was apparently over. He started to let her up, but she pushed with her dagger, and he was forced to slam her down again.

"Stop now, Breeg. Stop."

Laying a forearm heavily across her throat to ensure compliance, he threw his blade aside and pried the dagger from her grip.

Something wet shimmered in the corner of her eyes, and for a moment it stopped him cold.

"Gansükh!" Dagmer called, breathless.

Beside her in the thinning crowd stood the khan and his brother. Rage flickered in Batu's gaze. Sartaq was distinctly amused.

"Broken her to the bit, have you brother?"

"What is the meaning of this?"

"Batu Khan," Gansükh began, easing the pressure on her neck, but not daring to let go.

"She wanted to train," Dagmer put in hastily. "She's unharmed, my lord."

Batu took one menacing step forward. Bayanaa took a protective step forward as well, though to shield the khan, Briga, or Gansükh he couldn't say.

"Gansükh."

There was a peculiar note of command in her voice. She was clear-eyed now, calm and resolute. Warily he let her up. Batu paused, reassessing.

"Thank you for the instruction," she panted, still catching her breath.

"Of course, mistress," he replied automatically in his usual terse tone.

Any confusion was carefully leashed as he helped her to her feet and handed her the dagger, hilt first. Dagmer watched Briga. She didn't dare look away. The khan stepped closer, lowering his voice so even his brother would not hear. When he spoke, his expression was calm, but his voice was cold.

"What is the first law, Gansükh?"

"Loyalty to the khan."

"How dare you raise a naked blade to a royal wife?"

Briga blinked. Had she heard that correctly? There was no time to reflect on it at the moment.

"It was my choice to spar with live blades," she cut in smoothly, voice low and face schooled into casual pleasantry.

The crowd had nearly dispersed, but she didn't dare break the public image Batu had cast. He wouldn't argue with a kheshig or with his…woman publicly. Not over a matter such as this.

"He should have refused."

"I didn't grant him the opportunity." She smiled sweetly. "You yourself said I needed training. I'm too reckless and unprotected in battle. I wanted to improve."

"Come with me."

He smiled pleasantly and rested one hand at the back of her neck, guiding her into the tent. Inside, out of view of the camp, he allowed the leash on his control to slip completely and shoved her forward.

"You have made a spectacle of yourself," he growled.

His anger was evident, but he couldn't give it full voice without alerting the entire camp.

"It was only a practice fight, Batu," she replied, exasperated. "Why are you so upset?"

"The men saw."

"What did they see?" she demanded. "You yourself ordered me to train in archery and horsemanship. The men saw that, too."

When he didn't respond, she watched him closely, daring to reach out with her druid senses. What she felt confirmed what she had come to suspect, at least in part.

"This isn't about training, it's about Gansükh," she guessed. "Batu…"

"I am not blind. I see the way he looks at you. The way others look at you, as well."

She was on dangerous ground now and needed to play her role expertly. Warily, she placed a feather-light touch on his arm.

"Weak men covet the possessions of powerful men. As for Gansükh, what you see is loyalty. There's nothing to concern yourself over; he is my kheshig, and he takes his role seriously."

Batu looked unconvinced.

"Or would you rather I had a disloyal guardian?"

"Of course not."

"Then you must put this matter out of your mind. You are seeing threats where there are only shadows."

When he didn't move away from her touch, she took another step closer and rested her fingertips against his cheek. He stood rigid, watching her. She sensed he was beginning to relent and stepped closer still. Her other hand traced his collarbone lightly.

"If you wish me to appear strong before the men, you must allow me to train as I wish." Her tone was barely above a whisper, intimate and threatening and steady. "I will learn from my kheshig the ways of Drev'an combat, and from Dagmer, the proper use of my daggers and ax. Or am I still a prisoner here?"

Batu didn't answer. She didn't require an answer. Somewhere nearby, a wolf howled. She took half a step back and raised her eyes to meet his gaze directly.

"I don't know what you plan to do with the birds, but tonight is not the time."

Batu nodded, but there was still something unpleasant in his gaze.

"Tomorrow, I think."

Pretending more confidence than she felt, she stepped away to grab the wolfskin from where it had fallen and resettled it around her shoulders.

"Where are you going?" he asked, grabbing her by the elbow.

"I must seek the gods. This plan of yours requires sacrifice if it is to succeed."

When he didn't let go, she added, "Gansükh will stay here if you wish. I only require the slave girl."

After waiting a moment longer, she stepped out of his grasp and out of his tent.

"My lady," Dagmer began, rising, but Briga motioned for silence.

"Bring a torch."

The thrall did as she was asked. Briga smiled reassuringly at her two kheshig, and then set off toward a stand of trees near the river.

"Is everything all right?" the thrall ventured when they were out of earshot.

Briga sighed. "Fine."

It was not yet dark when they reached the trees, but Briga knew it might be a long night.

"Have we been followed?"

The thrall glanced over her shoulder. "Not that I can tell."

Briga cleared her mind and reached out with her senses. She could feel…something, but it was masked by a stronger *tug* from

340

the city. She settled herself on a dry, relatively frost-free patch of earth and regarded Dagmer calmly.

"I can't endure much more of this. My destiny lies within the city."

Dagmer thought for a moment. "My lady, you're in danger."

Briga looked at her, but there was no surprise evident on her face.

"You must make Sartaq and the khan fear you. Fear your magic and your connection to the gods."

"They don't fear Sartaq's shaman."

"They respect Sartaq's shaman. But she doesn't have the same gifts as you, and only has knowledge of the Drev'an gods. You don't have this limitation. You have already shown it. This makes you a target, and a prize. You must make their fear stronger than their greed."

When Briga said nothing, she continued, "I don't know if your gods have favored you in your captivity, but you have borne the mark of the red god of the tree. I saw it."

Briga glanced down to her own wrist reflexively, where the mark had been. "Sartaq's shaman doesn't please this god?"

"It's never revealed itself to her."

The she-wolf contemplated a moment, then irritably waved her hand. "Enough, Dagmer. I must pray."

She knew better than to reach out with anger in her heart, and took a few slow breaths to clear her mind, then shut her eyes. She still felt vaguely unsettled and couldn't quite shake the sensation away. One palm rested flat to the cold earth, as she'd learned to do so long ago. Gradually her senses stretched outward, through her hand, the ground, the air. She could feel Dagmer distantly, as she moved to light a fire. She could feel the heartbeats of the small, sleeping trees around them. Satisfied that no one was near enough to disturb them, she tried to relax her senses. The smell of sweet herbs drifted to her from where Dagmer fed the fire, and she felt the familiar dizziness of surrendering herself to the unseen world.

She called to Epona, the horse goddess, and Remi, a god of battle. She flattered and cajoled fair Lugus to lend cunning to the foreign Drev'an, that whatever their plan, it would succeed quickly and with minimal bloodshed. Tentatively, fearing insult to the Velkcic gods, she beckoned Tengri, god of the horselords.

There was no telling how long she spoke to the gods; time had no meaning in this place. She sensed they were satisfied, or at least that they were tiring of her flattery. Exhausted, she allowed herself to rest as she sensed the divine presence drifting away.

Briga sat quietly, willing the small tremors of fatigue to fade as she regained her breath.

"Dagmer," she rasped, holding out a hand for water.

When she opened her eyes, the girl was gone. The world had gone dark and silent around her. Startled, she surged to her feet, grasping for her dagger. Something hot brushed against her hand, making her jump. She looked down to see the red god, the divine creature from the red tree. The spirit gaze balefully at her.

"This is another vision," she breathed, understanding.

Fire pulsed mildly in her healing wounds. She remembered suddenly how it had attacked her at their first meeting, biting her shoulder and slashing her leg.

"But why?"

The creature growled, disliking being questioned. Her eyes were drawn beyond, to the Magyun city. She noticed thousands of threads. She was seeing the Pattern.

"Cathbad," she breathed.

How long had it been since she'd thought of them? Some threads were bright and luminous, others dark or weak. Gradually she became aware of one thread near her vibrating dully. Puzzled, she reached out a cautious hand to touch it.

The old druid gasped awake in a dark, crowded room and shuddered violently. Briga couldn't make out any details, but found herself suddenly there.

"Briga?" the old man gasped again, looking around blindly.

She tried to go to him, but could not move. His words sounded distant.

"Child, where are you?"

"I'm here!" she tried to call, but her words were lost in the darkness.

Someone came to his side. She strained to make them out. Could it be Amergin? She looked around desperately, hoping to find his threads, but they were all gone now.

"Briga…" the elder druid rasped weakly, allowing the other to guide him back to the floor.

She was struck with a profound sadness as the vision retreated, leaving her alone in the dark clearing once more. Gradually she became aware of someone standing close behind her. Their presence was an immense comfort, and she relaxed against it gratefully as two male hands wrapped around her shoulders. His scent was foreign and familiar all at once. When she opened her eyes, she found the red god before her with its teeth bared ferally, tails twitching. She tensed as one hand slid gently across her collarbone, and she felt soft lips press against the nape of her neck. Her body shivered in response. All at once, the hand at her chest changed to claws. She felt the sickening feeling of fangs closing around the back of her neck. The bear growled and lifted her by the neck as if she were a cub. She screamed, but no sound came out. She flailed at the bear uselessly. Golden hair caught her attention, and she turned in

343

the bear's maw to see her nemesis, the blond warrior from the Magyun city, standing where Cathbad had been before. His blade dripped gore as he stood scowling at her. His lips slowly twitched into a grin as the bear bit harder to carry her off.

"Cathbad," she squeaked, but he was far away in some other place.

The bear grunted, and the blond warrior took one step toward her.

When she opened her eyes, her throat felt raw, and the world was a confusion of darkness. Someone clutched at her sword arm. Someone else held her from behind, attempting to still her thrashing. She gasped, trying to make sense of what she saw, to determine whether this was another vision.

"Let her go, she stopped! Mistress, you must be calm!"

Dagmer. Dagmer with a panicky note to her voice. Briga took a shuddering breath. If Dagmer was here, then it must be Gansükh or Bayanaa restraining her. She looked over her shoulder, but the face that greeted her was unfamiliar. One of Sartaq's men. A grip of fear seized her, raw and instinctual.

"No," she breathed and struggled to free herself from his clamping limbs.

"Let her go!" Dagmer pleaded.

A low snarl sounded from across the small space. Briga gasped against the man's choking arm and looked to the creature. She expected to see the god, but instead there stood a wolf, lean and feral. The creature locked eyes with her attacker and stalked toward him menacingly. A second man behind them breathed a curse, and Briga could hear him fumbling for his bow. The wolf sprang forward, jaws snapping at the man holding Briga. He released her in an instant, scrambling to his feet to defend himself. The wolf's teeth tore the sleeve of his robe, but it stopped and took up a defensive stance between Briga and Sartaq's men.

Briga gasped a lungful of air, sinking back on her hands. The second man started to raise his sword, but paused uncertainly as the wolf flickered a glance at him. Dimly Briga was aware that other men were approaching, but they were muffled. She couldn't tell whether or not it was her druid sense at work. She felt trapped between the worlds. Slowly her eyes fell on the wolf, and she felt a quiver go through her as she noted a dark patch on his fur. A patch in the shape of a letter in ogham.

Dagmer let out the breath she'd been holding and regarded the scene wide-eyed. Briga was the first to break the silence, her voice raw.

"Where are my kheshig?"

"You left them with the khan." Dagmer peered closely at her. "You don't remember?"

The she-wolf squinted, trying to force her mind back into this reality, this time and place.

"Yes…I remember. What happened? Why are these men here?"

Sartaq's men were frozen, watching her and the wolf, uncertain what to do. Behind them, the commotion was growing louder. The wolf flicked an ear in irritation and backed one step toward Briga.

"You were screaming, thrashing on the ground as if you were in pain. I couldn't calm you, and eventually the sentries came."

The thrall was pale. Briga had frightened her. The she-wolf blinked in surprise and watched Dagmer for a long moment before turning to the Drev'an.

"You can go. I am all right now."

The men exchanged a look.

"You must come back to the camp."

345

"The shaman is praying," Dagmer retorted, shaky and indignant.

She flinched when the wolf's ear flicked in her direction. Briga silenced her with a gesture.

"I'm finished, Dagmer. I've seen enough."

The men relaxed slightly. So did the wolf. Shakily, Briga pushed herself to her feet. She took a few stiff, unsteady steps toward the men, who lowered their weapons, but kept a careful eye on the wolf. The beast looked up at her once, then fell into step at her side.

"Lead the way," she called to them, summoning a proper shaman's bearing.

Dagmer smothered the embers of their fire and rushed to walk with her lady, careful to remain on the other side of her from the wolf.

"Why does it not attack? Or leave?" one of the men asked, clearly unnerved.

"He is a free creature; he'll do as he likes."

But as Briga glanced down at the wolf and the mark on its side, she knew that wasn't true. Not any longer. The thought caused a pang of sadness.

"How long have we been out here?" she asked Dagmer quietly.

"All night. It'll be dawn before long."

Briga frowned and looked up at the sky. A few sparse clouds had gathered in the night, but were beginning to clear. Ahead, a group of men approached through the brush, drawn by her screaming, no doubt. Batu strode at their head, shirtless from sleep, and with his blade drawn.

"Breeg," he managed when he saw her, voice tight with controlled anger or fear.

His eyes flashed over her, searching for signs of injury. Then to Dagmer. Then to Sartaq's men.

"What has happened?"

He reached out to take her arm, but the wolf lunged at him, snapping its jaws. Batu raised his blade, and two kheshig appeared at his sides, wide-eyed, but poised to strike.

"Wait!" Briga called out, holding out her hand to shield the animal.

"Brother," she whispered to the wolf in Velkcic, "you must be calm now."

A hush fell over the Drev'an as the wolf shook itself grudgingly and retreated a few steps behind her. For a long moment, no one moved. Briga's hand faintly trembled, so she slowly lowered it. Dizziness washed over her suddenly, as it sometimes did when she visited that other place.

"Batu Khan," she beckoned quietly, remembering once more the role she must play.

The khan was slightly pale, his attention divided between the she-wolf and the actual wolf. But he remembered himself as well and came to her aid. One strong arm slid around her back, lending his strength. When she faltered again, he lifted her easily.

"Are you all right?" he asked quietly. "What happened?"

"A vision," she admitted, frowning, but glad now for his protectiveness.

The word was hardly adequate for the intensity of her experience. "It was…powerful. I didn't mean to worry you."

He glanced pointedly at Sartaq's men, who looked on in bewilderment, then to the wolf. His gaze traveled around the circle of men, standing silent and uneasy after this display.

"My shaman has received a rare blessing from Tengri himself. He has sent this wolf, his messenger, to protect and favor his prophet. Our victory is assured!"

The men hesitated but reluctantly broke their silence with cheers. Some called the god's name, some called out the khan's. A few called for the she-wolf. She felt a subtle shift in Batu at that.

"Tonight," she told him quietly. "The gods will favor your plan tonight."

Batu smiled faintly at her, then turned to lead the entire group back to the camp. After a token protest, Briga surrendered to sleep.

Chapter 30

"Amergin."

The druid blinked awake and stretched a kink out of his neck.

"Come and rest."

"Is that not what I've been doing?"

He glanced around blearily. He was seated before the fire. Cathbad was laid out beside him, worry creasing his brow despite being asleep. A sheen of sweat glistened on his skin. Amergin reached out and touched the back of his hand to the chief druid's face.

"How is he?"

Amergin shook his head and looked up at his chieftain. "He sat up once in the night, calling for Briga, and has been like this ever since."

Eamon handed him a mug of something warm, then reached down to help him stand.

"You need to rest, Amergin. The clan can't afford to lose all its druids."

In truth, he was gravely worried about the old priest. Cathbad had exhausted himself to protect the clan, and Amergin had watched him do it. He was in danger of giving too much. Hearing that thought spoken aloud by the chieftain chilled his blood, and he felt his face drain of color. There was a gasping, choking noise from beside the fire, and Cathbad struggled to rise onto his elbows. Amergin shook out of Eamon's grasp and crouched at the old priest's side.

"Briga," he rasped.

Amergin wasn't certain if Cathbad could see him; his attention seemed to be fixed on something distant. Hearing her name sent a lance of pain through his heart, but there was something about the way he said it.

"Have you…?"

Cathbad shook his head and waved off the question. "She is near, Amergin. I have seen her."

The younger druid frowned. "Where?" he asked gently.

"Beyond the walls," he rasped, body tense with effort. Or madness.

"Cathbad," Amergin began, laying a soothing hand over his teacher's. "She's a prisoner, but—"

"No."

The word was clear, and the chief druid's gaze fixed on him with a sudden, clear intensity.

"I've seen her, too," Eamon added quietly.

Amergin turned to look at him. Hadn't the chieftain said something similar on the wall? Amergin had dismissed him out of hand at the time, concerned for his health, but perhaps there was something more to it. Eamon stood looking down at the two druids with a haunted, grim expression.

"At least I think I did. With the Drev'an."

"I don't understand."

"Neither do I," Eamon agreed.

"She will return to us soon. I have seen it."

Cathbad looked from one man to the other, his face suddenly showing age and weariness. And sorrow. Amergin returned his attention to the chief druid.

"Brother, you've been praying all night. I believe you; I can feel the truth of it. Please rest now, you've exhausted yourself. We will speak more of this later."

Cathbad nodded and patted his hand. "You will make a fine chief druid someday. Remember always to keep the old ways."

"Rest," he urged again, but smiled sadly at the praise.

Cathbad watched him for a long moment before finally nodding. Something about that look unsettled Amergin, but he arranged a blanket over the old druid and finally rose to his feet once more.

"You need to rest as well," Eamon chided quietly.

Amergin closed his eyes tiredly and made a sound of agreement. "Aye, but first I must fetch more fresh water. The basin is half empty."

"I'll send Rorik and Connor to do that. Go and rest."

Amergin hesitated. He couldn't explain the sudden urge to top off their supply and the compulsion to do it himself, but there was a new look of desperation in the chieftain's eye that finally swayed him.

"As you wish, my lord."

With a final glance to Cathbad and to the warriors preparing to fetch water, he crossed the room to a relatively clean pile of straw and hoped he wouldn't dream.

***

Ambrus had been restless all day. He'd checked and rechecked his supplies, sharpened and polished all his weapons three times over. He had half a mind to flee the city tonight,

351

rather than wait for it to fall and hope to forge an opportunity amid that chaos. But he hadn't quite worked out how to smuggle Sitric out with him without drawing attention, and he couldn't leave Amergin and the clan to fend for themselves. There was also a score to settle with the she-devil. Could he really walk away from that? He touched the amulet carefully hidden beneath his shirt, seeking a sign. He could almost sense the gods watching him, delighting in the predicament he'd gotten himself into. If only he could get word to his crew. They must be wondering what to do, not having heard from him in so long now. He could hardly blame them if they'd sailed back to Krevaland, though they would have to answer to his father. That thought brought a bitter smile to his lips.

By dusk he was ready. He shouldered two small packs and set off into the creeping darkness, alert to any sound or warning of more severed limbs raining down on them. Months ago he'd scouted for potential escape routes. He'd decided, when it was time, he would escape through the southwest corner of the city. It would be farthest from any likely vector of attack, thereby giving him the most time to reach it. Patrols would be light there, which would make it easier to hide supplies. The downside was, it was nearer the palace than he would prefer. Fighting would inevitably concentrate there, if and when the city fell.

Rather than head directly there to stash supplies, he'd head north and plant one more bag there in case he needed an alternate escape route. He had learned early in life to always have two routes of escape whenever possible. He wound his way through the city, taking much the same path he usually took when patrolling on his own. It could well have been any other night, except for a mild anxious feeling that still fluttered about his gut unpleasantly.

Cursing himself, he lowered his head and soldiered on. One hand rose to touch the dagger's hilt, and he traced the sigil there with his thumb. He'd debated showing the knife to Siggi, but instinct had warned him not to. Not yet. The sigil was that of Jarl Ravn, he was certain. But what was it doing here? He both dreaded and hoped one of the Drev'an had been carrying it as a spoil of war and not some trade. That would all but confirm their suspicions. That knowledge alone would do little enough good, however. He would need a Drev'an prisoner to question. And not just any Drev'an, he needed one who had knowledge of the raids on Ravn's lands.

Ambrus had been so engrossed in these musings that he was surprised to find himself at the north wall already. Strolling quietly and casually, he made his way west along the wall until he came to a place where the wall formed a shallow corner, limiting the observable area to a few dozen paces. Doublechecking to be certain there was no one around, he crouched and ran his hands over the stone until he found a series of deep scratches, as if something had fallen against the wall here and done minor damage. He'd found the loose blocks months ago while searching for future hiding spots should they prove necessary. Working quickly, he pried loose one of the large stones, and stuffed one of his bags deep into the void. He clenched his teeth to keep from grunting as he lifted the stone carefully back into place, wincing as it scraped quietly against its mates. The bag contained a length of rope, a rolled blanket, and dried foods. Ambrus waited a moment to see if he'd been heard, but only muted silence greeted him. Carefully he balanced two small stones between the block and its neighbor. He would be able to tell quickly if his cache had been disturbed by checking to see if the rocks had been knocked loose. Satisfied, he glanced around once more to ensure he had not been observed, then set off east toward the northern gate to continue his "patrol".

He'd expected that vague sense of dread to lessen after hiding the first of his packs, but irritatingly, it did not. Ambrus glanced up at the emerging stars, seeking an omen, but the gods were quiet. He wished Tostig were there with him. The man had a nose for omens to rival any priest.

"Ambrus?"

The familiar voice pulled his attention to the present, and he glanced up to see Braxus atop the wall.

"What are you doing on this side of town?"

The blond man shrugged. "Just out for a walk. I needed to clear my mind."

"Come up, if you don't mind company."

Ambrus had no easy excuse, despite wanting to be on his way to store the other bag, and soon found himself climbing the nearest ladder. Braxus offered a hand politely at the top, which Ambrus accepted. He noted the way the Emorian's gaze rested on his remaining pack for a time, but neither of them said anything about it. Instead, Ambrus paced to the wall and looked out at the Drev'an campfires.

"Is anything happening?"

"The usual," Braxus responded blandly. "Nothing out of the ordinary."

"No?" Ambrus asked again, nodding toward the river.

In the fading twilight they could just barely make out a light haze forming over the water. The mist was barely more substantial than ghostly figures, but Ambrus didn't like it.

"Normal for this time of year," Braxus explained, following his gaze. "It won't amount to anything."

Ambrus felt his lips press into a thin line, but he had no response. Braxus was looking at him.

"Instinct again?"

"No, just...restless."

The Emorian chuckled darkly, but Ambrus saw a slight edge of tension leave him. "You Kith don't take to confinement very well, do you?"

Ambrus shot him a look. That was answer enough. Though under that careful, stoic mask he wondered if the Emorian knew about the man rotting in the dungeons.

"You're like the Velkcic clans that way. Quite uncivilized."

The blond warrior laughed quietly, surprising Braxus with his lack of argument. "I like the sound of them."

"You would." The Emorian sniffed. "No matter. They'll be brought to heel soon enough."

Ambrus eyed him curiously then, suddenly wondering if *this* was the source of tension he'd felt from Amergin before. Did Emoria harbor designs on the Velkcic?

"First, my friend," he steered the conversation smoothly, "we must bring these horselords to heel."

Braxus grunted his response and turned to look toward the gate and its watchtowers. Taking that as a cue, Ambrus stepped back from the ramparts and took up an easy, strolling pace beside the captain as they made their way leisurely toward the gate.

"Did you hear the screaming last night?" Braxus asked a bit too casually.

"Screaming?"

"From the camp. Sounded like a mountain cat…but I don't suppose you've heard one of those."

Ambrus sidestepped the question. It vexed Braxus that he didn't know much about the Kith, and he'd become famous for trying to get information out of him indirectly like this. Ambrus was well aware of the ploy, and it irked him. Braxus knew damn well there were no mountain cats in the North Lands, and he was seeking to either highlight his own travels or determine where the Kith might have ventured. The Emorian was crafty, but not so sly as he believed himself to be.

"I was…otherwise occupied last night."

There. Let him make of that what he will. The corner of Braxus' mouth twitched into a grin, but just barely.

"Have you finally found yourself a woman?" he asked, eyes falling briefly again to the sack Ambrus carried.

"Yes. Your sister is wonderful in bed, did you know that?"

Braxus moved to cuff him on the back of the head, but Ambrus dodged smoothly, laughing. The tension broken, they walked on together to the gate. Calling it the North Gate was not entirely accurate. The city boasted two gates, one to the south, and one to the north, but in truth this one lay on the northeast portion of the city, and faced in roughly the same direction. Its towers therefore were called the north and south towers. As they approached the north tower, a few of the soldiers called friendly greetings to Ambrus, which drew another sly smile from the captain. Braxus knew he hated the attention.

"If you have nowhere particular to be, come join me for a cup of ale."

Another probing question, but Ambrus nodded. In truth, a drink sounded like a good idea. They made their way to an open space on the tower directly south of the gate. Calling it a tower was generous. The structure and its twin were only perhaps a story higher than the wall itself, to afford a lookout position, and to house the mechanisms that controlled the various gates. Ambrus turned over an empty wooden crate and seated himself where he could look southward along the wall, as well as out toward the Drev'an camp. Braxus poured them each a cup from a small cask.

"It's amazing, isn't it? That the city should practically starve, yet we still have ale."

Braxus chuckled quietly. "Soldiers will endure many hardships if they have ale. A good commander always keeps a healthy reserve."

He passed a full cup to the Kith and pulled out a camp stool for himself.

"But I make no promise as to the quality."

"Ale is ale," Ambrus returned, and in a situation such as this, that was the truth of it.

Though after one sour mouthful, he was tempted to revise his statement. Still, sharing a cup afforded them both a much-needed sense of normalcy and took the bite out of the night's chill.

"Have you been through a siege before, Braxus?"

"Only from the other side of it."

Ambrus was silent a moment, contemplating the ways this thing could end. A breakout seemed unlikely, even if the army were still at full strength. It wasn't Bela's style to take such a risk. He knew from watching the horde they couldn't hope to outlast them on their quickly dwindling stores. Already the city folk were showing thinness. It was a wonder not many had died yet.

"Do you think Emoria knows what's happening?"

Now it was Braxus' turn to think. "Almost certainly, though I've heard of no birds coming from the south."

"Nor I," Ambrus confirmed.

"Even if she does know, they won't march until spring. If it were me, I'd strike the winter camps at first thaw, and move quickly, without sending a bird to betray my intentions."

Ambrus nodded as he evaluated the strategy. It was the best chance for a large body to hold the element of surprise, though if they lasted until spring, the Drev'an must surely expect a response. Ambrus had no intention of being here in the spring to see for himself. As he took another sip of the sour ale, a streak of light glinted at the edge of his vision. He looked to where the falling star had been, feeling a cold prickle crawl across his skin. The gods were watching.

"I have a wife back home. Did you know that, Ambrus?"

The blond man looked up curiously, distracted from his thoughts of the gods. "I did not."

"Beautiful woman, but with a shrew-tongue." The Emorian paused to sip his ale with a wistful expression. "She'd like you."

"Why didn't you bring her to Magyuna?"

"She is well respected in the capital. This is a two-year posting. It wouldn't do for her to be away so long…to have to rebuild her influence and standing. We decided she would wait for me in Atulari."

"Well," Ambrus began when Braxus fell into brooding silence once more, "when you see her in the spring, tell her hello for me."

Braxus shot him a look and smiled thinly. "If God wills it."

Suddenly serious, Ambrus leaned forward and lowered his voice to a harsh whisper that only the captain could hear.

"Don't talk like that where the men can hear you. Besides," he resumed at a normal tone and patted the armor around the Emorian's stomach, "*you* have no worry of starving."

"Pah!" He swatted Ambrus' hand away indignantly, but laughed.

A second shooting star drew the Kith's attention down the wall again so he was looking slightly south and eastward. Something else held his attention there, something his senses registered, but his mind hadn't recognized yet. He peered into the darkness, focusing on nothing in particular in an effort to let any motion draw his eye.

"Ambrus?"

After a few moments, he saw it again. Just a slight movement of someone climbing a ladder perhaps a few hundred feet down the wall from them.

"What is it, Ambrus?"

"When is shift change, Braxus?"

"Not for another few hours. Why?"

The Emorian followed his gaze, but the figure had stopped moving now.

"I thought I saw something. Probably just a curious citizen..."

Nevertheless, Ambrus drained the remainder of his ale and stood, his attention remaining fixed on the spot.

"Call it instinct."

"Then I'm coming with you."

"No need," Ambrus reasoned, but there was no dissuading Braxus when his mind was set.

The two men stalked the wall, one behind the other. Braxus spotted the movement for himself after a few minutes and fell into a hunter's silence. The figure seemed to be unaware of them. After carefully climbing a scaling ladder, it paused at the top of the wall to look for soldiers patrolling. Satisfied, it slowly crossed to the ramparts and now stood doing...something. With its attention turned in the other direction, Ambrus picked up his pace to close the distance between them.

Ambrus and Braxus drew ever closer as the figure fumbled with something on the ramparts. They couldn't afford to jog and draw attention from the other soldiers in case this person was no more than just curious about what was happening beyond the walls. The unneeded suspicion was likely to make the soldiers even more anxious, which would have poor results. Or worse, if the figure were up to no good, the soldiers might scare them away before Ambrus could determine what they were doing. When they'd closed to within fifty feet, the figure stepped back and turned to go. It might be nothing, but something about this prickled at Ambrus.

"You, there," he called out.

The figure looked at him sharply, startled, its features hidden within the hood of a cloak. But it only froze for a moment, then dashed for the ladder.

"Stop!" Ambrus called, running now.

Descending the ladder in a cloak slowed the figure down, and it was nearly at the bottom when Ambrus reached the ladder himself. He attempted to slide his feet down the outside of the ladder's arms and ended up jumping most of the way down.

He ignored the bark of protest in his knees and drew his sword as he turned and gave chase. The figure was quick, but not quick enough, and Ambrus caught up with it in a few strides. He grabbed an arm and spun the stranger around, bringing his sword across their throat as he slammed them against the nearest wall. The hood fell away, and Ambrus' eyes opened wide in shock and recognition.

"Ambrus, are you all right?"

"Yes," he called up to Braxus, who was still on the wall, without tearing his attention from his prisoner. "Dianna, what are you doing?"

The dark-haired girl trembled in his grasp, gazing up at him with fearful green eyes.

"I-I was just looking," she stammered, and he eased the blade off her throat a bit. "I look out most nights to see what is happening. I live just over there—"

"Braxus, check the ramparts," he called. Then more quietly, "Were you trying to escape?"

Her eyes widened once more, incredulous.

"There's a candle on a ledge," Braxus called down.

"A candle?"

Ambrus thought he could smell the faint scent of something burning and tightened his grip on Dianna once more. "Or were you signaling?"

She flinched at the touch of the blade and squirmed as if to escape it. "Signaling? Signaling who? I do not know what you are talking about!"

Something fell on his shoulder, and he looked up reflexively. Above, the thatched roof seemed to be...*smoking?*. As he watched, a small patch burst into flame.

"What...?"

A second later, the roof of a house a little ways down the street flared into sudden flame as well. In the same instant, he felt Dianna move under his hands and looked back just as she drew a short dagger and plunged it up under his ribs, aiming for his heart. He gasped at the sudden pressure, and she tried to twist away, but Ambrus had been wearing his usual mail-coat under his cloak, and the finely-wrought rings caught and turned the blade. He grabbed for her wrist with his free hand and slammed her against the wall again.

"Braxus!"

But the captain had already spotted the strange fires and was raising the alarm. Fire was the worst thing that could happen now. Even the stone buildings had thatched roofs, and it would spread quickly in the dry winter air.

"Is this an attack?" Ambrus growled uselessly.

There were no sounds of arrows in flight. He could only hear the sounds of screaming as more houses caught fire, and a growing chorus of terrified birdcalls as the beasts were roused from their overwinter nests in the thatch by fire.

"Come on," he snarled, pinning both her wrists in one of his hands and trapping her against him.

She struggled, but he was stronger, and they started back toward the gate. A new cry of birds caught his attention, and he looked up, awed to see dim streaks of fire lancing the night…like deadly falling stars.

***

"Now," Batu ordered calmly as he watched the soldiers atop the wall turn inward to address the fires.

And there were countless fires. The Drev'an had tied a wax shingle to every bird they'd caught. At Batu's direction, they had set fire to the wax and set the birds free. The terrified creatures had flown straight to their nests, to the warm eaves and thatch they'd learned over generations were easy places to spend their winters. Batu knew from his spies how close together the buildings were, and from what they were constructed. Now it was time to finish this. Sartaq nodded to a band of carefully chosen men, who loped off on foot. The rest of the army, mounted atop their blowing horses, started forward with the siege ladders.

Briga watched the streaks of fire stoically, understanding now what had been in her visions. It had been a warning—all of it. Batu sat to her left, watching as his men advanced rapidly toward the growing glow of the city. To her right, the wolf waited patiently. It hadn't let her out of its sight since the previous evening, waiting protectively outside the tent opening when Batu had refused to let it come in.

As she watched the city and the advancing Drev'an, a cold determination settled in her bones. There was no avoiding this, so she accepted it. Now it would be important to take the city quickly, in response to whatever that curious *tug* commanded.

Her hair had been tied back in elaborate plaits, thanks to Dagmer's help, and sported a few raven feathers tied in. Bayanaa had also brought her a long white feather with a black tip. He said it was from a strange eagle he was nursing, but the creature had been full of fight, and her feather might be a token of luck.

Dagmer had woven the feather into one of the braids. Her face wasn't painted with charcoal tonight, but with blood from the sacrifice of a prized mare. Batu had been opposed, but had eventually relented to her insistence, and the growling of her wolf. She hadn't practiced the coupling magic with the khan; there was no need. Tengri was with them, as well as the red god. The sacrifice was to draw the favor of any other gods watching, to ensure a quick victory. Watching the last of the birds streak away into the city, she could indeed feel the eyes of some unnamed god, and her flesh pebbled in response. Withdrawing her ax, she set Singer off toward the city gate.

***

Dozens of fires had mysteriously sprung to life, and those were only the ones he could see. Citizens were fleeing their homes, running to the nearest wells for water, but the flames took quick hold in the dry thatch. There was hardly a puff of air to help lay them down, but mercifully this would also slow their spread. Somewhat. Several roofs were fully engulfed now, and it must have been worse seen from above, because the soldiers on the wall were descending now to help with the fires.

"Braxus!" he called again, now contending with the cacophony around him.

But Braxus had the same thought and was desperately trying to restore order to his troops and keep them on the wall. There was precious little Ambrus could do to help while restraining this traitor; he needed to stash her somewhere. A group of people knocked into him as the street began to fill with panicked townsfolk, and Dianna nearly escaped from his grasp.

"What about Amergin?" she pleaded.

Ambrus looked to the south. Was the barn on fire? Did this madness stretch across the whole city? Dianna felt his attention slip and tried to pull away, effectively dragging his thoughts back to the present.

"You!" he called to the nearest soldier.

The young man turned to him, eyes wide with fear at this seeming witchcraft with the fire.

"Go and fetch General Larsson, now!"

The man nodded and dashed off into the fray.

"Please, let me go," Dianna tried again, "my mother will need help!"

"You don't have a mother, you little bitch," he snarled.

He began drag-walking her toward the gate once more, cursing as more animals and people began filling the narrow street.

"I should slit your scrawny throat and be done with it."

She fought him at every opportunity, stepping on his feet, kicking at him, and trying to get her hands free to grab one of his weapons. He didn't dare try to dig the rope out of his pack to restrain her.

"Keep struggling, and I will."

But he removed the sword from her neck again and used it to force a path through the crowd. Rather than fight as he expected, she stopped suddenly and froze. He doubted she had suddenly decided to comply and looked over his shoulder warily. Inconceivably, he saw a man squeezing through a tiny crack in the city wall. It had once been concealed by a tangle of dead vines and a pile of broken things, but the man had shoved them out of the way. It took precious moments for his mind to register what he was seeing. There was a strangled sound from above, and a Magyun soldier fell down into the street nearby, causing a fresh wave of panic and noise from the crowd. Ambrus turned to see men in dark cloaks atop the wall. They were making quick work of any Magyun soldiers they encountered, moving steadily toward the north gate.

"Why have you done this?" Ambrus asked in equal parts rage and horror.

For he was certain now the candle was a signal. It had been directly above that crack in the wall. This was no coincidence. But before she could answer, a great weight slammed into his back, and they both tumbled to the ground. He struggled to rise, and Dianna finally snaked out of his grasp before he could slither out from under the mysterious weight himself. Someone stepped on his neck, and he saw the point of a curved blade near his face.

"No!" Dianna called out in Drev'an, stepping between Ambrus and the stranger. "Batu wants all foreigners taken alive."

"He is a soldier," the man grunted, shoving her aside.

She withdrew something from beneath her tunic and flashed it at the warrior briefly. "And Commander Sartaq wants *this* foreigner alive."

Ambrus gritted his teeth, wondering at their conversation and whatever she had said to stay the man's blade. The man pushed the tip of his sword against Ambrus' cheek and reached down to remove the body he'd dropped on them. But whatever he had intended to happen next, it was not to be. A red-fletched arrow sprouted from the Drev'an's neck, and Ambrus flinched as hot blood spattered his face. A second arrow took him in the eye, and the man fell across Ambrus, adding more weight. Dianna didn't even scream. She backed away slowly, then turned and fled, disappearing into the crowd in seconds.

Cursing eloquently, Ambrus struggled to kick the two bodies off of him. He finally freed his shield arm and shoved at the dead weight until he, his weapon, and his sack of provisions were finally extricated. Panting, he looked toward the gate, where archers had finally noticed the threat and were attempting to pick off the Drev'an advancing across the wall. It must have been one of them who had saved him. The first group of Drev'an had reached the east tower, and more were still struggling through the crack.

"Ladders!" he heard a hoarse voice call out above the din, echoed by those who were still atop the wall.

The city was in burning chaos. Soldiers were streaming to the area from all over, some helping with the fire or rescuing people trapped in their homes, some pushing madly through the crowd to get to the wall and figure out what was happening. Ambrus looked south, and for the briefest moment considered running. Instead he found himself climbing the nearest ladder and rushing to the ramparts.

He immediately regretted his decision. A dozen scaling ladders had already been propped against the ramparts as a swarm of Drev'an below jostled one another to climb. Behind the mob he could see what looked like siege towers advancing, as well. Ambrus dared to look over his shoulder at the city. Every quarter seemed to be afire, the wooden structures blazing the strongest, as countless little blazes spread.

Dread sat like a stone in his belly, but he shook it off and called for someone, anyone to bring spears. Grabbing the nearest scaling ladder, he shoved, hoping to push it off the wall and send it toppling backward. A hail of black-fletched arrows sent him ducking back for cover. He dug the point of his sword into one arm of the ladder, hoping to use the blade's reach to more safely push the ladder. He needed two hands to handle the weight, but managed to push the structure past its balance point, sending the ladder and its cargo of climbers toppling backward onto the horde below.

On either side of him, other ladders were being defended against by soldiers, and in some cases, unarmed citizens. But in other places, the Drev'an were cresting the ramparts unchecked. The position was untenable, but there was nowhere to fall back and regroup. He glanced quickly backward toward the gate to assess the situation there. Braxus was nowhere to be seen, however the defenders seemed like they were trying to organize themselves. If the gates were opened, all would be lost. Another motion nearby caught his attention, and he brought up his sword reflexively to block. One of the horselords who'd already gotten past the wall was challenging him.

The warrior had caught him off-balance, and Ambrus pivoted to face him. It was an unnerving thing, not knowing who was at your back. Ambrus immediately regretted having his sword out and not the long knife instead, it would have been better in a close fight, but already the horselord was swinging at him again. Ambrus turned the blade, then aggressively closed the distance, stomping on the barbarian's foot and punching the hilt of his sword into the Drev'an's face. The horselord reeled and grabbed for Ambrus' throat with his free hand. Ambrus was already slashing a reverse stroke across the man's neck. He felt the tip of another blade cut across his back, breaking a few rings of his mail, and turned low, spinning the first Drev'an with him and shoving him at the second attacker. The first one crashed into the second one's knees, buckling them. Ambrus stabbed down into the space where shoulder met neck, then leapt past them both, not waiting to see where the next swing would come from. If he had any chance of getting Sitric and making his escape, it had to be now, there was no longer any doubt. Heedless of the risk, he leapt from the wall and ran for the palace grounds.

Chapter 31

Briga stood before the city gates, looking up as the fight on the wall raged. Not a single arrow flew in their direction; the defenders were already overwhelmed by the Drev'an who'd infiltrated the city. Sartaq's forces would be clearing the ramparts by now, removing any resistance to the scaling ladders. She could see fighting atop the wall near where they had entered, but there were more ladders that remained upright than those which were pushed back.

The fires had grown into a peculiar glow beyond the walls. She could only imagine the chaos that waited there. Beside her the wolf waited calmly, snugged up close to Singer's side to avoid being trampled by the other horses. One ear twitched from time to time as he stared forward with the rest of them. A great cry suddenly went up from the gate towers, and a loud crashing sound as one side of the drawbridge fell. The chain holding the other side remained intact, for now, and prevented the entire gate from lowering, but Batu's men were ready. The entire front rank rode forward, swinging grappling hooks at their sides. At some indistinct signal, they all launched their missiles to hook onto the edge of the bridge. Those who successfully caught began hauling on the ropes, backing their horses to add their weight to the effort. Dozens more hooks lanced through the air to add their support. There was a groaning sound now as the mechanisms that secured the remaining chain resisted this strange new force, yet still more grappling hooks flew. Additional horsemen began hauling on the lines as well. The Magyun archers seemed uncertain of what to do. Arrows flew haphazardly, some aimed at the impossible mass hauling on the drawbridge, but most sought desperately to hold back the Drev'an who'd already made it past the wall and presented a more immediate threat to their lives.

Briga tightened her grip on her ax, watching. With an unearthly groan, the bridge suddenly dropped several feet as the Drev'an mass overpowered its mechanisms. A shudder seemed to roll through the horsemen in anticipation, but the chain had caught again, stubbornly resisting. Along the wall, several of the Drev'an siege towers had drawn near enough for dismounted Drev'an to swarm up and add their numbers against the dwindling host of defenders on the ramparts. One tower had been set afire by doomed Magyuns determined to take as may invaders with them as they could. A flickering glow at the base of the wall indicated the Drev'an had taken it upon themselves to enlarge the existing hole Batu's spy had marked for them. With a loud crack that shattered the night, the bridge fell several more feet, caught for a moment, and finally crashed against the ground. The front ranks of Drev'an had barely avoided being crushed and now spurred their rearing mounts forward, leading the charge into burning chaos with a loud and resounding battle cry.

***

Ambrus could feel as well as hear the moment the chain broke, dropping the gate to admit the invading horselords. He didn't dare look back. Instead he pushed through the crowd thronging the streets, unhesitating now to cut his way through, if that was what it took. But the main street was just too clogged with people, and he dashed into a side street. It was still crowded, but he was better able to run here. A new body of screaming erupted far behind him, where the horselords were bringing death into the city. His lungs burned with exertion and smoke, but still he ran, pointing groups of soldiers back toward the carnage whenever he came across them. Townsfolk grabbed at his arms and torn cloak, begging for help against the fire and the terror, but he couldn't stop now. There was a groaning sound, and with precious little warning, a wooden barn collapsed in front of him, blocking the way.

A woman shrieked and tried to run into the burning debris, and Ambrus was knocked aside by a group of men who surged to restrain her.

"Noooo! Maggie! My child!!"

Ambrus swore, regaining his footing and trying to move away, but the woman's hands were flailing in all directions. Touching him, she took in his bloodied sword and torn cloak and her hands latched on, eyes wild.

"My child!" she screamed at him, begging.

Ambrus turned to look at the inferno and could just make out a thin scream. Swearing again, he twisted out of her grasp and threw off his sack as he strode into the debris, wondering what in Hel's name he was doing. He could hear hoofbeats in the main street now but tried not to think of it as he shoved piles of burning wood away with his sword or his hands. He heard coughing and carefully moved toward the sound, holding the edge of his cloak against his face to breathe. At the base of what had once been a wall, he saw an overturned water trough. It smoked as the heat sought to overcome the soaked wood. A small hand poked out of the opening, and Ambrus rushed forward. The little girl was unconscious but coughing when he pulled her out, and he wrapped her in his cloak against the smoky air.

He was coughing himself when he finally stumbled out of the debris, and the girl's mother tore free of all those restraining hands to claim her child.

"Go," Ambrus urged them, "flee the city, the horselords have attacked!"

He could delay no longer. Abandoning the sack of provisions that had been lost amid the crowd, he chose to take his chances in the wider main street. Most of the crowd was running in that direction, and Ambrus ran with them, then scrambled back as a stream of horsemen barreled down the street, red cloaks streaming behind them, and swords brandished. They were from the palace. Ambrus had no doubt General Larsson was among them. He watched after them for only the briefest moment before turning and running in the direction from which they'd come.

***

Briga had taken part in numerous skirmishes with Eamon's clan, but had only seen true battle twice. The first was at Rowanar, and the second had been the bridge. What she saw now was unlike any of those situations. Inside the gate, the narrow streets were clogged with fighting. Or slaughter. She'd lost sight of Batu almost instantly and even the wolf had left her side to find safer ground. Bayanaa and Gansükh pressed their horses close to her flanks, giving her enough room to fight, but not to lose them in the throng. She caught an arrow on her shield without thinking about it and swung her ax to cleave the spear someone thrust at her horse's neck. Gansükh rammed the soldier with his own horse a moment later, and likely trampled him. She urged her horse forward, slashing at Magyun soldiers whenever Gansükh's horse drifted a little too far.

The man facing her now on her right seemed terrified, but stood his ground, angling a sword at her over the top of his shield. Someone fell against her left leg, but she slammed the edge of her shield against them and shoved them off. The soldier on her right cut at the same instant, and she knocked the blade aside with her ax. He raised his shield to block her reverse swing, turning with her as the horse moved, dancing with all the noise and fire and swinging steel. Thinking quickly, she kicked the top edge of his shield, driving it into his face. He staggered, spurting blood, and she buried her ax in his neck.

A sudden, strong *tug* on her senses lifted her attention, and she found herself looking down the wider main road facing them. A column of horsemen was thundering down the road, clashing now with the lead Drev'an who'd already fought their way there.

It was no use calling for her kheshig, they would never hear her over the din. Trusting them to stay near, she bared her teeth in a snarl and fought her way toward that street.

Batu fought beside his brother, the two of them scything through the Magyun soldiers like so much chaff. He had spotted the red-cloaked riders and knew they were no ordinary soldiers. He grinned ferally, setting his sights on one of the lead riders as the man cut down one horselord, then another.

"Sartaq!" he yelled over the noise and swung his sword to point at the lords, or generals, or whatever they were.

With a wordless battle cry, Sartaq focused his killing rage, and his men, on the red-cloaked ones. Batu dared a quick glance around. His Drev'an were spreading in all directions, flooding the city and killing all who stood in their path. The Magyuns were too late to contain them. Grinning again, he kicked his stallion, which surged forward, uncaring of anyone in its way. The great beast roared and bit, just as deadly in a fight as its rider. Ahead of him, Sartaq had already cut his way through the mob and was squaring off with one of the redcloaks.

Soldiers and townsfolk alike were scattering from his path now, unwilling to be caught between the two groups of mounted fighters. Taking advantage of the space, Batu unslung his bow and quickly nocked an arrow, then loosed at the man his brother was trading blows with. The Magyun turned his head at the last moment, and Batu's arrow glanced off his helmet with a clang. Sartaq turned a death-glare on his brother for attempting to steal his kill. Batu returned the look with a wolf's grin, and Sartaq resumed his fight. The khan shifted aim as his horse shoved forward and shot one of the redcloaks in the neck. They wore heavy metal armor, which made them difficult to kill, but also slow, and with predictable vulnerable points.

Batu's horse reared suddenly as a man thrust a spear at its neck. Furious, it lashed out with heavy hooves to destroy both the spear and the man holding it. Batu swiveled his drawn bow and loosed at point-blank range. At that distance, the arrow passed almost completely through the man's chest. He followed with a kick and pressed forward, noting that his archers atop the wall were targeting the redcloaks now. They must have cleared that section of any resistance.

The redcloaks presented more of a fight than the regular soldiery, confirming Batu's assumption that they were men of some distinction. Sartaq had managed to kill his opponent and was now facing another. Batu growled, watching as the redcloaks fanned out in layered lines to block entrance into the main street. The street that undoubtedly led straight to Bela's palace.

His horse screamed and kicked backward as an arrow buried itself in its haunch. Batu tore the arrow out and barked encouragement to the stallion. The arrow hadn't penetrated deeply, but the wound trickled a thin stream, and Batu's blood riders closed protectively in an arc around them. The khan pointed with his sword to the nearest redcloak, marking him for death. The man noticed and turned his own horse to accept the challenge, quickly dispatching the dismounted Drev'an who'd already attacked him. The man wore black mail beneath his plate armor, and a black plume flowed from the crest of his helmet. The khan noted with alarm that his she-wolf was also pressing forward on the other side of the square to challenge these riders, but there was no time to deal with that now. Her kheshig were near, but that was cold comfort.

The stallion charged forward at Batu's command, ears flat and teeth bared. He lowered his head and shoulder-checked the other horse as their two riders noisily clashed shields. The blows had each been an attempt to unhorse the other rider, but neither succeeded. Batu slashed powerfully at the seam where the soldier's metal shoulder plate overlapped with his chest plates. The metal there creased, but he seemed unharmed. Batu caught a strong return blow on his shield and allowed his mount to dance away briefly. From the corner of his eye he saw Sartaq still fighting but had no time to check on the she-wolf before the black-plumed soldier closed with him again.

Briga herself was closing the distance with the redcloaked riders, intent on getting past them at the direction of that dull, insistent *tug*.

"Druid!" someone yelled, and she turned her head toward the sound.

A swarthy man faced her, bloodied and blocking her path to the horsemen. He was dismounted and pointed a gladius at her. It was an Emorian weapon, and she recognized it instantly. A flicker of emotion ran through her—fear, and hatred, and something else.

"Emorian," she hissed, turning Singer toward him.

There was no time to wonder what he was doing here, or why he'd sought her out. He had a spear in one hand and flipped it over into a throwing hold, then hurled it at her with his whole body behind the throw. She raised her shield, knowing it would do little good. With a yell, Bayanaa was suddenly between her and the Emorian, between her and the spear. His horse screamed and fell, taking Bayanaa with it.

"Bayanaa!" she called in horror, but there was nothing she could do.

The Emorian ran at her, slashing with his gladius. Singer pivoted so his shoulder and side were out of reach, and Briga reached across awkwardly with her shield. The Emorian was nimble, far more agile than the Magyuns in their heavy plate armor. Singer danced aside as the Emorian lunged at them again, driving her toward the redcloaks side-on. She batted his short sword away with her shield and swiped at him with her ax. He twisted as the ax grazed his chest and shoulder armor, then reached up and seized her ax-wrist in a crushing grip. She moved to slam the edge of her shield against his arm, but he hauled backward, using his already low position compared to her atop the horse to pull her off balance. The Emorian was stronger and heavier, and unhorsed her easily enough. She sensed his gladius aiming for her side as she fell, and moved her shield to block, then allowed all her weight to crash against him. Somewhere she thought she heard Gansükh call out.

Batu closed yet again with the black-plumed rider, and his stallion reached out to bite the other horse's neck. The rider could do nothing to help as Batu relentlessly sought to drive the point of his sword through the seams of his armor. Changing tactics, the khan feinted for another stab, then shoved his shield against the other rider and stabbed downward instead, into the man's horse. The horse screamed and danced away. Batu caught the briefest glimpse of his brother as he broke through the thinning lines of redcloaks to lead a charge of Drev'an toward the palace. He smirked. Sartaq knew what to do next. The khan returned his attention to the wounded horse and its black-plumed rider. His own stallion dashed in, smelling blood, and kicked out with its hooves. Batu's next cut sank into the wounded horse's shoulder as he maneuvered his own mount to remain out of sword reach.

The Magyun horse staggered and finally rolled before its rider could dismount. His leg was caught now beneath the flailing horse, and he swung his sword to keep Batu at a safe distance. The khan's stallion reared, trying to stomp on the downed rider, but the man's sword presented too much threat. The soldier pushed with his free leg against the animal's back for leverage while Batu circled, taking swings whenever an opportunity presented itself. Batu considered taking out his bow and ending it, but there were still other fighters trying to break through the arc of his blood riders and engage him. He would need to keep his sword close at hand. He spotted a broken spear nearby on the ground and leaned down to grab it.

The black-plumed fighter saw his chance and struggled harder, finally freeing his trapped leg as Batu turned again to face him. The khan's stallion bared its teeth and charged, pulling up short as the soldier staggered back a step and slashed at the stallion's nose. The wounded horse rolled then, knocking into the back of his rider's legs and throwing him off balance. Batu didn't hesitate to drive his horse forward again, impaling the

375

man on the spear. His fine armor was no match for the spear's sharp point. The soldier grabbed the spear's shaft by reflex, and Batu cruelly drove it deeper. The sword fell from the soldier's hand as he crumpled over the spear, attempting weakly to withdraw it. Batu placed the tip of his sword on the exposed skin on the back of the soldier's neck and drove down. The man hadn't been a particularly skilled fighter, but the armor had made him difficult to kill. Idly, Batu wondered if he would have presented more of a challenge without all that extra weight. The khan looked up then, searching for his next opponent, but found instead an opportunity to chase after his brother.

"Ambrus told me they had a woman fighter," the Emorian growled in Velkcic. "I should have known you'd be a druid."

He had rolled as she fell so they both landed on their sides, and he ended up on top of her. Briga was partially pinned beneath her own shield, but so was his gladius, tangled as they were. Her ax hand was free, but he still held her wrist tightly.

Briga rammed her head forward, attempting to head-butt him, but he twisted to the side. She pushed with her opposite leg, trying to roll them both in the direction he'd ducked. She partially succeeded before the edge of her shield caught, and he rocked them both back the other way, slamming her hand against the ground in the process to try to break her grip on the ax. Something slammed into them from the side as another armored soldier was knocked from his horse, and Briga lost her grip on the ax handle with that impact. The Emorian had also let go of his gladius as he was knocked aside. Briga didn't hesitate. She dropped her shield and leapt onto him, straddling his chest with one hand around his throat as she pulled the fighting knife from its sheath at her waist.

"Bitch," he rasped. "Typical Velkcic, turning on your own kind."

That cooled her killing rage somewhat, and she paused, wondering what he was talking about. He felt the change in her and rushed to sit up, but she thrust her knife into his side, where

376

his vile legion armor laced together. The Emorian gasped in surprise, then surged forward to knock her off balance. She stabbed him again and scrambled to escape his grasp. There was a hand at the collar of her leather jerkin, which hauled her back and up. By instinct she brought one hand up, and a sword grated against the back of her reinforced leather bracer instead of her throat. With her other hand, she slashed backward with her knife, aiming low to avoid any armor, and felt flesh. The hand released her, and she spun, slamming the hilt of her knife into the side of his helmet. She then reversed it smoothly and sank the blade into his throat.

Briga stepped back as the man fell to his knees, glancing around quickly for the next threat. There was no immediate danger. She took a few deep breaths, trying to force her breathing to slow to a more normal pace, before stumbling over to retrieve her ax and shield. The gladius lay beneath her shield, and she looked to the huddled form of its owner briefly before taking it and thrusting it through her sword belt. The Emorian was still moving, curled in on his wounds.

She sensed someone coming and turned to fight, but a spear emerged suddenly from the soldier's unarmored chest, and he collapsed. Bayanaa stood behind the stranger, shaking and holding his side.

"Breeg…" he breathed, face crumping with relief.

"Bayanaa! You're hurt…"

The kheshig shook his head and showed her his hands. "No blood."

Beyond him she could see an ordinary Magyun soldier attempting to hold Singer's reins. The gelding reared and lashed out with its hooves. Gansükh thundered in and nearly cut the man in half. Forcing herself to be calm, she walked toward him. His furious eyes took in Bayanaa hiding his injury, then searched every inch of Briga, assessing her. Taking hold of Singer's bridle, he calmed the horse and brought it to her.

"Next time, stay in the saddle," he ordered before turning his attention to Bayanaa. "And you had better find another horse."

"I seem to have freedom of choice." Bayanaa attempted to smile despite his injury and moved off to catch the first riderless horse he saw.

Gansükh held the gray still as the she-wolf mounted, gently stroking its nose while they waited. His hands were shaking as much as hers. Around them, relative silence grew as the Drev'an spread out into the city, leaving destruction in their wake. There was still a sizeable group clashing with the redcloaks at the mouth of the main street, and pockets of fighting all around them, but the chaos had lessened.

"Are you all right?" he finally asked as Bayanaa caught the reins of a loose horse.

She nodded, tightening her grip on the reins to hide the tremor in her hands.

"It is normal," he assured her quietly. "You fought well."

"It isn't over yet."

An animal ferocity had returned to her eyes, as she stared up the street that led to the palace. She wiped the blade of her knife against her leg and sheathed it before taking a sticky, familiar grip on her ax. Without another word, she rode for the main street, ready to fight more redcloaks,

***

Amergin awoke slowly, uncertain what had roused him this time. He was still curled up in the relatively clean straw where he had lain down earlier. Around him, he became aware of the sounds of snoring. The warriors seemed to be asleep—it must be night. He blinked the sleep from his eyes, feeling uneasy for some reason. Smelling smoke, he glanced over to check the fire burning low in the makeshift hearth. Cathbad was asleep where

Amergin had left him. With a start, he noted there was *too much* smoke in the air. Suspecting the smoke-hold was blocked, he looked up and was surprised to see portions of thatch that appeared to be emitting more smoke. Belatedly he registered a low crackling sound and watched in fascination as a single spark drifted down from above. *A spark...*

Instinct warned him of what was happening, but he had to see for himself. Dreading each moment, he stood and crossed to the door. Steadying himself with a breath, he opened it and looked out into the night. At first he saw nothing, but gradually he realized there was a glow at the north end of the city. He stared for a moment, then registered that the glow was also coming from somewhere closer. Much closer. Small fires were beginning to flare up in the thatched roofs of the structures around them, and not just one or two, but *all* of the nearby buildings were affected. He looked up to see their roof smoking and sporting a tiny flame as well.

"Fire!" he called into the night. "Fire! Fire!"

Some of their neighbors were already awake and scurrying to the water well. He thought he could hear distant screaming, but there were more immediate dangers to worry about right now. The buildings here were wooden and packed close together; they were all in danger of the flames spreading and growing out of control. He dashed back inside to see the warriors already rousing themselves to his alarm.

"Eamon," he called, rushing to the chieftain. "The thatch is smoking. There's fire on the nearby buildings."

"Rorik, Kessan, Niall, clear out the rushes."

The three warriors nodded and dashed to fetch rakes. They would clear the floor and the stalls of straw to prevent them catching fire if the thatch ignited fully and dropped more sparks, or fell altogether into the structure. Rorik found it faster to gather great armfuls of straw and carry it to a far corner, away from the wooden walls.

"You others, climb onto the roof. Take buckets and wet the thatch."

Even with the extra supply Amergin had insisted on earlier, there wouldn't be enough to wet the whole roof, and they needed to keep a reserve in case fire did break out. But Eamon had already thought of that.

"Not that barrel," he stopped Connor with a gesture, "leave that one."

"My lord, there won't be enough—"

"Oisean!" Eamon called out. "Run to the well. Get water if you can, but find out what's happening."

"Aye, lord."

Oisean grabbed his sword belt and a few spare waterskins and ran out into the night. Eamon eyed his warriors grimly, assessing the situation for himself.

"Cathbad," he called next, but the chief druid wasn't hovering at his chieftain's shoulder.

Eamon and Amergin looked to the hearth fire, where the old druid was still laying on his side, facing the flames. Amergin felt suddenly cold all over.

"Cathbad?" Amergin ventured, feeling his skin pebble.

"Come on, old man," Rorik added good-naturedly. "I need to clear this straw."

But he still didn't move. Rorik leaned down to touch his shoulder, and his grin faded.

"Amergin…"

The younger druid felt his body move on its own, stiffly crossing a space that was simultaneously too large and too small to reach the small hearthfire. He already knew. He'd known for some time, but still his hand reached out to touch his master's shoulder. The chief druid was clutching a fistful of herbs in one hand and had died staring into the fire. Amergin gently closed his master's eyes, then let his own head drop as he rested a hand on Cathbad's forehead. Grief clutched at his heart, but there would be time for that later. The old druid's spirit had departed cleanly. He looked up at Eamon, who regarded him pale-faced and still. For a moment the world was devoid of any sound. Eamon looked around to see that his warriors had paused to watch in stunned silence.

"Carry on," he ordered quietly. "If the thatch catches fire, we'll all join him. He would not want that."

With shared glances, they resumed their tasks. Amergin held the chieftain's gaze. Cathbad had been like a second father to all of them. There was a new sound outside now that shattered the spell of the moment and they both looked to the door. It was a chorus of screaming, slowly growing louder.

"Get to the roof," Eamon barked to the two warriors who were already climbing up to the loft. "Find out exactly how far the fires have spread."

When he looked to the sole remaining druid once more, there was an edge to his gaze that spoke of impending trouble.

***

Sartaq had been expecting strong resistance when he approached the palace, but so far had been disappointed. A few good archers kept his men behind the modest cover of some burning stone buildings for the moment. The courtyard was largely deserted, however. Unlike the rest of the city, the palace alone was constructed entirely of stone. He watched the handful of figures scrambling about the courtyard and grounds, never taking his eyes off the distant forms.

"General Altan."

An especially fearsome-looking Drev'an rode forward at Sartaq's command. He rode a stout black horse with one white sock and a thin, crooked stripe up its nose.

"Fire the stables and the outbuildings. We will keep the archers busy for you."

Altan grinned and nodded. With a short whistle, he summoned a contingent of his men and carefully set off, weaving through areas of cover until Sartaq was ready for him to move.

"Archers," Sartaq ordered calmly. "Prepare to attack."

***

Lord Heinrich huddled in his quarters, listening to the screams of the city. He dared once to glance out the window, but the sight of General Larsson leading his cavalry charge toward the disturbance at the northern gate was enough to drive him quickly back into hiding. He was no fighter, he was a nobleman! With shaking fingers, he withdrew the little wooden cross from beneath his shirt and prayed.

He was eventually disturbed by someone pounding on his door. His heart skipped a beat at the sound, and he tried desperately to ignore it, to will it away.

"Lord Heinrich!" a feminine voice pleaded on the edge of hysteria.

"Hanna?"

Still trembling faintly, he found the courage to stand and make his way shakily to the door.

"Hurry!" she pleaded.

He fumbled with the latch and finally managed to pull it open. Hanna stood on his doorstep, dark hair loose and streaming rather than hidden beneath the shawl she usually wore for the sake of discretion when she visited him. Her terror-filled green eyes gazed up at him desperately.

"What are you doing here?"

Both of her hands latched onto his arm, dragging him outside. "Hurry! We must get to the palace, now!"

He resisted. "Stop! It's too dangerous!"

"There is no *time,* m'lord, the horselords are inside the city. We have to run!"

"What?"

"Now!" she insisted again, tugging him forward.

At the far end of the courtyard they saw a small pack of mounted Drev'an heading for the stables. They were carrying naked blades and blazing torches. It was enough to break his resistance, and he grabbed her hand and ran for the king's stronghold. Arrows flew in their general direction, and ahead they saw the palace guards pulling the two heavy doors shut.

"Wait!" they both called in panic.

One guard continued hauling on his door, while the other paused and waved them on urgently. He couldn't wait long. They ignored the arrows and the sound of hooves behind them completely as they blindly ran. They reached the door just in time, and the guard pulled it shut behind them. Then the pair of guards closed and locked an interior metal gate. The outside of the heavy doors had no handles; they could only be opened from the inside. Heinrich turned, panting, to look at Hanna, and she collapsed into his arms.

"You saved my life," he breathed, realizing all at once how close he had come to death by fire or a Drev'an blade.

She said nothing in return, instead burying her face in his chest for a moment, letting him hold her. After time enough for them to both calm themselves, she took a step back.

"Come, we had better see what news there is."

Heinrich nodded and led the way into the audience chamber. Several others had retreated here for safety as well, it seemed. Lord Heinrich noticed some of the other high lords scattered about the room, some with their ladies in tow. The king whirled at his entrance, a hand flying to the hilt of his sword. Heinrich raised his hands in a placating gesture, and Hanna half hid behind him.

"Only me, my lord."

"The doors are shut and locked, Your Grace," one of the guards reported.

The king visibly relaxed now, though tension was still evident in his posture. Reluctantly he let go of his sword hilt.

"Who is that?" he asked, nodding faintly to the woman sheltering behind Heinrich.

"This is my...er...this is Hanna. Your Grace."

Bela looked as if he was about to make some comment, but Hanna shyly stepped forward and offered an uncertain curtsy.

"You Grace...what will we do?"

There was a grief-stricken note in her voice, and Heinrich reached out to gently touch her shoulder. Even the king softened slightly.

"We shall wait, my child. Lord Larsson has taken the cavalry to stop this terrible threat."

"But there is fire everywhere, Your Grace, and we saw horselords in the palace courtyard!"

"She's right, Your Grace," called Lord Olechs, who had climbed atop some furniture to peer out a high, narrow window. "They've fired the stables and are working on the outbuildings now."

A few of the women whimpered.

"Where are all the guards?" one whispered.

"We're doomed!"

"We aren't doomed; we are safe in this building." Bela shot a look to a few of the high lords. He disliked this simpering.

"Father Henri, if you would be so kind as to lead us in prayer, it might do everyone some good."

Rubbing his temples briefly, the king moved off to sink onto his throne. Hanna drew closer to Heinrich and lowered her voice.

"Where *are* the guards?" she questioned.

"I imagine many went out to help with the fires."

"But I only saw two in here. Two!"

He took her hand and patted it reassuringly. "There will be more in the inner rooms, fear not. Those doors can't be opened from the outside; it's impossible by design. Guards are better placed at the stairwells and other vulnerable points."

She shook him off, unwilling to be so easily placated. "Surely we are not to sit here and just wait—"

"Keep your voice down," Heinrich cautioned. "The king knows best, trust his judgement."

But she was angry now, and he could see the mild panic welling in her at their predicament. He reached for her, but she stepped back and turned away, striding back toward the antechamber.

"Where are you going?" he demanded, lowering his tone abruptly at a glance from the chanting priest.

"I need to walk."

"Wait…"

385

But she was already moving, crossing into the antechamber, where she barely glanced at the two guards before picking a hallway and striding off.

"Wait, Hanna, you can't just go wandering off," Heinrich protested with an apologetic look to the guards to convey that he would retrieve her. "She's distraught...you know how women panic."

He set off at a brisk but dignified pace and finally caught up with her.

"I know you're upset dearest but—"

"Upset!" She broke off suddenly and hugged herself, trying to stave off the trembling that consumed her. "I am terrified. The whole city is burning, and we are trapped here in the palace. The one place they are sure to come. We should never have come here, we should have fled!"

As if to emphasize her point, someone screamed outside, and the sound caused her to flinch. Her fear tore at Heinrich like a knife, and wordlessly he moved to take her in his arms again. One hand moved to gently raise her chin so she was looking at him.

"All will be well, you'll see. We are safe here."

Her eyes searched his face, emotion still brimming there. She leaned forward to kiss him then, one hand coming up to touch his cheek. He was startled, but embraced her and kissed her back. There was a desperate need in her touch, and she deepened the kiss, pushing him backward into a shadowed corner.

"Here?" he breathed against her, only mildly protesting.

She ignored the question and reached under her cloak to remove it. He made a small sound, and it changed slightly as she slipped her knife between his ribs, angling for his heart. He opened his eyes in shock to find her watching him with a hateful gaze. She drove the blade in again, twisting this time to end him quickly, before he could call out. She felt the knife scrape against his ribs and willed herself to ignore the sensation. As he sank down the wall, she sank with him so he wouldn't fall and alert the guards. There were none in sight. She'd chosen this corner for that reason, risking that no one would be patrolling, given the situation in the city.

Heinrich died quickly. She wiped her blade on his tunic and sheathed it back in its hiding place, then carefully cleaned her hands on his clothing as well. After a quick glance around to ensure there were still no guards within view, she walked back toward the audience chamber, wringing her hands. She watched the floor as she paced, studiously avoiding the fire-glow emanating through all the high windows. The very picture of female anxiety.

"Where's Lord Heinrich?" one of the guards asked when she wandered back into view alone.

"He went to find me a glass of water."

She looked over her shoulder, searching for his return. Her hands were shaking—she didn't have to feign that.

"Go back into the audience chamber, my lady, it's not safe to be walking around."

Panic flared in her gaze at his comment, and she bit her lip for just a moment.

"I *cannot* just wait in there like a penned lamb…will you walk with me?"

The guard shook his head regretfully. "I must stay here…for your safety. Go inside. Your-ah…Lord Heinrich will be back shortly."

Inwardly she cursed, but outwardly she nodded in grudging acceptance. She needed *that* guard, and soon. Once Heinrich's body was discovered, she was certain to be accused. She allowed the guard to guide her by the elbow for a few steps and then crumpled in on herself, hand raised to mask quiet sobs.

"My lady?" the guard asked awkwardly, having no idea what to do, but taking her shoulders to steady her.

"We quarreled," she confessed, laying hands on him anxiously. "He blames me for trapping him here."

"It'll be all right," he soothed clumsily. "It's only the stress speaking. Come, I will take you to the priest, and you'll feel better with prayer."

She nodded acceptance and took a few deep breaths to steady herself.

"My apologies," she ventured after a moment. "I just…"

She gestured around vaguely, indicating the entire situation. He tucked her under one arm, and she allowed him to take her back to the audience chamber, slowly regaining her composure.

"Thank you," she murmured as he led her across the threshold and gently let her go. "I am all right now."

He patted her shoulder kindly. She hugged herself and leaned against the nearest wall, sliding down to a sitting position, and deftly tucked away the keys she'd taken from the guard's belt.

Hanna lost track of time in developing her options, but it wasn't long before a clamor rose outside as more Drev'an assaulted the courtyard. By now they had probably set fire to every building they could and would be looking for ways to infiltrate the palace itself. She could hear running feet in the corridor, but it was impossible to determine direction. The king was restless. He sat tapping his foot one moment, then paced the next.

"You. Hanna, was it?" he eventually called irritably.

"Yes, Your Grace?"

"Where is Lord Heinrich?"

"I-I do not know, Your Grace."

"Damn coward," he muttered. "Lord Olechs, what do you see?"

Olechs had stacked more objects beneath the window to make it easier to look out, and now checked obediently. "The doors I can see have all been blocked with debris and set aflame."

"Where are the horselords?"

"They seem to have fallen back, my lord. No...they're dragging something."

There was a palpable increase in the room's tension.

"Siege engines? A ram?" someone asked.

"A body," Olechs stated after a moment. "I think it's General Larsson."

"No..."

"What now?"

"Guards!" someone cried out in distress, and Hanna felt her blood run cold. "It's Lord Heinrich!"

The two guards pulled their swords. One dashed off toward the alarm, while the other paused long enough to tell the king to conceal himself. Hanna couldn't delay. Hoping not to draw attention, she quickly slipped out of the room as the others sought hiding places and crossed the antechamber to the door gates. With shaking fingers, she withdrew the keys from concealment and fumbled with the lock. One precious second. Two. Three. Her heart was pounding so loud she was sure someone could hear it.

"What are you doing?" This from the far end of the hall, near where she'd left Heinrich's body.

The lock clicked loudly as it released, and she flung the gates open.

"Someone, stop her!"

She didn't dare stop to look. She threw her shoulder into the heavy door and pushed with all her might. It moved maddeningly slow, but it moved. A clear signal. She could hear the guards now almost upon her and shoved with all the strength she could muster. The door swung open, and she fell with the effort, rolling aside just in time to avoid being trampled by the first of the Drev'an riders. More horses followed, surging straight into the palace. A few dismounted warriors rushed forward to pull open the other door as well. Two advanced on her with ready blades, but she hastily withdrew the khan's seal secreted around her neck. They looked at each other uncertainly, then left her alone and ran into the palace with their brothers.

She nearly sobbed with relief, pushing herself up on her hands and knees, grateful to be in one piece. Grateful to be alive. She staggered a little further from the door, and one of the horsemen peeled off and reined to a sudden stop beside her. Sartaq leaned down and kissed her thoroughly as her shaking hands twined behind his neck.

"My beautiful, brilliant Davaa. That could not have been more perfect if we had planned it."

She laughed, tears glistening in the corners of her eyes, still not quite believing she was alive.

"How did you do it?"

He'd seen her rush across the courtyard with the fat Magyun, but had no idea what she had planned.

"Heinrich proved to be useful after all. They would never have let me in without a high lord."

He kissed her again, and his horse danced impatiently. "We will celebrate later. Now I must deliver that swine of a king to my brother."

Chapter 32

Ambrus was making slow progress, which made him more and more aggravated by the minute. He needed to stay ahead of the Drev'an, who were clearing the city as they advanced, but he was delayed by fleeing townsfolk thronging the streets and alleys. More than once he'd turned a corner to see a band of Drev'an in his path and had to fight his way through. Frustrated, he had even attempted to make his way across the rooftops, but the fire and unstable patches where fires had burnt out were proving too dangerous to traverse.

The congestion thinned as he approached the palace, and for good reason. The mounted Drev'an were beginning to mass there. It was a natural target, after all, to destroy King Bela's stronghold and capture or kill him. Ambrus picked his way carefully. He couldn't afford a fight here; he'd be badly outnumbered. He crept carefully to each corner, diligently checking any open spaces he would have to cross before simply barging out. He could hear the Drev'an talking now and knew he was getting close to a group of them. Crouching, he peeked out quietly to assess how to get around and eventually past them. He had become disoriented in the smoke and maze of narrow alleys, and found himself at the last row of structures lining the palace courtyard. Closer than he'd intended…much closer. Drev'an were milling at the edge of archery range from the palace or were otherwise snugged up close against the palace's stone walls. They seemed largely unconcerned with any threat of counterattack.

Ambrus ducked into a blackened house to hide while assessing the situation he found himself in. Moving quietly, he picked his way through charred furniture and dim embers still faintly glowing until he reached a window and could look out across the courtyard. He swore. Every building had been put to the torch. Not even the entrance to the dungeon, which had no wood or thatch to burn, had been spared. They'd mounded up anything that would burn in the doorway and set it ablaze. He could faintly see the outline of the intact iron gate through the inferno. The dungeons would be full of smoke by now. Even if they were not, there were Drev'an warriors *everywhere*. It would be impossible for him to sneak in and out with an unwilling prisoner, even if he could have created an opportunity to try it.

He had no choice now, he would have to abandon Siggi to fate, and hope he died from the smoke. He was about to turn away, when something caught his eye. Some faint movement near the palace's heavy doors. He squinted, trying to make out what had drawn his attention. In the glow from the firelight, he thought he might have seen the door shudder slightly. As he watched, it began inching outward. He blinked, uncertain of what he was seeing. The mounted horselords nearby had noticed it as well and readied themselves for whatever might happen. Ambrus couldn't make sense of what he was seeing. Those doors were impregnable from the outside. The king would be cowering within. He doubted Bela would choose to come out and fight now. Judging by the rooftop archers, there was no indication some other entry had been breached, either.

In a sudden rush, one door swung open all at once, and the nearest of the horselords wasted no time rushing in with drawn swords. Ambrus had known since seeing those first Drev'an atop the ramparts that the city was lost. It was only a matter of time. But seeing them now, surging into the palace, he knew the city had finally fallen. His mission was a failure; there was nothing left now but to escape. He touched the hilt of the Kithian dagger by reflex, seeking luck, and backed away from the window. He re-crossed the burnt-out room carefully, mentally assessing his options. He had no provisions now, except those he had stored near the north gate. With the Drev'an essentially running loose, he didn't dare try to cross the main street again. He would have to continue south and hope to improvise along the way.

At the door, he cautiously looked out to determine if the horselords from earlier were still nearby, or if they had joined their brothers at the palace. A quick peek confirmed they had not moved, though their attention was fixed on the activity in the courtyard. Ambrus glanced beyond them reflexively. He saw another group clustered around a few prone forms and guessed they were captured or slain noblemen. He was turning to go when one rider broke from the pack, drawing Ambrus' attention. The man rode to the open doorway but stopped short beside a standing figure. He leaned down for a moment, and when the two finally parted, the Kith's blood turned to ice. By firelight he recognized the shorter, standing form with the hood of her cloak thrown back. He regretted now not killing her when he had the chance, the treacherous bitch. For it was Dianna standing there with her hand on the horselord's thigh. Dianna, who turned to watch the Drev'an ride off into the palace. Dianna, who stared after the rider for a moment, then shakily sank to a seated position against the stone wall, her green gaze turned lazily around the group of horsemen guarding their prizes.

Ambrus wasn't aware he had moved, but when he regained control of his senses, he was several houses away from the burnt-out husk, and moving south. He had to leave, but he could at least try to warn Amergin on the way, if the fates allowed.

***

Davaa sat with her back against the damp stone wall trying to stop the shaking in her legs and hands. She had hated many men before, but she had never had to kill. She took a few deep breaths to steady herself, watching the group surrounding General Larsson's body. They were dragging others up now and arranging them in a neat row. She shuddered once, then forced the anxiety from her mind for now. There was still work to do.

She could hear fighting and the clash of blades within. Bela wouldn't surrender easily, now that he was certain of his death. She suspected there was likely another barricaded room, or even a concealed passageway at the rear of the audience chamber.

394

There almost had to be, but she had never found a suitable excuse to investigate the area for herself. Not without drawing undue suspicion. By the sounds of it, more soldiers had rushed to the audience chamber from elsewhere within to protect the king.

There was a new disturbance near the row of bodies as a new group of horsemen emerged. She recognized Batu by his black stallion, noting the creature was lightly wounded, but the khan himself seemed unscathed. Likely he'd ridden up with the bodies initially and would have held back as the palace doors swung open, in case of a counterattack. She knew he would wait now and allow his brother the honor of taking the palace before he claimed the city for the Drev'an and dealt with King Bela himself.

Davaa rose on surprisingly steady legs and began crossing the courtyards toward the khan. No archers remained atop the palace now; they were needed more urgently within. The khan saw her coming and jogged his mount to her. She remembered to bow respectfully at his approach.

"My lord," she offered with a smile in her voice for once.

"Davaa. You have done well."

"Thank you, Batu Khan. The commander is inside the palace now."

"Yes, I saw him enter."

Davaa schooled her features, wondering what else he had seen. But he said nothing of what he might have suspected.

"Where is a good place to corral the foreigners until I decide what to do with them?"

Davaa hesitated a moment, considering. The dungeon was an obvious choice, but one glance at its inferno of an entrance dismissed that notion. Where else to house a sizeable group temporarily? She frowned at the answer when it finally came. The khan was watching her expectantly.

"There…is a barn not far from here," she began, uncertain. "I should caution you, it is made of wood, and may not still stand."

Batu waved a hand dismissively.

"There is a group of Velkcic there now," she continued with obvious reluctance.

She knew from Sartaq that the khan had a keen interest in the Velkcic, but revealing this information felt…ill-timed, perhaps. Not quite right.

"Velkcic?"

"Yes. I believe they are survivors from Rowanar. They are near the south gate, which may also be an option if the barn is too badly burned."

The khan's face darkened at that into something menacing, but in a flash, he recovered himself.

"Where?"

She gestured in the direction of the barn, suddenly feeling a slight dread. The khan watched her a moment more, then nodded.

"Take me there."

"My lord, I…they will recognize me. One in particular."

"That will not matter soon."

Her face paled, and she moved on reflex to grip his arm, but stopped short as she remembered herself. "Please, Batu Khan, do not kill them."

His face darkened again, and he allowed a tinge of irritation to show. "Why?"

"Two of them are shaman," she explained, feeling inadequate. "They have no love for Magyuns; they are simply trapped here."

Batu forced calmness back into his demeanor. "What kind of shaman?"

"Healers. I do not know what other skills they might possess."

"We could use more healers," he acknowledged tepidly. "Do they have a leader?"

Davaa breathed a sigh of relief inwardly. She felt guilty jeopardizing Amergin, especially when he had produced no greater intelligence value than to bring her closer to the Kith. But he was kind-hearted, and that had endeared him to her. The rest were unimportant.

"He is called Eamon."

A muscle bunched in the khan's jaw, a strange expression she'd never seen on him before.

"My lord?" she ventured uncertainly.

The khan watched her a moment longer, assessing something, then turned in his saddle to gesture to two of his generals. Khuyag and Burd were quick to obey.

"Instruct the men. All foreigners will be brought to a barn at the south end of the city. We will sort them out there." He paused and turned a cold glance to his spy. "Davaa, you will show us the way."

She opened her mouth to protest again about being recognized, but he stayed her with a gesture.

"You may leave before we get too close. If the shaman trust you, there is still value in hiding your identity. Burd, inform the men. Khuyag, come with me to learn the way to this structure."

Something cold settled in her gut, but Davaa pushed the feeling aside and accepted the khan's hand to swing up behind him on the saddle. She pulled the deep hood of her cloak low over her eyes for good measure.

"That way," she instructed with a gesture.

***

Briga could taste blood in her mouth, though whether it was human, animal, or her own, she couldn't say. She had lost herself to the numb focus of combat for a time and spat now to clear her mouth and her mind. Her horse closed with another mounted rider again and they clashed shields, shoving one another for control, hacking uselessly. When they became locked, she hooked the beard of her ax over the top rim of his shield and yanked it down and toward her. She then swung her own shield around and slammed its edge into his exposed face. The soldier was spared serious damage by his nasal guard and the fatigue weakening her arm, but the blow still emitted a satisfying *clang*, and his head rocked with the impact.

She followed up by tearing away his shield, or at least that was what she attempted to do. It was lashed to his arm. Before he could regroup to counterattack, a dismounted Drev'an grabbed him from the other side and pulled him from his horse. She watched in shock as his booted foot flew past her face as he tumbled off. Furious, she kicked Singer to move around the now-riderless horse and pursue her opponent. The Drev'an had made short work of the soldier once he was on the ground, and she beat the spine of her ax against her shield in impotent fury. The blood-streaked face that looked up at her was familiar, smiling in a way that was at once impressed and mischievous.

"Jinghim," she growled.

He merely laughed, twisted his blade in the soldier for good measure, then stood and patted her on the leg in a comradely way. An arrow scythed the air between them, and Jinghim leaned back reflexively. Briga turned to track its origin and found

Bayanaa sitting atop a new horse with his empty bow in the rapidly clearing space. She scolded him with a look, understanding that he'd been warning the other Drev'an just as much as he had been targeting some Magyun, and she did not appreciate the gesture. Jinghim raised his hands in supplication, winked at the she-wolf, and then melted away to fight on.

Still angry, she glanced around for the next target. They had been caught in a small pocket of fighting that resurged when Sartaq and the khan had broken through the line of defending horsemen. Dismounted soldiers and armed townsfolk alike had converged at the mouth of the street to attempt to contain the remaining Drev'an, and she'd been forced to cut a path through them. The pocket of resistance had been largely subdued now, and she scanned what remained. The fires were still burning, but some had already run their course. More Drev'an were streaming into the city, and they dispersed in all directions to deal with any resistance they encountered, or to assist in the fighting elsewhere. In the absence of clashing steel, she could hear a new sound rending the night. It was the cries of the survivors, the women and children mostly, as they dealt with new horrors.

The Drev'an were going house to house, not looting, but killing. Briga was physically exhausted, and her arms and legs trembled faintly. Unlike earlier, these tremors were from the constant exertion of battle. She forced herself to lift her ax and shield once more and rode to join up with Bayanaa. The kheshig watched her approach, an arrow nocked loosely in his bow, but the weapon rested across one thigh.

"What are they doing?" she asked, watching a group of Drev'an dragging men from the nearby structures. "Those men aren't soldiers."

"They are carrying out the khan's wishes."

"But they aren't fighting us."

There was no joy in the killing, no ceremony or dark satisfaction. What she witnessed was the cold efficiency of a simple task being carried out. A cull.

"They are Magyun," was his even reply. "This is war."

It seemed to be mostly women and young children who were spared, and they were left for the time being to scream over their slain kin. Occasionally a man was spared and dragged off instead, or a woman killed who would not submit. Briga had no energy left to spare for the fate of the odd survivors at the moment. Outraged, she rode up to the nearest group, with Bayanaa scrambling to follow.

"Stop!" she called out, but it was too late, and her voice was too raw.

They had killed any fighting aged males and moved on. A number of the women had been gutted as well, she noticed, as her mount skidded to a halt and she vaulted off.

"Why?" she breathed, uncomprehending.

These people had been trying to flee, by the looks of them, not fight. Why kill them? She shed her shield and sheathed her ax as she approached the slaughter. She wasn't sure why she had come here, but heeded her instincts. Her eye was drawn to one woman who was still alive, clutching at her side. Briga dropped to her knees, rushing to help. The woman made some animal sound of fear and feebly tried to defend herself.

"No..." Briga soothed in Velkcic, knowing the woman couldn't understand, but sensing the Drev'an tongue would frighten her more. "Hush...let me help you."

The woman was indeed injured, but Briga realized it wasn't her side she was holding, but an infant child. The child was dead, and likely had been for some time now, but the mother refused to let it go. She bled badly from a gut wound. Briga knew at a glance she could not save this woman. She crept forward anyway, showing the woman her palms. Perhaps she could do something to ease her terror.

Another small form slid through the mud and fell at the woman's other side. The boy-child was old enough to wield a thin wooden club and swung it to hold Briga at bay. The sight of his too-small hand wrapped around the club's grip stunned her with a flash of memory. *Her brother held a man's sword in his too-small hand before their mother.* As quickly as it had come, the memory faded, leaving her feeling dizzy and off-balance. Bayanaa had stepped in and kicked the club away.

"Stop!" she stayed him with a gesture and looked to the boy again.

"Is this your mother?" she asked gently, still in Velkcic.

Bayanaa growled but stepped back a few paces. The boy lost all resolve then, and fell weeping upon his mother's shoulder. Briga inched back as well. There was nothing to be done here. The boy wept a moment longer, then began calling out to those still in hiding. She imagined he was probably calling for help. Feeling numb, she rocked back on her heels for a moment and surveyed the carnage. If there were other survivors nearby, they didn't wish to make themselves known. She caught Bayanaa's eye and read his disapproval. With a sigh, she finally stood and turned to go.

"Where's Gansükh?"

He gestured wordlessly to where the last of the redcloaks fought on. Gansükh was done with his fight and riding toward them. Briga nodded, suddenly bone tired.

"Go and fetch Dagmer. I expect we're nearly done here, and I will need her."

He opened his mouth to protest, but she cut him off. "Gansükh will stay with me."

"…yes, mistress."

401

Reluctantly he mounted and trotted off toward the north gate, exchanging a look and a few words with Gansükh as they passed one another. Briga had one foot in the stirrup when something the little boy said caught her attention. She couldn't speak much Magyun, but there was a familiar word. Pausing, she looked at him and waited to see if he would repeat it again. He was speaking to his mother now, desperately. But she heard it. A name amid the unintelligible Magyun tongue.

"What did you say?" she questioned uselessly.

The boy ignored her and turned his tear-streaked face away, calling to anyone that would help.

"Did you say 'Amergin'?"

They boy looked at her hatefully, then continued his plea.

"Gansükh!" she called as her kheshig neared. "You speak Magyun, yes?"

"A few words."

"That boy. What is he saying?"

Gansükh wiped blood and sweat from his brow with the back of his hand and flung it aside as he listened.

"I think he is calling for a healer," he finally responded.

Briga felt lightning crackle through her. A warning.

"What's the healer's name?"

Gansükh looked at her sharply hearing the tightness in her voice. "What is wrong?"

"The name! What is the name?"

The warrior listened a moment longer but didn't take his eyes from her. "Amergin, I think."

402

It can't be… She was nearly certain her heart had stopped, but she found her mind to be clear. Or at least as clear as she could manage.

"Is this healer Magyun?"

Her kheshig didn't like where this was leading, but when he could not glean this information passively, he decided to ask the boy outright.

"No, my lady. He is a foreigner of some kind."

She *knew*. She could feel the truth of her knowledge as plainly as she could feel her own heartbeat. With that knowledge also came a sense of impending danger. Something perilous and unstoppable that raised every hair on the back of her neck.

"Where?"

***

There had been to time to attend to Cathbad. The warriors were all seeing to their fire prevention tasks, and it had only taken a few moments longer for chaos to erupt outside. Embers flared into flame on several structures nearby, and judging by the screams and the faint glow, it extended much further. Amergin whispered a few words to Cathbad, then rushed to the doorway to see what he could. The gods had been with him earlier in compelling him to fetch more water ahead of the conflagrations. People were thronging the streets now, all scrambling toward the nearest well in a panic. The fires would prove to be devastating in no time, that much was obvious. But there was another noise behind the scramble and panic of fire, a sound that caused a great sense of foreboding in his very bones. It was a sound of malevolence. Amergin recognized a different sort of panic in the surge of people in the street now, and realized not everyone was headed for the well. Quite a few were fleeing in the other direction, toward the south gate. Fleeing…that was precisely what they were doing.

"Eamon!" he called over his shoulder.

But the clan warriors had recognized the danger already, and he could hear the rasp of their steel being drawn.

"To me!" the chieftain responded, already running up the ladder to the roof.

Rorik and Niall were already moving to take Amergin's place at the door, naked blades glinting in the fire glow as Amergin himself attended to his chieftain. Eamon was already pulling himself through the loose thatch when Amergin was only halfway up the ladder, and he hastened to catch up. When he finally clambered up onto the roof, Eamon was stone-faced as he looked over the city. Amergin rose to his feet slowly, uncertain of where to look. All around them was chaos. Theirs was one of the few buildings not aflame, and the destruction extended as far as he could see. A horde of townsfolk were thronging the south gate, some with possessions or animals in tow. The gate was closed, but the people were swarming, attempting to force it open. The druid couldn't see soldiers on the wall, but with sudden horror, he recognized the dark forms of Drev'an on the ramparts in their unfamiliar armor, killing indiscriminately, and attempting to hold the gate.

"It that...?" he breathed, unwilling to give voice to what he knew to be truth.

Eamon was looking the other way, toward the flaming heart of the city. He couldn't see it yet, but he could hear the clang of steel that indicated fighting in the streets. There were Magyun soldiers rushing below, but to Eamon's practiced eye, there was no indication of any kind of organized defense.

"Amergin," he began, not taking his eyes off the approaching threat, "are there other ways out of the city besides the north and south gates?"

The druid wracked his brain, thinking of anything he might have seen or heard. "No, my lord, unless you want to try climbing down the wall."

The chieftain was quiet for a long moment, watching the city. His jaw was tight, and he gripped his sword with a warrior's casual confidence. There was something somber about the way the fire glow limned his hair and features.

"The city has fallen, Amergin. The horselords have entered somehow and are sacking it now."

Amergin felt the sense of dread hardening in his gut, and by instinct he looked to the south gate again. The Drev'an there were holding strong, repelling or outright killing the masses who sought to force it open.

"You must escape."

"What?" Amergin questioned, snapping his head back around.

"There's plenty of rope in the barn. Ready your sword, you'll need to fight," Eamon continued as if he hadn't spoken, and turned his gaze to the far end of their street, where he could see the first of the marauders emerge into view. "We will protect you."

"My lord," he began, incredulous, but Eamon rounded on him then.

"You are a bard and the last remaining druid of our clan. If you don't survive to tell our story, the clan will well and truly cease to exist. Your duty is to the histories."

Amergin felt numb all over, but he could sense the truth of Eamon's words. For the briefest moment he had a glimpse of their Patterns, how they'd always been meant to part. He rocked back on his heels slowly, nodding once.

"Go and find the others," Eamon continued in a kinder voice as he laid a reassuring hand on the priest's shoulder. "If they still survive, they will need leadership. Take them across the sea. I have kin there, somewhere."

"Your grandfather's clan," Amergin confirmed quietly, recalling the tale.

"You are a wise druid and a natural leader, Amergin. Lend them your strength."

The druid nodded, but was unable to hold Eamon's gaze. A clash of steel nearer up the street broke the spell of the moment, and Amergin forced himself to move and scrabble through the hole in the thatch to descend the ladder once more.

***

"There," she told the khan, pulling on his arm to gain his attention and pointing to a relatively large structure in the near distance. "The one with the men on the roof."

With a jerk of the reins, Batu swung his horse around to wait for Khuyag, his vanguard following suit in a protective fan.

"No fire," he commented blandly, eyeing the structure.

Davaa squinted into the night. Fire glow illuminated the barn and the men atop it, but she couldn't make it out well enough to make that distinction. Batu frowned, perhaps wondering if the Velkcic gods had a protective hand in this. Khuyag was at his side a moment later, awaiting direction. Behind him, Batu's vanguard began clashing with some of the Magyuns. They were near one of the wells, which had drawn many of the townsfolk, yet unaware of the greater danger.

"There," Batu indicated to his general. "That one. The one unburned. Bring all foreigners there."

Khuyag nodded once, curtly, then wheeled off to spread the khan's direction. Davaa regarded the khan curiously for a moment. Surely he didn't intend to spare every non-Magyun in the city. She had thought only the Velkcic interested him, but now she wondered what he was planning. Batu remained unreadable, however, as he glanced around to consider his next move. Without warning, he spurred off toward the barn once more, and Davaa gripped him urgently.

"Wait!"

Batu ignored her.

"My lord, any closer and one of them might recognize me. They might have sent someone to the well."

Having just realized this possibility as she voiced it, she glanced around in a near panic, scanning the nearby faces. There was at least one head of lime-washed hair she could see clustered near the well itself. Only the Velks did that. She didn't know the warrior by name, but he was certainly one of Eamon's. Had he seen her? Would he recognize her if he had? He'd been carrying two jugs of water, but dropped them now to pull his sword.

"There is one of them by the well."

Batu snapped his head in that direction, seeking the warrior. He recognized the peculiar hair treatment amid the dark-haired Magyuns, then finally nodded.

"How will I know Eamon?"

"He wears warrior mustaches."

"They all do," Batu snapped irritably, recalling that distant encounter at Rowanar.

Davaa wracked her brain for a distinguishing characteristic. She had only encountered the man once or twice. "A scar on the side of his head. From Rowanar, I think."

He eyed her dubiously, but finally offered her an arm to swing down. "Wait for me at the palace."

She slid off the stallion gracefully and immediately raised the hood of her cloak, allowing the khan's sigil to hang on its chain in plain view about her neck. Moving away from the Velkcic, there should be no one left to identify her, though she needed safe passage through the bands of pillaging Drev'an, lest she be mistaken for a local and rounded up…or worse. The hood would mask her features well enough, while the sigil spoke for her. She could feel the thunder of hoofbeats behind her as the khan set off, but she did not glance back. She didn't dare.

***

Ambrus heard the riders coming and ducked into a smaller, more crowded alley to avoid them. Here on the south end of the city, the fighting was still fresh, and he found himself caught amid packs of frightened and confused townsfolk, uncertain of what was actually happening. The only difference was a lack of Magyun soldiers compared to the battle near the north gate. Most had been killed or scattered by now. The area wasn't completely devoid of resistance, however what defenders there were existed singly or in small groups, not as an organized response. They would only slow the Drev'an, and not long at that. Dimly he registered that the hoofbeats sounded as if they were going in the wrong direction, but he dismissed the thought as a trick of the sound bouncing around the enclosed and crowded spaces here.

He thought he heard one of the soldiers call his name, but his commitment to their forces had been wholly spent now. Ambrus didn't even bother to glance in that direction as he continued to push his way south. A pang of regret ate at him, but this was about survival now, and the greater goal.

An arrow lanced mere inches in front of him as he turned a corner and embedded itself in the wall beside his head. He ducked, turning in the direction of the arrow's source in one quick motion, hoping to rush the archer before the man could reload and fire. He saw the archer bare his teeth in a snarl as he attempted to bring his bow up to a firing position before Ambrus could close with him. Their contest was interrupted suddenly as another Drev'an speared into Ambrus from the side, driving his shoulder into the blond warrior's torso and wrapping both arms around him in a wrestler's grab.

408

Ambrus hadn't anticipated the second fighter and grunted as he was driven aside, bracing with his leg to stop himself from falling. He tried to turn, pulling the second Drev'an between himself and the archer, but the bowman had already rushed forward and was swinging his weapon like a club. Ambrus ducked back, dragging the second man with him. That fighter slammed the pommel of his sword into the space between Ambrus' shoulder blades. It hurt, but the Drev'an couldn't generate enough force to drop him in his compromised position, wrapped up with Ambrus as he was. Likewise Ambrus knew his own sword was nearly useless this close against Drev'an armor.

Instead, he hacked at the man's legs, hoping to cut away his balance as he continued to avoid swings of the bow. His left arm was wrapped up in the tackle, but he tried to reach for his fighting knife anyway. The Drev'an recognized what Ambrus was trying to do and pivoted them both in a wrestler's throw designed to take both men to the ground. The Drev'an was successful, slamming Ambrus on his back in the mud despite his attempt to turn and brace somewhat. The wind was knocked out of him, and it took Ambrus a moment to gather his wits and react. The fighter grabbed for Ambrus' sword hilt, as the archer danced back a step and drew. He didn't have a clear shot during the struggle that ensued as Ambrus fought to keep his long blade. He should have let go and reached for the dagger, but the thought came to him too late. He cursed his fatigue from all the fighting. Ambrus head-butted the Drev'an forcefully, feeling a satisfying slackening of the other man's limbs, but two other Drev'an entered the fray now and leapt to restrain his arms. He snarled, trying to turn and throw one of them off, but one punched him squarely across the jaw and took tighter hold.

The archer looked on stoically, arrow held taut, but he didn't fire. Instead he barked an order to the two Drev'an. Five more emerged in the small space, weapons drawn, but waiting patiently. When Ambrus continued to fight, two more approached to drag him up to a sitting position and pull his arms behind his back.

Ambrus growled in fury, recognizing they meant to capture and not kill him. He thrashed, but the Drev'an only kicked and punched him until one finally managed to secure bindings around his wrists. Dimly he was aware that one fighter seemed to be arguing with the archer, but the Drev'an indicated his blond hair and said something that ended the discussion. They took his sword, but left the dagger sheathed at his side, which Ambrus noted with more than a little surprise. One Drev'an grabbed him by the hair and hauled him upright. Ambrus refused to flinch and only bared his teeth in a snarl, promising death the moment he got free. But the Drev'an only smiled thinly and spoke something in return, then nodded his chin at the others, who pulled Ambrus roughly away.

***

Amergin only had time for a quick glance at Cathbad's body as he rushed for the door. Rorik was readying himself for whatever it was he saw in the street beyond, but Niall turned to look at him. There was a knowing look on his young face, and for a moment Amergin felt time slow.

"Best draw that blade, bard," was all he said, nodding once to the sword Amergin had hastily tied around his hips.

Amergin rested his hand on the hilt and nodded grimly. He could fight…all Velkcic could fight, but he wasn't a warrior. He spared another moment to glance around the barn, searing his clanmates into his considerable memory before blowing out a breath and rushing to the entrance.

"That way," Niall indicated down the street toward the well. "Fewer horselords."

The druid nodded but didn't dare linger; there was no time or purpose for sentimentality. He glanced right, toward the south, where he could just glimpse Drev'an warriors fighting at the end of the street, then ran in the opposite direction, toward the well. There would be more townsfolk here to clog the way, but he hoped Niall was right and there'd be less chance of encountering any horselords.

Ahead he could already see the area around the well was crowded, but with dismay, he recognized a line of riders steadily cutting their way through the throng. He glanced to the sides, searching for an alley that might be passable, but the area around him was clogged with fleeing Magyuns, or fire.

Grimacing in frustration, he slowed his pace and deliberated what to do. A sharp *tug* on his senses drew his attention backward, to the barn. Was he meant to return there? To die with them?

Feeling hopeless and frustrated, he turned and dashed for the nearest alley that would take him in the direction of the well. He'd take his chances trying for escape. His height compared to the Magyuns gave him an advantage, as he shouldered his way through the crowd, however he was stopped abruptly by a hand fisted in his long hair. He reeled back painfully, one hand flying to his head in reflex, but he didn't reach for his sword. He was yanked back against the side or shoulder of a horse as some Drev'an growled above him. The rider exchanged a few words with another, then kicked his horse and dragged Amergin along with him. Both hands were raised to his head now to alleviate the pain, and he had little choice but to attempt to pace the horse, lest he be dragged. He considered making a grab for his sword and attempting to fight, but the barbarian on the horse pulled sharply and nearly lifted the druid off his feet.

After a few dozen paces, the riders stopped. The one holding him swung easily from the saddle and held his blade across Amergin's throat. He braced for the cut, bending awkwardly against the slightly shorter man, but he realized with sudden alarm they were back at the barn now. The clan was fighting from the doorway, and Amergin's captor marched him forward as a warning. The Drev'an didn't hesitate to fight, but held their distance slightly. A man of some apparent importance stalked forward, weapon low, ready but unhurried.

411

"Priest," he called out in thick Velkcic, gesturing to Amergin with his sword.

The warriors looked at each other uncertainly, but none of them stood down. Niall was looking at Amergin strangely, which the druid took as a message to slowly and carefully pull his sword. The instant he tried to move, however, the apparent leader's sword tip flicked up threateningly. The Velkcic warriors tensed in response, which caused the Drev'an to raise their swords and arrow tips, but the leader stayed everyone with a gesture.

"No," he commanded both groups. "No fight."

His cold, calculating eyes searched the faces present before finally settling on Amergin. "Not Magyun, yes?"

"Yes," the druid answered as calmly as he could.

The Drev'an leader gave him a frankly expectant look. Amergin wasn't sure what was being asked of him, but acted on instinct.

"Put your swords down," he called to his clan, summoning more confidence than he felt.

"Amergin," Rorik protested in return.

"They only care for the Magyun. They don't want to fight us."

"Why?"

"I don't know."

"Give us the...priest," ordered a voice behind Rorik in a negotiating tone.

Eamon. The Drev'an leader looked to this new voice, considering.

"Leader? Chief?" he finally asked.

412

Eamon stepped forward into view and nodded once, regally. The barbarian leader sized Eamon up, then nodded once as well, satisfied. At some unseen signal, Amergin was abruptly released. He staggered forward a step, uneasy and uncertain. Eamon commanded him with a glance, and the druid crossed to his chieftain as if this were all perfectly normal.

"Weapons away," he commanded quietly, returning a steady gaze to the Drev'an leader.

"My lord," the druid warned quietly, but Eamon ignored him.

Reluctantly the clansmen obeyed and sheathed their blades. The Drev'an gestured to the barn's interior, clearly indicating that he wished to talk, out of the street and fighting. Amergin saw the chieftain clench his jaw, but he agreed. In reality, the Velkcic could have put up a decent fight, but ultimately the horselords could simply fire the building and kill them that way. It wasn't a good warrior's death. Perhaps they were being given an option here that might yet preserve the clan, and its sole druid.

Though his whole being protested, Amergin entered the barn with his clanmates and tried not to flinch as the still-armed Drev'an followed them inside. The two leaders waited as their men arranged themselves inside, while still more horselords held a cordon along the street in either direction.

Inside, Eamon's men arranged themselves in a fan of sorts, though the horselords drove them deeper into the space. Finally the two leaders stepped inside. The Drev'an looked around the space in a sweeping gaze, as if marveling that this structure alone had escaped the fires. His gaze settled briefly on Cathbad, then at last rested on the Velkcic chieftain.

"Eamon," he intoned with an odd note of smugness.

"Khan Batu," Eamon returned, confirming that he too knew with whom he was parlaying.

The khan smiled in grim amusement. Then he shook his head almost wistfully

"Drev'an," he began, gesturing vaguely to his men, "no need to fight Velkcic. Velkcic…Magyun enemy, yes?"

Eamon nodded once, his face guarded. The Drev'an took a step closer, and Amergin could feel the protective tension rising from his warriors.

"Drev'an and Velkcic not enemies," he confirmed, looking past the chieftain to his clan. "Good fighters."

Eamon saw his men glance at one another in question or distrust. He had been about to ask after Briga, but Batu spoke sharply to his men.

"Take them," the khan ordered in Drev'an.

The horselords sprang into action, physically throwing themselves at the larger Velkcic and producing lengths of cord from their belts. With sheathed blades and fewer numbers, the Velkcic had no real hope.

"What?" Eamon questioned at the sudden activity, then stopped suddenly as a sword point smoothly entered his side.

"But *you* are *my* enemy," Batu growled quietly, privately.

Turning in shock, Eamon grabbed the naked blade with his bare hand as if not quite believing it was real. Rorik shrieked like a demon, having been the first to see what had happened, and shook three horselords off him in sheer rage. The room was chaos, but Batu hardly noticed. He twisted the blade and drove it deeper, seeking the heart.

Eamon had always expected to die in battle, but not like this. He could taste blood and bared his teeth in impotent rage as his body refused to fight or respond. He fell to one side, and Batu followed his movement, twisting the blade again.

"Breeg is mine now."

414

Eamon turned an incredulous and rage-filled gaze on the khan.

"What?" he sputtered, disbelieving.

Around him he was vaguely aware of his men struggling, but he knew they would be overcome shortly. He rasped again as the khan withdrew the sword and tried feebly to stop himself from slumping to the ground. His eyes found Amergin's, and he fought to hold the gaze as long as he could. The druid stared right back, heedless of anyone else in the room. He was pale-faced and frightened, but managed to set his jaw before his chieftain.

Silently Eamon cursed himself for a fool, hoping Amergin didn't blame himself. The clan would need him now more than ever. There would be no room for doubt or regret. The space remained strangely muted around the two men. Eamon didn't even notice as Batu turned to leave, or that his men stayed behind to subdue the Velkcic. All he could see was the grimly determined face of the young druid.

***

Briga raced blindly through the streets with Gansükh trailing at her heels. She didn't care who got in her way. Her gray gelding was war-mad and willing to shove, bite, or trample anyone in their path. The crowd was relatively thin behind the Drev'an front line, but she was still slowed by the odd townsfolk or soldier wishing to fight. Mostly she broke contact and spurred on, attempting to follow the confused directions of the Magyun boy. Gansükh had tried and failed twice to curb her recklessness, and now resigned himself to attempting to keep pace with her, tangling with or dispatching any fighters foolish enough to try her. He nearly lost her at least once when she sped around a corner while he was fighting, but despite the uncomfortable gap, he mostly kept her in sight.

For her part, Briga was hardly aware of the chaos around her. Her only thought was reaching the barn, to see for herself if it was true. If they were really here. If they were still alive. Turning another corner, she scanned her surroundings hastily, but finding one particular barn in the dark and among the fires was proving incredibly difficult. She felt a peculiar sense of urgency, and with effort, forced herself to slow down and calm down. To think. The Velkcic were near the south gate, allegedly, in a large barn. Singer slowed reluctantly and danced beneath her in agitation. She had no idea how close to the south gate she might be, but she could see fleeing townsfolk headed in roughly the same direction. They were almost certainly heading for the gate in an effort to escape their doomed city. Swiveling her head, she couldn't make out any large structures in the area amid the flames and decided to continue south.

The crowd condensed the further south she rode until she could no longer keep up a canter. The Magyuns were fleeing desperately, trying to avoid the invaders at all costs. The Drev'an were thicker here as well, though they seemed to be milling more than fighting. She heard one of them giving orders regarding a "large barn", and her heart froze in her chest for a moment. She questioned him harshly, and he responded in kind, but with instructions on how to reach it. Briga felt the truth of his words and felt a touch of fate that unnerved her. Without bothering to scold him for his tone, she dug her heels into Singer's sides, and he readily dashed off, rearing and turning on his back legs agilely.

They were reckless again, storming up the main street and counting off the side roads, two, three, *there*. The gray gelding turned without needing direction, and even in the darkness, Briga was struck by the sight of the barn. It was completely unburnt, despite carnage all around, and eerily lit by those other blazes. A group of Drev'an were outside, but she hardly noticed. Her horse slid to a stop in front of the building, and Briga had already dismounted without conscious thought. Her gaze was fixed on the doorway, nothing else in this world existed at that moment. She moved with agonizing slowness, then suddenly through the door.

At once her gaze snagged on two supine forms near the fire. Her blood froze when she recognized Cathbad laying so still. As if he were only sleeping. Cathbad...her teacher, her brother, her second father. There wasn't enough air in the barn. She couldn't even whisper his name, but took two staggering steps toward him. *Too late...* She had found them. They were here. But she was too late. An agonized gasp wrung from her. But then the other form moved. Just barely, but enough to draw her attention. She focused on the other body, the familiar but scarred face, and her heart froze again.

Amergin watched as the female entered, her face streaked in blood and soot and...paint? All his small hairs stood on end watching her as she took two staggering steps into the room, then froze as her gaze fell on Eamon. She seemed to stare at the chieftain for an eternity, then all at once crossed the space in a rush and fell on him. *Could it be...?*

The Velkcic warriors thrashed against their captors when she fell on Eamon, but she responded to them with a feral, inhuman cry and drew a short, bloodied fighting knife from her waist. Amergin recognized the knife, he was sure of it. But the face of its wielder?

Briga cried out in rage, crouched protectively over Eamon. His wound was grievous, but for the moment, he lived. The Drev'an guards were quick to subdue the others, and Briga shifted her attention back to Eamon.

"Eamon," she rasped, barely audible.

Amergin wasn't certain if he heard her or simply imagined it. Her face grew pale under the paint and gore, and she reached out with trembling fingers to touch his chest. Eamon's breathing was shallow and frighteningly irregular. She let out a strangled cry and brushed strands of faded lime-washed hair back from his forehead. One hand lightly touched the healing scars on his temple and cheek.

"Briga?" Amergin breathed, quiet and uncertain.

The leather armor was right, as was her hair color and complexion. But the Drev'an robes? And she seemed somehow leaner, bigger too. Not at all like the wisp she had been all those months ago. Kessan was the closest to Amergin and looked over at him questioningly.

Briga felt as if she were teetering on the brink of unconsciousness. Her vision narrowed as she scanned Eamon and assessed his injuries, old and new. She felt oddly disconnected from her own body, a peculiar sort of numbness. Eamon gasped painfully, struggling for breath, and his eyes fluttered open. There was fear there. Her hands trembled, and she withdrew from him slightly. His eyes found hers and locked on, but what she saw in them was hatred and confusion.

"Eamon," she breathed again in anguish and disbelief.

For a moment a look of puzzlement came over his features, followed slowly by the light of recognition. He *saw* her, she was certain, and a tear escaped the corner of her eye then. He stared at her for another long moment, an eternity, and mouthed a word. His breath caught painfully in his throat, and that sense of clarity faded from his eyes. And just like that, he was gone.

Briga stared for a moment, struggling to breathe. Then she wailed, a low, mournful sound, and fell slowly forward until her forehead rested between her hands on his chest. She had been too late. They had been here in the city. She'd known it, somehow, had done everything in her power to bring about a swift victory that might spare them, but she had been too late.

Amergin watched in mute shock, now certain this was their lost sister. Her raw grief over Eamon shook him to the core. What had happened to her? One of the Drev'an stepped forward and laid a hand on her shoulder, saying something quietly in his own tongue. She stiffened for a moment, then slashed at him with that bloody knife still clutched in her hand and snarled a response in the same language. The warrior let go of her, but only retreated out of knife range. A second warrior stepped forward then, holding a drawn blade. It was bloodied like the rest, and he flicked it to motion the first horselord back. Amergin tensed, trying frantically to glean some information or intuition about what was happening.

***

Ambrus used the walk to very carefully loosen the bindings at his wrists. Usually one or more of the Drev'an guards griped him tightly by the upper arm, robbing him of more meaningful chances to improve his situation. After a few blocks, he noted grimly they were marching him in a generally southward direction, away from the palace. His mind churned though multiple possibilities, working on escape plans and options, but also urging himself to be patient. To observe and wait for the opportune moment. If they'd simply wanted him dead, it would have happened already, so he intended to make good use of the time he had been granted.

After turning the next corner, it became clear they were heading for the Velkcic barn. Ambrus could not begin to guess why, but he was dismayed at the number of Drev'an outside in the street. He spotted a few other prisoners trussed as he was also being shepherded to the barn, and wondered why they had been singled out.

Any thought he had of trying one last time to wrench free before they reached the barn vanished at the sound of an inhuman cry from within. He stopped dead in his tracks at the sound, and even his captors seemed wary. But they only paused for a moment and shuffled him along, exchanging a few words with one of the warriors who seemed to be in charge here. The man barely looked at Ambrus and gestured vaguely to the doorway beyond. For the first time he noticed that the structure had somehow escaped burning, and he marveled briefly at their luck. Cautiously he allowed himself to wonder if Amergin and the clan had survived.

Entering the space, he looked around quickly for any sign of Amergin or the others. They were here. They were *here*. Prisoners, but alive. All of them were focused on some spectacle in the center of the room. He felt a peculiar prickle of fate and turned to look.

***

Briga was aware of Gansükh somewhere behind her, but little else penetrated her thoughts. Eamon was dead. Killed. *Murdered*. 'Who did this?' she'd wanted to ask, but hesitated. A sharp *tug* on her senses abruptly drew her attention to the doorway, and she wondered if the world was indeed shifting beneath her feet.

Ambrus regarded the scene with a moment of numb shock as his mind struggled to process the sight. The blonde she-devil was here. Her presence was so incongruous, he had difficulty absorbing the information. Her eyes were red rimmed from smoke and fatigue, her face streaked in blood and bearing an expression more animal than human. She was crouched over a still form, a bloody dagger still clutched tightly in her fist. It was the chieftain she was crouched over, Eamon, he realized in mounting rage.

"Murderer!" he challenged, moving in slow motion to shake free of his guards and slip one wrist free of its ties to draw his knife.

"You," she snarled, voice raw and distorted from smoke and screaming.

In equal slow motion, she rose to her feet, stepping over Eamon's body and raising her blade in answer. A big Drev'an with his sword out had already moved to intervene as Ambrus' guards reached for him again, but she waved them all off with a gesture. Ambrus wasn't thinking of survival any longer, his only thought was killing her. For Eamon. For Amergin. For himself. He rushed forward, giving himself to the moment.

"No!" a commanding and terrified voice from beside them called out, and another prisoner dashed forward past his guards.

420

Ambrus recognized Amergin and saw the demoness turning to gut him first. He took his chance, throwing himself at her with that same agonizing slowness. Gritting his teeth, the druid reached out to shove Ambrus off the mark. The blond warrior looked at his friend in shock, anticipating a death blow from the she-demon, but Amergin was staring at the woman, who stared back at him wide-eyed.

The big Drev'an moved now, wrenching the knife away from Ambrus and bear-hugging him in restraint.

"Briga, don't kill him," was all Amergin could say before the guards dragged him back again.

"Amergin?" she asked, eyes still wide and fixed on him.

Gansükh brought his sword up to his captive's throat.

"Wait," Briga managed, tearing her gaze away from Amergin with marked difficulty.

The big Drev'an flashed his teeth in a snarl of annoyance, but waited. Briga took a steadying breath, looking up as Dagmer and Bayanaa entered the dim space as well. Dagmer watched wide-eyed while the other kheshig remained mostly stoic, uncertain of what was happening. Briga took a second steadying breath and beckoned them closer with a look. Summoning what remained of her strength, she straightened into the commanding persona of the khan's shaman.

"This man would have killed me on the bridge," she began in low tones.

Amergin frowned. She was speaking in Drev'an, and he couldn't understand her words, but the tone was not one he had ever heard from her.

"Kill him," one of the Drev'an opined.

She paused and eyed the blond warrior coolly. After a moment she raised her blade and stepped toward him.

"No!" Amergin interjected again, but she only looked at him.

There was something hard in that gaze, but she conveyed a silent message with its directness. The druid suddenly understood, or thought he did. She turned her attention once again to the blond warrior.

"This death would be too quick. Gansükh," she commanded, fixing her kheshig with a meaningful gaze bearing a silent command.

He handed his prisoner off to another Drev'an and stepped to his mistress's side. Ambrus watched her with cold fury. She sheathed her knife without cleaning it and placed a hand casually on Gansükh's arm. Then she tilted her head slightly as if considering some new thought.

"Dagmer, you have no further use for that slave collar. Have it removed and placed on this prisoner."

Ambrus felt something cold settle in his core as she looked at him with a viper's smile.

"You are mine now, slave," she intoned in Velkcic.

The she-wolf stepped past him without another word, two Drev'an warriors in tow. Gansükh was acutely aware of how tightly she gripped his arm. He was familiar enough with her now to recognize when she was play-acting. Something was wrong. He said nothing, aware too of the role he must play.

"Search him for all weapons this time," was his only instruction to the guards.

"See that these other prisoners are treated comfortably," she instructed Bayanaa discreetly.

She cast one last weighted glance at Amergin, searching his eyes for understanding in that all-too-brief moment before anyone might realize her interest. But then the moment passed, and she continued outside.

The world was bright and unstable beneath her, but she willed herself to walk confidently, one step at a time. She would never have guessed it was still night. Her head throbbed, and there was a roaring sound in her ears not caused by the crowds or the fires. Suitably far out into the street and out of sight of the barn's doorway, she paused, trying to focus her vision.

"Gansükh," she called unsteadily, loosening her grip on his arm.

And then her world went black.

Chapter 33

There was a roaring sound all around her. It was everywhere, it was the whole world. Sand and sea and sky and air all jumbled hopelessly into one confused entity. She was cold. She couldn't breathe. She no longer cared. Her small body tumbled in the surf, tossed and dragged and scraped along the rock-strewn seabed. Or was it the shore? It didn't matter. She closed her eyes and waited for Ran's daughters to claim her.

***

"It was a good match, Diarmot," the chief druid assured his chieftain.

The chieftain pulled his mustache through his fingers, an old habit of his when thinking or uncertain. Diarmot was watching his son exploring the path before them, but the druid knew his thoughts were still with his daughter.

"She will be happy here," he said finally, though with a note of sadness in his voice, "and we need the alliance."

The druid held his tongue, though he agreed. The Avernic, as they'd taken to calling themselves, were an old branch of Velkcic people who lived far to the north of Diarmot's clan. The clans had once relied upon one another for trade and key goods. Diarmot still wondered sometimes why the self-bestowed name persisted, though chief Averna had died at least four generations earlier. The Avernic clan sent fish and exotic clay vessels south to Diarmot's people, who had no special name for themselves, in exchange for cattle or bundles of wheat. The alliance had faded over time as the Avernic conquered some bits of arable land, but Diarmot was still reliant on them for trade. And with the growing number of incursions by the Emorians to the south into Velkcic lands, Diarmot also needed them for mutual protection. Marrying his daughter to their chieftain's son seemed a small price, despite his fondness for her.

"Eamon," his father called out, and the boy turned to regard him.

Diarmot was struck suddenly that Eamon was a boy no longer but nearly a man. What was he now, fourteen at least? Every now and again he still saw glimpses of the boy shining through and he wondered when it would be time to test him.

"How would you like to marry an Avernic girl?"

Eamon scrunched up his face in a way that was decidedly boyish, and Diarmot laughed for the first time in days. The high druid smiled as well. It was good to see Diarmot adjusting to his burden.

"Did you know the sea is just beyond those hills over there?"

The boy shook his head and turned to look up the path. He'd never been to the sea. He had never been anywhere except Rowanar before this journey.

"Go to the shore and find some pretty shells. We will make a necklace for your sister."

The boy nodded eagerly and dashed off, carrying his spear.

"Be mindful of the water!" his father called after him.

He chuckled quietly to himself and glanced to the druid, who regarded him with a faint look of amusement.

"What?"

"You did not want to marry Tara off at all, and now you entertain the idea of both your children married to the Avernic?"

Diarmot only laughed and clapped him on the shoulder. "Go and keep an eye on the boy, would you Cathbad? I have duties to attend before the marriage ceremony."

The druid bowed his head respectfully and watched Diarmot move off back toward the village before he turned and walked leisurely toward the shore. The path was well worn, and he didn't need to concentrate at all to follow it. He wandered slowly, allowing his thoughts to drift as he scanned the sides of the path for any interesting herbs or berries, perhaps.

Nearing the crest of the small hill, he had the subtle feeling something was wrong. Worried about Eamon, he quickened his place when the boy suddenly appeared atop the hill, wide-eyed and serious.

"Father! Oh…Cathbad. Come quick!"

"What is it?" the druid asked, frowning as he quelled a flare of alarm and gathering up the hem of his robes to walk more freely.

"A sea monster, I think."

Cathbad blinked in puzzlement, but the boy was quite serious. Cresting the hill himself, he scanned the beach for any signs of trouble. The shore was a narrow strip of coarse sand dotted with rocks here and there. Cold waves gently crashed against the beach in foamy curls of water. He followed Eamon with his eyes while picking his way carefully down the sandy slope. The boy loped off a few paces to where a large rock lay in the surf, gesturing at it with his spear. No, not a rock, what was it? As Cathbad moved closer, he reached out with his druid senses. He was skilled with animals, and if this were some sort of creature, perhaps he could sense something.

"Eamon, stop that," he scolded as the boy tried to prick it with his spear, then wondered aloud as he recognized a wet clump of fur. "A wolf?"

It shifted, and Eamon readied his spear like a proper warrior. He eyed his quarry seriously, but after a moment, threw down his weapon and rushed forward.

"Eamon!"

But the boy ignored him. Cathbad abandoned dignity and ran forward. Eamon crouched beside the wet bundle and gently turned it over. It was a girl, white with cold, and bedraggled. Eamon looked up and met his teacher's eyes with a questioning blue gaze. There was no sign of his boyishness now.

"Is she alive?" he asked, sliding a knee beneath her neck and shoulders to support her.

Cathbad dropped to a crouch with uncharacteristic haste and touched her neck, then opened each of her eyes in turn.

"She is, but only just."

How old was she? Eight? Ten? It was difficult to say in her present condition. Cathbad scanned up and down the beach, searching for a nearby house that might know her.

"Where did she come from?" Eamon asked.

"I—"

The girl shuddered suddenly and coughed, curling onto her side as she expelled water from her lungs and sat up. Eamon supported her, just in case, and carefully moved a tangled strand of tawny hair from her face. The girl took a ragged breath or two and opened her eyes, blinking away the salt. She seemed confused, not quite there with them.

"Pol?" she asked, slowly focusing on Eamon's face.

Her blue-gray eyes were striking, but they soon widened in fear as she realized she didn't recognize either of them. She scrambled backward away from them in the surf on legs that refused to obey properly. With a fear sound, she snatched a long dagger from somewhere under the ragged wolf pelt she was

427

wearing as a cloak and brandished it menacingly at them. Cathbad stilled and placed his hands on his knees. Eamon showed her both his palms in a placating gesture.

"Calm down...you are all right, we mean you no harm."

She flashed her teeth at them in a wolf-like snarl and waved the knife to keep them back. The blade seemed too large for her small form.

"Are you hurt?" Eamon tried again, noting the way her legs seemed a bit limp beneath her.

She growled again and spat a string of words neither of them recognized. Eamon raised his eyebrows in surprise and dared a quick look at Cathbad.

"Do you understand Velkcic, child?" the druid tried gently.

His tone and posture seemed to confuse her, and the tip of her knife dipped a few inches uncertainly. She tilted her head in puzzlement.

Eamon moved, and she snapped her attention and her blade to him instantly. He stopped and showed her his palms again, then more slowly this time, reached into the pouch at his hip and withdrew a wedge of hard cheese. Carefully he held it out to her.

"Here...take it."

She watched him for a long moment, weighing her options. Showing her teeth once more, she growled a few more words that sounded distinctly threatening, before cautiously edging toward him with her knife poised to strike. Eamon kept perfectly still. She waited a moment longer before snatching the cheese and scrambling back to a safe distance. Watching Eamon closely, she sniffed the morsel, then tasted it. A change came over her at the familiar taste, and she allowed herself to relax somewhat as she wolfed down the treat.

"Hungry, eh?" Eamon asked with a soft chuckle.

She regarded him quizzically and asked him something. Eamon shook his head, not understanding.

"Harald?" she tried again. "Hverr es ykkarr jarl?"

"What's she saying, Cathbad?"

The druid shook his head. "I don't know."

The girl appeared terribly forlorn for a moment when they didn't answer and looked over her shoulder out to sea. Eamon shifted uncomfortably. The water was cold. She was shivering, but ignoring it.

"Eamon," he offered, laying a hand on his own chest.

She looked at him again with that curious head tilt.

"Eamon," he repeated and then gestured to the druid. "Cathbad."

"Eamon," she repeated slowly, as if testing the word, then pointed at him with her dagger, though there was no threat in the gesture now.

"Yes," he nodded. "Eamon. He's Cathbad."

"Kabad," she mimicked,

The druid smiled. "Close enough."

"Bricia," she offered, touching her own chest hesitantly.

"Briga," Eamon repeated, smiling.

She shook her head. "Bricia. Brick-ah."

"Breeg-ah," he tried again.

She sighed in exasperation and half-smiled.

"Are you cold?" he asked, miming hugging himself and shivering.

The girl giggled uncertainly, and Cathbad wondered again how young she might be.

"Here," the boy stood and removed his cloak, holding it out to her. "It's dry at least."

She regarded the garment uncertainly, as if expecting a trick. Eamon smiled reassuringly, and she shifted toward them, but was unable to stand.

"Here, Cathbad, hold this," he instructed, handing his mostly dry cloak to the chief druid.

Cathbad stood slowly, watching the scene with mild trepidation. There was something about this girl that niggled at him. Eamon gently took her by the arm to help her stand, waiting for her tension to fade before moving any further. Cathbad pulled the sodden wolf pelt from her shoulders and flung the woolen garment in its place. She made a sound of distress and reached for the pelt, but Cathbad smiled kindly and picked it up. Eamon scooped the girl up into his arms. She still held her knife, and he made no protest, only smiled at her kindly.

"What now?" he asked the druid as he stepped onto the beach and stooped to retrieve his discarded spear.

"Bring her to the Avernic. Maybe they know her."

"She's so cold," Eamon remarked, glancing down at her.

"Briga," Cathbad belatedly repeated. "I don't recognize the name."

"I wonder what happened to her?"

"Poor child."

She was asleep before they reached the low hill.

***

Not knowing what else to do with her, they placed her in the guest house with Diarmot, Eamon, and their small element of household warriors. All had agreed if she was not Velkcic, she should remain with a familiar face until her origins could be determined. Cathbad was staying in the house of druids, and it would be inappropriate to bring her there. Especially with Odri the Sacrificer making comments about her arrival on the eve of the wedding, and not so subtly suggesting she be submitted to his talents. Sacrificers were always like that, but thankfully the other druids urged caution until they could assign meaning to her sudden appearance.

Diarmot was worried this might sour his painstakingly negotiated wedding arrangement. As it happened, she slept all that night, the entire following day, and through all the night ceremonies following that as well. Cathbad and one of the Avernic druids had examined her, and except for a few minor scrapes, declared her uninjured. She'd been in the water for quite some time, it seemed, and her legs had been numb with cold at their first meeting, but it was nothing more than that. The druids expected no lasting effects there. They speculated that she had been swept out to sea in a storm, or perhaps was in a shipwreck. A single wooden slat was found on the beach, which might have been from a boat of some kind, or might not. Nothing to provide any clues to her origin, anyway.

Briga had no effect on the marriage or the alliance, but both chieftains and their chief druids sat down to discuss what to do with her.

"She could be from anywhere," commented Gentrix, the Avernic chieftain. "If she's from a seafaring people, they are unknown to my shores, Diarmot."

Diarmot was stroking his long mustache thoughtfully. "What if they come looking for her?"

"What if they don't?"

"She is very young," Cathbad remarked. "Too young to be alone. That cannot speak well for any other survivors."

431

"*If* there was something to survive. If she was perhaps swept out to sea?"

The group was silent a moment, considering the numerous possibilities and their ramifications.

"Gentrix, may I have a private word with my chieftain?" Cathbad asked with respectful formality.

It would have been unspeakably rude to offer private consult in another chieftain's hall without leave to do so. Gentrix gestured placidly.

"My lord, I think we should take her with us," he counseled quietly.

"Why?"

"Well, for one, she is somewhat comfortable around Eamon and myself. The Avernic are strangers to her, and we have already established that she is not Velkcic."

Diarmot appeared dubious. It wasn't that he shunned charity, but she would be another mouth to feed, and there was no way of knowing what she might be able to give back to the clan in return. However Diarmot was a wise chieftain and would hear his chief druid out before making his decision.

"And," Cathbad dropped his voice further as he continued, "I think she has druid gifts."

That got Diarmot's full attention. Those born with the gifts were not so common as they once were, and a clan's relative strength and power was marked by the number of druids they retained.

Cathbad had come in to check on the girl that morning and found her sitting cross-legged on a bare patch of dirt. Her palms were pressed to the soil, and her eyes were closed in concentration. In that moment he understood the prickling sensation he'd felt about her. This strange, foreign girl harbored gifts.

432

Diarmot stroked his mustaches for several long moments, considering. Finally he turned back to his host and nodded.

"As it was my son who found her, I will take responsibility for her."

Gentrix narrowed his eyes, perhaps wondering if she had some value of which he was unaware.

"Cathbad is wise," Diarmot went on. "Under the laws of hospitality, it would not be honorable to burden you with her care."

"I agree," offered the Avernic chief druid, who was a trained brehon, a judge, himself. "Besides, Odri is still making noise about spilling her entrails for his divinations. I fear she wouldn't be safe here, in spite of my orders to leave her be."

Cathbad nodded sagely and regarded the other druid with respect. If he had sensed her potential, he was more concerned with her safety, which marked him as a true priest of the old ways.

"What if her people come looking?" Gentrix asked warily.

"She will be treated honorably as a member of my clan until her people come to claim her. We're friends, a message would be easy to send to my lands."

Gentrix sat back. He didn't seem wholly convinced, but he had already accepted a new daughter into his own clan in the form of the bride Tara, and this would remove one responsibility from his shoulders. He nodded his agreement and called for ale to mark the occasion.

"To daughters." He smiled wryly in salute.

***

Briga blinked in the soft light, confusion blanketing her like a shroud. Where was she? There was something soft under her. But also something firm and comforting. A voice whispered from somewhere. Gradually she became aware that there were arms around her. She was cradled in someone's lap. That's right, they had saved her. She looked up, expecting to see the reassuring face of Eamon. The tanned face and dark hair startled her, and she stiffened in fear.

"My lady," the words drifted to her from the too-bright haze, concern and reassurance mingling in the familiar voice.

Dagmer. She was in the "now" time. Relaxing slightly, she looked up at Gansükh again. Her head ached, as did her stomach, and her throat felt raw.

"What happened?" she croaked, still unsettled by the dream—the memory—that had gripped her.

Dagmer and Gansükh exchanged a look, but the slave crept forward and offered a cup of something.

"Drink this," she instructed softly.

No, not a slave. Briga had freed her. She took the cup, her eyes lingering on the spot where the slave collar had once been. The drink was warm, fragrant and sweet.

"Honey," the girl explained.

Briga glanced around as she sipped, attempting to regain her bearings, to orient herself to the present once more. They were in an unfamiliar stone-walled room, well-lit, with large windows. She was curled on her side in a large, soft bed, cradled in Gansükh's lap.

Gansükh! She sat up abruptly, creating panicked distance between them.

"Batu," she breathed, feeling oddly guilty.

"Outside," Gansükh explained in a strained but calm tone.

"Shh…it's all right," Dagmer soothed. "He knows."

Briga paled further, uncertain what she meant.

"You collapsed after—" Dagmer stopped herself awkwardly, "...ah Gansükh brought you to the Magyun palace. You wouldn't let anyone else touch you. Not even the khan."

She looked at Gansükh, concerned for his safety in the face of Batu's insane jealousy.

"There are guards outside the door," he explained mildly, "for your safety."

And the khan's peace of mind, he didn't say, but she heard the silent words anyway.

"Are you all right?" he asked.

His face was slightly pale. Had he stayed awake with her the whole time?

"How long?" she asked, taking another draw of the honey-sweetened beverage.

"A few hours perhaps. It is only mid-morning."

She frowned, taking stock of her stiff and sore muscles. It felt as if she'd been asleep for days.

"Where is Bayanaa?"

"Seeing to your new slave," Dagmer stated with a peculiar note of venom.

Briga looked at her, wondering if she'd offended the former slave somehow. "You disapprove of my taking him?"

To Briga's surprise, the girl laughed, low and bitter. "No, my lady. He deserves far worse. He had this."

She tossed an item on the bed between them and grinned like a hunting feline. Briga reached down to take the object, cold anger settling on her as her fingers closed around the smooth, familiar ivory of her lost fighting knife. Oh, yes...Amergin had some explaining to do.

"Amergin!" she recalled suddenly. "Dagmer, those slaves in the barn, what will happen to them?"

"The khan will keep any who might be useful. The rest will be sold."

No…to come so far only to lose them again?

"The khan will never allow you to have them," Gansükh cautioned, correctly reading her thoughts.

"They're your clan?" Dagmer asked, puzzled.

Briga only nodded, not trusting herself to speak until she had a plan. She couldn't bring herself to ask how many were left.

"One is a…shaman," was all she said.

"Like you?" Gansükh asked.

"In some ways."

Something dark briefly crossed his features, but he schooled stoicism back onto his face.

"The others, though…"

There was a curious, rhythmic clanging outside, which intruded unpleasantly on Briga's thoughts. An idea suddenly lit Dagmer's face, and she smiled tentatively.

"I may have a plan," she confirmed with a quick warning glance to the door.

Whatever her thoughts, she didn't want the guards to overhear. They might inform the khan and ruin her chances. Dagmer wasn't sure if Briga's interest in the prisoners might reveal them to be her clansmen and put them in further danger. She too was aware of the dangerous sense of possession the khan had over his she-wolf. Dagmer's eyes scanned Gansükh discreetly. The kheshig had been shaken at the she-wolf's sudden collapse and the behavior that followed. She'd been like an animal in her grief, mad and withdrawn by turns. She had clung to Gansükh as if he were a tether, as if without that leash she might vanish into her grief and be consumed. He had scooped her onto his horse and rode with her straight for the palace.

Batu had been busy overseeing matters there, but he stopped when he saw Gansükh ride up with Briga slung in his arms. Her refusal to allow him near at first drew a cold and terrifying mask of dark fury over the khan, but they'd earnestly assured him this was some sort of shaman's trance, brought on by the ordeal of battle and the killing of so many. Surely the gods were gorged on blood and revelry. And was it not true? She wasn't with them, not truly, which was clear to all.

"Where are we?" she finally asked, intruding on Dagmer's thoughts.

"The Magyun palace."

Briga gathered herself and carefully slid out of bed, crossing to the window. Blood marked the linens where she had lain. Gansükh started, but Dagmer touched his arm to still him. It could wait. Briga held herself stiffly, focusing on the courtyard below. Iron rings were being fastened to the stone. A group of mounted Drev'an milled closer to the center of the space, between the palace and two neat rows of dead Magyun.

"What are they doing?"

It was Gansükh who answered. "The king has barricaded himself in one part of the building. He is dug in like a tick."

She watched the activity silently, returning her attention to the riders. Dagmer had quietly crossed to the door and addressed one of the guards in low tones.

"Fetch water and clean linens."

"Is she injured?" came the equally quiet response.

Dagmer nodded. If Briga had heard, she showed no signs of concern. In fact there was a faint smile curling one corner of

437

her mouth. The sight unnerved Dagmer. They said nothing while they waited. Briga just watched the scene below, while Gansükh, relieved of his burden, began cleaning his sword with an oiled rag produced from somewhere. Briga was still clutching her second dagger, the mug forgotten. The kheshig's eyes flicked up to the two women discreetly. When the guard finally returned with the requested items, Briga cast Dagmer a sidelong glance.

"We should go to Batu."

Dagmer nodded. "After we get you cleaned up. Gansükh—"

But the kheshig had already stood and was crossing to the door.

"I will be waiting outside."

Briga finally came away from the window and seated herself on a stool. Dagmer wetted one of the rags and began cleaning the dust and blood from her face.

"I'm not wounded." It wasn't a question.

Dagmer half smiled. "No. But I thought you might appreciate a moment alone."

Some of the tension left her then. She took a breath, then held her hand out for one of the rags. Dagmer obliged silently, then resumed cleaning scrapes and scratches along her lady's face and neck, while Briga pulled open her robe to attend to her more private areas.

"What happened to the wolf?" Dagmer asked curiously.

Briga examined the rag, which held only dirt and soot, and frowned. Had she misinterpreted the cause of her stomach pain? Refusing to dwell on that idea, she allowed herself to be distracted by Dagmer's question.

"I don't know," she replied, turning the rag on her hands and wrists instead. "He will turn up when he's ready."

Dagmer said nothing. The wolf made her uneasy. When she finished with her own ministrations, Briga picked at her soiled robes. They were soot-stained, and blood-streaked from the battle. There was a hollowness in her heart she couldn't allow herself to think about. Not until the rest of the Velkcic were safe. Only then could she allow herself the grief Eamon and Cathbad deserved. She knew she could ask Dagmer to find out what had happened, but there would be no peace in the knowledge. No, that would have to wait.

"All your training with Gansükh has left me with less to clean up." Dagmer laughed hesitantly, turning her lady's mind from wherever it dwelt.

"It has," Briga agreed, rubbing the sore muscles in her legs.

She paused, watching Dagmer from the corner of her eye.

"I meant it, you know."

"Meant what, my lady?"

"You're no longer a slave. You are a free woman among the Drev'an."

Dagmer hesitated briefly. "There are no free women among the Drev'an."

Briga had no response. Dagmer was right. Until they broke free of the Drev'an, they had only exchanged chains and collars for finder bindings.

"I...would stay with you, my lady," Dagmer added quietly.

There was no resignation in her tone, only hope, and Briga turned to look at her fully. "You don't need—"

"I'm yours to command," she interrupted with more confidence. "It's my choice."

Briga was touched by emotion and took Dagmer's hand gratefully, then dragged the other woman into a hug.

439

"We'll escape this," the she-wolf whispered.

There was a knock at the door, and Gansükh tentatively poked his head in.

"We should go down to the khan," he prompted.

Briga nodded. With effort, she shoved all her emotions and worries to the corners of her mind. There was too much to handle all at once; grief alone would shatter her if given the chance, and she couldn't afford to be off-balance now. Dagmer watched as the she-wolf appeared to don a mask of herself, forcing calm composure onto her face through force of will. But she could see the traces of exhaustion and sorrow around her edges.

***

Batu hadn't slept. He ran a hand across his face to clear away dust and sweat and glanced to the open doors of the audience chamber once more. Sartaq was still in there; he could hear his brother trying to break down the doors to King Bela's hiding place.

"Coward," he spat, cursing the Magyun aloud.

His eyes drifted again to the palace wing, where they'd secured a block of quarters. Where he had sent Breeg and her kheshig to recover. This was taking longer than anticipated, but Bela couldn't survive in his den forever. The city was his now. He turned to survey the smoking ruins around him, grinning with one side of his mouth.

"General Burd!"

The general rode up to his khan dutifully. He hadn't slept, either.

"Take as many men as you need and round up all surviving livestock. We will need to know how much remains. Have your men salvage and stockpile any fodder as well, though I doubt they had any left even before the attack."

"Yes, Batu Khan."

Burd saluted and rode away, calling his captains to him. General Tseren had already set about organizing defenders along the walls and gates in case any Magyun allies were foolish enough to march in winter to come to their aid. Batu's eye was drawn to motion, and he turned his head to catch sight of his she-wolf walking across the palace grounds. She bore fresh war paint. He waited as they approached, regarding her small entourage blandly.

Briga felt a peculiar flare of gooseflesh as she regarded the khan, then looked past him to assess the state of the rest of the courtyard. Approaching within arm's length, she nodded respectfully before returning a cold, unsettling gaze on him. Batu cupped her chin in his hand and examined her, not unkindly. There was a gleam of triumph in his eyes, Briga noted.

"Are you well?"

"Well enough," she confirmed. "Congratulations on your victory, Batu Khan."

Her smile was cold, hollow. Predatory, perhaps. Batu wasn't entirely sure what to make of it.

"No victory yet. The coward has locked himself in. Sartaq has been worrying at the door all night like a dog with a bone. Ah, you found your missing knife?" he added, noticing both hilts gleaming at her waist.

"A gift from my new pet," she returned, and this time her smile was one of cold cruelty. "Is the king alone?"

"No," Batu answered, returning his thoughts to the matter at hand. "He has a priest and two lords in there with him."

She angled her head slightly in thought. "Without food or water, it won't matter for long."

Her gaze drifted to the iron rings set into the ground nearby. "Ah...you need him alive. Has Sartaq tried bargaining?"

441

Batu hesitated. "They abandoned their women."

Briga arched a brow, and her face darkened after a moment. She could imagine what he was implying. They would have been used as threat or bargaining chips, most likely. Unsuccessfully, it seemed. The impulses of men after war were distasteful enough, but that was the way of things. To use a woman that way was far worse.

"They care only for their own lives, then," she noted, forcing her mind away from those dark thoughts and onto the cowards who'd created such a situation.

Something sparked in Batu's gaze as he realized what she had given him. He smoothed her hair and leaned down to kiss her quickly.

"Davaa!" he called, favoring Briga with a guarded, grateful look, then he turned to find his spy, who was no doubt holed up out of sight.

Briga watched him ride off, her shoulders set stiffly. After a moment, she turned to her former slave.

"Dagmer, I believe you had a task to see to for me?"

The dark-haired girl nodded. "Of course, my lady."

Gansükh alone had not turned his attention from Briga once since they'd come outside. He watched Dagmer from the corner of his eye for the first few steps as she took her leave, so he was aware of the tiny sag to the she-wolf's shoulders. She turned her face up to the sky slightly and closed her eyes, a small frown marring her painted features.

"Is something wrong?"

She opened her eyes after a moment, though the creases remained. "I'm not sure…something…"

But she trailed off before finishing the thought. He followed her gaze to see Bayanaa leading a chained and angry-looking blond prisoner. Gansükh tightened his grip on the hilt of his sword. This man was a natural fighter. Dangerous. He did not like the idea of the she-wolf taking him as her slave. The man glowered. He still wore the same blood-and-fire-marred clothing, but Gansükh knew the other kheshig had thoroughly searched him for hidden weapons this time. Bayanaa carried something slung over his shoulder as he led the new slave.

"Another gift for you, mistress," Bayanaa called as he neared, jerking the chain to bring her slave forward and unslinging the item from his shoulder.

He held a long garment made of gleaming, interlocking metal rings. She reached out to touch it, her fingers exploring a section of broken rings gently.

"Armor," she said quietly, half question but half not.

"He was wearing it," Bayanaa added unnecessarily.

She cast him a look but said nothing. Something cold and wet brushed against her hand, and she knew without looking the mysterious wolf had returned. She let her fingers twine in its fur briefly. Finally she turned to the blond man, allowing the full weight of her cold gaze to rest on him. Her fingers itched at the proximity, longing for revenge. Beside her the wolf growled once. He had a handsome face. Hate-filled green eyes, not unlike her own with their touch of gray, glared steadily back at her. There was a presence to him that seemed undiminished despite the chains and slave collar.

"Kneel," she commanded in Drev'an.

When he didn't respond, Bayanaa yanked violently on the chains. Ambrus fell to his knees painfully but stifled a grimace and kept his eyes locked on the demoness. She held his gaze, then smiled in faint amusement.

"Fighting won't do you any good," she began again, in Velkcic this time, taking a step closer to Gansükh without

443

shifting her gaze. "I have won the loyalty of all manner of beasts. You are no different."

She reached up with one hand to caress Gansükh's cheek, then glanced meaningfully to the wolf. Gansükh didn't so much as flinch, merely watched the prisoner. He spoke no Velkcic, but recognized she was acting again, and settled into his role. Slowly she let her hand drop and stalked closer to the slave.

"The only reason you're still alive is because of my love for Amergin."

There was no warmth or amusement in her tone now, only cold venom.

"You betrayed him," he growled, and Bayanaa backhanded him across the face.

"I may yet change my mind."

"Murderer..." he growled.

Bayanaa moved to strike him again, but she held up her hand. Narrowing her eyes, she examined his face, wondering what had transpired between him and Amergin to thwart her vengeance. She reached out with one finger to touch that strong jawline, hating herself for doing it. When he twitched away, she grabbed a fistful of short, unkempt beard beneath his chin.

"You will regret not killing me," she vowed, holding and matching his hate-filled gaze.

"Take him to my quarters," she ordered Bayanaa in Drev'an, releasing his beard with a violent gesture.

Chapter 34

Davaa found Sartaq blowing on a fire he'd lit before the king's strongroom, attempting to force smoke through the narrow slit at the base of the door. She watched for a moment, amused.

"They are dug in like ticks," he commented over his shoulder by way of greeting.

She smiled thinly, allowing her gaze to travel from Sartaq to his men idly ringed around the area. Some sharpened or cleaned weapons, but most just looked bored, waiting for something to happen.

"Might I have a word, commander?"

Sartaq sighed irritably and motioned for one of his men to continue directing smoke under the door. She drew him aside somewhat. She had no concern about being overheard by his men, but didn't want the king and whoever was with him to hear her voice. They might recognize her. What she proposed required trust, and she could never secure that now, not if they recognized the voice of Hannah.

"What have you tried?"

Sartaq ran a hand across his scalp. He'd removed his helmet, and the gesture mussed the ridge of hair he styled down the center of his head.

"Brute force. Threats."

He looked at her briefly, and she knew by his expression there was something he'd withheld. No matter.

"The door cannot be opened from the outside," he went on. "Either they choose to come out, or they starve in there."

Her eyes flickered to the fire and back again. "Who is with him in there?"

"A priest and two others. Lords, I think."

She searched her memory for who she had seen in the audience chamber before betraying them, examining the faces in her mind.

"I know something about most of their nobility." She paused, organizing her thoughts.

Sartaq eyed her with a look that was equal parts weariness, irritation, and curiosity.

"Depending on who is there, we may be able to…negotiate."

The commander studied her as the words and their meaning sank in. "You think one of them might turn on him."

She nodded. "It is possible. But it depends on who is there. You need to do the talking; they might recognize my voice, and they will never trust me."

Sartaq grunted his understanding and willingness to try, motioning her to follow. At the door, he sent his man back to the bored semi-circle and violently kicked the fire away. He waited a moment, then banged on the door with his fist.

"Are you tired of breathing smoke yet?"

A few muffled coughs could be heard beyond the thick door, but no one spoke.

"Ah, but where are my manners? We have been here for hours without introduction."

Davaa smiled slightly, encouraging him.

"I am Sartaq, brother of the khan, and commander of his forces. Perhaps you have heard of me."

A few of the Drev'an chuckled—many of Sartaq's hand-chosen could speak Magyun. Someone scoffed on the other side of the door.

"Who is there with you, King Bela?"

Several minutes passed with no answer. Sartaq *tsk*ed.

"This does not have to be unpleasant. We have one of your lords. He is asking after who still lives."

They could hear muffled conversation followed by a single clear word. "Who?"

Sartaq looked at Davaa, who mouthed a name.

"Lord Larsson."

"Liar! I saw his body. Larsson is dead."

Davaa recognized the voice as belonging to Lord Olechs.

"He is injured, but he lives," Sartaq assured them. "We are not savages, whatever you might think. Let him have hope his fellow nobles may yet survive this...ordeal."

Davaa smiled coldly as Sartaq laid the bait. A slim chance of survival. Fragile hope. Olechs was a coward, as was the king. There was more muffled conversation and some sounds of dissent. Sartaq allowed them time to discuss.

"Larsson truly still lives?"

"He does."

"Tell him...Lord Olechs and Lord Janus remain."

Davaa nodded to herself while Sartaq issued nonsense orders to a fictional messenger in Drev'an. Commander and spy moved away from the door together to let the men inside think for a while in silence. Davaa brought her lips close to Sartaq's

447

ear and whispered the plan, what he must convince them to do. He nodded. The silence stretched on, until finally a voice Davaa did not recognize raised a question. She supposed it might be the priest.

"Will you kill him?"

"That depends on King Bela," Sartaq answered coolly.

"What do you mean?" This after a startled silence.

"Come out, surrender, and I will spare what nobles remain.

"As prisoners," Olechs scoffed.

Sartaq let a heavy silence stretch for a moment, as if weighing his options.

"The khan has duties elsewhere that cannot remain unattended indefinitely. As do I. We will require a ruler in our absence, to keep the peace, and defend what citizens remain."

The king laughed harshly. "You wish me to swear allegiance to Khan Batu in exchange for our lives? Never."

"Not you, King Bela."

There was another startled silence.

"My brother offered you that chance before, and you refused him. He promised to raze your city, did he not?"

No response. None was expected.

"My brother is a man who keeps his promises. You will die, Bela. 'The Strong'," Sartaq added with velvet coldness.

"Hardly a compelling argument, Commander. I will not open this door to die."

Sartaq shrugged. "You will die of hunger or thirst in there. Have you ever been hungry, Bela? Starving? No, I imagine not. It is a slow, torturous death. You will linger for days. Weeks even, if you are unlucky. Wallowing in your own filth. Perhaps I will have my men give you water, just to prolong your suffering."

The commander was pacing before the door now, slow and calculating.

"I am certain your priest is salivating at the prospect of becoming a martyr, but what about Lords Janus and Olechs?"

He didn't bother to glance at Davaa for reassurance now. He was like a wolf scenting blood.

"My lords, I offer you a chance to avoid this painful, ignoble death, but I only offer it once. Open the door. Give me the king, and I will spare you to assume power of the Magyun kingdom."

Sartaq watched the door, imagining he could see what transpired beyond. They might have rejected his offer outright, but he didn't think so. Instead he pictured the king turning a fearful and suspicious gaze on his subjects. He imagined the priest preparing his words to encourage them to martyrdom. He sensed the two lords sneering at his offer. But only at first. One would eventually look to the other, assessing.

"You have one hour," he informed them, then stepped away to let them argue.

Already his mind was churning, trying to develop another option if this should fail. But Davaa was regarding him calmly, unconcerned.

"Every young rider grabs the mane when his horse bolts," she counseled quietly. "They fear falling."

"Hmm."

"Give them time. Olechs is a coward. I do not know if he is ambitious enough to act, but Janus might be."

They could hear the muffled sounds of an argument through the door, but the words were indistinct.

"Where *is* my brother?" he finally asked.

"Outside, seeing to matters of governance. He wishes it to be your honor to capture Bela."

Surprise flared but was quickly subdued on Sartaq's face. Davaa's eyes sharpened in faint amusement, but she refrained from commenting. She only leaned forward and dared to kiss his cheek softly.

"I think I shall fetch a plate of roasted meat for your men. The scent might help our guests arrive at their decision."

In the end it took three quarters of an hour before they heard the hiss of steel beyond the door. The warriors stirred themselves to alertness and traded glances.

"This is treason!" Bela shouted clearly.

"This is your fault," a voice remarked coldly.

Janus, maybe. Sartaq didn't recognize it.

"You were warned about killing those emissaries."

"You think this is about the *emissaries*?" Bela balked amid some scrabbling noises.

"The khan might have stayed away. At a distance, he was no real worry to us."

"You all but invited him here," Olechs squeaked.

Sartaq recognized the sound of a man desperately clinging to life. To hope. He smiled and let the argument drag on a while longer. The priest was praying now. There were a few clangs of steel, then a scraping sound, and a choked growl. A gauntleted fist banged on the inside of the door.

"Are you ready to give me your decision?" Sartaq prompted, mildly concerned they might be forced to kill Bela if he resisted.

"Stop this!" the priest gasped to more sounds of struggle.

There was a moment more of hesitation before a voice finally rasped, "Yes."

Sartaq smiled thinly. Davaa drew up the hood of her cloak and melted into the shadows.

"Give me your word," the voice choked, sounding conflicted.

"You doubt me?" Sartaq bristled.

"No…but—"

"Open the door. Give me the king, and my men will not harm you."

"I will see you in hell, traitor," Bela growled, but the sound was choked. Impotent.

Sartaq drew his sword as he heard someone manipulating the lock mechanism. His men readied their own blades, taking their cue from the commander. There was a grinding sound, and then a click, and the door swung outward fractionally. At a glance, two Drev'an rushed forward and pried the heavy door open. Sartaq entered the doorway, flanked by his kheshig, as others flooded the space.

The priest was on his knees, notionally guarded by one lord, while the other had his sword point to Bela's throat. The king was pressed against a wall, one arm slowly dripping blood. Drev'an rushed in before the Bela could think to take his own life, disarming the king and taking him roughly into custody.

"Lord Janus?" Sartaq guessed, addressing the lord who had held his own king at bay.

The man nodded, tight-lipped and grimly angry.

"Your sword," Sartaq prompted coldly, holding out his hand.

The lord hesitated another moment, then finally handed it over hilt-first. His hard eyes bored into Sartaq. The commander didn't gloat, merely accepted the weapon and signaled his men. Janus was released outside the door, though the Drev'an remained close. Olechs was shoved out, also disarmed, while the king remained firmly under control. For the first time, Sartaq smiled a thin, genuine smile.

"A wise decision, Lord Janus. It seems we will all get what we want. The king is mine, you two will live, and the priest…will get his martyrdom."

The priest looked up sharply as the Drev'an shoved him back into the room and shut the door.

"No!" he called, frantic, and beat weakly on the door.

Already the horselords were moving various heavy debris to block the exit. Janus watched silently, and Olechs visibly paled, but neither uttered a sound.

"Now," Sartaq began, flinging a comradely arm over each lord's shoulder. "Let us go and see my brother."

***

Batu Khan was in the center of the courtyard, still astride his stallion. The beast must be tired, but it gave no indication, other than blowing and shaking its mane irritably. The she-wolf stood beside him, her hand upon his knee. They both looked toward the door as Sartaq emerged before his strange entourage.

"Brother!" Sartaq called triumphantly, his eyes sweeping over the she-wolf and dismissing her for now.

His own shaman was nowhere to be seen. One arm was still draped around Olechs' shoulders while his other clutched a rope. At the other end of the rope was a bound and disgruntled-looking king being led out by the neck, like a common dog. Batu stifled the grin he felt and reached down to rest his non-sword hand atop the she-wolf's.

The commander didn't bother masking *his* grin as he tugged the rope, dragging the king off balance.

"I have a gift for you, Batu Khan."

Batu finally smiled, a thin, cruel expression, and swept his gaze over Sartaq's entourage.

"You have done well, commander."

There was a genuine note of praise in his voice. All eyes had turned to the khan and his brother now, watching the moment. Batu clasped his brother by the arm and shared a private look with him before turning his attention to the prisoner.

"King Bela, we meet at last."

Whatever Bela had been about to growl in response was lost when one of Sartaq's men punched him squarely across the jaw using the hilt of his sword. Bela fell to one knee, unable to maintain balance with his hands tied, and spat blood.

"I did warn you what would happen if you defied me," he warned in Magyun. "Khuyag, take him."

Hateful eyes flared up at him, but only for a moment, before General Khuyag and two of his men stepped forward and took hold of the prisoner. Batu hadn't even bothered to dismount. Bela was a prize, but not worth any measure of deference. Bela struggled as Khuyag drew a knife, but he only cut the bindings from his wrists after his men took firm hold of his arms. Then the trio marched him away in the direction of the iron rings.

Batu watched them coolly, then turned back to his brother. "What else have you brought me?"

The two lords shifted uncomfortably under the khan's gaze, and Sartaq regarded them stoically for a moment, calculating.

"Lords Janus and Olechs. They were holed up with Bela."

Batu eyed them but continued speaking in Drev'an. "I heard there was also a priest?"

"There was." Sartaq nodded. "He chose to become a martyr."

The khan scoffed. "Foolish. How did you get these two out?"

Sartaq paused and smiled with one side of his mouth. He stepped back to Lord Olechs and slung an arm across the man's shoulders again.

"I offered an incentive, and in return they surrendered the king to me."

Olechs seemed distinctly uncomfortable beside Sartaq. His gaze flicked around the group, landing on Briga curiously, but he immediately looked away when she returned his gaze. Though he couldn't speak Drev'an, he appeared to take comfort from Sartaq's friendly demeanor.

"Incentive?" Batu asked in a flat tone that instantly captured Briga's attention.

Sartaq shrugged slightly and let his arm fall. "Survival. Someone needs to watch over the city when we are done here."

Batu's spine stiffened, seeming to grant him an additional inch or two of height.

"And just where do you need to be? You will watch over the city if necessary."

The khan switched to Magyun and focused the weight of his gaze on the two lords. "Kill them."

Janus paled instantly. Olechs panicked. Sartaq did nothing, but his men pulled their weapons free of their scabbards. Olechs clutched at Sartaq's arm desperately.

"Lord Sartaq! You gave your word!"

"So I did," the commander agreed, motioning for his men to sheath their weapons again.

A few glanced uncertainly between the commander and the khan. Briga dared to glance at Batu and noted the small muscle feathering in his jaw, but he otherwise restrained his anger. There was a cold cast to Sartaq's eyes as he drew his own blade.

"What did you promise?" Batu asked flatly, still in Magyun.

"That my men would not harm them," he answered carelessly, a slight grin returning to his features. "But I never claimed to speak for the khan."

Olechs paled even further and took a stumbling step back from Sartaq. Cold anger stole over Janus' face, though to his credit, he didn't move. Briga hadn't realized she had been holding her breath, nor did she realize her fingers had tightened on Batu's thigh until he reached down to loosen them. She looked up at him, uncertain if something else had just happened here.

"Might they still be of some use to you?" she asked quietly.

"What use?"

Sartaq paused, listening to their exchange.

"The location of any remaining food stores? Weapons?" she paused, wracking her brain. "Wasn't there talk of some Magyun ally? Do we know if anyone is coming to their aid even now?"

Batu sat back, considering. Even Sartaq seemed surprised. Olechs, trembling, looked on guardedly. He couldn't understand what was being said but recognized a possible chance to survive this. Batu flickered his gaze over the two lords, assessing them briefly before looking beyond them to someone lingering near the door. Briga couldn't make out who it was through the small crowd of Sartaq's warriors. Sartaq did not follow his brother's gaze, assuming he was checking for Davaa. The hooded figure nodded once in confirmation, then nodded again to indicate one of the prisoners. The khan squeezed Briga's fingers discreetly, then let out a short huff of breath.

"I have only one inviolate law in my Khanate," he began again in Magyun, releasing Briga to pace his horse forward. "What is that law, Commander Sartaq?"

"Never betray your khan."

Batu met his eyes for a moment, then moved his horse to face Olechs.

"My shaman thinks I should spare you," he continued, glancing over his shoulder at the she-wolf in her fearsome paint and foreign leather armor.

Janus flicked his gaze to her briefly but kept his cold focus on the khan. Olechs looked at her as well, but his gaze lingered.

"Yes, she is a pagan," he confirmed with a dark smile. "Our gods have proven stronger than yours...perhaps I should consider her request."

Briga could only partially follow the Magyun words but kept her face schooled into stoicism. She allowed one hand to rest on the hilt of a dagger. Olechs visibly swallowed.

"You betrayed your king. How could I ever trust you not to betray me?"

"My lord, I could never—" Olechs was cut off mid-sentence by a guard cuffing the back of his head.

"Khan," he corrected roughly.

Sartaq watched passively, clearly amused by the situation.

"Batu Khan," the commander interjected, "they were responsible for your ultimate victory."

"Which of them laid hands on their king?"

"Him!" Olechs blurted in a panic, pointing to the still-glowering Janus.

The stallion reared and lashed out with its front legs. Heavy hooves clipped Olechs on the head and shoulders, then trampled him as they fell to earth together.

"Coward," Batu spat when it was over.

Sartaq laughed mirthlessly and looked away. Batu drew his curved sword and pointed it at Janus.

"I have no use for cowards. Are you a coward, Lord Janus?"

With effort, he tore his fear-tinged gaze from the bloody pulp that remained of Olechs and met Batu's eyes.

"I am not, Batu Khan."

With a grunt and a nod, he sheathed the sword and commanded his dancing stallion to settle.

"I can see you are not. I will honor my brother's promise, then."

Still smiling in amusement, Sartaq clapped Janus on the shoulder. The lord blinked and exhaled, struggling to accept the reprieve and master his emotions.

"Find him quarters and see that he is fed and bathed. General Khuyag will dispatch two guards for his protection."

Sartaq's eyes steeled slightly at that last remark, but the frozen half-smile didn't fade. Briga did not fail to note the change and wondered at it. When Batu turned around to look at her, she saw a low fire smoldering in his gaze. She licked suddenly dry lips.

"You should rest," she advised quietly when he was close enough to hear.

"Later," he growled in husky tones and ran a rough finger up under her jaw. "There is still work to do."

The touch only lasted a moment before he rode past, toward two dismounted generals. It sent a shiver through her as she watched him ride off. Feeling eyes on her, she cast a sidelong look at Gansükh and inexplicably blushed. The feeling didn't cease and she turned to see the cloaked figure of a woman watching her from beside the palace doors. A chill spider-walked up her spine that was entirely different from the one Batu had caused.

***

Amergin twitched himself awake as one of the guards tossed a half-filled bowl of thin gruel at his feet. He ran a hand over his face, unaware of having fallen asleep. The last thing he could remember clearly was trying and failing to seek out his sister through the Pattern. He'd tried for hours, but the chaos of the city and their immediate situation stymied him at every attempt.

At some point during the night they had removed the bodies of Eamon and Cathbad, provoking a violent response from the Velkcic warriors, which was even more violently quelled. Kessan likely had a broken arm. Amergin tried to work a kink out of his neck as he looked around and took stock of the situation. More prisoners had arrived, crowding the space. He felt a touch on his shoulder and looked back to find dark-haired Niall watching him.

"First rule, druid. Eat. The gods only know if they'll feed us again."

"Or when," Kessan muttered.

Frowning, Amergin picked up the bowl and tipped its cold contents into his mouth.

"Slowly," Niall counselled. "Make it last a while."

"To trick the stomach," Kessan added, soliciting a warning look from both men.

He grunted but kept his mouth shut and returned attention to his meal, such as it was.

"Where's Rorik?" Amergin asked after choking down a bit more of the gruel. It was Kessan who answered.

"Bastards took him, Connor, and a few of those others earlier."

"Took them where?"

"Damned if I know," he growled.

Amergin turned to face him fully. Kessan's left forearm was swollen, and he kept it cradled in his lap.

"They took your friend Ambrus, too. The big one and the woman."

"The woman was Briga," he stated, too quietly.

The warriors stared at him, disbelieving, and shared a look.

"She was taken as a prisoner. And that head wound..."

Amergin only nodded, reluctantly meeting their eyes. He hadn't wanted to believe it either, but Cathbad knew she'd survived. Amergin himself had felt her presence as well. He'd *seen* her. Truly seen her. The two warriors must have been able to read the conviction in his face, as they sat back, attempting to absorb the information.

"No...the lass was a wee wisp of a thing at Rowanar."

"It was her," Amergin affirmed, a cold certainty coming over him now like a mantle.

"I think the druid's right, Kessan."

The big warrior looked between Niall and Amergin for a few moments, assessing their expressions. He then slammed his bowl down in fury, cracking it and earning a few hurled abuses and threats from their guards.

"Fuck!" he shouted, trying to stand.

Niall and Amergin grabbed him immediately and forced him back down.

"Stop before you get us killed," Niall hissed.

Kessan shook them both off but stilled, his anger banked to a more controllable level.

"Let me see that arm," Amergin instructed him quietly to distract his thoughts.

Kessan blew out a short breath, but obediently held out his arm to the druid.

"That bitch," he growled, undeterred.

Amergin glared up at him and might have let his fingers probe the injured arm a bit too firmly. Kessan hissed in pain but got the message and attempted to calm himself.

"Why is she helping them, then?"

Amergin was quiet a moment, concentrating on Kessan's arm. It was a question that had plagued him as well.

"I think she's a prisoner, like us."

Kessan scoffed. "She didn't act like a prisoner. I saw the way those horselords obeyed her."

The druid was silent, remembering the look she had given him before leaving. She'd been trying to tell him something, he was certain. Amergin shook his head.

"If she were free to leave, she would have done so. Something else is going on here. Niall, hand me that."

Niall grabbed a stick the druid had pointed at and handed it over. His expression was carefully guarded.

"She loved Eamon, we could all see that," he added quietly, aware the issue was taboo for druids. "She would never—"

460

"Who are these others?" Amergin asked, abruptly changing the conversation and tearing a strip of linen from the hem of his shirt.

"More prisoners," Niall answered, accepting the change of direction. "But…"

Amergin paused from winding the cloth around Kessan's arm and its makeshift brace long enough to look at the other warrior. "But?"

"I keep feeling there's a pattern here, but one I can't make out, aside from them all being men. Why single us out when they are killing survivors in the streets?"

Amergin had no good answer for that. Worse, he wondered what had happened to Dianna. Were there female prisoners being kept elsewhere? Was she even still alive? He looked around the room again. The prisoners spanned a range of ages and builds. He could divine no special commonality between them all. The druid frowned as he resumed work on Kessan's arm.

"I think Briga will help us, if she can command any of these horselords. We should be good prisoners for now. Escape if given the chance and if it won't endanger the others, but otherwise do as they ask."

Kessan looked hard at the druid, and Amergin had the peculiar sense he was searching for any signs of weakness, or doubt. After a long moment, he finally nodded.

"For now."

"For now," Niall agreed.

***

Ambrus had watched the proceedings in the courtyard below from the window for most of the day. King Bela had been stripped of his clothing, and each wrist had been fastened to an iron ring set into the ground by a length of chain. The chains

461

held just enough slack that he could sit on his knees and cover his nakedness.

He'd been forced to clean the she-demon's chambers for a good portion of the afternoon, and he tried to protest by emptying the chamber pot on her bed and throwing the vessel itself across the room. The dark-haired servant female had tried to attack him after that, fingers extended as if they were claws, and with a shriek of fury worthy of any Valkyrie. The male guard had been forced to restrain her, then had beaten Ambrus with his scabbard until he feared he might have broken an arm or a rib. He'd then been forced to clean up the mess with old rushes and his bare hands, and promptly decided the act of defiance had not been worth it.

They'd then forced him to change out the entire bed, dragging a clean straw mattress from another room down the hall. He'd been allowed to clean his hands before fetching the new bedding, which he regarded as a mixed blessing, really. After a short rest, they had fetched him again and forced him to haul first a bathing tub, then several scrawny stacks of firewood up to the room, and finally several bundles of candles. It was awkward with his hands and feet still chained.

When the sun started to set, they chained him to an iron ring set into the floor in a corner of the room. He couldn't tell if the fixture was old or newly installed while he was out fetching some item or another. No one lit the fire or any of the candles, they just left him chained in the dark, cooling room with at least two guards posted outside.

For a time he tested his restraints, searching for any exploitable weakness in the manacles themselves, individual links in the chain, the anchor bolt, or its setting. He'd tried to chip away at the stone with chain links, but that proved useless. If he rubbed one of the links against the coarser stones in the wall, he might wear away the metal in a week or two. *If* he could hide the marks. The idea wasn't much, but it was something.

462

As the sun sank below the horizon, the temperature dropped quickly. Without furs or his cloak, Ambrus was forced to abandon his slow progress at wearing away the chain link and instead attempt to rub warmth back into his arms and chest. The beginnings of despair edged in on his thoughts. Is this what it had been like for Siggi?

"Sitric..."

He climbed to his feet and got as close to the window as his chains would allow. Outside, numerous small fires dotted one side of the courtyard, leaving a wide berth around Bela. It was unclear if these were campfires or cook fires, but he supposed it didn't really matter.

He could hear the Drev'an celebrating. His gaze drifted across the yard to the dungeon entrance and he was slightly relieved to see it was still blocked and smoldering. Motion caught his eye and drew his attention to a group in the center of the Drev'an mass. He recognized the demoness in the group, flanked by the male and female guards who'd been tormenting him all day. The sight of her heated his blood with rage, and he found he was clenching his fists painfully. She looked up then, seeming to look directly at him.

They were eating something, and the tantalizing scent of roasted meat drifted up to taunt him. The Drev'an beside her noticed her attention and followed her gaze, then cupped her chin and turned her to face him. There was something...proprietary in the gesture.

Before he could watch more, the door crashed open behind him, and the large male guard who normally attached himself to the she-devil stomped in. He sniffed the air, then growled as if scenting the lingering traces of Ambrus' earlier act of defiance. He did not curse under his breath as he crossed to the corner, simply unlocked his chains from the eye ring and pointed to the pile of candles he'd left beside the bed earlier. He then held up a heel of bread, the first food Ambrus had been offered all day.

The implication was clear. Carry out his tasks without protest, and he could eat.

"I'd prefer meat."

"You will eat what my lady commands."

Ambrus regarded him with surprise. He'd assumed his guards didn't speak Magyun. He would have to guard his words around this one, at least.

"What's your name?"

"Start the fire, light the candles, fill the bath. It must be warm. This does not require talking."

With some difficulty, Ambrus restrained himself, and after blowing out a breath, he simply nodded.

Chapter 35

Briga frowned as she looked up toward her quarters. She couldn't see anyone there in the darkness, but his presence bothered her like a splinter in the skin of her perception. Not always, but there were moments…

Her thoughts were abruptly interrupted by a hand gripping the back of her head and neck and firmly turning her to face away from the darkened building. She found Batu regarding her, dark eyes glittering in question.

"I'm all right," she confirmed quietly.

By the thin line of his mouth, she knew he didn't believe her. She didn't believe herself. Since Eamon died, she'd been holding on to control by her fingernails. Something shifted in Batu's expression, and he offered her his own cup. She accepted and drank gratefully, surprised to taste golden ale instead of ayrak.

"They found quite a bit of that in a palace storeroom. I thought you might like it."

She flashed him a genuine smile and watched him over the rim of the cup as she drank again. One side of his mouth twitched into a brief grin as he watched her. He leaned forward and kissed her forehead. Briga felt wariness prick at her. Such a public display of real affection was unusual for the khan. His gaze swept the assemblage around them and she followed his attention.

"What's wrong?" she whispered.

He shook his head slightly and slid his hand down to her hip. His other hand beckoned to a servant to bring him a fresh cup.

"Stay beside me tonight." His voice was warm but edged with warning. "Their blood is up, and there are too few women slaves. Even your status is not enough for some to resist."

A shudder went through her, part fear, and part rage. His thumb stroked her hip bone lightly, focusing her attention somewhat, and drawing it inward, where she might control it. At the edge of her vision, she saw Dagmer edge closer to Bayanaa and simmered at the realization that they were not the only women under threat.

"Brother!" a voice called.

Sartaq was sidling toward them through the crowd, a cup of ayrak in one hand and a grin on his face. His steps were only slightly unsteady. Batu released her to clasp elbows with his brother. They exchanged a look, but there was no undercurrent of malice this time.

"Did I not promise you the city?" Batu called out, turning to his army.

The men cheered ferociously, raising their cups or bowls skyward in salute.

"There will be time for pretty speeches later, tonight we feast!"

The roar was louder still as the men shouted their approval.

"Plenty of time later for pretty things," Sartaq echoed, grasping Briga's chin lightly.

There was something unnerving and entirely sober in his gaze. Before Briga could shake him off or Batu could intervene, he released her.

"I have my own pretty thing waiting for me," he commented lazily, and by the way he took a swig of the ayrak, Briga wasn't sure if he meant a woman, a drink, or something else entirely.

"Sit," Batu offered, diffusing the tension. "Eat with me."

Sartaq obliged him and motioned for his kheshig to make themselves comfortable. A servant materialized with a plate of roasted horseflesh for the khan and his entourage to pick over. They had butchered all the dead and dying horses after the battle. There was more meat now than even the horde could devour in one sitting, so a good portion would be salted and dried for winter provisions. Briga stared at the meat, suddenly fearful.

"Singer is fine," Batu commented as if reading her mind.

Briga looked at him, surprised he knew the name.

"Singer?" Sartaq asked, puzzled.

"Her gelding."

The commander barked a laugh, but it wasn't entirely cruel. "She named it?"

"You haven't named yours?" Briga questioned.

"No," he answered simply, eyebrows drawn in mild surprise.

"And you, Batu?"

"Drev'an do not normally name their beasts."

"We name everything," she commented absently and sipped at her ale.

"Khuyag!" Batu called out, catching sight of his general. "Take a cup of ale to Bela out there, then come and join us."

Briga watched as the general nodded and set about his task. Her gaze flitted to the king. He had abandoned some dignity in favor of comfort and was sitting cross-legged between the chains now. She couldn't make out his expression. When she returned her attention to the khan, she found him watching her closely.

"Ale," he commanded the closest servant.

Sartaq was watching her, too. He seemed about to say something when motion over her shoulder caught his attention.

"Your pardon, brother," Sartaq slurred, tipping back the rest of his cup. "I am needed."

Briga watched him leave. She mistrusted the commander but was uncertain of exactly why. He made her feel uneasy and suspicious. Though she watched after him, she couldn't see who he went to meet.

"I heard," Batu began, not looking at her. "I heard about the Velkcic in the barn."

Her blood froze at his words, and there was an inexplicable catch in her throat.

"Is that why…? Did you know any of them?"

He was watching his men, both of them conscious of the tears threatening at the corners of her eyes. There was too little air, but Briga dragged in a breath anyway and fought to control herself. She considered lying. What would he do if he knew of their connection? Would the survivors be at more or less risk? If she lied…would he find out anyway?

"Yes," she finally answered in a breathy tone that surprised her.

He half looked at her, concern furrowing his brow.

"Two of them were…there was nothing I could do."

468

A single tear fell, and she sniffed, turning her face away and determined to master her emotions. To his credit, Batu allowed her the time she needed, half watching her as he directed a servant to leave a small cask of ale and refilled a bowl for her. When she eventually turned back to look over the crowd absently, he caught her eye and offered her the fresh drink. There was a rare softness to his gaze.

"War is a terrible thing, especially for those caught between the tides."

She nodded and accepted the bowl, drinking deeply. She didn't want to dwell on her sorrows, didn't want to wonder what had happened to them. Not now. Not yet. For the same reason she did not dare ask after the fates of the other prisoners. They had been here looking for her. She'd felt them searching. Because of her, Eamon and Cathbad had fallen in the resulting battle. Because of her.

"You fought well," he commented, something shifting in his eyes slightly.

Briga allowed herself to smile, allowed the distraction. She *had* fought well. She'd killed and had avoided major injury in the process.

"I think you killed more even than General Khuyag here," he teased with a grin in his voice as the general returned from his task.

"That is because I was too busy guarding *you*," Khuyag returned with good-natured venom.

Of all the generals, Briga found she liked Khuyag the best. She mustered a smile for him and lifted her bowl in salute.

"I am pleased to see Batu Khan taught you more than just pretty horsemanship. You seem fairly unscathed, she-wolf."

"You forget I was a fighter before, General," she responded sharply, irritation flashing through her unexpectedly.

Khuyag eyed her, but after a quick glance at the khan, he decided not to say whatever he'd been about to say. She suspected she knew anyway. Her injury trends were well-known to him, after all.

"Of course," he offered, smooth and placating, "I only meant fighting in the Drev'an style suits you."

She nodded, conciliatory. "It does."

A sudden, subtle *tug* drew her attention, and she scanned the crowd. It was fleeting, too brief to properly interpret.

"When the clan found me many years ago, they at first thought I was a wolf."

She spoke without realizing it and without knowing why. Batu and Khuyag regarded her curiously. She could feel Dagmer's eyes on her as well but did not turn to look, merely watched a group of warriors engaged in an impromptu wrestling competition.

"I had washed ashore, half-drowned and draped in wolfskin."

Her fingers absently touched the wolfskin cloak at her shoulders. The one Batu had gifted her.

"It seems we have named you well, then," Khuyag remarked. "Where did you come from?"

She shook her head. "I don't know. I have very few memories of the time before. Only these."

Her hand dropped to touch the hilt of one fighting knife. Khuyag seemed as if he were about to ask to see one of the knives more closely, but he was interrupted by a drunk warrior stumbling toward them. Bayanaa half rose, and Batu's guards moved to intercept, but the khan motioned them back.

"Batu Khan," he called out, grinning.

He was young. Briga eyed him, wondering if this was his first battle campaign.

"They said you have called for your mhorin khuur. I would be honored if you would take mine."

The young warrior sank down on one knee respectfully, holding out his horse-headed fiddle toward the khan. The instrument was well-kept, but plainer than Batu's own. The khan handed his cup to Briga and stood slowly. The area around them had grown quiet to watch, and he crossed the few paces separating them with ease.

"It was my father's," the warrior explained, not looking up.

Wordlessly Batu reached out to gently take the instrument, looking it over reverently. He lowered into a cross-legged position in front of the young man and placed the instrument in his lap.

"What is your name?"

"Zu'qi, Batu Khan."

The khan smiled. "A good name. My father was called Zu'qi."

The boy Zu'qi flashed a grin of his own, intelligence glinting through the drunken glaze of his eyes. "I know."

Batu chuckled at the impertinence, then gestured with the bow for him to sit. With a conspiratorial, sidelong glance to Briga, he dragged the bow across the neck of the instrument and started an upbeat tune. Briga recognized it after a few measures. It was one of the first he had played for her, so long ago now, when she'd been brought before him as a captive.

A crowd gathered around them, as it always did when the khan was among his men. At length, a runner finally returned from beyond the walls, bearing the khan's own instrument.

"Join me," Batu instructed as he wound down the song.

He motioned for the runner to hand his instrument over to Zu'qi. The young warrior seemed stunned for a moment, then accepted the mhorin khuur with reverent hands, belying his apparent intoxication. The khan nodded encouragingly and started a mournful tune. The boy listened respectfully for a few measures, adjusting his grip on the unfamiliar bow. Finally he joined in, familiar with the song. He played tentatively at first, matching Batu's timing. When he finally seemed relaxed, Batu let him carry the melody and improvised a harmony. The song was beautiful, and Briga felt herself sink into it, feeling at peace for the first time in days. Longer, perhaps. There was a subtle kind of magic in the music. She allowed herself to just be in the moment and release all else.

The song stretched on, or perhaps they began a new one, but eventually Batu stopped for a break. He kept the gifted mhorin khuur and made a gift of his own instrument to the young warrior.

"From one Zu'qi to another," he joked quietly.

Briga wasn't aware that time had passed until she felt a fresh bowl of ale nudged into her hand. She blinked, half-startling. Batu eased himself down beside her, setting his new instrument aside.

"What do you see?" he asked, watching her closely.

"No," she explained with a shake of her head. "I was just enjoying the music. You play beautifully."

"Do you play any instruments?" Khuyag asked.

Briga had almost forgotten he was there.

"Not well. I was taught the harp when they were judging our potential for bardic talent, but I've never had the skill. My talents are elsewhere."

"Then you must sing?"

She eyed him sharply but didn't contradict his half-statement. Khuyag smiled.

"Are your songs so different from ours? Sing for us."

"Now?" She blinked incredulously.

"Why not? It is a feast."

He was right. As she glanced around the courtyard, pockets of warriors clustered together, singing or playing or both amid the revelry. She'd seen them do this before, and it wasn't so different from Eamon's war bands after a successful raid. Thinking of Eamon sobered her. She looked to Batu. The khan was watching her expectantly and offered an encouraging nod.

"I…"

"Perhaps a shaman's chant…" the general suggested, noting her discomfort.

She nodded, gathering herself. She sang the rituals often, before and after her time with the Drev'an. There was no need to be self-conscious here.

"Very well. But I should like to hear you grace us with your talents when I'm done."

She grinned darkly, and both Drev'an laughed.

"She will fit in well back home." Khuyag laughed, turning his attention from the khan back to her. "It is a deal."

Briga felt a pang of dread at his words, but firmly pushed it aside for the moment. She thought through what songs she could remember, and a lament rose unbidden to her mind. It was a song she remembered from the bardic trials. Closing her eyes, she began to sing in Velkcic.

The song had been originally composed for an old Velkcic king, written by a famous bard who'd been loyal to the clan. The king had successfully repelled the Emorians from Velkcic lands, but the victory did not last. He was captured, dissolving the small alliance of clans he had forged, and was eventually killed. Briga sang the words dutifully, but in her heart they were meant for Eamon. It wasn't for the loss of that ancient clan and their culture, but a lament for the life she herself had left behind.

Sometime during the second verse, she felt the sting of another tear at the corner of her eye. She blinked it away, willing herself to anger for the loss rather than sorrow. She also became aware of a different mournful tone, complimenting her melody with slow, respectful notes. Khuyag had taken up the mhorin khuur and was playing her accompaniment. She met his eye; there was no hint of mirth there, only solemn respect.

When the song finally ended and she fell silent, she became uncomfortably aware of the hush that had fallen around them. The Drev'an had stopped to listen, or at least those within earshot.

"Powerful," Khuyag told her quietly. "What is it about?"

Briga smiled self-consciously, glancing at the staring faces.

"The death song for an ancient king. Perhaps too sorrowful for such a celebration. Do you have a drum?" she asked, trying to deflect some of the attention. "Oh. And that doesn't count as your playing, General. But find me a drum, and we'll play something happier together."

***

It took effort, such effort, to accept that he wasn't dead. His eyes peeled open with difficulty. They stung. The darkness had a different quality now. It was…thicker, somehow…denser. He gasped awake and immediately choked on the acrid air. His throat burned, and he gulped down what remained of his water bucket. It didn't taste fresh. How long had it been sitting there? He tried to rake his memory, still gasping around his raw throat. There had been screaming and smoke, but that was all he could remember. No one had come to open his cell, despite his efforts to gain the attention of the guards. He must have passed out.

474

Head throbbing, he lay back on the cold stone. The air was cleaner down here, with a tiny draft blowing through the crack below the door. He sucked in a breath to clear his lungs, still coughing.

Within a few minutes his mind cleared enough to handle thoughts broader than his own immediate survival, and he wondered what had happened. The dungeon beyond was utterly silent. He could hear no guards shuffling through the halls, no prisoners moaning or screaming. Not anymore. Only the slow drip, drip of water. The light flickering beneath the door was dim, as if a sole torch left somewhere was burning out. He wanted to hit something, kick down the door, but he knew it would be useless rage. Better to think, calculate, before acting. He closed his eyes for a moment to center himself and caught a different sound, strange and out of place. The faint strains of a distant female voice floated to him down the stone corridors. She was…singing. He focused on the voice, puzzled. Her song was beautiful and haunting. Was he really dead after all? This wasn't Valhalla; had he been denied a warrior's death? A warrior's honor? Or was it some messenger coming to claim him? Lacking the strength to fight fate, he lay still. Listening. Waiting.

In time the song faded, leaving him ill at ease. Silence reigned once more, broken only by the dripping of water. A different sound drifted to him now, something rhythmic. A drum? What was happening up there? It was then he recognized male voices, muted and indistinct, distorted by several floors of stone. It sounded vaguely like a war camp. Had someone attacked the city? And more importantly, who had won? Uneasy, he closed his eyes to think. To develop options.

***

Briga made a small, breathy sound as Batu pushed her back against the door to her new quarters, pinning her with his body as they kissed. They'd played for hours with Khuyag and the other Drev'an, feasting and drinking. She'd caught Batu watching her as she drummed, looking at her with the same

475

savage, dangerous look he'd given her after killing Lord Olechs. The expression electrified her to the core. She wanted him. More, she wanted *this*…the feeling of being so alive after all they'd witnessed. This wasn't just some duty or ceremony, it was something else. Her fingers slid up his neck into his hair as he pushed the door open behind her. One hand slid to her ribs, steadying her as the door fell away. She stifled a small laugh and allowed him to walk her backwards.

The candles had been lit, as had the hearth, but she barely registered that information as she arched her head back, exposing her throat and jaw to his grazing teeth. Batu obliged with a growl of sorts, bringing his other hand to her hip. He was still armored, and her fingers worked at the bindings inexpertly. He let go of her long enough to shrug out of it and let the tunic and arm pieces fall to the floor. She kissed him wildly, but he caught her by the throat with one hand, sliding his thumb up to her jaw to lift her chin. The gesture was more control than threat and she stilled, watching him. He took one of her wrists, silently commanding her to be still as he untied one, then the other bracer and pulled them off her forearms. She swayed a bit drunkenly but watched intently. His hands moved to remove her jerkin and wide leather sword belt, but when they drifted to the fastenings of her robe, she placed one hand on his chest.

A clink of metal drew their attention to the corner. There, crouched in the shadows, sat Briga's new slave. His wrists were shackled to the floor, and he seemed shocked and disgusted watching them.

"Who is that?" Batu rasped, studying him unpleasantly.

"My new slave," she purred, turning his chin and his attention back to her.

"Why is he here?"

"Because he tried to kill me. I don't trust him around the other slaves."

Batu bristled at that and turned a cold, savage gaze on the prisoner. "You should kill him."

"I haven't decided," she half-lied, then leaned in to sink her teeth lightly into his collarbone.

When he didn't look away from the slave, she laid her whole hand on his cheek and forced his head to turn. She kissed him then, fierce and demanding. Her hands went to the fastenings of her robe and allowed the whole garment to fall away. Batu paused to take in the sight of her, apparently forgetting the slave entirely now. She took a step back and turned from him, sauntering toward the bed. She flashed him a feral smile over her shoulder, and Batu stalked forward, a predator once more. She caught a strange look from the slave but only had a moment to puzzle over it before Batu was there pushing her onto the furs. She giggled in dark amusement and forgot all about the slave in the corner.

***

When she awoke in the gray light of pre-dawn, the hearth fire had gone out. She shivered and felt Batu curl around her reflexively, one arm draped over her waist. Her head swam, hungover or still drunk, she couldn't determine. Gauzy linens hung down and enclosed the bed itself, but she couldn't remember drawing them. Through a slit in the curtains, she spotted the blond slave huddled in the corner, shivering and attempting to sleep.

"Dagmer," she croaked quietly.

Batu stirred behind her but did not wake. His hand drifted up to her breast of its own volition. There was no response at the door, so she tried again.

"Guard?"

After a pause, there was a shuffling sound outside the door, and it slowly cracked open. The prisoner was watching her, and she self-consciously checked to ensure the skins covered her. Gansükh poked his head in, looking like he hadn't slept.

"Where's Dagmer?" she rasped in a whisper.

"Sleeping," he returned quietly, then glanced at the prisoner. "Is something wrong?"

"The fire is out."

He looked to the cold hearth, then grunted and stepped into the room toward the slave.

"No," she corrected, reading his intent. "I don't want him loose right now."

Gansükh regarded her for a moment through the sheer curtains, then left to retrieve fresh wood. She felt Batu's breath on the nape of her neck, and it sent a small thrill through her. She arched her back slightly, pushing her hips into him, and was rewarded with a light squeeze at her breast. She shifted onto her back and closed her eyes against the slow, dizzy spin of the room. His hand drifted to her stomach, and she traced the contours of his forearm lightly.

She lay like that with her eyes closed, listening when Gansükh came back and moved quietly through the room to relight the fire. It was warm enough beneath the skins, but she'd seen the slave shivering in the winter chill. Her hate and cruelty would only extend so far. The door issued a soft click as Gansükh resumed his place outside. Batu's hand slid down her stomach, as if he'd been waiting for the kheshig to leave, down to the place between her legs. She gasped softly, surprised. She still wanted for her own sake, and Batu made some sound deep in his throat at the knowledge. She looked at him, noting the hazy but strangely alert cast to his expression.

"You have your city, Batu Khan," she whispered hoarsely.

"So I do," he agreed, shifting slightly to trap her leg between his as he continued caressing her.

"What happens now?" she asked, closing her eyes but clearly talking about his strategic plans.

"Subdue the kingdom, deal with the Emorians if necessary. Then a trip home is in order."

"Home?"

"The steppe," he confirmed. "I have been away on this campaign for too long."

She paused, forcing order into her thoughts. "What will become of me?"

Batu stopped and looked at her coolly. "You will come with me, of course."

Panic flooded through her, cold and acute. She didn't know where the Drev'an steppe was, other than they'd come from far, far to the east. Farther than anyone she had known or even heard of had ever been. So far from her people and all the familiar gods…she couldn't possibly go. She wouldn't. They would make her a slave forever. Batu was watching her expression, triggering a sense of alarm. She forced herself to smile in feigned delight as her mind churned. Forced herself to kiss him. Forced herself to slide her leg over his waist.

When it was done, she lay on her side, facing away from him as if to doze. Her head still swam, but with more unease now than any lingering alcohol.

***

Ambrus was grateful for the fire. He hadn't slept much, shivering himself awake there in the corner. His gaze kept drifting to the she-devil and her lover for lack of anything else in the room to stare at. How was it possible that she was Amergin's kinswoman? He could plainly read her lust last night and didn't miss her pleasant smile again this morning. Amergin, who now sat in chains, as he did, while she whored herself to the horselords. Hate burned in his marrow.

Before long, the Drev'an roused himself and dressed. He splashed cold water from the useless bathing tub on his face and said something to the woman, who mouthed a response but didn't stir. The horselord then turned to look at him, and Ambrus misliked the hint of malice he saw in the man's eyes.

"Lucky man," the Drev'an rasped in Magyun before strapping on his sword and leaving the room.

Ambrus was wise enough not to respond, merely kept stoically to himself. Chained to the floor. The woman waited until her lover's footsteps could no longer be heard in the hall before hauling herself up to sit on the edge of the bed. He thought he saw a tear glistening at the corner of her eye. He did clearly see the scars he'd given her, and that rekindled his anger. She looked at him suddenly, as if feeling his gaze, and lifted a skin to cover herself. The gesture was oddly self-conscious, and he was puzzled to feel some of his anger drain away.

***

"Dagmer," she called, and this time the girl responded to her summons.

The former slave took in her lady's posture and frowned. "Are you all right?"

"He wants to take me back to the steppe," Briga told her, sounding a bit shaken.

Dagmer crossed to her quickly, not wanting the guards to overhear them.

"I can't," she continued flatly.

"Hush," Dagmer advised. "We'll figure this out together. Remember?"

Briga blinked, then nodded.

"Pull yourself together. We aren't doomed yet."

Dagmer was right. She was no good to herself or anyone else wallowing in fear or self-pity. She had to focus.

"I need to bathe."

The former slave called for Gansükh, who entered and released the current slave to build up a low fire around the basin. The kheshig watched him closely, not trusting their prisoner in the slightest. Briga was watching him now, too, the distant look in her eyes earlier now giving way to calculated curiosity. She observed the man as a cat might consider some fascinating new prey it had encountered.

"Who are his people?" she asked Dagmer.

"Difficult to say," the servant replied. "Shall I ask?"

"No," Briga commanded, shaking her head and acting on instinct. "Not yet. It isn't important right now."

When the water was warm enough, Gansükh dragged him back to the corner. Briga stopped him with a gesture before he could chain him up again.

"Take him with you," Briga instructed, not wanting the blond man to see her naked again. "And see that he's well fed."

A flicker of annoyance crossed Gansükh's face, but he hauled the man to his feet and took him along, leaving the women to their business.

***

Amergin awoke to Niall shaking his arm. He blinked blearily in the weak light. Some others around them were still sleeping, but most watched the horselords near the door with grim expressions. A group of three had entered and were talking with the guards. Amergin didn't recognize them, but that counted for precious little. He sniffed the air and was pleasantly surprised to scent warm broth of some kind. He hoped they would get a portion.

"Stop thinking with your stomach," Niall hissed.

The druid couldn't help but smile as he looked at Niall. "What then?"

"Rorik and Connor haven't come back. A small group returned right before that trio of horselords showed up."

"Oh?"

"I can't speak Magyun well enough to ask questions."

Amergin caught the thread of the idea at once and nodded his understanding. One of the horselords was coming around, ladling out warm soup, and Amergin's stomach rumbled. This one seemed kinder than the others, and the druid offered a small smile. There was no reaction beyond filling a bowl and passing it to him. Near the door, the three horselords seemed agitated, and one guard pointed at Amergin and his clanmates.

"Trouble," Niall murmured and nudged Kessan awake.

Amergin took a sip of his lukewarm broth to calm his mind and his stomach as the three picked their way over.

"You," one of them growled at Kessan. "Get up."

"He doesn't speak Magyun," Amergin explained, starting to rise himself. "Allow me—"

The second warrior turned to him in an instant, simultaneously freeing his blade and jerking the druid fully to his feet by the front of his shirt. Amergin raised his hands to placate both the warrior and his clanmates.

"Who are you?" the man snarled in rough Magyun.

"I am Amergin."

The man examined him critically, as if he suspected a lie.

"You are Kith," he finally declared, eyeing the tense warriors seated behind the druid.

"No, we are not Kith, we are—"

The man shook him violently, then pointed at Kessan. To the ruddy blond hair he sported. "Kith."

"Velkcic," Amergin returned firmly, silently wondering what a Kith was. "All Velkcic," he continued, pointing to himself, Niall, and Kessan in turn.

The third warrior barked something in their native tongue, and the three of them launched into an argumentative discussion. Amergin dared a tiny glance at Niall, who had a killing look about him, and silently willed him to be still. At length the horselord let him go.

"Are there any Kith here?" he growled, no less menacing for having released the druid. "Dead? Alive?"

Warning flared suddenly in his mind. Had not Ambrus once said he was a Kith? Amergin shook his head slowly.

"I don't know the Kith," he answered slowly.

"They have light hair, like that one," the warrior explained, gesturing curtly at Kessan.

"Not always," grated the first horselord.

"Usually."

"My people lighten their hair with lime paste, but it grows out." He gestured to Niall, whose dark roots were clearly visible.

The horselord peered at Niall curiously but shook his head. "Not like that."

"I haven't seen anyone here with light hair," he offered carefully.

All three warriors were watching him suspiciously now. They exchanged a look.

"If you change your mind, maybe remember seeing someone, you tell the guard. That one," he paused, pointing out a horselord with a distinctive scar across his temple. "Yes? Maybe we grant you freedom in exchange."

Amergin nodded, his throat suddenly dry. They watched him for another long moment before moving off to search the rest of the room.

"What was that about?" Kessan asked tightly when the trio had moved off.

"They didn't like your hair," Amergin replied distractedly as he sank back down to the floor, his mind reeling.

Beside him, the soup had been kicked over.

"My hair?" Kessan asked, incredulous.

The kinder guard returned and refilled Amergin's bowl. He glanced to the trio completing their circuit of the room, then back to Amergin, as if searching his expression for something. Refocusing, Amergin met and held his gaze. The guard's lips compressed into a thin line, then raked over the three remaining Velkcic in turn, swift and efficient. With a grunt he pointed at Niall and motioned for him to stand.

"Now what," the warrior mumbled, draining his soup as he complied.

He was taller than the Drev'an, but otherwise they had a similar build. The guard set down the serving pot and produced a length of rope to tie around Niall's neck like a leash. The Velkcic bristled, and Amergin caught a dangerous glint in his eye.

"Go with him, Niall," the druid cautioned. "Watch for the others."

Niall stared at him for a long moment, his jaw set tightly. But he nodded once and grudgingly allowed the horselord to lead him away.

Chapter 36

Dagmer walked with her head down, distracted. Gansükh had brought the slave back after Briga had finished bathing and dressing, and chained him once again to the floor. The she-wolf was uninterested in the proceedings with the chained king in the courtyard, and instead took Gansükh and Bayanaa with her to go train. Dagmer had excused herself. She'd intended to find Jinghim and ask about the request she'd made of him, but had become distracted by her own thoughts, and paced the streets aimlessly.

She had been a Drev'an slave for far longer than she cared to admit and craved freedom every bit as much as Briga did. More, perhaps. She hadn't been mistreated, but that was small consolation. If Briga was dragged east to the Drev'an steppe, she would be as well, and that thought chilled her blood. In the entirety of her captivity, they had never moved her out of this general region. Sartaq was clearly focused on this area and slightly north, and having been so long a part of his camp, she had enjoyed staying in relatively familiar lands. If she were taken from the area, returning would be exponentially more difficult. But she wasn't foolish enough to attempt escape. Not without a solid plan, at least. She had no doubt the she-wolf was already scheming something and drew comfort from the idea, but she wasn't helpless, either.

So deep in her own mind was she, that at first Dagmer wasn't sure what had nipped at her attention. She paused, listening, and attempted to focus on her surroundings. She had wandered into a series of alleys well off the main street and somewhat near the city wall. The acrid smell of smoke still clung to the charred walls. There was a rustle of paper as something changed hands within a group around the next corner.

"Who found this?"

She recognized Sartaq's voice and carefully edged to the corner where she might be able to peek around.

"Arban," another voice answered quietly. "He has been scouting to the north. They shot a white eagle carrying this."

Holding her breath, Dagmer stepped deeper into shadow and carefully looked around the corner. The commander was holding a scrap of paper, flipping it over briefly to check the back side. She couldn't make out the two men he was standing with.

"Did you read it?"

The two others looked at each other uncomfortably. "I cannot read Kith writing, Commander. The scouts could not, either. They did not even know it was Kith."

Sartaq nodded, turning the scrap over in his hand again. "Find me someone who can. Someone we can trust...or who would not be missed."

He handed the scrap back to the other speaker. The man and his companion bowed respectfully and turned to walk off. Dagmer recognized him then, the one who had been speaking, as he stepped briefly into a shaft of light. Nergüi had been among the group that had originally taken her as a Drev'an slave. Unlike the others, he actually talked to her on occasion and had helped her learn their language. She wouldn't call him a friend by any means, but there was no hostility there, either. Noting what direction they went, she drifted deeper into shadow to avoid Sartaq spotting her. She wanted to know what was on that paper.

"Nergüi," the commander called as an afterthought.

Dagmer froze in place.

"Keep checking the prisoners and the dead. I want the Kith found. If he is alive, bring him to me and only me. Not my brother."

"I understand, Commander."

Kith? Dagmer wondered to herself. They weren't talking about her, if they even realized she was Kith. They'd said, "he." Were they talking about the new slave the she-wolf had taken? Dagmer strongly suspected he was Kith, but couldn't be certain. Having been attached originally to Sartaq's camp for almost a year before being traded to the khan's, she had noticed an odd sense of secrecy in certain aspects. Until now she'd never thought much about it beyond sibling rivalry, but now she wondered. What could Sartaq want with some Kith…and why hide it from the khan?

She'd been distracted by these thoughts as she walked and nearly crashed bodily into two Drev'an as they rounded a corner. Hands reached out and took her by the shoulders to prevent the collision.

"Nergüi!" she gasped, genuinely surprised to cross paths with him so soon.

The Drev'an peered at her a moment, suspicious, before recognition flickered through his gaze.

"You are that slave," he fumbled for her name for a moment. "Dagmer?"

She nodded and flashed her teeth at him in a smile. "Slave no longer."

His eyes fell to her throat, noting the absent collar.

"What are you doing here?"

"I serve the khan's shaman now."

She thought she detected a flicker of tension in them and wondered if she shouldn't have mentioned the khan.

"I know that," he responded quietly. "What are you doing *here*?"

Dagmer's smile took on a hint of flirtation. "Running an errand for my lady."

"An errand?"

Her look flattened as if to question whether he truly expected her to divulge the she-wolf's secrets. After a moment he relented and smiled.

"Your Drev'an is much improved."

"I had a good teacher." She winked.

"So," he cleared his throat awkwardly. "The foreign shaman? What is she like?"

"Frightening at times," Dagmer admitted, "but a capable warrior. I can arrange for you to meet her. Perhaps she can read a dream for you, or a prophecy."

She let the offer hang in the air, knowing it would be tempting for two such as they to meet the exotic pet of the khan.

"A-as a repayment for your past kindness," she added timidly, worried they might still be suspicious of her ties to the khan.

Nergüi was staring at her in a peculiar way. He glanced to his friend for a moment before seeming to make up his mind about something.

"Dagmer, who are your people?"

"The Drev'an now." She shrugged as if it no longer mattered, but inwardly she was wary.

He seemed as if he would say something more, but only nodded instead.

"Well," she smiled, willing herself to blush slightly, "it was nice seeing you again after all this time."

She rested one hand on his forearm hesitantly, trying but failing to meet his gaze.

"Come to us later today if you'd like an audience with my lady."

His other hand lifted her chin until she was looking at him. There was neither threat nor tenderness in the gesture. Instead, she felt as if she was being assessed. Examined. She blushed in earnest at the uncertainty.

"I think I would enjoy meeting this creature who has delivered us victory. Thank you."

Wordlessly she nodded and stepped back, her gaze dropping again as her chin left his grasp. Gathering her confidence again, she turned to go, only looking back at them once before she disappeared down the lane. Her heart was racing with what she'd just done. She had seen him stuff the note into his gauntlet after leaving Sartaq, and while she hadn't managed to steal it, her fingers had managed to reveal a single, tiny word. Winter. It was useless without the rest of the paper, but with luck she might have another chance later.

She took a circuitous route back to the palace, her quest to find Jinghim temporarily forgotten. She didn't find Briga or the kheshig en route, but she hadn't really expected to, either. Dagmer stood now in the small room Bayanaa had claimed for himself, staring at the white eagle he was rehabilitating. Bayanaa's favorite bird and the winter eagle rested on perches on opposite sides of the room. One of the white bird's black-edged wings was still wrapped tightly in a brace. It turned to look in her direction, despite being hooded, and ruffled its feathers into agitated spikes. She regarded it coolly, recalling what Bayanaa had told her about it. The weight of certainty settled in her, and she *knew* this was the same bird Nergüi had referenced. The message canister had been removed, but she knew. Her mind made up, she snatched a knife from the small table beside Bayanaa's bed and marched out of the room.

***

Ambrus sat with his back to the wall, mindlessly rubbing a chain link against the stones. He looked up as the door opened, and the dark-haired female guard entered. She closed the door calmly, but he could see hatred smoldering in her features. He frowned watching her, wondering what she would order him to do now. With increasing concern, he watched as she pulled a knife from her belt and stalked toward him. Subtly he shifted so he might have at least some ability to react. She drew closer, threatening him with the weapon's point, though not quite close enough he could knock it from her grasp.

"Who are you?" she growled quietly.

Ambrus simply starred at her in shock for a moment, the knife forgotten.

"Answer me," she demanded, jabbing now with the blade's tip.

He understood her. She was speaking in Kith. *Impossible.* Warning chimes sounded in the back of his mind. If the wrong Drev'an discovered him, he was done for.

"What?" he tried in Magyun, hoping to throw her off.

"I know you are Kith," she pressed, though he thought he saw a tiny glimmer of doubt mar her steady gaze for a brief instant.

He studied her, wary, but didn't respond. Instead he tried to adopt the appearance of incomprehension, raising his hands slowly in response to the knife. She seemed frustrated now and edged closer, crouching to press the knife's tip into the hollow if his throat.

"Don't play games with me. No one would bat an eye if they returned to find you dead. Now who are you?"

491

She growled the words quietly, and for half a heartbeat he wondered why. Her eyes darted to the door and back again. It was only the briefest of distractions, but it was all Ambrus needed. His hands shot up and forward, catching the knife blade on his chains and shoving it away from his neck. At the same time, he kicked at her hip, knocking her off balance and onto one side. She flung out a hand instinctively to catch her fall, then immediately brought both hands to the hilt of her knife to retain it as one of his hands closed painfully over her wrist. She rolled to her side, more concerned with keeping the knife than her balance, and he moved with her to keep her pinned with his weight. Strong fingers squeezed the bones of her wrist, crushing them together. They could both feel the bones grinding. She lashed out with her foot, suddenly realizing the full extent of the danger she was in.

Hearing the scuffle, one of the guards opened the door to check what was happening. Ambrus only needed one hand to control the knife and reached out with the other to grab the front of her robes, hauling her closer as insurance against the newcomer. The guard shouted something and surged forward, drawing his blade.

"Shh…" he cautioned in her ear, eyeing the quickly approaching guards.

She was strong, but he was far stronger and overpowered her easily.

***

Briga rubbed at the pleasant soreness in her arm and shoulder, earned in combat practice with her kheshig. It was the distraction she'd needed to help calm and focus her mind. Turning the corner in the hallway outside of her quarters, she was surprised to see the guards turn to regard her door quizzically. One opened the door and peeked in, then quickly drew his sword and entered fully.

"What?" she wondered aloud, but the kheshig were already moving, blades drawn in an instant.

Gansükh was the first through the door, shoving aside the second guard, who was even now trying to enter.

"Stop," he warned Briga as she entered behind him, attempting to block her with one arm.

"Stay back!" the slave shouted in Magyun.

It took Briga a moment to absorb the scene before her. Her slave had somehow managed to take Dagmer as a hostage and was pressing the edge of a knife to her throat. Bayanaa pushed past all of them, more enraged than she'd ever seen him. Her initial shock gave way to cold rationalization as she registered the tension in the room. The situation was far too volatile. Too dangerous. Cold composure settled on her as she stepped past Gansükh and gestured for all the guards to hold.

"What's happening here?" she asked in Drev'an.

"She was in here alone, mistress, only for a moment," the first guard explained, his tone half shocked and half enraged.

"Dagmer," she demanded, her demeanor cold and distant now.

"He's Kith," the former slave growled in return, switching to Velkcic.

For some reason the revelation sent a chill of premonition down her spine, but she gave no outward sign of her unease. The slave shook Dagmer once in warning, drawing the weight of Briga's cold gaze in full. Her gut warned discretion. Uncertain of why, she nonetheless heeded the warning and finally turned her back on the slave to address the two door guards.

"Return to your posts. I will deal with you later."

The two exchanged a glance, then looked to Gansükh for guidance.

493

"I gave you an order," she snapped, her ire stoked in earnest now.

Gansükh didn't countermand her. He didn't so much as nod to undermine her authority, though he did glance at her briefly with surprise and clear disapproval. Uncomfortable but duly chastened, the guards returned to their posts and closed the door behind them.

Briga took a calming breath, glanced to each of her kheshig in turn to assess their state, and finally returned her attention to the blond prisoner.

"What was your plan, slave? Do you think we'll release you to simply walk free? Or were you just going to kill her and hope for the best?"

He'd watched the two guards leave and now regarded her distrustfully. His eyes settled on hers as she spoke in Velkcic, arousing a familiar hatred in his bones as she all but smirked down at him. While his command of the Velkcic tongue wasn't as strong as his command of Magyun, he understood well enough.

"Or perhaps you have no plan?"

She was right, though he was loathe to admit it. He'd reacted too quickly without considering his next steps, trapping himself in a near impossible predicament. If he killed his hostage, they would almost certainly kill him. If he let her go, they might decide he was too much trouble and kill him anyway. He didn't know how far her promise to Amergin might extend, and was reluctant to discover its limits.

"Dagmer, I'm disappointed in you." She glared down at his hostage, still speaking Velkcic. "How did this happen?"

"I came to question him," the girl, Dagmer, answered through gritted teeth.

"Alone? Foolish."

Dagmer tried to shift her weight, but Ambrus tightened his grip in warning. Her eyes darted to the two remaining guards before answering.

"I heard something I wasn't supposed to hear earlier. I was trying to find out more before I told you."

The demoness narrowed her eyes, considering. Ambrus wondered if this was some kind of trick. Why continue to speak in Velkcic? As if in answer, Dagmer said something in Drev'an. Ambrus decided he didn't like being left out of the conversation and pressed the knife harder against her throat in warning. Whatever she'd said provoked a flicker of response in the demoness, who blinked in surprise before regaining her composure. She studied the two guards for a moment, then calmly stepped closer to the slave. The guards tensed visibly but held their positions. Almost as an afterthought, she said something to the younger guard, who was clearly resistant to obey. She fixed him with a fierce stare for several moments before he angrily relented and left the room.

"What did she say?" he demanded of Dagmer in Velkcic, sensing they'd chosen this language over Magyun for a reason.

"She ordered Bayanaa to find wine or ale for her headache."

"He's fetching reinforcements," he growled, pricking her neck slightly.

"If she wanted reinforcements, she'd have brought the two outside back in, idiot," she growled in return.

The she-demon merely watched their exchange, aloof.

"What is your name?" she finally asked, studying him.

"Ivar," he answered grudgingly, uncertain why he'd given his father's name.

Her eyes bored into him, and he had the peculiar idea that she could sense the lie. He resisted the urge to squirm.

495

"Why are the Drev'an looking for you, Ivar?" she asked in a cool, quiet tone.

It was Ambrus' turn to be surprised. "Me?"

Dozens of questions surged through his mind, robbing him of the ability to remain quite as calm as his captor. She tilted her head curiously as she watched him.

"Dagmer tells me the Drev'an are hunting Kith in the city."

He was too stunned to deny being a Kith. How could they possibly have known he was here? Briga didn't need him to speak. The response was clear on his face. She was unsure why this information was important, but tucked it away nonetheless. She allowed a curtain of steel to envelop her once more. When she spoke again, her voice was a dangerously soft growl.

"It is only for the promise I made to Amergin that I didn't have you killed the moment I stepped into this room. If you kill my advisor, I will reveal you and hand you over to them without another thought."

She paused, allowing her words to sink in before continuing in a less harsh tone, "If you release her, I'll keep your identity hidden."

He eyed her distrustfully, wary of the opportunity not only to survive, but remain relatively unscathed. It seemed too good to be true...which usually meant it was. There had to be a catch. Suddenly, a disturbing thought occurred to him.

"Your guards don't speak Velkcic, do they?"

If she was caught off guard by his observation, she gave no indication of it.

"No."

He realized there was something in this arrangement for her as well, and suspected it was more than just her promise to his druid friend. He could retain a bit of leverage with that knowledge. Mindful of the enormous risk he was taking, he finally nodded and released his hold on Dagmer. The girl scrambled away, and the remaining guard relaxed slightly.

"Hand over the knife," the guard commanded in Magyun.

Grudgingly Ambrus tossed the knife aside, out of his reach. The guard moved forward to pick it up, following swiftly with a strong, lunging fist across the slave's jaw. Briga shot the guard a disapproving look but said nothing. Her mind was reeling, wondering exactly what Dagmer had overheard, and from who. She was clearly hesitant to provide details where the kheshig could overhear her. Was there some unknown feud between the Drev'an and these Kith she'd now been dragged into?

She watched as Gansükh sheathed the knife in his own belt and eyed Dagmer appraisingly before finally turning his attention to her.

"What happened?" he demanded in Drev'an.

Aware that Ivar was watching and able to interpret body language, even if he couldn't understand Drev'an, she stiffened her spine and fixed Gansükh with a mildly predatory gaze.

"When's the last time you fed him?"

"This morning."

"Was there meat?"

"No."

"He should be fed regularly. And well. Once I've decided what to do with him, he may need strength."

"I do not like—"

"I will not be questioned in this!" she snapped.

Gansükh flinched. She'd never spoken to him in true anger before. The door opened at that moment, giving them both an excuse to back down as Bayanaa entered carrying a wine skin.

His eyes went immediately to the slave, then to Dagmer when he saw she was no longer a hostage, then to Gansükh, seeking answers. But Gansükh was still watching the she-wolf. Subdued, Dagmer stepped forward to take the skin from Bayanaa and bring it to her lady. She knew Briga's indifferent treatment toward her earlier had been part of the net for Ivar's benefit, but she could sense the undercurrent of true disappointment for getting herself into that situation.

"We can expect company later," she informed Briga quietly as she handed over the skin, not meeting her eyes.

Briga, still quelling her anger, unstoppered the skin and took a healthy dose of its contents. She then tossed the skin to the slave.

"Gansükh. Take Bayanaa and discipline those two outside for allowing Dagmer to be overpowered by the prisoner."

"Leave you here alone?" he asked skeptically, tossing a threatening look in the slave's direction.

"I have nothing to fear from him."

"He tried to kill Dagmer. He has tried to kill *you*," he reminded her. "Several times."

"He's chained. I need a moment alone with Dagmer," she returned pointedly, fighting to control her irritation.

There was an obstinate set to his jaw, and for a moment she was afraid he would disobey. He'd sworn her an oath of loyalty, but she was afraid to test the limits and sincerity of that bond. After a moment he relented and took Bayanaa with him out into the hall. The moment the door was shut, Briga collapsed to sit on the edge of her bed.

Ambrus looked on curiously, uncertain what to make of her abrupt change in demeanor. He wasn't certain why she had offered him a level of protection, but he had no doubt it served her own interests. If he was careful, perhaps he could discern her intent and turn it to his own advantage.

"Tell me what happened," Briga began quietly to Dagmer in Drev'an.

Dagmer eyed their captive once before taking a seat beside Briga.

"I saw Sartaq talking to one of his captains. In secret."

Briga looked up in mild surprise. "What makes you think it was in secret?"

"He sent his men in search of our Kith friend here and told them to report directly to him. Not to the khan."

Briga turned to look at her slave, assessing. "What does Sartaq want with *him*?"

"I don't know. But they had a note taken from a messenger bird. It's written in Kith. Sartaq is trying to find someone who can read it for him."

Briga sat back, absorbing this information. All she knew for certain was that Sartaq was up to something he wanted to keep out of his brother's attention. Was he plotting something? Did he suspect his brother of some kind of treason? Or was there perhaps something else going on here? The possibilities flooded her mind.

"Did they see you?"

"No. Well, not exactly."

Briga looked at her sharply.

"I recognized one of them and found a reason to cross paths with him." She paused, not wanting to explain this piece of her history for the moment. "He was impressed that I serve you. I offered for him to come and meet you later. To have a prophecy read, perhaps. I think he'll do it."

"Why?"

"He has the paper. There are very few Drev'an who can read Kith. I'm gambling that he won't let the note out of his possession until he finds someone who can translate for the commander."

"You can't possibly expect me to allow Ivar to read it."

"No!" Dagmer replied in disgust. "Of course not. But *I* can read Kith."

Chapter 37

Rorik was furious He hadn't wanted to go when the guards came for him, but fighting only made things worse, and he and Connor were dragged off regardless. They had worked through the night hauling bodies to various collection points. The two Velkcic were both bigger than their Drev'an guards, which meant they were more closely watched than the other prisoners. However it also meant they were given wide berth. Rorik adjusted the strip of fabric he'd tied over his mouth and nose to help mask the smell and exchanged a look with Connor.

His hands and arms ached from the labor. Some of their group had been taken away just after dawn, presumably to exchange for a fresh batch, but the two Velkcic and several of the other, larger specimens were expected to keep working.

They had been instructed to lay the bodies out in neat rows. All the Drev'an dead went to one area, while the rest seemed to be grouped into Magyun or Other. Rorik wasn't always certain what distinguished a Magyun from something else. Sometimes age, hair color, or gender seemed to be the deciding factor. Other times, it seemed to depend on whether or not the man had a warrior's build.

It was Connor who'd found Oisean. The lad had been among a mass of bodies near the well. Rorik had come over to help carry their comrade. He noted with grim satisfaction that Oisean had died with a sword in his hand. They'd taken a few minutes to grieve for their brother, and to the horselords' credit, no one interrupted them. Rorik himself had closed the lad's eyes. He had then closed Oisean's hands around the sword's hilt and left it there atop his body, marking him as a warrior. Frowning, one of the horselords had stepped forward to strip away the

501

weapon, but both Velkcic fixed him with silent, murderous glares. An older Drev'an stopped his comrade with a strong grip on his arm and a shake of the head. Rorik nodded once, one fighter to another, then he and Connor moved off to return to their duties. Now they had finally been given food and a break.

"We should have heeded Cathbad," Connor voiced bitterly, thinking back to a time before they'd ever left for Rowanar.

Rorik flashed a grim smile but shook his head. "It was fate."

"I will not die here as a slave," he growled.

"Calm yourself. If we have any chance to escape and save the others, we'll take it, but acting rashly will do no good at all."

Connor lapsed into wrathful silence, chewing the tough but tasty horseflesh they'd been given.

"That woman," he said at length, calmer now. "Was it really Briga?"

"Looked like her," Rorik agreed.

"She seemed...something. Different."

"I can't begin to imagine what she's been through."

Rorik had the peculiar sense there was more to their collective situation than he could perceive, and the thought preoccupied him.

"The last time I saw her," Connor commented, "she was in the thick of battle. I saw her close with that horselord. The one under the banner, remember?"

Rorik did remember. He too had seen her charge and marveled at the bravery and stupidity of it. She was no trained warrior, what had she been thinking?

"It's a small miracle she survived that blow."

The red-haired warrior watched again in his mind's eye as the horselord grinned, fending off her attacks until he finally slammed the hilt of his blade into her temple. Rorik had seen blood as she crumpled. The fighter had grabbed the front of her tunic, hauling her across his own horse's withers and striking her again on the back of the head to still her token remaining struggle. Rorik had tried to rush forward to help, but Eamon had been dragged from his horse at the same instant, and his duties were to the chieftain. The big man shook himself to rid his mind of the memories.

"Is that Niall?" he asked suddenly, spotting a roped figure in the distance.

Connor squinted. "How do you see better with only one eye than I do with two?" he asked in wonder.

Rorik didn't bother to answer, just marked their sword-brother's progress. He would try to maneuver their work in the same direction if he could.

***

Gansükh watched the she-wolf as she crossed the courtyard with measured, regal steps. Dagmer was at her side, he and Bayanaa trailing a pace behind. The khan had summoned her, likely to make some spectacle of the chained king. Sartaq hadn't yet arrived, and several of the generals were only now beginning to filter in. Despite this, Gansükh watched the she-wolf. He was suspicious. She was plotting something, he was certain of it, but thus far she had excluded her kheshig from the plans. He would have to ask Dagmer what she knew of it.

Her exchange with the dangerous blond slave was the most puzzling piece of it. Many of her foreign ways still confused him, but he'd seen her cruel streak and wondered why she hadn't killed him immediately. Gansükh couldn't speak Velkcic, but he'd heard her do so often enough to recognize the language, and wondered why she spoke with this Magyun dog in that tongue. He could think of only two reasons. Either the man wasn't Magyun, and the she-wolf did not want to use a translator, or she didn't want anyone else to understand what was said.

The implications troubled him.

He threw out an arm reflexively as she faltered mid-step and nearly stumbled. Her face was pale, and she darted a wide-eyed gaze across the courtyard. It only lasted the span of a heartbeat before she regained control and composure

"Are you all right?"

"Fine," she answered distractedly, a clear sign one of the gods had reached out and touched her.

The knowledge prickled the hairs along the back of his neck. She touched his shoulder absently and he had the disturbing thought she might be reassuring herself of being in the mortal world. The idea was absurd, but he'd seen may inexplicable things these months spent at her side.

Sartaq arrived a few moments later, flanked by two of his generals. Briga tossed him a look by reflex, though she was still focused on something else. She was unimpressed with the spectacle surrounding King Bela and was tired of being summoned to Batu's side for the sake of ceremony. She wanted to investigate whatever kept beckoning to her from across the courtyard. She wanted to return and question Ivar more. But most of all, she wanted to engineer her escape. She counseled herself sternly. If she became rushed and desperate, she was likely to make a critical mistake. It had been months already, she could last a few more weeks. Pasting a smile on her features, she took her place beside the khan to observe his pageantry.

"How long do you plan to toy with him?" she asked quietly.

"There is no purpose in keeping him alive any longer. It ends today."

Movement near them caught her eye, and she glanced to her right. General Khuyag was escorting the sole surviving Magyun lord toward them. She watched him mildly, wondering if Batu truly intended to honor his brother's offer of power.

"Lord Janus," he offered evenly by way of greeting.

The Magyun was pale and looked as if he hadn't slept, but to his credit, he maintained a stoic and somewhat distant demeanor. He was wearing a heavy gold chain draped around his neck, likely some gaudy symbol of his new station. *How appropriate*, Briga thought to herself. He wore a fresh velvet cape as well. Briga noted the way he stared disdainfully when his gaze fell on Bela.

The naked, fallen king rested on his knees again. He was pale from the cold, but his eyes burned with defiant fury despite his humiliation. Briga noted the group of mounted and fully armored warriors on the far end of the courtyard, noted the open ground around them, and frowned slightly. But she noticed something else across the open space as well. Jinghim was there, leading a roped prisoner casually along the street. With a start she recognized Niall and had to concentrate on her breathing to avoid reacting. Niall looked angry but unhurt and carried a pail of some kind. He looked toward her, perhaps sensing her attention. Briga forced her gaze to continue drifting over the crowd. Inwardly she felt the grim satisfaction that at least one of them was safe. For the moment, anyway. She would have to try and get a message to them. When she looked again, they were gone, vanished into the crowd.

With the generals assembled, Batu strode forward. A hush descended on the crowd by unspoken command. The khan stalked forward until he stood directly before Bela, looking down on the chained king coldly. He didn't waste a single word on the defeated foe, merely turned to face his army and the pockets of Magyun survivors who'd been allowed to congregate. He raised his arms in silent acknowledgement of their total victory, and the Drev'an erupted into cheers. Bela flinched only slightly at the sudden, unbidden noise, then spat at the khan's feet when Batu half turned to give him a last, derisive sneer. Batu didn't respond to the insult. What meaning did an insult from a dead man hold? Instead he simply turned and walked back to the line of generals, denying Bela any reaction.

Unbidden, Sartaq's shaman stepped forward, clearly preparing to make a ritual and offering out of their enemy's death. Briga noted a flicker of surprise in Batu's expression and stepped forward as well. If Sartaq was trying to undermine his brother, she would do well to protect the khan's image. The shaman didn't seem offended and offered a curt nod that they should begin.

Though Briga was unfamiliar with the Drev'an rituals, she fell into rhythm with the shaman's drum and chanting, modifying her movements into a dance of sorts as she offered sacrifice and blood to whatever gods might be present to accept. Briga avoided looking at the king. She was never comfortable with this sort of sacrifice and didn't want to meet the wrath and judgement she knew would be in his eyes. When the invocations were complete, the two shaman walked together, stride for eerie stride, back to the khan and his commander. Batu flashed her an approving glance as she returned to her place beside him, still silently beseeching her own gods and the red god to aid her, to create an opportunity to craft her escape.

At a nod from the khan, the horsemen moved en masse, kicking their mounts into a gallop and sprinting toward the king.

"You have guaranteed your own death, Batu!" the king screamed in rage as the horses bore down on him.

For a man who lacked courage in war, it was a commendable final act. The riders trampled him with their first pass, then rode a wide arc around the courtyard for two more passes.

Briga did not look at what was left of the king's body. There was no reason to. Instead, in the shadows beside the palace doors, she spotted a familiar woman's face staring back at her. Her senses prickled as the two of them held gazes for a moment, but Briga wasn't certain how to interpret the sensation. She sensed Batu shifting at her side, following her gaze. The woman nodded respectfully, then shifted her attention to someone else.

"One of my spies," Batu offered quietly from beside her. "The one who opened that hole in the wall, actually."

"Her?" Briga blurted without thinking.

There were so few women in the camp, she'd assumed the Drev'an had no use for them outside of domestic capacities, excluding the shaman and herself. Batu merely nodded once, then surveyed his warriors.

Sartaq clapped his brother on the shoulder, exchanging a satisfied look with Batu before drifting off in the spy's general direction. Briga watched after him with narrowed eyes.

"What is it?" Batu asked, noting her attention again.

For one breathless moment, she thought she could feel the red god's lashed tails curling around her leg. She dared not look down.

"He's up to something."

The khan's grim expression didn't change, but he watched after his brother. "He thinks he can win her for himself."

Perhaps. Had she been the "sweet thing" Sartaq was talking about during the feast?

"They are discreet, but little happens in my war band that is beneath my notice."

She glanced at him sidelong, wondering by the tone if he was warning her, or simply boasting.

"What about in your brother's camp?"

He rounded on her suddenly, and she sensed a flare of restrained violence. Unfazed, she met his gaze directly.

507

"What are you implying?" he growled quietly, suddenly aware he might be drawing attention.

"He's up to something. I can feel it."

She was only half lying, but she kept her expression steady. Batu's expression changed suddenly. She only caught a brief flicker of it, but he regarded her with a curious, guarded air before glancing in the direction his brother had gone.

"We will speak more of this later."

Perhaps Batu hadn't been boasting earlier. She seemed to have correctly guessed at some subtle subterfuge between the brothers. One that neither wanted to address publicly. She filed away the knowledge for future use and nodded her understanding.

"You did well," he offered, changing the subject, "accompanying the other shaman."

Both of them would have been undermined in allowing Sartaq's shaman the sole honor. Before the khan had acquired his she-wolf, it was necessary to use his brother's shaman in formal ceremonies, but that was no longer the case. She'd suspected a subtle power struggle between the brothers, and had acted to protect her own position, as well as support the khan, and further garner his trust. She needed him to believe her to be fully loyal to him if her fledgling plan had any hope of succeeding.

But she only nodded demurely in response, both of them aware of what her actions signified. He lingered a moment, awkwardly and Briga offered a small smile.

"See to your men. I'll be all right."

Batu nodded slightly and eyed her a moment longer before turning his attention to Khuyag and Lord Janus, who both waited at a respectful distance. Briga eyed the Magyun curiously, wondering how long he would survive as the khan's puppet ruler, now that she understood how deep the current of brotherly distrust might flow.

She didn't care to stay and listen to their conversation. Instead she turned in a slow circle, inspecting the courtyard and their surroundings. The crowd had thinned slightly, but mostly it had congealed into groups. Groups of warriors stood talking, some still looking or gesturing in the direction of the mess that had once been a king, others inwardly focused. A small group of Magyuns stood huddled together, the women consoling one another. She could see the occasional slave or prisoner, but none of them were Niall, or any of the other Velkcic. Sartaq was gone, vanished into the throng with that woman. His shaman stood near the king's remains, seemingly in a trance. No one was paying any special attention to Briga now, except for Dagmer and her kheshig. Satisfied, she turned slowly and sauntered through the crowd, making her way in the general direction of the periodic draw on her druid's senses.

Gansükh glanced to Dagmer as they followed behind the she-wolf at a suspiciously casual pace. She answered the silent question with a shrug, not knowing if this was some plan or merely boredom.

"My lady?" the former slave questioned timidly.

"Everything's fine," Briga assured her with a thin smile. "Just…stretching my legs."

They slowly crossed the open space to a row of scorched stone buildings flanking one end of the courtyard. Briga admired them curiously. She'd never seen such a place as this, with entire buildings made of stone. Fences and walls were occasional sights in the areas surrounding Eamon's lands, and in Rowanar, but entire buildings? And so many of them.

"It's marvelous, isn't it?" she asked Dagmer, reaching out gingerly to touch the wall in front of her.

Dagmer watched with concern as Briga drew her hand back abruptly, as if stung. Her eyes sharpened with sudden focus, and

509

she studied the wall in front of her with less wonder and more purpose.

"What is this building?" she asked Dagmer finally.

Dagmer didn't have time to answer before Briga moved down the wall, seemingly searching for something. An entrance of sorts was nearby, but the opening was choked with charred debris. Behind that was an iron gate. Briga frowned, visually inspecting it. There was a locking mechanism that seemed to have melted forever into place. For a moment she almost seemed to be listening to something. Then just as abruptly as it had started, her features softened, and she resumed her casual, wandering pace.

"We need to get in there," she told Dagmer quietly, switching to Velkcic.

"Horses can pull open that gate."

"No. Something discreet. Our new *friend* was somewhat highly ranked, I believe. I'd wager he knows another way in."

"What's in there?" Dagmer asked curiously, turning to admire the stone edifice briefly.

"Not what. Who. There's someone there, I can feel it. Someone best kept hidden for now."

***

Amergin had been dozing again, the consequence of failed attempts to meditate. Like Cathbad, he found he sometimes required the aid of special herbs thrown on the fire to help him seek out answers in the Pattern, particularly when there were distractions. And he could think of few settings more distracting than his imprisonment in the barn. With a sigh, he finally abandoned the effort and blinked to clear his mental haze.

By the light he guessed it was sometime in the afternoon. Glancing around, he noted that while some of the prisoners had returned, none of his Velkcic brothers were among them. It was still only himself and Kessan. The warrior was doing his best to exercise without drawing too much attention to himself, but the broken arm limited him somewhat.

Idly, Amergin looked up as the door creaked open. His blood froze for a moment, then surged as he recognized the figure who entered and lowered the hood of her cloak.

"Dianna," he breathed, unbelieving.

"Eh?" Kessan looked up, oblivious to the druid's utter shock.

She saw him through the gloom, freezing in place for a moment as well before taking up a water pail and nearly rushing across the space to him, heedless of the prisoners around her reaching out for a drink. When she reached him, she abandoned all propriety, setting the pail down carelessly and throwing her arms around his neck.

"You are alive," she breathed into his shoulder.

The druid's hands came up awkwardly to fold around her as well, still not quite believing this was real and not some trance. Her breath hitched, and she finally pulled back to look at him. Tears glistened in the corners of her eyes.

"I thought you were dead!"

She touched his face, and he took her hand in his, moving it away, but not unkindly. He was chief druid now, despite his wants.

"Where are the others?" she asked suddenly, glancing around. "Eamon?"

"Dead," he offered quietly.

"What?"

"Eamon is dead," he amended, "and Cathbad. The others are prisoners."

"Oh, I am so sorry, Amergin."

She squeezed his hands comfortingly, and he allowed his thumbs to play over her knuckles.

"Are you all right?"

He nodded, then looked at her sharply. "Are *you* all right?"

"Fine," she confirmed, though he noted she'd averted her eyes.

"Did anyone...hurt you? I have medicine—"

"No, no, none of them have touched me."

He felt a surge of anger he hadn't been aware of holding subside. Near the door, one of the guards looked over in irritation at Dianna's lack of progress watering the other prisoners.

"Any news of Ambrus?" she asked, noting the guard's look.

"He's alive."

A peculiar sense of unease lanced through him at the question.

"I think. I haven't seen him since the night of the battle, however," he amended.

"I hope he is all right."

"Me too," Amergin agreed, still puzzling at the source of his discomfort.

Jealousy perhaps? He pushed the feeling aside to study later.

She watched him quietly for a moment. "I am on water duty. I will try to come back to you soon."

"Watch for him," he suggested. "We'll do the same."

"I will," she promised, then impulsively she leaned forward and kissed him on the cheek, standing quickly with her pail as two guards began yelling.

"So your woman is alive, eh, druid?" Kessan asked after they both watched her continue her rounds.

"She's not my woman," the druid snapped, though his eyes still tracked her progress.

"I'm surprised to see her alive."

"As am I."

"Did she have any news?"

Amergin paused. He hadn't thought to ask her for news, and now he cursed himself for a missed opportunity.

"No," he answered finally. "Maybe next time."

He would have to keep his mind clear, or try. She had a singular way of distracting him. Not for the first time, he wondered how things would be were he not a druid. By the look on Kessan's face, he knew the other man could read his thoughts as clearly as if they were his own.

***

Briga had lingered in the courtyard long enough to convince anyone watching that she had no special interest in any of the buildings. Gansükh had watched her careful progression with his usual stoic expression, but inwardly his frustration was mounting. When she was satisfied she'd remained long enough, she turned to make her way back to their new quarters. Discreetly, Gansükh pulled the other kheshig aside.

"Bayanaa, go find something to eat. For the prisoner as well. Take Dagmer with you; I will stay with the she-wolf."

Bayanaa read the additional, unspoken order in Gansükh's gaze and nodded in acknowledgement. The older kheshig watched him go. Bayanaa was also aware that the she-wolf was keeping something from them and would try to pry the information from Dagmer. His primary concern was keeping them and the khan safe from whatever her scheming involved. He suspected Dagmer had only risked being alone with the prisoner thanks to whatever the lady had charged her with. He felt protective over Dagmer, but her connection to Bayanaa was different. He'd been aware that there was some kind of bond between Dagmer and Bayanaa for some time, but had never suspected how strong it might have been until he'd seen the younger kheshig react to her capture earlier. He would grant them time to themselves as they hadn't had a moment alone since the incident, but later he needed to talk to Bayanaa about it. He couldn't allow anyone to cloud his judgement.

Alone, he trailed the she-wolf back into the palace.

"We need to talk," he bit out after glancing around to ensure no one was within earshot.

Briga paused and looked back over her shoulder at him.

"I know you are planning something."

She scoffed and continued walking.

"If your plans will harm the khan—" he began in a warning tone before she wheeled around and cut him off in a harsh whisper.

"I'm trying to protect the khan."

"Then tell me your plans. I can help you."

She held his gaze a moment, eyes fierce, before shaking her head and turning to walk away again. A surge of anger flared through him, and for once he didn't try to hold it back. He grabbed her by the upper arm and dragged her into the corridor beside them, shoving her back against the wall and stepping close to keep their voices down, and keep her there.

"I saved your life. If you do not trust me, you should find another kheshig," he growled in quiet rage.

Hurt flashed in her eyes, quickly replaced by a cold anger he was beginning to recognize all too well.

"Let go of me," she growled back.

He did, but he didn't step away. His gaze drifted down to her mouth. She was breathing faster, some part of his brain registered in startled surprise. So was he. Her expression softened a shade, making him uncomfortably aware of how close he was standing. He had a sudden, incongruous memory of holding her half-frozen body against himself and felt suddenly off-balance.

"I trust you..."

He took a step back, hoping to mask his self-consciousness behind his usual stoic mien.

"...but we can't talk about this here."

He nodded to himself, taking another half step back, and broke her gaze to glance sideways into the hall. Still empty. As he watched, he could see her come to some decision, donning her composure like a cloak and stepping away from him, out into the hall. Gansükh followed. He looked again in both directions, satisfied that no one had seen him accost a royal wife. That was dangerous. He needed to control his emotions better. He needed to stop allowing this...*she-wolf* to get under his skin.

Though she wouldn't admit it, Briga was shaken. Whether by Gansükh himself or the implications of him knowing she was scheming, she could not say. She wasn't sure if she *could* trust him, certainly not with the full extent of her plan. Her heart was still hammering in her chest as she led the way back to her quarters, trying to put the encounter out of her mind.

The sight of Ivar crouched placidly in the corner when she entered her room was enough to spike her blood with the familiar animosity she felt toward him, lending her focus.

"Bayanaa is fetching your food," Gansükh told him curtly before taking up a distinctly expectant and predatory stance near Briga.

She was staring out the window, her focus landing on the stain that had once been Bela, and the men bathing their horses beyond. Her gaze flickered once to the gated building.

"Well?" Gansükh asked impatiently.

She narrowed her eyes, disliking his demanding approach. Turning, she eyed him closely, debating what and how much to tell him. Her eyes flickered to the door, ensuring it was shut. With a sigh, she finally relented.

"What do you know of this tension between Batu and his brother?"

Her voice was quiet, not daring to be overheard by the guards in the hall. Gansükh's only reaction was a hardening of his features.

"Tension?"

She narrowed her eyes again. "I'm not blind. I can see their rivalry plain enough."

Gansükh shrugged. "Sartaq is the elder brother, but Batu was chosen as Khan."

"There's something more than just jealousy."

"Why are you asking this?"

"Sartaq is plotting something."

"That is between the brothers."

"No," she corrected sharply. "If there is a power struggle between them, it affects all of the Drev'an."

He merely watched her, unwilling or unable to concede the point.

"And it affects me," she continued, hoping the dread she felt didn't sound in her words.

"You?"

She fixed him with a dubious glare. "I'm a khan's wife, am I not?"

There it was. The horrible truth she had suspected for so long but had refused to give voice. Gansükh blinked in shock. They had all been so careful to shield her from this knowledge.

"You are more than simply a war-bride," he offered, softening.

"Yes, yes, I'm a shaman as well," she snapped, holding back a growing sense of fury at this confirmation.

She felt half sick but refused to give in to it.

"Any threat to the khan's position is also a threat to mine."

And to my life, she added silently. She had no doubt Sartaq would have her killed, or at the least sold as a very dangerous and exotic slave, if he managed to usurp his brother.

"Confronting Sartaq is dangerous. Very dangerous."

"I have no intent of confronting him, only ferreting out his scheme and presenting it to the khan."

His expression shifted to one of suspicion. "By yourself."

"No," she answered, meeting his gaze directly.

She shifted her attention to Ivar abruptly, who sat there watching their exchange closely. No doubt trying to glean what

517

he could from tone and posture, as she herself had done in the early days of her own captivity.

"Our friend here is part of it."

"Him?" he asked skeptically, shifting his own gaze to the prisoner with a frown. "Why him?"

"*That* is exactly the question."

Chapter 38

"Ivar," she said, switching to Velkcic, not so much to mask the conversation from Gansükh, as to reinforce trust between them, or at least what would pass as trust for now. "Will you tell me now why the Drev'an are looking for you?"

"I have no idea."

"Some feud perhaps between your people and theirs?"

Ambrus suppressed the lance of shock that went through him and laughed dismissively. "Feud? We are people of the sea. They rule the grasslands, how could we possibly feud?"

He shook his head. This woman was too clever by half.

Briga regarded him flatly, assessing. "Nevertheless, they are searching for Kith. Or perhaps they're only searching for you?"

"There are no other Kith here," he insisted, "apart from your advisor."

"Then they must be hunting you."

Ambrus couldn't argue with her conclusion, but it made no sense. True, he'd been hunting Drev'an himself, but he had never even met one before they attacked this city. There was no way his task was worth so much notice.

"How did you come to be here" she asked, changing tactics.

Inwardly he cringed. Half-truths. He would feed her only enough to satisfy the questions.

"I left my crew and needed work. So I came inland where the Kith...ah, reputation might not be an issue."

"Alone?"

"No."

Anger darkened his features at the memory, more so when he realized he'd trapped himself into answering. "A man and his son came with me."

"I thought you were the only Kith here?"

"I am now."

"Where are the other two?"

"Dead. You killed the boy," he growled, venom lacing his words as he recalled his reason for hating her.

She blinked in surprise. "I did?"

"Caleb. On the bridge."

She squinted into the distance, trying to call up the memory. Her recollections of the battle were hazy at best, and she'd been focused on trying to kill *him*. His anger simmered when he realized she had no memory of the action. It hadn't been worthy of notice. Finally she shrugged.

"He shouldn't have been there if he was not yet ready for battle."

Rage flared white-hot for a moment before he forced it back under control. "Amergin tried to save him, but he died without a sword in his hand."

She merely watched him, refusing to be baited.

"What's that building over there?" She pointed out the window to the gated stone building, abruptly changing topics once more.

Grudgingly he sat up to look. She thought she detected a faint reaction but couldn't be certain, given his agitated state.

"The gate is melted shut," she continued. "I wonder if you might know another way in. Something…discreet."

"Why should I help you, murderess?"

"Because if you do not, I'll hand you over to Batu Khan."

Ambrus paused for a moment, trying to assign meaning to the name. Wasn't khan their term for leader?

"Batu Khan," he sneered, calling her bluff. "Just hand me right over."

She regarded him curiously for a moment, dark amusement flickering in her gaze.

"Who do you think was sharing my bed?"

He couldn't help but laugh at the absurdity of it. Her gamble deserved appreciation for its audacity, but it was ultimately ridiculous. She was searching for leverage, attempting to take advantage of his lack of knowledge or acquaintance with the Drev'an leadership. The guard was glowering at him now, which sobered him, until he remembered the man couldn't speak Velkcic.

"Why do you want to go into a fire-ruined Magyun building?" he scoffed, though a measure of his curiosity was genuine.

Briga paused before answering, her gaze taking on a peculiar, distant look, as if she might have been somewhere else.

"There's something in there," she finally responded, her voice mirroring that strange, far-away sense.

Something in her tone caused gooseflesh to ripple on his arms.

"Something important."

All trace of humor left him then. How could she possibly know? It had to be a well-aimed guess. She lingered in that distant place for a few eerie moments, then slid her gaze to him without moving her head. He found the gesture very serpent-like, and unsettling.

"It will only be a matter of days before the Drev'an pry it open for themselves, looking for stockpiles of food or weapons. Treasure of another sort, perhaps."

One hand rubbed her arm as if she'd suddenly become chilled, and she turned away.

"I suppose I'll have to be patient."

She sighed and drew the wolfskin cloak tighter around her shoulders. Turning, she fixed Gansükh with a subtly frustrated look.

"Let's give him time to consider," she commented in Drev'an, absently rubbing the space between her eyes to ward off a headache.

Ambrus was careful to maintain an outward mask of studied neutrality, but his mind was reeling. She had to be guessing about Sitric. It was impossible that she somehow knew of him; she'd have just said so if that were the case. What if Sitric was alive down there? How much longer before he died of thirst or starvation…and did he have enough time to wait? No, that was an ignoble death for a warrior, even someone like Siggi. Worse, what if the Drev'an discovered him still alive? Would they kill him outright? Or would it put his objective in danger, maybe even his own life? He may have shed blood with Siggi, but given the man's past, he didn't trust him. Not fully. Not even by half, perhaps.

Frowning, he tried to determine what benefits there might be in allowing the she-devil to get to him first. What should he tell her to maintain control of the situation…and what might make things worse? If Siggi was dead, he could explain things away. But if he was in fact alive? Ambrus struggled through the options and various outcomes for each course of action.

The only thing he could be certain of was that she wasn't bluffing about the timeline. Undoubtedly the Drev'an would tear apart what remained of the city to find every last usable scrap.

"Why do you speak to him in that language?" Gansükh asked quietly, his tone controlled.

She eyed the kheshig for a moment as if debating what to say. "He's not Magyun."

"He was in their army."

"I know."

"Why is he here?"

She turned her gaze on the slave once more, but he was clearly lost in his own thoughts.

"I don't know. Not the truth of it anyway. But I will."

***

Davaa blinked as she stepped out into the afternoon light. She paused to set down the empty water pail and once again raise the hood of her cloak, then waited a few moments longer to organize her thoughts. She took a breath, then set off at a casual pace, wending her way through the streets, making her indirect path toward the south gate. Sartaq would be in there somewhere, waiting for her. She glanced around by habit, checking her surroundings before entering the structure. The Drev'an warriors eyed her dubiously, but with the khan's sigil prominently displayed at her throat, none dared question her.

She found Sartaq in a room near the top of one tower. The room had a large window that looked out over the wide field beyond the city. The commander was watching as Drev'an and slaves carried the dead out, placing them well beyond the walls. Drev'an custom was to leave their dead for the predators and scavengers to consume, if they were worthy, but so many dead would draw sickness. These would have to be burned, therefore they were being moved far enough away that drifting smoke wouldn't be a problem. They were kept far enough from the river to prevent contamination, as well.

"Well?"

He did not turn to look at her. She didn't answer right away, merely lingered in the doorway a moment. His head turned slightly in her direction, and she stepped forward to join him at the window. Ash or snowflakes swirled lightly on the breeze; she wasn't certain she knew which. She wasn't certain she wanted to know.

"He knows more than he is saying."

Sartaq clenched his jaw thoughtfully and watched her from the corner of his eye.

"He said he might be dead, but I do not think he believes that."

"We have not found any Kith among the dead," he responded in low tones.

She studied him for a moment. The scowl, the tense set to his shoulders.

"I can serve you better if I understand your goals."

She risked laying her fingers lightly on his arm. Rather than flinch away, he shook his head and looked out at the field of bodies again.

"Are there any others?"

"None that I saw or knew of, but then my tasking was not about finding Kith."

Sartaq nodded once in acknowledgement. It was a reminder that she worked for the khan and was here as his spy. The commander hadn't tasked her with anything specific. In fact, Kith had been the farthest thing from his mind until she mentioned it idly that time outside the walls. Davaa watched him a moment longer, then stepped closer to lean her body lightly against his arm and her cheek against his shoulder.

"Who is that woman?" she asked at length in carefully neutral tones.

"Hmm?"

"With the khan."

"Ah. His new pet."

"Pet?"

He shifted finally, draping an arm around her shoulders. "Be careful of that one. She is a shaman."

"A foreigner…?"

"She has Tengri's attention."

Davaa frowned, puzzled. "Strange."

"Do not," he warned, sensing her thoughts. "She is dangerous, and I have other tasks for you."

Barely moving, she slipped her dagger from its hidden sheath and pressed the tip into his side. "So am I."

He laughed despite himself, though it was a dark sound, and grabbed her wrist to push the blade away. Smiling darkly herself, she slipped the knife back into its sheath. The memory of Heinrich's blood flowing over her hands hit her suddenly, and she felt herself pale. She blinked to clear her mind. If Sartaq noticed, he didn't say anything.

"Where would he go?" Sartaq asked. "The Kith?"

"If he is alive and somehow avoided capture, I imagine he would have fled the city. Or attempt to flee. But I did not know him well."

Sartaq nodded, accepting this. "Then I suppose we shall keep searching."

***

Braxus gasped awake at the searing pain in his side. He struggled to breathe around what must be broken ribs, then became slowly aware of a crushing weight on his legs and torso. The air was cold and tainted by the smell of death. Death, and the distinct acrid stench of the burning dead. He could feel frozen, crusted blood on him, but it was impossible to tell what was his, and what had oozed from the bodies stacked on top of him. He blinked several times to wet his eyes and clear his vision, squinting against a gritty feeling he didn't want to contemplate. The Drev'an must have mistaken him for dead. He was in a pile of corpses with his head, left arm, and left shoulder exposed. His armor and weapons had been stripped. Around him, dozens more piles of corpses were arranged in semi-orderly rows. In the distance he could see fire glow and knew he had to escape or be burned with the rest of them.

Drev'an patrolled the stacks at random, likely examining the bodies for overlooked armor, weapons, or anything else of value. He could see a few, but none were in his immediate vicinity, and more importantly, none were looking in his direction. Gritting his teeth against a variety of pains, he tried to wiggle his legs free. They wouldn't move. Braxus took a breath to gather himself, then pushed with his free hand to try and wriggle his other arm and shoulder out instead. Pain seared his trapped wrist, but he continued to pull anyway until his elbow emerged, and finally his hand. The wrist was purple and swollen and would make holding a gladius difficult if it wasn't outright broken. His body shook faintly with pain or fatigue, and he closed his eyes for a moment to rest.

When he opened them again, the sun was low on the horizon, its light taking on faint gray tones. The Emorian glanced around cautiously before daring to move. When he was certain the vicinity was safe from observation, he collected himself and braced his hands on the half-frozen corpses

526

trapping him to push himself free. His breath caught, and it took raw willpower to stop the cry of pain bubbling up his throat at the grinding sensation in his side. Broken ribs, certainly. There was a feeling of slickness that warned of renewed bleeding from somewhere, and a brief flash of disorientation.

Grinding his teeth together, he braced again, attempting to bring one knee up. It was a task of inches, moving one leg at a time into any space he could gain. Something caught and gouged the skin of his legs as he moved, but he couldn't give up. As sparkles began to mar his vision, he tried to simply accept the pain rather than fight against it.

Braxus paused to catch his breath and calm his shaking body. He didn't dare close his eyes this time. Three rows away he could see flames. While he'd freed much of his torso, everything below his hips was still trapped. His knees wouldn't raise any further. They wouldn't even move. He tried again. Nothing. Again, straining more. Again. Again. *Again*. Quelling a desperate sob of pain and fear, he pushed with all the strength he could muster, striving to bring one knee forward even fractionally, straining until he was on the verge of passing out again. It wasn't enough. Helpless now, and dizzy from renewed blood loss, he surrendered. The warrior thought of his wife, picturing her so perfectly, waiting in the doorway for him, standing strong and beautiful in the sun. Tears pricked at his eyes as he allowed his head to fall back against the rest of the dead and allowed the vision to claim him.

Bright sunlight surrounded him, blotting out all the cold and death. Blotting out the image of his wife. He didn't know how long it had been, but gradually he began to feel the sun's warmth faintly on his face. He thought he could smell grass. Horses. Braxus frowned, trying to remember, trying to summon the face of his beloved.

There was a sharp tug on his hair as someone lifted his head, then let it drop after a moment. He remembered suddenly where he was and held his breath. The horse smell clung to the Drev'an, who must be searching his corpse pile one last time.

The warmth on his face wasn't from the sun, but a torch. For a moment he contemplated grabbing one of them. A sword to the throat would be a better death than burning. But before he could resolve himself to the task, he felt a shift in the bodies above him, a change in the weight. It tested the very limits of his will not to attempt to shift one leg, not while the Drev'an were still present. They searched for several minutes more. Braxus waited until he thought they might be on the far side before daring to crack open an eye fractionally. At least one Drev'an stood nearby, but he wasn't looking in his direction. At a command from someone out of sight, the Drev'an touched his torch to the bunches of dry grass at the base of the stack, then touched it to a few exposed cloaks, or other scraps of clothing that might be flammable. The task completed, they all moved on to another pile.

The Emorian sucked in a breath and looked around cautiously. No one was near except those searching the next pile, but they were close enough that moving now was still risky. The fire was catching, but not yet spreading fast enough to truly worry him. Not yet. He couldn't afford to wait long. Carefully he moved one leg to test the shifted weight. It moved several inches. He seemed to have a pocket of space to work with. Keeping his upper body still, he watched the closest Drev'an while slowly working his legs free. His mind no longer registered any pain, it was fixated completely on the situation around him, and on the renewed possibility of escape.

The fire was creeping closer. He couldn't wait any longer without risk of remaining trapped. Bracing, he shoved with hands and feet to push his hips free. It worked. It *worked*! Only his legs were still caught, but he could tell by the weight they would be easy to extricate now. He glanced around again, looking for Drev'an, but for the moment he didn't see any. Setting his jaw against the pain that must return soon, he yanked out one leg, then the other, and tumbled to the frozen ground.

Cold air struck him like a fist, sending bolts of pain through his wounds. His legs were cut and bleeding from whatever they'd been caught on. His wrist throbbed. He could feel his side bleeding now that there was no longer pressure on the wound. The irony of dead men keeping him alive with their weight wasn't lost on him, but there was no time to deal with any of that. His stiff legs wouldn't stand, so he half crouched, half crawled to another pile, away from the party of Drev'an. Braxus threw himself on the nearest corpses as another group walked by, idly chatting. None spared him more than a cursory glance. When they had gone, he crept to the next stack, working his way toward the edge of this field of death. Beyond this point, all the pyres were lit. Braxus paused for a moment to take a cloak from one of the bodies and tore several strips from another's tunic. He wrapped his torso as tightly as he could, tying several of the strips in layers to hopefully staunch the bleeding. Finally he took a pair of boots, his own having been taken or trapped in the corpse pile. He was beginning to feel faint again and dashed off between the pyres, confident no Drev'an would be patrolling that area.

The heat and the smell choked him, but he shambled forward, entirely fixated on the last row and freedom beyond. When he stumbled past the last row of fires, he didn't bother to look for sentries. He could think only of the line of low trees ahead, and the river beyond, and could see nothing but that objective. Somewhere an eagle screamed, and he thought it must be the Aquila, urging him onward. When he finally reached the brush line, his legs would carry him no further, and he collapsed on the frozen mud.

Braxus awoke sometime later, surprised that there was still fading light in the sky. He rolled onto his back, struggling to breathe around the searing pain in his ribs. The cloth bandage was soaked through, so he added another, his last, over the top of the others. If he survived, he would need to pack the wound with moss and re-bind it, but not here. He was still too close to the Drev'an. No one had evidently come after him, but that didn't mean he would not encounter some patrol or scout party. Sucking in a breath, he rolled onto his hands and knees and crawled forward. He could smell the river, crisp and clean and cold. If he could follow the river, he would eventually find himself in Emorian lands, might even find a winter camp, if he was lucky. If he could survive that long. Still dizzy from blood loss, he pulled himself forward again and slid down a small, muddy slope. He tried to get his feet under him and stand, but his legs wouldn't obey.

A low, menacing growl sounded behind him. Moving slowly, the Emorian looked over his shoulder. A thin, feral-looking wolf stood there, watching him with flattened ears and bared fangs. A strange dark shape marred one of its otherwise silver haunches.

"Peace, friend," he called quietly, not moving.

The creature flicked one ear and lowered its head, hackles bristling. Braxus slowly raised one hand to turn and face the wolf, but it darted forward at that moment and closed its jaws around his arm. Thanks to a quick withdrawal, the wolf ended up with a mouthful of his cloak. It dragged him off balance, shaking him. The animal was stronger than Braxus realized, and he fell forward as the wolf dragged him again. Grabbing the edge of the fabric, he tugged back, trying to regain his balance. The wolf adjusted its grip as well, clamping its jaws over his injured wrist, and slashing with its claws. Braxus gathered the end of the cloak in his good hand and punched the animal's snout until it released him. It lunged for his throat, and he stumbled backwards, sliding further down the embankment with the wolf chasing after him. It bit his shoulder, but the cloak and his thick winter tunic dulled the impact where his shoulder armor had been torn away. The wolf abruptly let him go as the embankment rapidly fell away, and he plunged into icy water.

Cold sucked all the air from his lungs, and the fabric of the cloak and weight of his mangled lorica dragged him down. As he struggled to unfasten the heavy wool with nerveless fingers, and to keep his head above water, he caught sight of the wolf's yellow eyes watching as he was swept downriver and below the surface.

***

Ambrus cursed every step he took. Why was he doing this? What good could possibly come from this? What danger could he face by *not* doing this? Ultimately that had been what swayed him.

"Wait," he'd called as the she-devil and her guardian were about to leave the room.

She paused, exchanging an unreadable look with the guard, then slowly turned to face him.

"Closer," he requested, still not trusting that the guard was as unstudied in Velkcic as they implied.

She narrowed her eyes suspiciously but approached. When he still hesitated, she crouched down and crept closer, but remained out of his reach.

"If I take you there, I'm putting myself at great risk. How do I know this isn't some trap?"

His voice low and guarded.

"Why go to all this trouble?" she returned. "Why not just hand you over? Or simply kill you."

"Because you promised Amergin."

Anger flared in both of them at the reminder and they held each other's glares for a few moments.

"I am doing this, enduring this, because I wish to see Amergin and the others freed."

Her voice was a quiet hiss. He could tell by the steady gaze that she was resolutely avoiding looking at her guard. He wasn't sure how to interpret that.

"You have power, simply take them as slaves for yourself. Then release them."

531

Her eyes blazed with what might have been tears if she allowed them. Ambrus felt a slight, unexpected pang of sympathy. She shook her head slowly.

"You do not understand what's transpiring here."

"Then tell me."

He sat forward suddenly, causing the guard to tense, but the woman did not react. Instead she studied him closely, clearly struggling with whether or not to say what she was thinking.

"If I acknowledge them, pay them the slightest interest, their lives will be in danger."

"Their lives are already in danger."

"You don't *understand*," she snapped again, becoming frustrated. "A pretty bird in a golden cage. That is what I am."

Ambrus sat back, noting the sincerity in her eyes, and weighed his options one last time.

"If I take you, and he is still alive, you must hide him from the other Drev'an. If he's discovered…it could well mean the deaths of innocent people. People I care about. If their lives are in danger, I no longer care what happens to me, and I will take you down."

She raised her brows slightly at the venom in his tone, attempting to decipher meaning in his words. But for the moment she only nodded once, curtly.

"What's your name?" he asked.

She regarded him skeptically.

"I won't make a bargain with someone I only know as she-devil."

"She-devil. I like that sound of that." Cool amusement spread over her features now. "Briga."

"Briga," he echoed. "Very well then."

They had waited until dusk before he led them through the audience chamber, back to a series of servant's corridors. Only the woman, Briga, and her guard accompanied him. The other guard and advisor hadn't turned up, despite their orders to bring food, but he noted Briga seemed unconcerned with their absence. They'd left his wrists shackled, but he still calculated his chances of defeating them and making a run for it. Not yet, though, still too great a chance of blundering into armed patrols. As if reading his thoughts, the guard edged closer. He led them on a winding path back to General Larsson's strategy rooms, deep in the palace. The corridors had been sporadically lit to this point, but they had left the light behind at the last turn. Briga frowned in the gloom as Ivar stepped into the dark room and fumbled for a torch.

"Do you have a striker?" he asked the guard.

"Where are we?" Briga asked flatly.

They weren't far underground, and she sensed this wasn't the right direction to have brought them to the stone building with its melted gate.

"We need keys," he explained, taking a flint and striker from the guard and lighting the torch.

True, there were more direct ways to get here than the way he'd led them, but he wanted them disoriented and dependent on him for direction. He stepped away from the door and toward the general's large desk. There were oil lamps there, but he didn't bother lighting any of them. They wouldn't be here long enough to need them. Briga and the guard were examining the room in the ambient light. Briga seemed particularly enthralled by a map hanging on one wall. Ambrus said nothing, merely skirted behind the desk and began opening drawers. Perhaps Larsson had left a knife in here somewhere. The big Drev'an drifted closer, watching his actions intently.

Shelving the effort, he opened one more drawer containing five keys. He withdrew two of them and placed them in the guard's outstretched hand.

"Ready?"

The she-devil was examining a shelf of small war trophies and nick-knacks the general had collected over time, but looked up at the sound of his voice and nodded.

Ambrus led them on an equally winding route through cold and empty halls. They slipped behind a heavy tapestry into another series of cold and dusty halls. This one had no torches lit at all. None of the Drev'an had apparently thought to search this deep into the palace, or to look for hidden doorways. Yet.

He'd discovered this path by accident and used it only once when he had first gained Larsson's trust after handing Sitric over. It had been crafted such that the king, or anyone of significant importance, might visit some of the more sensitive prisoners discreetly. The path was little used in recent times, and was protected by a special key different from any the jailers carried.

When they came to a locked iron door at the bottom of a stairwell, Ambrus took one of the keys from the Drev'an and pushed it into the lock. With effort, it turned, squealing loudly in the gloom. The trio froze, waiting to see if anyone had heard. No sounds echoed through the corridors to meet them. They waited a moment longer anyway, just to be certain. Ambrus took a breath and pushed the door open, bracing for the screech of hinges. As it happened, the hinges were in better shape than the locking mechanism, and they barely made a sound.

"After you," he offered to the she-devil, standing aside to let her pass.

"No," the guard stepped forward. "You first."

Ambrus shrugged and held out the torch before him as he stepped into the gloom. The hallway stank of smoke, and he stifled the urge to cough. That couldn't be a good sign. They were in the dungeons now, and passed a series of barred metal doors. None of the prisoners above had survived, he could tell by the utter silence. The Kith knew there had been no prisoners on this level, but superstitiously resisted looking into the cells nonetheless. At the end of the hall, he led them down two flights of stairs to the level where Siggi alone was kept.

It's a dungeon, Briga realized silently, gazing at the barred doors as they passed. The torch light did not penetrate far into the cells, but she could sense they were empty. Smoke hung on the air, thick enough that she could see it in the halo of torch light. All her senses prickled, uncomfortably aware and alert.

Gansükh hovered at her side, his presence a comforting shadow in the stale air and darkness. They followed wordlessly behind the slave, down more stairs and into another damp, dark hallway. The smoke was much less prevalent here, but she could still smell it.

The doors on this level weren't barred, but solid. Her eyes fell on the third one instinctively as a creeping numbness slowly stole up her limbs. She may have shuddered once, but neither male noticed. Ivar stopped at the third door, as she knew he would, and turned to take the second key from Gansükh. This lock did not shriek in protest and the hinges moved smoothly as her slave pushed the door open.

With only the slightest hesitation, she stepped into the doorway. Ivar held the torch into the room, its orange-yellow glow revealing a pair of boots. A dirty pair of breeches. Her gaze picked out a man sitting propped against the far wall, the torch failing to illuminate his features. For a moment nothing happened. Then he shifted subtly and slowly leaned forward. Long brown hair hung stringy and limp around a gaunt face and dirty beard. But the eyes that stared out of that face were piercingly clear and blue. She could feel the sharp gaze that traveled over her. When he spoke, the voice was a deep rasp, but it was his words that made her blood freeze.

"My my…Don't you look exactly like your father."

Afterword

The inspiration for this story occurred during a solo trip to Mongolia—my first solo vacation ever. The circumstances surrounding that trip are a story for another day; suffice it to say I was able to really get off the grid and spend a few weeks riding with my nomad guides across the steppe to the vicinity of Kharakhorum. I was very nervous at the scale of my insane undertaking, and one of the first nights of our journey featured some local, traditional musicians who treated us to an amazing concert. Briga's reaction to music the first time she heard Batu play was in many ways my experience at this first brush with traditional Mongolian culture. Many of the characters in this novel are inspired by people I met on that journey, as is inspiration for the very real language barrier. I'd like to thank my Mongolian guides for the incredible experience, and for inadvertently sending me on this literary journey, in addition to the very real journey in the ancestral heart of the Mongolian people.

While many names have been changed, no doubt my readers who have an interest in history will have noted the cultural inspirations for many of the peoples I've created in this novel. I must beg indulgence for many of these, particularly the Mongolian influences. I'm aware that I am oversimplifying many social constructs and not using strictly correct translations or interpretations of titles. While I attempted to keep many of the historical and linguistic references accurate (across all my fictitious cultures), this was ultimately fiction, and not truly historical. Therefore I've taken liberties in preventing unnecessary complexity within the world I've created, as well as for literary purposes. For those gods who actually existed in those cultures, I chose not to take as many liberties, and to leave their names, mythology, and theology intact to the best of my ability. The gods demand respect in this way.

Which brings me to my final point. When I began writing this story—which, by the way, was never with the intent of publishing—I had little knowledge of the historical context I'd stumbled across. I named Batu and Bela before I learned of the historical figures, the existence of the historical Magyars, or the battle of the Mohi Bridge. While I later took loose inspiration from that battle, a series of eerie coincidences have developed my Batu to be very like the historical Batu Khan. In this vein, I opted to keep some of those similarities, though it wasn't always intentional. As I began to research the historical Batu, the similarities to my fictional character were uncanny, which made the development and evolution of his character extremely delicate. While similar, I'd like to reiterate that this is NOT a representation of the historical Batu Khan, and his likeness and ideals remit themselves to historical fiction at best.

Acknowledgements

Thank you to my Mongolian guides for the incredible experience, and for inadvertently sending me on this literary journey, in addition to the very real journey into the ancestral heart of the Mongolian people. Thank you also to my family for their fanatical support during this process. And finally, I would like to thank my friend Heather. Without her encouragement, several of these characters would never have been developed at all, and there's no chance this would have ever been a publication effort. Her support and enthusiasm for my story has meant more than I could ever convey, and I'd never have been able to weave this tangled web of thoughts into something orderly and interesting.

About the Author

K. W. Kenny began writing in 2015 during a trip to Mongolia, where she had gone for some personal reflection and to take a break from the ordinary for a while. The Wolf's Shadow is her first publication. When she's not writing, K. W. demonstrates her disregard for free time as a circus aerialist and avid full distance triathlon competitor. She is a military veteran with two schnauzers, and calls Florida home – no matter where she is living at the time.

Made in United States
Orlando, FL
25 February 2022

15125099R00326